# PARNASSUS ON WHEELS

## AND

# THE HAUNTED BOOKSHOP

By CHRISTOPHER MORLEY

Parnassus on Wheels and The Haunted Bookshop
By Christopher Morley

Print ISBN 13: 978-1-4209-7893-3
eBook ISBN 13: 978-1-4209-8028-8

Cover Image: a detail of "Horse Drawn Cabs at Evening, New York", by Childe Frederick Hassam, c. 1890 (w/c and gouache on paper) / Photo © Christie's Images / Bridgeman Images.

Please visit *www.digireads.com*

# CONTENTS

*Parnassus on Wheels*

To
H. B. F. and H. F. M.
"Trusty, dusky, vivid, true"

A LETTER TO

David Grayson, Esq.

OF HEMPFIELD, U. S. A.

MY DEAR SIR,

Although my name appears on the title page, the real author of this book is Miss Helen McGill (now Mrs. Roger Mifflin), who told me the story with her own inimitable vivacity. And on her behalf I want to send to you these few words of acknowledgment.

Mrs. Mifflin, I need hardly say, is unskilled in the arts of authorship: this is her first book, and I doubt whether she will ever write another. She hardly realized, I think, how much her story owes to your own delightful writings. There used to be a well-thumbed copy of "Adventures in Contentment" on her table at the Sabine Farm, and I have seen her pick it up, after a long day in the kitchen, read it with chuckles, and say that the story of you and Harriet reminded her of herself and Andrew. She used to mutter something about "Adventures in Discontentment" and ask why Harriet's side of the matter was never told? And so when her own adventure came to pass, and she was urged to put it on paper, I think she unconsciously adopted something of the manner and matter that you have made properly yours.

Surely, sir, you will not disown so innocent a tribute! At any rate, Miss Harriet Grayson, whose excellent qualities we have all so long admired, will find in Mrs. Mifflin a kindred spirit.

Mrs. Mifflin would have said this for herself, with her characteristic definiteness of speech, had she not been out of touch with her publishers and foolscap paper. She and the Professor are on their Parnassus, somewhere on the high roads, happily engrossed in the most godly diversion known to man—selling books. And I venture to think that there are no volumes they take more pleasure in recommending than the wholesome and invigorating books which bear your name.

Believe me, dear Mr. Grayson, with warm regards,

Faithfully yours,
CHRISTOPHER MORLEY.

*Chapter One*

I wonder if there isn't a lot of bunkum in higher education? I never found that people who were learned in logarithms and other kinds of poetry were any quicker in washing dishes or darning socks. I've done a good deal of reading when I could, and I don't want to "admit impediments" to the love of books, but I've also seen lots of good, practical folk spoiled by too much fine print. Reading sonnets always gives me hiccups, too.

I never expected to be an author! But I do think there are some amusing things about the story of Andrew and myself and how books broke up our placid life. When John Gutenberg, whose real name (so the Professor says) was John Gooseflesh, borrowed that money to set up his printing press he launched a lot of troubles on the world.

Andrew and I were wonderfully happy on the farm until he became an author. If I could have foreseen all the bother his writings were to cause us, I would certainly have burnt the first manuscript in the kitchen stove.

Andrew McGill, the author of those books every one reads, is my brother. In other words, I am his sister, ten years younger. Years ago Andrew was a business man, but his health failed and, like so many people in the story books, he fled to the country, or, as he called it, to the bosom of Nature. He and I were the only ones left in an unsuccessful family. I was slowly perishing as a conscientious governess in the brownstone region of New York. He rescued me from that and we bought a farm with our combined savings. We became real farmers, up with the sun and to bed with the same. Andrew wore overalls and a soft shirt and grew brown and tough. My hands got red and blue with soapsuds and frost; I never saw a Redfern advertisement from one year's end to another, and my kitchen was a battlefield where I set my teeth and learned to love hard work. Our literature was government agriculture reports, patent medicine almanacs, seedsmen's booklets, and Sears Roebuck catalogues. We subscribed to *Farm and Fireside* and read the serials aloud. Every now and then, for real excitement, we read something stirring in the Old Testament—that cheery book Jeremiah, for instance, of which Andrew was very fond. The farm did actually prosper, after a while; and Andrew used to hang over the pasture bars at sunset, and tell, from the way his pipe burned, just what the weather would be the next day.

As I have said, we were tremendously happy until Andrew got the fatal idea of telling the world how happy we were. I am sorry to have to admit he had always been rather a bookish man. In his college days he had edited the students' magazine, and sometimes he would get discontented with the *Farm and Fireside* serials and pull down his bound volumes of the college paper. He would read me some of his youthful poems and stories and mutter vaguely about writing something himself some day. I was more concerned with sitting hens than with sonnets and I'm bound to say I never took these threats very seriously. I should have been more severe.

Then great-uncle Philip died, and his carload of books came to us. He had been a college professor, and years ago when Andrew was a boy Uncle Philip had been very fond of him—had, in fact, put him through college. We were the only near relatives, and all those books turned up one fine day. That was the beginning of the end, if I had only known it. Andrew had the time of his life building shelves all round our living-room; not content with that he turned the old hen house into a study for himself, put in a stove, and used to sit up there evenings after I had gone to bed. The first thing I knew he called the place Sabine Farm (although it had been known for years as Bog Hollow) because he thought it a literary thing to do. He used to take a book along with him when he drove over to Redfield for supplies; sometimes the wagon would be two hours late coming home, with old Ben loafing along between the shafts and Andrew lost in his book.

I didn't think much of all this, but I'm an easy-going woman and as long as Andrew kept the farm going I had plenty to do on my own hook. Hot bread and coffee, eggs and preserves for breakfast; soup and hot meat, vegetables, dumplings, gravy, brown bread and white, huckleberry pudding, chocolate cake and buttermilk for dinner; muffins, tea, sausage rolls, blackberries and cream, and doughnuts for supper—that's the kind of menu I had been preparing three times a day for years. I hadn't any time to worry about what wasn't my business.

And then one morning I caught Andrew doing up a big, flat parcel for the postman. He looked so sheepish I just had to ask what it was.

"I've written a book," said Andrew, and he showed me the title page—

PARADISE REGAINED
BY
ANDREW MCGILL

Even then I wasn't much worried, because of course I knew no one would print it. But Lord! a month or so later came a letter from a publisher—accepting it! That's the letter Andrew keeps framed above his desk. Just to show how such things sound I'll copy it here:

DECAMERON, JONES AND COMPANY
PUBLISHERS
UNION SQUARE, NEW YORK

January 13, 1907.
DEAR MR. MCGILL:

We have read with singular pleasure your manuscript "Paradise Regained." There is no doubt in our minds that so spirited an account of the joys of sane country living should meet with popular approval, and, with the exception of a few revisions and abbreviations, we would be glad to publish the book practically as it stands. We would like to have it illustrated by Mr. Tortoni, some of whose work you may have seen, and would be glad to know whether he may call upon you in order to acquaint himself with the local colour of your neighbourhood.

We would be glad to pay you a royalty of 10 percent upon the retail price of the book, and we enclose duplicate contracts for your signature in case this proves satisfactory to you.

Believe us, etc., etc.,

DECAMERON, JONES & CO.

I have since thought that "Paradise Lost" would have been a better title for that book. It was published in the autumn of 1907, and since that time our life has never been the same. By some mischance the book became the success of the season; it was widely commended as "a gospel of health and sanity" and Andrew received, in almost every mail, offers from publishers and magazine editors who wanted to get hold of his next book. It is almost incredible to what stratagems publishers will descend to influence an author. Andrew had written in "Paradise Regained" of the tramps who visit us, how quaint and appealing some of them are (let me add, how dirty), and how we never turn away any one who seems worthy. Would you believe that, in the spring after the book was published, a disreputable-looking vagabond with a knapsack, who turned up one day, blarneyed Andrew about his book and stayed overnight, announced himself at breakfast as a leading New York publisher? He had chosen this ruse in order to make Andrew's acquaintance.

You can imagine that it didn't take long for Andrew to become spoiled at this rate! The next year he suddenly disappeared, leaving only a note on the kitchen table, and tramped all over the state for six weeks collecting material for a new book. I had all I could do to keep him from going to New York to talk to editors and people of that sort. Envelopes of newspaper cuttings used to come to him, and he would pore over them when he ought to have been ploughing corn. Luckily the mail man comes along about the middle of the morning when Andrew is out in the fields, so I used to look over the letters before he saw them. After the second book ("Happiness and Hayseed" it was called) was printed, letters from publishers got so thick that I used to put them all in the stove before Andrew saw them—except those from the Decameron Jones people, which sometimes held checks. Literary folk used to turn up now and then to interview Andrew, but generally I managed to head them off.

But Andrew got to be less and less of a farmer and more and more of a literary man. He bought a typewriter. He would hang over the pigpen noting down adjectives for the sunset instead of mending the weather vane on the barn which took a slew so that the north wind came from the southwest. He hardly ever looked at the Sears Roebuck catalogues any more, and after Mr. Decameron came to visit us and suggested that Andrew write a book of country poems, the man became simply unbearable.

And all the time I was counting eggs and turning out three meals a day, and running the farm when Andrew got a literary fit and would go off on some vagabond jaunt to collect adventures for a new book. (I wish you could have seen the state he was in when he came back from these trips, hoboing it along the roads without any money or a clean sock to his back. One time he returned with a cough you could hear the other side of the barn, and I had to nurse him for three weeks.) When somebody wrote a little booklet about "The Sage of Redfield" and described me as a "rural Xantippe" and "the domestic balance-wheel that kept the great writer close to the homely realities of life" I made up my mind to give Andrew some of his own medicine. And that's my story.

## Chapter Two

It was a fine, crisp morning in fall—October I dare say—and I was in the kitchen coring apples for apple sauce. We were going to have roast pork for dinner with boiled potatoes and what Andrew calls Vandyke brown gravy. Andrew had driven over to town to get some flour and feed and wouldn't be back till noontime.

Being a Monday, Mrs. McNally, the washerwoman, had come over to take care of the washing. I remember I was just on my way out to the wood pile for a few sticks of birch when I heard wheels turn in at the gate. There was one of the fattest white horses I ever saw, and a queer wagon, shaped like a van. A funny-looking little man with a red beard leaned forward from the seat and said something. I didn't hear what it was, I was looking at that preposterous wagon of his.

It was coloured a pale, robin's-egg blue, and on the side, in big scarlet letters, was painted:

R. MIFFLIN'S
TRAVELLING PARNASSUS
GOOD BOOKS FOR SALE
SHAKESPEARE, CHARLES LAMB, R. L. S.
HAZLITT, AND ALL OTHERS

Underneath the wagon, in slings, hung what looked like a tent, together with a lantern, a bucket, and other small things. The van had a raised skylight on the roof, something like an old-fashioned trolley car; and from one corner went up a stove pipe. At the back was a door with little windows on each side and a flight of steps leading up to it.

As I stood looking at this queer turnout, the little reddish man climbed down from in front and stood watching me. His face was a comic mixture of pleasant drollery and a sort of weather-beaten cynicism. He had a neat little russet beard and a shabby Norfolk jacket. His head was very bald.

"Is this where Andrew McGill lives?" he said.

I admitted it.

"But he's away until noon," I added. "He'll be back then. There's roast pork for dinner."

"And apple sauce?" said the little man.

"Apple sauce and brown gravy," I said. "That's why I'm sure he'll be home on time. Sometimes he's late when there's boiled dinner, but never on roast pork days. Andrew would never do for a rabbi."

A sudden suspicion struck me.

"You're not another publisher, are you?" I cried. "What do you want with Andrew?"

"I was wondering whether he wouldn't buy this outfit," said the little man, including, with a wave of the hand, both van and white horse. As he spoke he released a hook somewhere, and raised the whole side of his wagon like a flap. Some kind of catch clicked, the flap remained up like a roof, displaying nothing but books—rows and rows of them. The flank of his van was nothing but a big bookcase. Shelves stood above shelves, all of them full of books—both old and new. As I stood gazing, he pulled out a printed card from somewhere and gave it to me:

ROGER MIFFLIN'S
TRAVELLING PARNASSUS

Worthy friends, my wain doth hold
Many a book, both new and old;
Books, the truest friends of man,
Fill this rolling caravan.
Books to satisfy all uses,
Golden lyrics of the Muses,
Books on cookery and farming,
Novels passionate and charming,
Every kind for every need
So that he who buys may read.
What librarian can surpass us?

MIFFLIN'S TRAVELLING PARNASSUS

By R. Mifflin, Prop'r.

Star Job Print, Celeryville, Va.

While I was chuckling over this, he had raised a similar flap on the other side of the Parnassus which revealed still more shelves loaded with books.

I'm afraid I am severely practical by nature.

"Well!" I said, "I should think you *would* need a pretty stout steed to lug that load along. It must weigh more than a coal wagon."

"Oh, Peg can manage it all right," he said. "We don't travel very fast. But look here, I want to sell out. Do you suppose your husband would buy the outfit—Parnassus, Pegasus, and all? He's fond of books, isn't he?

"Hold on a minute!" I said. "Andrew's my brother, not my husband, and he's altogether *too* fond of books. Books'll be the ruin of this farm pretty soon. He's mooning about over his books like a sitting hen about half the time, when he ought to be mending harness. Lord, if he saw this wagonload of yours he'd be unsettled for a week. I have to stop the postman down the road and take all the publishers' catalogues out of the mail so that Andrew don't see 'em. I'm mighty glad he's not here just now, I can tell you!"

I'm not literary, as I said before, but I'm human enough to like a good book, and my eye was running along those shelves of his as I spoke. He certainly had a pretty miscellaneous collection. I noticed poetry, essays, novels, cook books, juveniles, school books, Bibles, and what not—all jumbled together.

"Well, see here," said the little man—and about this time I noticed that he had the bright eyes of a fanatic—"I've been cruising with this Parnassus going on seven years. I've covered the territory from Florida to Maine and I reckon I've injected about as much good literature into the countryside as ever old Doc Eliot did with his five-foot shelf. I want to sell out now. I'm going to write a book about 'Literature Among the Farmers,' and want to settle down with my brother in Brooklyn and write it. I've got a sackful of notes for it. I guess I'll just stick around until Mr. McGill gets home and see if he won't buy me out. I'll sell the whole concern, horse, wagon, and books, for $400. I've read Andrew McGill's stuff and I reckon the proposition'll interest him. I've had more fun with this Parnassus than a barrel of monkeys. I used to be a school teacher till my health broke down. Then I took this up and I've made more than expenses and had the time of my life."

"Well, Mr. Mifflin," I said, "if you want to stay around I guess I can't stop you. But I'm sorry you and your old Parnassus ever came this way."

I turned on my heel and went back to the kitchen. I knew pretty well that Andrew would go up in the air when he saw that wagonload of books and one of those crazy cards with Mr. Mifflin's poetry on it.

I must confess that I was considerably upset. Andrew is just as unpractical and fanciful as a young girl, and always dreaming of new adventures and rambles around the country. If he ever saw that travelling Parnassus he'd fall for it like snap. And I knew Mr. Decameron was after him for a new book anyway. (I'd intercepted one of his letters suggesting another "Happiness and Hayseed" trip just a few weeks before. Andrew was away when the letter came. I had a suspicion what was in it; so I opened it, read it, and—well, burnt it. Heavens! as though Andrew didn't have enough to do without mooning down the road like a tinker, just to write a book about it.)

As I worked around the kitchen I could see Mr. Mifflin making himself at home. He unhitched his horse, tied her up to the fence, sat down by the wood pile, and lit a pipe. I could see I was in for it. By and by I couldn't stand it any longer. I went out to talk to that bald-headed pedlar.

"See here," I said. "You're a pretty cool fish to make yourself so easy in my yard. I tell you I don't want you around here, you and your travelling parcheesi. Suppose you clear out of here before my brother gets back and don't be breaking up our happy family."

"Miss McGill," he said (the man had a pleasant way with him, too—darn him—with his bright, twinkling eye and his silly little beard), "I'm sure I don't want to be discourteous. If you move me on from here, of course I'll go; but I warn you I shall lie in wait for Mr. McGill just down this road. I'm here to sell this caravan of culture, and by the bones of Swinburne I think your brother's the man to buy it."

My blood was up now, and I'll admit that I said my next without proper calculation.

"Rather than have Andrew buy your old parcheesi," I said, "I'll buy it myself. I'll give you $300 for it."

The little man's face brightened. He didn't either accept or decline my offer. (I was frightened to death that he'd take me right on the nail and bang would go my three years' savings for a Ford.)

"Come and have another look at her," he said.

I must admit that Mr. Roger Mifflin had fixed up his van mighty comfortably inside. The body of the wagon was built out on each side over the wheels, which gave it an unwieldy appearance but made extra room for the bookshelves. This left an inside space about five feet wide and nine long. On one side he had a little oil stove, a flap table, and a cozy-looking bunk above which was built a kind of chest of drawers— to hold clothes and such things, I suppose; on the other side more bookshelves, a small table, and a little wicker easy chair. Every possible inch of space seemed to be made useful in some way, for a shelf or a hook or a hanging cupboard or something. Above the stove was a neat little row of pots and dishes and cooking usefuls. The raised skylight made it just possible to stand upright in the centre aisle of the van; and a little sliding window opened onto the driver's seat in front. Altogether it was a very neat affair. The windows in front and back were curtained and a pot of geraniums stood on a diminutive shelf. I was amused to see a sandy Irish terrier curled up on a bright Mexican blanket in the bunk.

"Miss McGill," he said, "I couldn't sell Parnassus for less than four hundred. I've put twice that much into her, one time and another. She's built clean and solid all through, and there's everything a man would need from blankets to bouillon cubes. The whole thing's yours for $400—including dog, cook stove, and everything—jib, boom, and spanker. There's a tent in a sling underneath, and an ice box (he pulled up a little trap door under the bunk) and a tank of coal oil and Lord knows what all. She's as good as a yacht; but I'm tired of her. If you're so afraid of your brother taking a fancy to her, why don't you buy her yourself and go off on a lark? Make *him* stay home and mind the farm!... Tell you what I'll do. I'll start you on the road myself, come with you the first day and show you how it's worked. You could have the time of your life in this thing, and give yourself a fine vacation. It would give your brother a good surprise, too. Why not?"

I don't know whether it was the neatness of his absurd little van, or the madness of the whole proposition, or just the desire to have an adventure of my own and play a trick on Andrew, but anyway, some extraordinary impulse seized me and I roared with laughter.

"Right!" I said. "I'll do it."

I, Helen McGill, in the thirty-ninth year of my age!

## Chapter Three

"Well," I thought, "if I'm in for an adventure I may as well be spry about it. Andrew'll be home by half-past twelve and if I'm going to give him the slip I'd better get a start. I suppose he'll think I'm crazy! He'll follow me, I guess. Well, he just shan't catch me, that's all!" A kind of anger came over me to think that I'd been living on that farm for nearly fifteen years—yes, sir, ever since I was twenty-five—and hardly ever been away except for that trip to Boston once a year to go shopping with cousin Edie. I'm a home-keeping soul, I guess, and I love my kitchen and my preserve cupboard and my linen closet as well as grandmother ever did, but something in that blue October air and that crazy little red-bearded man just tickled me.

"Look here, Mr. Parnassus," I said, "I guess I'm a fat old fool but I just believe I'll do that. You hitch up your horse and van and I'll go pack some clothes and write you a check. It'll do Andrew all the good in the world to have me skip. I'll get a chance to read a few books, too. It'll be as good as going to college!" And I untied my apron and ran for the house. The little man stood leaning against a corner of the van as if he were stupefied. I dare say he was.

I ran into the house through the front door, and it struck me as comical to see a copy of one of Andrew's magazines lying on the living-room table with "The Revolt of Womanhood" printed across it in red letters. "Here goes for the revolt of Helen McGill," I thought. I sat down at Andrew's desk, pushed aside a pad of notes he had been jotting down about "the magic of autumn," and scrawled a few lines:

DEAR ANDREW,
    Don't be thinking I'm crazy. I've gone off for an adventure. It just came over me that you've had all the adventures while I've been at home baking bread. Mrs. McNally will look after your meals and one of her girls can come over to do the housework. So don't worry. I'm going off for a little while—a month, maybe—to see some of this happiness and hayseed of yours. It's what the magazines call the revolt of womanhood. Warm underwear in the cedar chest in the spare room when you need it.

                                                With love,
                                                HELEN.


    I left the note on his desk.
    Mrs. McNally was bending over the tubs in the laundry. I could see only the broad arch of her back and hear the vigorous zzzzzzz of her rubbing. She straightened up at my call.
    "Mrs. McNally," I said, "I'm going away for a little trip. You'd

better let the washing go until this afternoon and get Andrew's dinner for him. He'll be back about twelve-thirty. It's half-past ten now. You tell him I've gone over to see Mrs. Collins at Locust Farm."

Mrs. McNally is a brawny, slow-witted Swede. "All right Mis' McGill," she said. "You be back to denner?"

"No, I'm not coming back for a month," I said. "I'm going away for a trip. I want you to send Rosie over here every day to do the housework while I'm away. You can arrange with Mr. McGill about that. I've got to hurry now."

Mrs. McNally's honest eyes, as blue as Copenhagen china, gazing through the window in perplexity, fell upon the travelling Parnassus and Mr. Mifflin backing Pegasus into the shafts. I saw her make a valiant effort to comprehend the sign painted on the side of the van— and give it up.

"You going driving?" she said blankly.

"Yes," I said, and fled upstairs.

I always keep my bank book in an old Huyler box in the top drawer of my bureau. I don't save very quickly, I'm afraid. I have a little income from some money father left me, but Andrew takes care of that. Andrew pays all the farm expenses, but the housekeeping accounts fall to me. I make a fairish amount of pin money on my poultry and some of my preserves that I send to Boston, and on some recipes of mine that I send to a woman's magazine now and then; but generally my savings don't amount to much over $10 a month. In the last five years I had put by something more than $600. I had been saving up for a Ford. But just now it looked to me as if that Parnassus would be more fun than a Ford ever could be. Four hundred dollars was a lot of money, but I thought of what it would mean to have Andrew come home and buy it. Why, he'd be away until Thanksgiving! Whereas if I bought it I could take it away, have my adventure, and sell it somewhere so that Andrew never need see it. I hardened my heart and determined to give the Sage of Redfield some of his own medicine.

My balance at the Redfield National Bank was $615.20. I sat down at the table in my bedroom where I keep my accounts and wrote out a check to Roger Mifflin for $400. I put in plenty of curlicues after the figures so that no one could raise the check into $400,000; then I got out my old rattan suit case and put in some clothes. The whole business didn't take me ten minutes. I came downstairs to find Mrs. McNally looking sourly at the Parnassus from the kitchen door.

"You going away in that—that 'bus, Mis' McGill?" she asked.

"Yes, Mrs. McNally," I said cheerfully. Her use of the word gave me an inspiration. "That's one of the new jitney 'buses we hear about. He's going to take me to the station. Don't you worry about me. I'm going for a holiday. You get Mr. McGill's dinner ready for him. After dinner tell him there's a note for him in the living-room."

"I tank that bane a queer 'bus," said Mrs. McNally, puzzled. I think the excellent woman suspected an elopement.

I carried my suit case out to the Parnassus. Pegasus stood placidly between the shafts. From within came sounds of vigorous movement. In a moment the little man burst out with a bulging portmanteau in his hand. He had a tweed cap slanted on the back of his head.

"There!" he cried triumphantly. "I've packed all my personal effects—clothes and so on—and everything else goes with the transaction. When I get on the train with this bag I'm a free man, and hurrah for Brooklyn! Lord, won't I be glad to get back to the city! I lived in Brooklyn once, and I haven't been back there for ten years," he added plaintively.

"Here's the check," I said, handing it to him. He flushed a little, and looked at me rather shamefacedly. "See here," he said, "I hope you're not making a bad bargain? I don't want to take advantage of a lady. If you think your brother...."

"I was going to buy a Ford, anyway," I said, "and it looks to me as though this parcheesi of yours would be cheaper to run than any flivver that ever came out of Detroit. I want to keep it away from Andrew and that's the main thing. You give me a receipt and we'll get away from here before he comes back."

He took the check without a word, hoisted his fat portmanteau on the driver's seat, and then disappeared in the van. In a minute he reappeared. On the back of one of his poetical cards he had written:

Received from Miss McGill the sum of four hundred dollars in exchange for one Travelling Parnassus in first class condition, delivered to her this day, October 3rd, 19—.   Signed

ROGER MIFFLIN.

"Tell me," I said, "does your Parnassus—*my* Parnassus, rather—contain everything I'm likely to need? Is it stocked up with food and so on?"

"I was coming to that," he said. "You'll find a fair supply of stuff in the cupboard over the stove, though I used to get most of my meals at farmhouses along the road. I generally read aloud to people as I go along, and they're often good for a free meal. It's amazing how little most of the country folk know about books, and how pleased they are to hear good stuff. Down in Lancaster County, Pennsylvania...."

"Well, how about the horse?" I said hastily, seeing him about to embark on an anecdote. It wasn't far short of eleven o'clock, and I was anxious to get started.

"It might be well to take along some oats. My supply's about exhausted."

I filled a sack with oats in the stable and Mr. Mifflin showed me where to hang it under the van. Then in the kitchen I loaded a big basket with provisions for an emergency: a dozen eggs, a jar of sliced bacon, butter, cheese, condensed milk, tea, biscuits, jam, and two loaves of bread. These Mr. Mifflin stowed inside the van, Mrs. McNally watching in amazement.

"I tank this bane a queer picnic!" she said. "Which way are you going? Mr. McGill, is he coming after you?"

"No," I insisted, "he's not coming. I'm going off on a holiday. You get dinner for him and he won't worry about anything until after that. Tell him I've gone over to see Mrs. Collins."

I climbed the little steps and entered my Parnassus with a pleasant thrill of ownership. The terrier on the bunk jumped to the floor with a friendly wag of the tail. I piled the bunk with bedding and blankets of my own, shook out the drawers which fitted above the bunk, and put into them what few belongings I was taking with me. And we were ready to start.

Redbeard was already sitting in front with the reins in hand. I climbed up beside him. The front seat was broad but uncushioned, well sheltered by the peak of the van. I gave a quick glance around at the comfortable house under its elms and maples—saw the big, red barn shining in the sun and the pump under the grape arbour. I waved goodbye to Mrs. McNally who was watching us in silent amazement. Pegasus threw her solid weight against the traces and Parnassus swung round and rolled past the gate. We turned into the Redfield road.

"Here," said Mifflin, handing me the reins, "you're skipper, you'd better drive. Which way do you want to go?"

My breath came a little fast when I realized that my adventure had begun!

## Chapter Four

Just out of sight of the farm the road forks, one way running on to Walton where you cross the river by a covered bridge, the other swinging down toward Greenbriar and Port Vigor. Mrs. Collins lives a mile or so up the Walton road, and as I very often run over to see her I thought Andrew would be most likely to look for me there. So, after we had passed through the grove, I took the right-hand turn to Greenbriar. We began the long ascent over Huckleberry Hill and as I smelt the fresh autumn odour of the leaves I chuckled a little.

Mr. Mifflin seemed in a perfect ecstasy of high spirits. "This is certainly grand," he said. "Lord, I applaud your spunk. Do you think Mr. McGill will give chase?"

"I haven't an idea," I said. "Not right away, anyhow. He's so used to my settled ways that I don't think he'll suspect anything till he finds my note. I wonder what kind of story Mrs. McNally will tell!"

"How about putting him off the scent?" he said. "Give me your handkerchief."

I did so. He hopped nimbly out, ran back down the hill (he was a spry little person in spite of his bald crown), and dropped the handkerchief on the Walton Road about a hundred feet beyond the fork. Then he followed me up the slope.

"There," he said, grinning like a kid, "that'll fool him. The Sage of Redfield will undoubtedly follow a false spoor and the criminals will win a good start. But I'm afraid it's rather easy to follow a craft as unusual as Parnassus."

"Tell me how you manage the thing," I said. "Do you really make it pay?" We halted at the top of the hill to give Pegasus a breathing space. The terrier lay down in the dust and watched us gravely. Mr. Mifflin pulled out a pipe and begged my permission to smoke.

"It's rather comical how I first got into it," he said. "I was a school teacher down in Maryland. I'd been plugging away in a country school for years, on a starvation salary. I was trying to support an invalid mother, and put by something in case of storms. I remember how I used to wonder whether I'd ever be able to wear a suit that wasn't shabby and have my shoes polished every day. Then my health went back on me. The doctor told me to get into the open air. By and by I got this idea of a travelling bookstore. I had always been a lover of books, and in the days when I boarded out among the farmers I used to read aloud to them. After my mother died I built the wagon to suit my own ideas, bought a stock of books from a big second-hand store in Baltimore, and set out. Parnassus just about saved my life I guess."

He pushed his faded old cap back on his head and relit his pipe. I clicked to Pegasus and we rumbled gently off over the upland, looking down across the pastures. Distant cow bells sounded tankle-tonk among the bushes. Across the slope of the hill I could see the road winding away to Redfield. Somewhere along that road Andrew would be rolling back toward home and roast pork with apple sauce; and here was I, setting out on the first madness of my life without even a qualm.

"Miss McGill," said the little man, "this rolling pavilion has been wife, doctor, and religion to me for seven years. A month ago I would have scoffed at the thought of leaving her; but somehow it's come over me I need a change. There's a book I've been yearning to write for a long time, and I need a desk steady under my elbows and a roof over my head. And silly as it seems, I'm crazy to get back to Brooklyn. My brother and I used to live there as kids. Think of walking over the old Bridge at sunset and seeing the towers of Manhattan against a red sky! And those old gray cruisers down in the Navy Yard! You don't know how tickled I am to sell out. I've sold a lot of copies of your brother's books and I've often thought he'd be the man to buy Parnassus if I got tired of her."

"So he would," I said. "Just the man. He'd be only too likely to—and go maundering about in this jaunting car and neglect the farm. But tell me about selling books. How much profit do you make out of it? We'll be passing Mrs. Mason's farm, by and by, and we might as well sell her something just to make a start."

"It's very simple," he said. "I replenish my stock whenever I go through a big town. There's always a second-hand bookstore somewhere about, where you can pick up odds and ends. And every now and then I write to a wholesaler in New York for some stuff. When I buy a book I mark in the back just what I paid for it, then I know what I can afford to sell it for. See here."

He pulled up a book from behind the seat—a copy of "Lorna Doone" it was—and showed me the letters *a m* scrawled in pencil in the back.

"That means that I paid ten cents for this. Now, if you sell it for a quarter you've got a safe profit. It costs me about four dollars a week to run Parnassus—generally less. If you clear that much in six days you can afford to lay off on Sundays!"

"How do you know that *a m* stands for ten cents?" I asked.

"The code word's *manuscript*. Each letter stands for a figure, from 0 up to 9, see?" He scrawled it down on a scrap of paper:

$$m \quad a \quad n \quad u \quad s \quad c \quad r \quad i \quad p \quad t$$
$$0 \quad 1 \quad 2 \quad 3 \quad 4 \quad 5 \quad 6 \quad 7 \quad 8 \quad 9$$

"Now, you see *a m* stands for 10, *a n* would be 12, *n s* is 24, *a c* is 15, *a m m* is $1.00, and so on. I don't pay much over fifty cents for books as a rule, because country folks are shy of paying much for them. They'll pay a lot for a separator or a buggy top, but they've never been taught to worry about literature! But it's surprising how excited they get about books if you sell 'em the right kind. Over beyond Port Vigor there's a farmer who's waiting for me to go back—I've been there three or four times—and he'll buy about five dollars' worth if I know him. First time I went there I sold him 'Treasure Island,' and he's talking about it yet. I sold him 'Robinson Crusoe,' and 'Little Women' for his daughter, and 'Huck Finn,' and Grubb's book about 'The Potato.' Last time I was there he wanted some Shakespeare, but I wouldn't give it to him. I didn't think he was up to it yet."

I began to see something of the little man's idealism in his work. He was a kind of traveling missionary in his way. A hefty talker, too. His eyes were twinkling now and I could see him warming up.

"Lord!" he said, "when you sell a man a book you don't sell him just twelve ounces of paper and ink and glue—you sell him a whole new life. Love and friendship and humour and ships at sea by night—

there's all heaven and earth in a book, a real book I mean. Jiminy! If I
were the baker or the butcher or the broom huckster, people would run
to the gate when I came by—just waiting for my stuff. And here I go
loaded with everlasting salvation—yes, ma'am, salvation for their little,
stunted minds—and it's hard to make 'em see it. That's what makes it
worth while—I'm doing something that nobody else from Nazareth,
Maine, to Walla Walla, Washington, has ever thought of. It's a new
field, but by the bones of Whitman it's worth while. That's what this
country needs—more books!"

He laughed at his own vehemence. "Do you know, it's comical,"
he said. "Even the publishers, the fellows that print the books, can't see
what I'm doing for them. Some of 'em refuse me credit because I sell
their books for what they're worth instead of for the prices they mark
on them. They write me letters about price-maintenance—and I write
back about merit-maintenance. Publish a good book and I'll get a good
price for it, say I! Sometimes I think the publishers know less about
books than any one else! I guess that's natural, though. Most school
teachers don't know much about children."

"The best of it is," he went on, "I have such a darn good time. Peg
and Bock (that's the dog) and I go loafing along the road on a warm
summer day, and by and by we'll fetch up alongside some boarding-
house and there are the boarders all rocking off their lunch on the
veranda. Most of 'em bored to death—nothing good to read, nothing to
do but sit and watch the flies buzzing in the sun and the chickens
rubbing up and down in the dust. First thing you know I'll sell half a
dozen books that put the love of life into them, and they don't forget
Parnassus in a hurry. Take O. Henry, for instance—there isn't anybody
so dog-gone sleepy that he won't enjoy that man's stories. He
understood life, you bet, and he could write it down with all its little
twists. I've spent an evening reading O. Henry and Wilkie Collins to
people and had them buy out all their books I had and clamour for
more."

"What do you do in winter?" I asked—a practical question, as most
of mine are.

"That depends on where I am when bad weather sets in," said Mr.
Mifflin. "Two winters I was down south and managed to keep
Parnassus going all through the season. Otherwise, I just lay up
wherever I am. I've never found it hard to get lodging for Peg and a job
for myself, if I had to have them. Last winter I worked in a bookstore in
Boston. Winter before, I was in a country drugstore down in
Pennsylvania. Winter before that, I tutored a couple of small boys in
English literature. Winter before that, I was a steward on a steamer; you
see how it goes. I've had a fairly miscellaneous experience. As far as I
can see, a man who's fond of books never need starve! But this winter
I'm planning to live with my brother in Brooklyn and slog away at my

book. Lord, how I've pondered over that thing! Long summer afternoons I've sat here, jogging along in the dust, thinking it out until it seemed as if my forehead would burst. You see, my idea is that the common people—in the country, that is—never have had any chance to get hold of books, and never have had any one to explain what books can mean. It's all right for college presidents to draw up their five-foot shelves of great literature, and for the publishers to advertise sets of their Linoleum Classics, but what the people need is the good, homely, honest stuff—something that'll stick to their ribs—make them laugh and tremble and feel sick to think of the littleness of this popcorn ball spinning in space without ever even getting a hot-box! And something that'll spur 'em on to keep the hearth well swept and the wood pile split into kindling and the dishes washed and dried and put away. Any one who can get the country people to read something worth while is doing his nation a real service. And that's what this caravan of culture aspires to.... You must be weary of this harangue! Does the Sage of Redfield ever run on like that?"

"Not to me," I said. "He's known me so long that he thinks of me as a kind of animated bread-baking and cake-mixing machine. I guess he doesn't put much stock in my judgment in literary matters. But he puts his digestion in my hands without reserve. There's Mason's farm over there. I guess we'd better sell them some books—hadn't we? Just for a starter."

We turned into the lane that runs up to the Mason farmhouse. Bock trotted on ahead—very stiff on his legs and his tail gently wagging—to interview the mastiff, and Mrs. Mason who was sitting on the porch, peeling potatoes, laid down the pan. She's a big, buxom woman with jolly, brown eyes like a cow's.

"For heaven's sake, Miss McGill," she called out in a cheerful voice—"I'm glad to see you. Got a lift, did you?"

She hadn't really noticed the inscription on Parnassus, and thought it was a regular huckster's wagon.

"Well, Mrs. Mason," I said, "I've gone into the book business. This is Mr. Mifflin. I've bought out his stock. We've come to sell you some books."

She laughed. "Go on, Helen," she said, "you can't kid me! I bought a whole set of books last year from an agent—'The World's Great Funeral Orations'—twenty volumes. Sam and I ain't read more'n the first volume yet. It's awful uneasy reading!"

Mifflin jumped down, and raised the side flap of the wagon. Mrs. Mason came closer. I was tickled to see how the little man perked up at the sight of a customer. Evidently selling books was meat and drink to him.

"Madam," he said, "'Funeral Orations' (bound in sackcloth, I suppose?) have their place, but Miss McGill and I have got some real books here to which I invite your attention. Winter will be here soon, and you will need something more cheerful to beguile your evenings. Very possibly you have growing children who would profit by a good book or two. A book of fairy tales for the little girl I see on the porch? Or stories of inventors for that boy who is about to break his neck jumping from the barn loft? Or a book about road making for your husband? Surely there is something here you need? Miss McGill probably knows your tastes."

That little red-bearded man was surely a born salesman. How he guessed that Mr. Mason was the road commissioner in our township, goodness only knows. Perhaps it was just a lucky shot. By this time most of the family had gathered around the van, and I saw Mr. Mason coming from the barn with his twelve-year-old Billy.

"Sam," shouted Mrs. Mason, "here's Miss McGill turned book pedlar and got a preacher with her!"

"Hello, Miss McGill," said Mr. Mason. He is a big, slow-moving man of great gravity and solidity. "Where's Andrew?"

"Andrew's coming home for roast pork and apple sauce," I said, "and I'm going off to sell books for a living. Mr. Mifflin here is teaching me how. We've got a book on road mending that's just what you need."

I saw Mr. and Mrs. Mason exchange glances. Evidently they thought me crazy. I began to wonder whether we had made a mistake in calling on people I knew so well. The situation was a trifle embarrassing.

Mr. Mifflin came to the rescue.

"Don't be alarmed, sir," he said to Mr. Mason. "I haven't kidnapped Miss McGill." (As he is about half my size this was amusing.) "We are trying to increase her brother's income by selling his books for him. As a matter of fact, we have a wager with him that we can sell fifty copies of 'Happiness and Hayseed' before Hallowe'en. Now I'm sure your sporting instinct will assist us by taking at least one copy. Andrew McGill is probably the greatest author in this State, and every taxpayer ought to possess his books. May I show you a copy?"

"That sounds reasonable," said Mr. Mason, and he almost smiled. "What do you say, Emma, think we better buy a book or two? You know those 'Funeral Orations.'..." "Well," said Emma, "you know we've always said we ought to read one of Andrew McGill's books but we didn't rightly know how to get hold of one. That fellow that sold us the funeral speeches didn't seem to know about 'em. I tell you what, you folks better stop and have dinner with us and you can tell us what we'd ought to buy. I'm just ready to put the potatoes on the stove now."

I must confess that the prospect of sitting down to a meal I hadn't cooked myself appealed to me strongly; and I was keen to see what kind of grub Mrs. Mason provided for her household; but I was afraid that if we dallied there too long Andrew would be after us. I was about to say that we would have to be getting on, and couldn't stay; but apparently the zest of expounding his philosophy to new listeners was too much for Mifflin. I heard him saying:

"That's mighty kind of you, Mrs. Mason, and we'd like very much to stay. Perhaps I can put Peg up in your barn for a while. Then we can tell you all about our books." And to my amazement I found myself chiming in with assent.

Mifflin certainly surpassed himself at dinner. The fact that Mrs. Mason's hot biscuits tasted of saleratus gave me far less satisfaction than it otherwise would, because I was absorbed in listening to the little vagabond's talk. Mr. Mason came to the table grumbling something about his telephone being out of order—(I wondered whether he had been trying to get Andrew on the wire; he was a little afraid that I was being run away with, I think)—but he was soon won over by the current of the little man's cheery wit. Nothing daunted Mifflin. He talked to the old grandmother about quilts; offered to cut off a strip of his necktie for her new patchwork; and told all about the illustrated book on quilts that he had in the van. He discussed cookery and the Bible with Mrs. Mason; and she being a leading light in the Greenbriar Sunday School, was pleasantly scandalized by his account of the best detective stories in the Old Testament. With Mr. Mason he was all scientific farming, chemical manures, macadam roads, and crop rotation; and to little Billy (who sat next him) he told extraordinary yarns about Daniel Boone, Davy Crockett, Kit Carson, Buffalo Bill, and what not. Honestly I was amazed at the little man. He was as genial as a cricket on the hearth, and yet every now and then his earnestness would break through. I don't wonder he was a success at selling books. That man could sell clothes pins or Paris garters, I guess, and make them seem romantic.

"You know, Mr. Mason," he said, "you certainly owe it to these youngsters of yours to put a few really good books into their hands. City kids have the libraries to go to, but in the country there's only old Doc Hostetter's Almanac and the letters written by ladies with backache telling how Peruna did for them. Give this boy and girl of yours a few good books and you're starting them on the double-track, block-signal line to happiness. Now there's 'Little Women'—that girl of yours can learn more about real girlhood and fine womanhood out of that book than from a year's paper dolls in the attic."

"That's right, Pa," assented Mrs. Mason. ("Go on with your meal, Professor, the meat'll be cold.") She was completely won by the travelling bookseller, and had given him the highest title of honour in her ken. "Why, I read that story when I was a girl, and I still remember it. That's better readin' for Dorothy than those funeral speeches, I reckon. I believe the Professor's right: we'd ought to have more books laying around. Seems kind of a shame, with a famous author at the next farm, not to read more, don't it, now?"

So by the time we got down to Mrs. Mason's squash pie (good pie, too, I admit, but her hand is a little heavy for pastry), the whole household was enthusiastic about books, and the atmosphere was literary enough for even Dr. Eliot to live in without panting. Mrs. Mason opened up her parlour and we sat there while Mifflin recited "The Revenge" and "Maud Muller."

"Well, now, ain't that real sweet!" said Emma Mason. "It's surprising how those words rhyme so nicely. Seems almost as though it was done a-purpose! Reminds me of piece day at school. There was a mighty pretty piece I learned called the 'Wreck of the Asperus.'" And she subsided into a genteel melancholy.

I saw that Mr. Mifflin was well astride his hobby: he had started to tell the children about Robin Hood, but I had the sense to give him a wink. We had to be getting along or surely Andrew might be on us. So while Mifflin was putting Pegasus into the shafts again I picked out seven or eight books that I thought would fit the needs of the Masons. Mr. Mason insisted that "Happiness and Hayseed" be included among them, and gave me a crisp five-dollar bill, refusing any change. "No, no," he said, "I've had more fun than I get at a grange meeting. Come round again, Miss McGill; I'm going to tell Andrew what a good show this travelling theayter of yours gives! And you, Professor, any time you're here about road-mending season, stop in an' tell me some more good advice. Well, I must get back to the field."

Bock fell in under the van, and we creaked off down the lane. Mifflin filled his pipe and was chuckling to himself. I was a little worried now for fear Andrew might overtake us.

"It's a wonder Sam Mason didn't call up Andrew," I said. "It must have looked mighty queer to him for an old farm hand like me to be around, peddling books."

"He would have done it straight off," said Mifflin, "but you see, I cut his telephone wire!"

## Chapter Five

I gazed in astonishment at the wizened little rogue. Here was a new side to the amiable idealist! Apparently there was a streak of fearless deviltry in him besides his gentle love of books. I'm bound to say that now, for the first time, I really admired him. I had burnt my own very respectable boats behind me, and I rather enjoyed knowing that he, too, could act briskly in a pinch.

"Well!" I said. "You are a cool hand! It's a good job for you that you didn't stay a schoolmaster. You might have taught your pupils some fine deviltries! And at your age, too!"

I'm afraid my raillery goes a little too far sometimes. He flushed a bit at my reference to his age, and puffed sharply at his pipe.

"I say," he rejoined, "how old do you think I am, anyway? Only forty-one, by the bones of Byron! Henry VIII was only forty-one when he married Anne Boleyn. There are many consolations in history for people over forty! Remember that when you get there.

"Shakespeare wrote 'King Lear' at forty-one," he added, more humorously; and then burst out laughing. "I'd like to edit a series of 'Chloroform Classics,' to include only books written after forty. Who was that doctor man who recommended anæsthetics for us at that age? Now isn't that just like a medico? Nurse us through the diseases of childhood, and as soon as we settle down into permanent good health and worldly wisdom, and freedom from doctors' fees, why he loses interest in us! Jove! I must note that down and bring it into my book."

He pulled out a memorandum book and jotted down "Chloroform Classics" in a small, neat hand.

"Well," I said (I felt a little contrite, as I was sincerely sorry to have offended him), "I've passed forty myself in some measurements, so youth no longer has any terrors for me."

He looked at me rather comically.

"My dear madam," he said, "your age is precisely eighteen. I think that if we escape the clutches of the Sage of Redfield you may really begin to live."

"Oh, Andrew's not a bad sort," I said. "He's absentminded, and hot tempered, and a little selfish. The publishers have done their best to spoil him, but for a literary man I guess he's quite human. He rescued me from being a governess, and that's to his credit. If only he didn't take his meals quite so much as a matter of course...."

"The preposterous thing about him is that he really can *write*," said Mifflin. "I envy him that. Don't let him know I said so, but as a matter of fact his prose is almost as good as Thoreau. He approaches facts as daintily as a cat crossing a wet road."

"You should see him at dinner," I thought; or rather I meant to think it, but the words slipped out. I found myself thinking aloud in a rather disconcerting way while sitting with this strange little person.

He looked at me. I noticed for the first time that his eyes were slate blue, with funny birds' foot wrinkles at the corners.

"That's so," he said. "I never thought of that. A fine prose style certainly presupposes sound nourishment. Excellent point that... And yet Thoreau did his own cooking. A sort of Boy Scout I guess, with a badge as kitchen master. Perhaps he took Beechnut bacon with him into the woods. I wonder who cooked for Stevenson—Cummy? The 'Child's Garden of Verses' was really a kind of kitchen garden, wasn't it? I'm afraid the commissariat problem has weighed rather heavily on you. I'm glad you've got away from it."

All this was getting rather intricate for me. I set it down as I remember it, inaccurately perhaps. My governess days are pretty far astern now, and my line is common sense rather than literary allusions. I said something of the sort.

"Common sense?" he repeated. "Good Lord, ma'am, sense is the most uncommon thing in the world. I haven't got it. I don't believe your brother has, from what you say. Bock here has it. See how he trots along the road, keeps an eye on the scenery, and minds his own business. I never saw him get into a fight yet. Wish I could say the same of myself. I named him after Boccaccio, to remind me to read the 'Decameron' some day."

"Judging by the way you talk," I said, "you ought to be quite a writer yourself."

"Talkers never write. They go on talking."

There was a considerable silence. Mifflin relit his pipe and watched the landscape with a shrewd eye. I held the reins loosely, and Peg ambled along with a steady clop-clop. Parnassus creaked musically, and the mid-afternoon sun lay rich across the road. We passed another farm, but I did not suggest stopping as I felt we ought to push on. Mifflin seemed lost in meditation, and I began to wonder, a little uneasily, how the adventure would turn out. This quaintly masterful little man was a trifle disconcerting. Across the next ridge I could see the Greenbriar church spire shining white.

"Do you know this part of the country?" I asked finally.

"Not this exact section. I've been in Port Vigor often, but then I was on the road that runs along the Sound. I suppose this village ahead is Greenbriar?"

"Yes," I said. "It's about thirteen miles from there to Port Vigor. How do you expect to get back to Brooklyn?"

"Oh, Brooklyn?" he said vaguely. "Yes, I'd forgotten about Brooklyn for the minute. I was thinking of my book. Why, I guess I'll take the train from Port Vigor. The trouble is, you can never get to Brooklyn without going through New York. It's symbolic, I suppose."

Again there was a silence. Finally he said, "Is there another town between Greenbriar and Port Vigor?"

"Yes, Shelby," I said. "About five miles from Greenbriar."

"That'll be as far as you'll get to-night," he said. "I'll see you safe to Shelby, and then make tracks for Port Vigor. I hope there's a decent inn at Shelby where you can stop overnight."

I hoped so, too, but I wasn't going to let him see that with the waning afternoon my enthusiasm was a little less robust. I was wondering what Andrew was thinking, and whether Mrs. McNally had left things in good order. Like most Swedes she had to be watched or she left her work only three quarters done. And I didn't depend any too much on her daughter Rosie to do the housework efficiently. I wondered what kind of meals Andrew would get. And probably he would go right on wearing his summer underclothes, although I had already reminded him about changing. Then there were the chickens... Well, the Rubicon was crossed now, and there was nothing to be done.

To my surprise, little Redbeard had divined my anxiety. "Now don't you worry about the Sage," he said kindly. "A man that draws his royalties isn't going to starve. By the bones of John Murray, his publishers can send him a cook if necessary! This is a holiday for you, and don't you forget it."

And with this cheering sentiment in my mind, we rolled sedately down the hill toward Greenbriar.

I am about as hardy as most folks, I think, but I confess I balked a little at the idea of facing the various people I know in Greenbriar as the owner of a bookvan and the companion of a literary huckster. Also I recollected that if Andrew should try to trace us it would be as well for me to keep out of sight. So after telling Mr. Mifflin how I felt about matters I dived into the Parnassus and lay down most comfortably on the bunk. Bock the terrier joined me, and I rested there in great comfort of mind and body as we ambled down the grade. The sun shone through the little skylight gilding a tin pan that hung over the cook stove. Tacked here and there were portraits of authors, and I noticed a faded newspaper cutting pinned up. The headlines ran: "Literary Pedlar Lectures on Poetry." I read it through. Apparently the Professor (so I had begun to call him, as the aptness of the nickname stuck in my mind) had given a lecture in Camden, N.J., where he had asserted that Tennyson was a greater poet than Walt Whitman; and the boosters of the Camden poet had enlivened the evening with missiles. It seems that the chief Whitman disciple in Camden is Mr. Traubel; and Mr. Mifflin had started the rumpus by asserting that Tennyson, too, had "Traubels of his own." What an absurd creature the Professor was, I thought, as I lay comfortably lulled by the rolling wheels.

Greenbriar is a straggling little town, built around a large common meadow. Mifflin's general plan in towns, he had told me, was to halt Parnassus in front of the principal store or hotel, and when a little throng had gathered he would put up the flaps of the van, distribute his cards, and deliver a harangue on the value of good books. I lay concealed inside, but I gathered from the sounds that this was what was happening. We came to a stop; I heard a growing murmur of voices and laughter outside, and then the click of the raised sides of the wagon. I heard Mifflin's shrill, slightly nasal voice making facetious remarks as he passed out the cards. Evidently Bock was quite accustomed to the routine, for though his tail wagged gently when the Professor began to talk, he lay quite peaceably dozing at my feet.

"My friends," said Mr. Mifflin. "You remember Abe Lincoln's joke about the dog? If you call a tail a leg, said Abe, how many legs has a dog? Five, you answer. No, says Abe; because calling a tail a leg doesn't make it a leg. Well, there are lots of us in the same case as that dog's tail. Calling us men doesn't *make* us men. No creature on earth has a right to think himself a human being if he doesn't know at least one good book. The man that spends every evening chewing Piper Heidsieck at the store is unworthy to catch the intimations of a benevolent Creator. The man that's got a few good books on his shelf is making his wife happy, giving his children a square deal, and he's likely to be a better citizen himself. How about that, parson?"

I heard the deep voice of Reverend Kane, the Methodist minister: "You're dead right, Professor!" he shouted. "Tell us some more about books. I'm right with you!" Evidently Mr. Kane had been attracted by the sight of Parnassus, and I could hear him muttering to himself as he pulled one or two books from the shelves. How surprised he would have been if he had known I was inside the van! I took the precaution of slipping the bolt of the door at the back, and drew the curtains. Then I crept back into the bunk. I began to imagine what an absurd situation there would be if Andrew should arrive on the scene.

"You are all used to hucksters and pedlars and fellows selling every kind of junk from brooms to bananas," said the Professor's voice. "But how often does any one come round here to sell you books? You've got your town library, I dare say; but there are some books that folks ought to own. I've got 'em all here from Bibles to cook books. They'll speak for themselves. Step up to the shelves, friends, and pick and choose."

I heard the parson asking the price of something he had found on the shelves, and I believe he bought it; but the hum of voices around the flanks of Parnassus was very soothing, and in spite of my interest in what was going on I'm afraid I fell asleep. I must have been pretty tired; anyway I never felt the van start again. The Professor says he looked in through the little window from the driver's seat, and saw me sound asleep. And the next thing I knew I woke up with a start to find myself rolling leisurely in the dark. Bock was still lying over my feet, and there was a faint, musical clang from the bucket under the van which struck against something now and then. The Professor was sitting in front, with a lighted lantern hanging from the peak of the van roof. He was humming some outlandish song to himself, with a queer, monotonous refrain:

*Shipwrecked was I off Soft Perowse*
*And right along the shore,*
*And so I did resolve to roam*
*The country to explore.*
*Tommy rip fal lal and a balum tip*
*Tommy rip fal lal I dee;*
*And so I did resolve to roam*
*The country for to see!*

I jumped out of the bunk, cracked my shins against something, and uttered a rousing halloo. Parnassus stopped, and the Professor pushed back the sliding window behind the driver's seat.

"Heavens!" I said. "Father Time, what o'clock is it?"

"Pretty near supper time, I reckon. You must have fallen asleep while I was taking money from the Philistines. I made nearly three dollars for you. Let's pull up along the road and have a bite to eat."

He guided Pegasus to one side of the road, and then showed me how to light the swinging lamp that hung under the skylight. "No use to light the stove on a lovely evening like this," he said. "I'll collect some sticks and we can cook outside. You get out your basket of grub and I'll make a fire." He unhitched Pegasus, tied her to a tree, and gave her a nose bag of oats. Then he rooted around for some twigs and had a fire going in a jiffy. In five minutes I had bacon and scrambled eggs sizzling in a frying pan, and he had brought out a pail of water from the cooler under the bunk, and was making tea.

I never enjoyed a picnic so much! It was a perfect autumn evening, windless and frosty, with a dead black sky and a tiny rim of new moon like a thumb-nail paring. We had our eggs and bacon, washed down with tea and condensed milk, and followed by bread and jam. The little fire burned blue and cozy, and we sat on each side of it while Bock scoured the pan and ate the crusts.

"This your own bread, Miss McGill?" he asked.

"Yes," I said. "I was calculating the other day that I've baked more than 400 loaves a year for the last fifteen years. That's more than 6,000 loaves of bread. They can put that on my tombstone."

"The art of baking bread is as transcendent a mystery as the art of making sonnets," said Redbeard. "And then your hot biscuits—they might be counted as shorter lyrics, I suppose—triolets perhaps. That makes quite an anthology, or a doxology, if you prefer it."

"Yeast is yeast, and West is West," I said, and was quite surprised at my own cleverness. I hadn't made a remark like that to Andrew in five years.

"I see you are acquainted with Kipling," he said.

"Oh, yes, every governess is."

"Where and whom did you govern?"

"I was in New York, with the family of a wealthy stockbroker. There were three children. I used to take them walking in Central Park."

"Did you ever go to Brooklyn?" he asked abruptly.

"Never," I replied.

"Ah!" he said. "That's just the trouble. New York is Babylon; Brooklyn is the true Holy City. New York is the city of envy, office work, and hustle; Brooklyn is the region of homes and happiness. It is extraordinary: poor, harassed New Yorkers presume to look down on low-lying, home-loving Brooklyn, when as a matter of fact it is the precious jewel their souls are thirsting for and they never know it. Broadway: think how symbolic the name is. Broad is the way that leadeth to destruction! But in Brooklyn the ways are narrow, and they lead to the Heavenly City of content. Central Park: there you are—the centre of things, hemmed in by walls of pride. Now how much better is Prospect Park, giving a fair view over the hills of humility! There is no hope for New Yorkers, for they glory in their skyscraping sins; but in Brooklyn there is the wisdom of the lowly."

"So you think that if I had been a governess in Brooklyn I should have been so contented that I would never have come with Andrew and compiled my anthology of 6,000 loaves of bread and the lesser lyrics?"

But the volatile Professor had already soared to other points of view, and was not to be thwarted by argument.

"Of course Brooklyn is a dingy place, really," he admitted. "But to me it symbolizes a state of mind, whereas New York is only a state of pocket. You see I was a boy in Brooklyn: it still trails clouds of glory for me. When I get back there and start work on my book I shall be as happy as Nebuchadnezzar when he left off grass and returned to tea and crumpets. 'Literature Among the Farmers' I'm going to call it, but that's a poor title. I'd like to read you some of my notes for it."

I'm afraid I poorly concealed a yawn. As a matter of fact I was sleepy, and it was growing chilly.

"Tell me first," I said, "where in the world are we, and what time is it?"

He pulled out a turnip watch. "It's nine o'clock," he said, "and we're about two miles from Shelby, I should reckon. Perhaps we'd better get along. They told me in Greenbriar that the Grand Central Hotel in Shelby is a good place to stop at. That's why I wasn't anxious to get there. It sounds so darned like New York."

He bundled the cooking utensils back into Parnassus, hitched Peg up again, and tied Bock to the stern of the van. Then he insisted on giving me the two dollars and eighty cents he had collected in Greenbriar. I was really too sleepy to protest, and of course it was mine anyway. We creaked off along the dark and silent road between the pine woods. I think he talked fluently about his pilgrim's progress among the farmers of a dozen states, but (to be honest) I fell asleep in my corner of the seat. I woke up when we halted before the one hotel in Shelby—a plain, unimposing country inn, despite its absurd name. I left him to put Parnassus and the animals away for the night, while I engaged a room. Just as I got my key from the clerk he came into the dingy lobby.

"Well, Mr. Mifflin," I said. "Shall I see you in the morning?"

"I had intended to push on to Port Vigor to-night," he said, "but as it's fully eight miles (they tell me), I guess I'll bivouac here. I think I'll go into the smoking-room and put them wise to some good books. We won't say good-bye till to-morrow."

My room was pleasant and clean (fairly so). I took my suit case up with me and had a hot bath. As I fell asleep I heard a shrill voice ascending from below, punctuated with masculine laughter. The Pilgrim was making more converts!

## Chapter Six

I had a curious feeling of bewilderment when I woke the next morning. The bare room with the red-and-blue rag carpet and green china toilet set was utterly strange. In the hall outside I heard a clock strike. "Heavens!" I thought, "I've overslept myself nearly two hours. What on earth will Andrew do for breakfast?" And then as I ran to close the window I saw the blue Parnassus with its startling red letters standing in the yard. Instantly I remembered. And discreetly peeping from behind the window shade I saw that the Professor, armed with a tin of paint, was blotting out his own name on the side of the van, evidently intending to substitute mine. That was something I had not thought of. However, I might as well make the best of it.

I dressed promptly, repacked my bag, and hurried downstairs for breakfast. The long table was nearly empty, but one or two men sitting at the other end eyed me curiously. Through the window I could see my name in large, red letters, growing on the side of the van, as the Professor diligently wielded his brush. And when I had finished my coffee and beans and bacon I noticed with some amusement that the Professor had painted out the line about Shakespeare, Charles Lamb, and so on, and had substituted new lettering. The sign now read:

H. MCGILL'S
TRAVELLING PARNASSUS
GOOD BOOKS FOR SALE
COOK BOOKS A SPECIALTY
INQUIRE WITHIN

Evidently he distrusted my familiarity with the classics.

I paid my bill at the desk, and was careful also to pay the charge for putting up the horse and van overnight. Then I strolled into the stable yard, where I found Mr. Mifflin regarding his handiwork with satisfaction. He had freshened up all the red lettering, which shone brilliantly in the morning sunlight.

"Good-morning," I said.

He returned it.

"There!" he cried—"Parnassus is really yours! All the world lies before you! And I've got some more money for you. I sold some books last night. I persuaded the hotel keeper to buy several volumes of O. Henry for his smoking-room shelf, and I sold the 'Waldorf Cook Book' to the cook. My! wasn't her coffee awful? I hope the cook book will better it."

He handed me two limp bills and a handful of small change. I took it gravely and put it in my purse. This was really not bad—more than ten dollars in less than twenty-four hours.

"Parnassus seems to be a gold mine," I said.

"Which way do you think you'll go?" he asked.

"Well, as I know you want to get to Port Vigor I might just as well give you a lift that way," I answered.

"Good! I was hoping you'd say that. They tell me the stage for Port Vigor doesn't leave till noon, and I think it would kill me to hang around here all morning with no books to sell. Once I get on the train I'll be all right."

Bock was tied up in a corner of the yard, under the side door of the hotel. I went over to release him while the Professor was putting Peg into harness. As I stooped to unfasten the chain from his collar I heard some one talking through the telephone. The hotel lobby was just over my head, and the window was open.

"What did you say?"

"———— ———— ———— ————"

"McGill? Yes, sir, registered here last night. She's here now."

I didn't wait to hear more. Unfastening Bock, I hurried to tell Mifflin. His eyes sparkled.

"The Sage is evidently on our spoor," he chuckled. "Well, let's be off. I don't see what he can do even if he overhauls us."

The clerk was calling me from the window: "Miss McGill, your brother's on the wire and asks to speak to you."

"Tell him I'm busy," I retorted, and climbed onto the seat. It was not a diplomatic reply, I'm afraid, but I was too exhilarated by the keen morning and the spirit of adventure to stop to think of a better answer. Mifflin clucked to Peg, and off we went.

The road from Shelby to Port Vigor runs across the broad hill slopes that trend toward the Sound; and below, on our left, the river lay glittering in the valley. It was a perfect landscape: the woods were all bronze and gold; the clouds were snowy white and seemed like heavenly washing hung out to air; the sun was warm and swam gloriously in an arch of superb blue. My heart was uplifted indeed. For the first time, I think, I knew how Andrew feels on those vagabond trips of his. Why had all this been hidden from me before? Why had the transcendent mystery of baking bread blinded me so long to the mysteries of sun and sky and wind in the trees? We passed a white farmhouse close to the road. By the gate sat the farmer on a log, whittling a stick and smoking his pipe. Through the kitchen window I could see a woman blacking the stove. I wanted to cry out: "Oh, silly woman! Leave your stove, your pots and pans and chores, even if only for one day! Come out and see the sun in the sky and the river in the distance!" The farmer looked blankly at Parnassus as we passed, and then I remembered my mission as a distributor of literature. Mifflin was sitting with one foot on his bulging portmanteau, watching the tree tops rocking in the cool wind. He seemed to be far away in a morning muse. I threw down the reins and accosted the farmer.

"Good-morning, friend."

"Morning to you, ma'am," he said firmly.

"I'm selling books," I said. "I wonder if there isn't something you need?"

"Thanks, lady," he said, "but I bought a mort o' books last year an' I don't believe I'll ever read 'em this side Jordan. A whole set o' 'Funereal Orations' what an agent left on me at a dollar a month. I could qualify as earnest mourner at any death-bed merry-makin' now, I reckon."

"You need some books to teach you how to live, not how to die," I said. "How about your wife—wouldn't she enjoy a good book? How about some fairy tales for the children?"

"Bless me," he said, "I ain't got a wife. I never was a daring man, and I guess I'll confine my melancholy pleasures to them funereal orators for some time yet."

"Well, now, hold on a minute!" I exclaimed. "I've got just the thing for you." I had been looking over the shelves with some care, and remembered seeing a copy of "Reveries of a Bachelor." I clambered down, raised the flap of the van (it gave me quite a thrill to do it myself for the first time), and hunted out the book. I looked inside the cover and saw the letters *n m* in Mifflin's neat hand.

"Here you are," I said. "I'll sell you that for thirty cents."

"Thank you kindly, ma'am," he said courteously. "But honestly I wouldn't know what to do with it. I am working through a government report on scabworm and fungus, and I sandwich in a little of them funereal speeches with it, and honestly that's about all the readin' I figure on. That an' the Port Vigor Clarion."

I saw that he really meant it, so I climbed back on the seat. I would have liked to talk to the woman in the kitchen who was peering out of the window in amazement, but I decided it would be better to jog on and not waste time. The farmer and I exchanged friendly salutes, and Parnassus rumbled on.

The morning was so lovely that I did not feel talkative, and as the Professor seemed pensive I said nothing. But as Peg plodded slowly up a gentle slope he suddenly pulled a book out of his pocket and began to read aloud. I was watching the river, and did not turn round, but listened carefully:

*"Rolling cloud, volleying wind, and wheeling sun—the blue tabernacle of sky, the circle of the seasons, the sparkling multitude of the stars—all these are surely part of one rhythmic, mystic whole. Everywhere, as we go about our small business, we must discern the fingerprints of the gigantic plan, the orderly and inexorable routine with neither beginning nor end, in which death is but a preface to another birth, and birth the certain forerunner of another death. We human beings are as powerless to conceive the motive or the moral of it all as the dog is powerless to understand the reasoning in his master's mind. He sees the master's acts, benevolent or malevolent, and wags his tail. But the master's acts are always inscrutable to him. And so with us.*

*"And therefore, brethren, let us take the road with a light heart. Let us praise the bronze of the leaves and the crash of the surf while we have eyes to see and ears to hear. An honest amazement at the unspeakable beauties of the world is a comely posture for the scholar. Let us all be scholars under Mother Nature's eye.*

"How do you like that?" he asked.

"A little heavy, but very good," I said. "There's nothing in it about the transcendent mystery of baking bread!"

He looked rather blank.

"Do you know who wrote it?" he asked.

I made a valiant effort to summon some of my governessly recollections of literature.

"I give it up," I said feebly. "Is it Carlyle?"

"That is by Andrew McGill," he said. "One of his cosmic passages which are now beginning to be reprinted in schoolbooks. The blighter writes well."

I began to be uneasy lest I should be put through a literary catechism, so I said nothing, but roused Peg into an amble. To tell the truth I was more curious to hear the Professor talk about his own book than about Andrew's. I had always carefully refrained from reading Andrew's stuff, as I thought it rather dull.

"As for me," said the Professor, "I have no facility at the grand style. I have always suffered from the feeling that it's better to read a good book than to write a poor one; and I've done so much mixed reading in my time that my mind is full of echoes and voices of better men. But this book I'm worrying about now really deserves to be written, I think, for it has a message of its own."

He gazed almost wistfully across the sunny valley. In the distance I caught a glint of the Sound. The Professor's faded tweed cap was slanted over one ear, and his stubby little beard shone bright red in the sun. I kept a sympathetic silence. He seemed pleased to have some one to talk to about his precious book.

"The world is full of great writers about literature," he said, "but they're all selfish and aristocratic. Addison, Lamb, Hazlitt, Emerson, Lowell—take any one you choose—they all conceive the love of books as a rare and perfect mystery for the few—a thing of the secluded study where they can sit alone at night with a candle, and a cigar, and a glass of port on the table and a spaniel on the hearthrug. What I say is, who has ever gone out into high roads and hedges to bring literature home to the plain man? To bring it home to his business and bosom, as somebody says? The farther into the country you go, the fewer and worse books you find. I've spent several years joggling around with this citadel of crime, and by the bones of Ben Ezra I don't think I ever found a really good book (except the Bible) at a farmhouse yet, unless I put it there myself. The mandarins of culture—what do they do to teach the common folk to read? It's no good writing down lists of books for farmers and compiling five-foot shelves; you've got to go out and visit the people yourself—take the books to them, talk to the teachers and bully the editors of country newspapers and farm magazines and tell the children stories—and then little by little you begin to get good books circulating in the veins of the nation. It's a great work, mind you! It's like carrying the Holy Grail to some of these way-back farmhouses. And I wish there were a thousand Parnassuses instead of this one. I'd never give it up if it weren't for my book: but I want to write about my ideas in the hope of stirring other folk up, too. I don't suppose there's a publisher in the country will take it!"

"Try Mr. Decameron," I said. "He's always been very nice to Andrew."

"Think what it would mean," he cried, waving an eloquent hand, "if some rich man would start a fund to equip a hundred or so wagons like this to go huckstering literature around through the rural districts. It would pay, too, once you got started. Yes, by the bones of Webster! I went to a meeting of booksellers once, at some hotel in New York, and told 'em about my scheme. They laughed at me. But I've had more fun toting books around in this Parnassus than I could have had in fifty years sitting in a bookstore, or teaching school, or preaching. Life's full of savour when you go creaking along the road like this. Look at today, with the sun and the air and the silver clouds. Best of all, though, I love the rainy days. I used to pull up alongside the road, throw a rubber blanket over Peg, and Bock and I would curl up in the bunk and smoke and read. I used to read aloud to Bock: we went through 'Midshipman Easy' together, and a good deal of Shakespeare. He's a very bookish dog. We've seen some queer experiences in this Parnassus."

The hill road from Shelby to Port Vigor is a lonely one, as most of the farmhouses lie down in the valley. If I had known better we might have taken the longer and more populous way, but as a matter of fact I was enjoying the wide view and the solitary road lying white in the sunshine. We jogged along very pleasantly. Once more we stopped at a house where Mifflin pleaded for a chance to exercise his art. I was much amused when he succeeded in selling a copy of "Grimm's Fairy Tales" to a shrewish spinster on the plea that she would enjoy reading the stories to her nephews and nieces who were coming to visit her.

"My!" he chuckled, as he gave me the dingy quarter he had extracted. "There's nothing in that book as grim as she is!"

A little farther on we halted by a roadside spring to give Peg a drink, and I suggested lunch. I had laid in some bread and cheese in Shelby, and with this and some jam we made excellent sandwiches. As we were sitting by the fence the motor stage trundled past on its way to Port Vigor. A little distance down the road it halted, and then went on again. I saw a familiar figure walking back toward us.

"Now I'm in for it," I said to the Professor. "Here's Andrew!"

*Chapter Seven*

Andrew is just as thin as I am fat, and his clothes hang on him in the most comical way. He is very tall and shambling, wears a ragged beard and a broad Stetson hat, and suffers amazingly from hay fever in the autumn. (In fact, his essay on "Hay Fever" is the best thing he ever wrote, I think.) As he came striding up the road I noticed how his trousers fluttered at the ankles as the wind plucked at them. The breeze curled his beard back under his chin and his face was quite dark with anger. I couldn't help being amused; he looked so funny.

"The Sage looks like Bernard Shaw," whispered Mifflin.

I always believe in drawing first blood.

"Good-morning, Andrew," I called cheerfully. "Want to buy any books?" I halted Pegasus, and Andrew stood a little in front of the wheel—partly out of breath and mostly out of temper.

"What on earth is this nonsense, Helen?" he said angrily. "You've led me the deuce of a chase since yesterday. And who is this—this person you're driving with?"

"Andrew," I said, "you forget your manners. Let me introduce Mr. Mifflin. I have bought his caravan and am taking a holiday, selling books. Mr. Mifflin is on his way to Port Vigor where he takes the train to Brooklyn."

Andrew stared at the Professor without speaking. I could tell by the blaze in his light-blue eyes that he was thoroughly angry, and I feared things would be worse before they were better. Andrew is slow to wrath, but a very hard person to deal with when roused. And I had some inkling by this time of the Professor's temperament. Moreover, I am afraid that some of my remarks had rather prejudiced him against Andrew, as a brother at any rate and apart from his excellent prose.

Mifflin had the next word. He had taken off his funny little cap, and his bare skull shone like an egg. I noticed a little sort of fairy ring of tiny drops around his crown.

"My dear sir," said Mifflin, "the proceedings look somewhat unusual, but the facts are simple to narrate. Your sister has bought this van and its contents, and I have been instructing her in my theories of the dissemination of good books. You as a literary man..."

Andrew paid absolutely no attention to the Professor, and I saw a slow flush tinge Mifflin's sallow cheek.

"Look here, Helen," said Andrew, "do you think I propose to have my sister careering around the State with a strolling vagabond? Upon my soul you ought to have better sense—and at your age and weight! I got home yesterday and found your ridiculous note. I went to Mrs. Collins, and she knew nothing. I went to Mason's, and found him wondering who had bilked his telephone. I suppose you did that. He had seen this freight car of yours and put me on the track. But my God! I never thought to see a woman of forty abducted by gypsies!"

Mifflin was about to speak but I waved him back.

"Now see here Andrew," I said, "you talk too quickly. A woman of forty (you exaggerate, by the way) who has compiled an anthology of 6,000 loaves of bread and dedicated it to you deserves some courtesy. When *you* want to run off on some vagabond tour or other you don't hesitate to do it. You expect me to stay home and do the Lady Eglantine in the poultry yard. By the ghost of Susan B. Anthony, I won't do it! This is the first real holiday I've had in fifteen years, and I'm going to suit myself."

Andrew's mouth opened, but I shook my fist so convincingly that he halted.

"I bought this Parnassus from Mr. Mifflin fair and square for four hundred dollars. That's the price of about thirteen hundred dozen eggs," I said. (I had worked this out in my head while Mifflin was talking about his book.)

"The money's mine, and I'm going to use it my own way. Now, Andrew McGill, if you want to buy any books, you can parley with me. Otherwise, I'm on my way. You can expect me back when you see me." I handed him one of Mifflin's little cards, which were in a pocket at the side of the van, and gathered up the reins. I was really angry, for

Andrew had been both unreasonable and insulting.

Andrew looked at the card, and tore it in halves. He looked at the side of Parnassus where the fresh red lettering was still damp.

"Well, upon my word," he said, "you must be crazy." He burst into a violent fit of sneezing—a last touch of hay fever, I suspect, as there was still goldenrod in the meadows. He coughed and sneezed furiously, which made him madder than ever. At last he turned to Mifflin who was sitting bald-headed with a flushed face and very bright eyes. Andrew took him all in, the shabby Norfolk jacket, the bulging memorandum book in his pocket, the stuffed portmanteau under his foot, even the copy of "Happiness and Hayseed" which had dropped to the floor and lay back up.

"Look here, you," said Andrew, "I don't know by what infernal arts you cajoled my sister away to go vagabonding in a huckster's wagon, but I know this, that if you've cheated her out of her money I'll have the law on you."

I tried to insert a word of protest, but matters had gone too far. The Professor was as mad as Andrew now.

"By the bones of Piers Plowman," he said, "I had expected to meet a man of letters and the author of this book"—he held up "Happiness and Hayseed"—"but I see I was mistaken. I tell you, sir, a man who would insult his sister before a stranger, as you have done, is an oaf and a cad." He threw the book over the hedge, and before I could say a word he had vaulted over the off wheel and ran round behind the van.

"Look here sir," he said, with his little red beard bristling, "your sister is over age and acting of her own free will. By the bones of the Baptist, I don't blame her for wanting a vacation if this is the way you treat her. She is nothing to me, sir, and I am nothing to her, but I propose to be a teacher to you. Put up your hands and I'll give you a lesson!"

This was too much for me. I believe I screamed aloud, and started to clamber from the van. But before I could do anything the two fanatics had begun to pummel each other. I saw Andrew swing savagely at Mifflin, and Mifflin hit him square on the chin. Andrew's hat fell on the road. Peg stood placidly, and Bock made as if to grab Andrew's leg, but I hopped out and seized him.

It was certainly a weird sight. I suppose I should have wrung my hands and had hysterics, but as a matter of fact I was almost amused, it was so silly. Thank goodness the road was deserted.

Andrew was a foot taller than the Professor, but awkward, loosely knit, and unmuscular, while the little Redbeard was wiry as a cat. Also Andrew was so furious that he was quite beside himself, and Mifflin was in the cold anger that always wins. Andrew landed a couple of flailing blows on the other man's chest and shoulders, but in thirty seconds he got another punch on the chin followed by one on the nose that tumbled him over backward.

Andrew sat in the road fishing for a handkerchief, and Mifflin stood glaring at him, but looking very ill at ease. Neither of them said a word. Bock broke away from me and capered and danced about Mifflin's feet as if it were all a game. It was an extraordinary scene. Andrew got up, mopping his bleeding nose.

"Upon my soul," he said, "I almost respect you for that punch. But by Jove I'll have the law on you for kidnapping my sister. You're a fine kind of a pirate."

Mifflin said nothing.

"Don't be a fool, Andrew" I said. "Can't you see that I want a little adventure of my own? Go home and bake six thousand loaves of bread, and by the time they're done I'll be back again. I think two men of your age ought to be ashamed of yourselves. I'm going off to sell books." And with that I climbed up to the seat and clucked to Pegasus. Andrew and Mifflin and Bock remained standing in the road.

I was mad all the way through. I was mad at both men for behaving like schoolboys. I was mad at Andrew for being so unreasonable, yet in a way I admired him for it; I was mad at Mifflin for giving Andrew a bloody nose, and yet I appreciated the spirit in which it was done. I was mad at myself for causing all the trouble, and I was mad at Parnassus. If there had been a convenient cliff handy I would have pushed the old thing over it. But now I was in for it, and just had to go on. Slowly I rolled up a long grade, and then saw Port Vigor lying ahead and the broad blue stretches of the Sound.

Parnassus rumbled on with its pleasant creak, and the mellow sun and sweep of the air soon soothed me. I began to taste salt in the wind, and above the meadows two or three seagulls were circling. Like all women, my angry mood melted into a reaction of exaggerated tenderness and I began to praise both Andrew and Mifflin in my heart. How fine to have a brother so solicitous of his sister's welfare and reputation! And yet, how splendid the little, scrawny Professor had been! How quick to resent an insult and how bold to avenge it! His absurd little tweed cap was lying on the seat, and I picked it up almost sentimentally. The lining was frayed and torn. From my suit case in the van I got out a small sewing kit, and hanging the reins on a hook I began to stitch up the rents as Peg jogged along. I thought with amusement of the quaint life Mr. Mifflin had led in his "caravan of culture." I imagined him addressing the audience of Whitman disciples in Camden, and wondered how the fuss ended. I imagined him in his beloved Brooklyn, strolling in Prospect Park and preaching to chance comers his gospel of good books. How different was his militant love of literature from Andrew's quiet satisfaction. And yet how much they really had in common! It tickled me to think of Mifflin reading aloud from "Happiness and Hayseed," and praising it so highly, just before fighting with the author and giving him a bloody nose. I remembered that I should have spoken to Andrew about feeding the hens, and reminded him of his winter undergarments. What helpless creatures men are, after all!

I finished mending the cap in high good humour.

I had hardly laid it down when I heard a quick step in the road behind me, and looking back, there was Mifflin, striding along with his bald pate covered with little beads of moisture. Bock trotted sedately at his heels. I halted Peg.

"Well," I said, "what's happened to Andrew?"

The Professor still looked a bit shamefaced. "The Sage is a tenacious person," he said. "We argued for a bit without much satisfaction. As a matter of fact we nearly came to blows again, only he got another waft of goldenrod, which started him sneezing, and then his nose began bleeding once more. He is convinced that I'm a ruffian, and said so in excellent prose. Honestly, I admire him a great deal. I believe he intends to have the law on me. I gave him my Brooklyn address in case he wants to follow the matter up. I think I rather pleased him by asking him to autograph 'Happiness and Hayseed' for me. I found it lying in the ditch."

"Well," I said, "you two are certainly a great pair of lunatics. You both ought to go on the stage. You'd be as good as Weber and Fields. Did he give you the autograph?"

He pulled the book out of his pocket. Scrawled in it in pencil were the words *I have shed blood for Mr. Mifflin. Andrew McGill.*

"I shall read the book again with renewed interest," said Mifflin. "May I get in?"

"By all means," I said. "There's Port Vigor in front of us."

He put on his cap, noticed that it seemed to feel different, pulled it off again, and then looked at me in a quaint embarrassment.

"You are very good, Miss McGill," he said.

"Where did Andrew go?" I asked.

"He set off for Shelby on foot," Mifflin answered. "He has a grand stride for walking. He suddenly remembered that he had left some potatoes boiling on the fire yesterday afternoon, and said he must get back to attend to them. He said he hoped you would send him a postal card now and then. Do you know, he reminds me of Thoreau more than ever."

"He reminds me of a burnt cooking pot," I said. "I suppose all my kitchenware will be in a horrible state when I get home."

Christopher Morley    41

## Chapter Eight

Port Vigor is a fascinating old town. It is built on a point jutting out into the Sound. Dimly in the distance one can see the end of Long Island, which Mifflin viewed with sparkling eyes. It seemed to bring him closer to Brooklyn. Several schooners were beating along the estuary in the fresh wind, and there was a delicious tang of brine in the air. We drove direct to the station where the Professor alighted. We took his portmanteau, and shut Bock inside the van to prevent the dog from following him. Then there was an awkward pause as he stood by the wheel with his cap off.

"Well, Miss McGill," he said, "there's an express train at five o'clock, so with luck I shall be in Brooklyn to-night. My brother's address is 600 Abingdon Avenue, and I hope when you're sending a card to the Sage you'll let me have one, too. I shall be very homesick for Parnassus, but I'd rather leave her with you than with any one I know."

He bowed very low, and before I could say a word he blew his nose violently and hurried away. I saw him carrying his valise into the station, and then he disappeared. I suppose that living alone with Andrew for all these years has unused me to the eccentricities of other people, but surely this little Redbeard was one of the strangest beings one would be likely to meet.

Bock yowled dismally inside, and I did not feel in any mood to sell books in Port Vigor. I drove back into the town and stopped at a tea shop for a pot of tea and some toast. When I came out I found that quite a little crowd had collected, partly owing to the strange appearance of Parnassus and partly because of Bock's plaintive cries from within. Most of the onlookers seemed to suspect the outfit of being part of a travelling menagerie, so almost against my will I put up the flaps, tied Bock to the tail of the wagon, and began to answer the humorous questions of the crowd. Two or three bought books without any urging, and it was some time before I could get away. Finally I shut up the van and pulled off, as I was afraid of seeing some one I knew. As I turned into the Woodbridge Road I heard the whistle of the five o'clock train to New York.

The twenty miles of road between Sabine Farm and Port Vigor was all familiar to me, but now to my relief I struck into a region that I had never visited. On my occasional trips to Boston I had always taken the train at Port Vigor, so the country roads were unknown. But I had set out on the Woodbridge way because Mifflin had spoken of a farmer, Mr. Pratt, who lived about four miles out of Port Vigor, on the Woodbridge Road. Apparently Mr. Pratt had several times bought books from the Professor and the latter had promised to visit him again.

So I felt in duty bound to oblige a good customer.

After the varied adventures of the last two days it was almost a relief to be alone to think things over. Here was I, Helen McGill, in a queer case indeed. Instead of being home at Sabine Farm getting supper, I was trundling along a strange road, the sole owner of a Parnassus (probably the only one in existence), a horse, and a dog, and a cartload of books on my hands. Since the morning of the day before my whole life had twisted out of its accustomed orbit. I had spent four hundred dollars of my savings; I had sold about thirteen dollars' worth of books; I had precipitated a fight and met a philosopher. Not only that, I was dimly beginning to evolve a new philosophy of my own. And all this in order to prevent Andrew from buying a lot more books! At any rate, I had been successful in that. When he had seen Parnassus at last, he had hardly looked at her—except in tones of scorn. I caught myself wondering whether the Professor would allude to the incident in his book, and hoping that he would send me a copy. But after all, why should he mention it? To him it was only one of a thousand adventures. As he had said angrily to Andrew, he was nothing to me, nor I to him. How could he realize that this was the first adventure I had had in the fifteen years I had been—what was it he called it?—compiling my anthology. Well, the funny little gingersnap!

I kept Bock tied to the back of the van, as I was afraid he might take a notion to go in search of his master. As we jogged on, and the falling sun cast a level light across the way, I got a bit lonely. This solitary vagabonding business was a bit sudden after fifteen years of home life. The road lay close to the water and I watched the Sound grow a deeper blue and then a dull purple. I could hear the surf pounding, and on the end of Long Island a far-away lighthouse showed a ruby spark. I thought of the little gingersnap roaring toward New York on the express, and wondered whether he was travelling in a Pullman or a day coach. A Pullman chair would feel easy after that hard Parnassus seat.

By and by we neared a farmhouse which I took to be Mr. Pratt's. It stood close to the road, with a big, red barn behind and a gilt weathervane representing a galloping horse. Curiously enough Peg seemed to recognize the place, for she turned in at the gate and neighed vigorously. It must have been a favourite stopping place for the Professor.

Through a lighted window I could see people sitting around a table. Evidently the Pratts were at supper. I drew up in the yard. Some one looked out of a window, and I heard a girl's voice:

"Why, Pa, here's Parnassus!"

Gingersnap must have been a welcome visitor at that farm, for in an instant the whole family turned out with a great scraping of chairs and clatter of dishes. A tall, sunburnt man, in a clean shirt with no collar, led the group, and then came a stout woman about my own build, and a hired man and three children.

"Good evening!" I said. "Is this Mr. Pratt?"

"Sure thing!" said he. "Where's the Perfessor?"

"On his way to Brooklyn," said I. "And I've got Parnassus. He told me to be sure to call on you. So here we are."

"Well, I want to know!" ejaculated Mrs. Pratt. "Think of Parnassus turned suffrage! Ben, you put up the critters, and I'll take Mrs. Mifflin in to supper."

"Hold on there," I said. "My name's McGill—Miss McGill. See, it's painted on the wagon. I bought the outfit from Mr. Mifflin. A business proposition entirely."

"Well, well," said Mr. Pratt. "We're glad to see any friend of the Perfessor. Sorry he's not here, too. Come right in and have a bite with us."

They were certainly good-hearted folk, Mr. and Mrs. Ben Pratt. He put Peg and Bock away in the barn and gave them their supper, while Mrs. Pratt took me up to her spare bedroom and brought me a jug of hot water. Then they all trooped back into the dining-room and the meal began again. I am a connoisseur of farm cooking, I guess, and I've got to hand it to Beulah Pratt that she was an A-1 housewife. Her hot biscuit was perfect; the coffee was real Mocha, simmered, not boiled; the cold sausage and potato salad was as good as any Andrew ever got. And she had a smoking-hot omelet sent in for me, and opened a pot of her own strawberry preserve. The children (two boys and a girl) sat open-mouthed, nudging one another, and Mr. Pratt got out his pipe while I finished up on stewed pears and cream and chocolate cake. It was a regular meal. I wondered what Andrew was eating and whether he had found the nest behind the wood pile where the red hen always drops her eggs.

"Well, well," said Mr. Pratt, "tell us about the Perfessor. We was expectin' him here some time this fall. He generally gets here around cider time."

"I guess there isn't so much to tell," I said. "He stopped up at our place the other day, and said he wanted to sell his outfit. So I bought him out. He was pining to get back to Brooklyn and write a book."

"That book o' his!" said Mrs. Pratt. "He was always talkin' on it, but I don't believe he ever started it yet."

"Whereabout do you come from, Miss McGill?" said Pratt. I could see he was mighty puzzled at a woman driving a vanload of books around the country, alone.

"Over toward Redfield," I said.

"You any kin to that writer that lives up that way?"

"You mean Andrew McGill?" I said. "He's my brother."

"Do tell!" exclaimed Mrs. Pratt. "Why the Perfessor thought a terrible lot of him. He read us all to sleep with one of his books one night. Said he was the best literature in this State, I do believe."

I smiled to myself as I thought of the set-to on the road from Shelby.

"Well," said Pratt, "if the Perfessor's got any better friends than us in these parts, I'm glad to meet 'em. He come here first time 'bout four years ago. I was up working in the hayfield that afternoon, and I heard a shout down by the mill pond. I looked over that way and saw a couple o' kids waving their arms and screamin'. I ran down the hill and there was the Perfessor just a pullin' my boy Dick out o' the water. Dick's this one over here."

Dick, a small boy of thirteen or so, grew red under his freckles.

"The kids had been foolin' around on a raft there, an' first thing you know Dick fell in, right into deep water, over by the dam. Couldn't swim a stroke, neither. And the Perfessor, who jest happened to be comin' along in that 'bus of his, heard the boys yell. Didn't he hop out o' the wagon as spry as a chimpanzee, skin over the fence, an' jump into the pond, swim out there an' tow the boy in! Yes, ma'am, he saved that boy's life then an' no mistake. That man can read me to sleep with poetry any night he has a mind to. He's a plumb fine little firecracker, the Perfessor."

Farmer Pratt pulled hard on his pipe. Evidently his friendship for the wandering bookseller was one of the realities of his life.

"Yes, ma'am," he went on, "that Perfessor has been a good friend to me, sure enough. We brought him an' the boy back to the house. The boy had gone down three times an' the Perfessor had to dive to find him. They were both purty well all in, an' I tell you I was scared. But we got Dick around somehow—rolled him on a sugar bar'l, an' poured whiskey in him, an' worked his arms, an' put him in hot blankets. By and by he come to. An' then I found that the Perfessor, gettin' over the barb-wire fence so quick (when he lit for the pond) had torn a hole in his leg you could put four fingers in. There was his trouser all stiff with blood, an' he not sayin' a thing. Pluckiest little runt in three States, by Judas! Well, we put *him* to bed, too, and then the Missus keeled over, an' we put *her* to bed. Three of them, by time the Doc got here. Great old summer afternoon that was! But bless your heart, we couldn't keep the Perfessor abed long. Next day he was out lookin' fer his poetry books, an' first thing you know he had us all rounded up an' was preachin' good literature at us like any evangelist. I guess we all fell asleep over his poetry, so then he started on readin' that 'Treasure Island' story to us, wasn't it, Mother? By hickory, we none of us fell asleep over that. He started the kids readin' so they been at it ever since, and Dick's top boy at school now. Teacher says she never saw such a boy for readin'. That's what Perfessor done for us! Well, tell us 'bout yerself, Miss McGill. Is there any good books we ought to read? I used to pine for some o' that feller Shakespeare my father used to talk about so much, but Perfessor always 'lowed it was over my head!" It gave me quite a thrill to hear all this about Mifflin. I could readily imagine the masterful little man captivating the simple-hearted Pratts with his eloquence and earnestness. And the story of the mill pond had its meaning, too. Little Redbeard was no mere wandering crank—he was a real man, cool and steady of brain, with the earmarks of a hero. I felt a sudden gush of warmth as I recalled his comical ways.

Mrs. Pratt lit a fire in her Franklin stove and I racked my head wondering how I could tread worthily in the Professor's footsteps. Finally I fetched the "Jungle Book" from Parnassus and read them the story of Rikki-Tikki-Tavi. There was a long pause when I had finished.

"Say, Pa," said Dick shyly, "that mongoose was rather like Professor, wasn't he!"

Plainly the Professor was the traditional hero of this family, and I began to feel rather like an impostor!

I suppose it was foolish of me, but I had already made up my mind to push on to Woodbridge that night. It could not be more than four miles, and the time was not much after eight. I felt a little twinge of quite unworthy annoyance because I was still treading in the glamour of the Professor's influence. The Pratts would talk of nothing else, and I wanted to get somewhere where I would be estimated at my own value, not merely as his disciple. "Darn the Redbeard," I said to myself, "I think he has bewitched these people!" And in spite of their protests and invitations to stay the night, I insisted on having Peg hitched up. I gave them the copy of the "Jungle Book" as a small return for their hospitality, and finally sold Mr. Pratt a little copy of "Lamb's Tales from Shakespeare" which I thought he could read without brain fever. Then I lit my lantern and after a chorus of good-byes Parnassus rolled away. "Well," I said to myself as I turned into the high road once more, "drat the gingersnap, he seems to hypnotize everybody... he must be nearly in Brooklyn by this time!"

It was very quiet along the road, also very dark, for the sky had clouded over and I could see neither moon nor stars. As it was a direct road I should have had no difficulty, and I suppose I must have fallen into a doze during which Peg took a wrong turning. At any rate, I realized about half-past nine that Parnassus was on a much rougher road than the highway had any right to be, and there were no telephone poles to be seen. I knew that they stretched all along the main road, so plainly I had made a mistake. I was reluctant for a moment to admit that I could be wrong, and just then Peg stumbled heavily and stood still. She paid no heed to my exhortations, and when I got out and carried my lantern to see whether anything was in the way, I found that she had cast a shoe and her foot was bleeding. The shoe must have dropped off some way back and she had picked up a nail or something in the quick. I saw no alternative but to stay where I was for the night.

This was not very pleasant, but the adventures of the day had put me into a stoical frame of mind, and I saw no good in repining. I unhitched Peg, sponged her foot, and tied her to a tree. I would have made more careful explorations to determine just where I was, but a sharp patter of rain began to fall. So I climbed into my Parnassus, took Bock in with me, and lit the swinging lamp. By this time it was nearly ten o'clock. There was nothing to do but turn in, so I took off my boots and lay down in the bunk. Bock lay quite comfortably on the floor of the van. I meant to read for a while, and so did not turn out the light, but I fell asleep almost immediately.

I woke up at half-past eleven and turned out the lamp, which had made the van very warm. I opened the little windows front and back, and would have opened the door, but I feared Bock might slip away. It was still raining a little. To my annoyance I felt very wakeful. I lay for some time listening to the patter of raindrops on the roof and skylight— a very snug sound when one is warm and safe. Every now and then I could hear Peg stamping in the underbrush. I was almost dozing off again when Bock gave a low growl.

No woman of my bulk has a right to be nervous, I guess, but instantly my security vanished! The patter of the rain seemed menacing, and I imagined a hundred horrors. I was totally alone and unarmed, and Bock was not a large dog. He growled again, and I felt worse than before. I imagined that I heard stealthy sounds in the bushes, and once Peg snorted as though frightened. I put my hand down to pat Bock, and found that his neck was all bristly, like a fighting cock. He uttered a queer half growl, half whine, which gave me a chill. Some one must be prowling about the van, but in the falling rain I could hear nothing.

I felt I must do something. I was afraid to call out lest I betray the fact that there was only a woman in the van. My expedient was absurd enough, but at any rate it satisfied my desire to act. I seized one of my boots and banged vigorously on the floor, at the same time growling in as deep and masculine a voice as I could muster: "*What the hell's the matter? What the hell's the matter?*" This sounds silly enough, I dare say, but it afforded me some relief. And as Bock shortly ceased growling, it apparently served some purpose.

I lay awake for a long time, tingling all over with nervousness. Then I began to grow calmer, and was getting drowsy almost in spite of myself when I was aroused by the unmistakable sound of Bock's tail thumping on the floor—a sure sign of pleasure. This puzzled me quite as much as his growls. I did not dare strike a light, but could hear him sniffing at the door of the van and whining with eagerness. This seemed very uncanny, and again I crept stealthily out of the bunk and pounded on the floor lustily, this time with the frying pan, which made an unearthly din. Peg neighed and snorted, and Bock began to bark. Even in my anxiety I almost laughed. "It sounds like an insane asylum," I thought, and reflected that probably the disturbance was only caused by some small animal. Perhaps a rabbit or a skunk which Bock had winded and wanted to chase. I patted him, and crawled into my bunk once more.

But my real excitement was still to come. About half an hour later I heard unmistakable footsteps alongside the van. Bock growled furiously, and I lay in a panic. Something jarred one of the wheels. Then broke out a most extraordinary racket. I heard quick steps, Peg whinneyed, and something fell heavily against the back of the wagon. There was a violent scuffle on the ground, the sound of blows, and rapid breathing. With my heart jumping I peered out of one of the back windows. There was barely any light, but dimly I could see a tumbling mass which squirmed and writhed on the ground. Something struck one of the rear wheels so that Parnassus trembled. I heard hoarse swearing, and then the whole body, whatever it was, rolled off into the underbrush. There was a terrific crashing and snapping of twigs. Bock whined, growled, and pawed madly at the door. And then complete silence.

My nerves were quite shattered by this time. I don't think I had been so frightened since childhood days when I awakened from a nightmare. Little trickles of fear crept up and down my spine and my scalp prickled. I pulled Bock on the bunk, and lay with one hand on his collar. He, too, seemed agitated and sniffed gingerly now and then. Finally, however, he gave a sigh and fell asleep. I judged it might have been two o'clock, but I did not like to strike a light. And at last I fell into a doze.

When I woke the sun was shining brilliantly and the air was full of the chirping of birds. I felt stiff and uneasy from sleeping in my clothes, and my foot was numb from Bock's weight.

I got up and looked out of the window. Parnassus was standing in a narrow lane by a grove of birch trees. The ground was muddy, and smeared with footprints behind the van. I opened the door and looked around. The first thing I saw, on the ground by one of the wheels, was a battered tweed cap.

### Chapter Nine

My feelings were as mixed as a crushed nut sundae. So the Professor hadn't gone to Brooklyn after all! What did he mean by prowling after me like a sleuth? Was it just homesickness for Parnassus? Not likely! And then the horrible noises I had heard in the night; had some tramp been hanging about the van in the hope of robbing me? Had the tramp attacked Mifflin? Or had Mifflin attacked the tramp? Who had got the better of it?

I picked up the muddy cap and threw it into the van. Anyway, I had problems of my own to tackle, and those of the Professor could wait.

Peg whinneyed when she saw me. I examined her foot. Seeing it by daylight the trouble was not hard to diagnose. A long, jagged piece of slate was wedged in the frog of the foot. I easily wrenched it out, heated some water, and gave the hoof another sponging. It would be all right when shod once more. But where was the shoe?

I gave the horse some oats, cooked an egg and a cup of coffee for myself at the little kerosene stove, and broke up a dog biscuit for Bock. I marvelled once more at the completeness of Parnassus' furnishings. Bock helped me to scour the pan. He sniffed eagerly at the cap when I showed it to him, and wagged his tail.

It seemed to me that the only thing I could do was to leave Parnassus and the animals where they were and retrace my steps as far as the Pratt farm. Undoubtedly Mr. Pratt would be glad to sell me a horse-shoe and send his hired man to do the job for me. I could not drive Peg as she was, with a sore foot and without a shoe. I judged Parnassus would be quite safe: the lane seemed to be a lonely one leading to a deserted quarry. I tied Bock to the steps to act as a guard, took my purse and the Professor's cap with me, locked the door of the van, and set off along the back track. Bock whined and tugged violently when he saw me disappearing, but I could see no other course.

The lane rejoined the main road about half a mile back. I must have been asleep or I could never have made the mistake of turning off. I don't see why Peg should have made the turn, unless her foot hurt and she judged the side track would be a good place to rest. She must have been well used to stopping overnight in the open.

I strode along pondering over my adventures, and resolved to buy a pistol when I got to Woodbridge. I remember thinking that I could write quite a book now myself. Already I began to feel quite a hardened pioneer. It doesn't take an adaptable person long to accustom one's self to a new way of life, and the humdrum routine of the farm certainly looked prosy compared to voyaging with Parnassus. When I had got beyond Woodbridge, and had crossed the river, I would begin to sell books in earnest. Also I would buy a notebook and jot down my experiences. I had heard of bookselling as a profession for women, but I thought that my taste of it was probably unique. I might even write a book that would rival Andrew's—yes, and Mifflin's. And that brought my thoughts to Barbarossa again.

Of all extraordinary people, I thought, he certainly takes the cake—and then, rounding a bend, I saw him sitting on a rail fence, with his head shining in the sunlight. My heart gave a sort of jump. I do believe I was getting fond of the Professor. He was examining something which he held in his hand.

"You'll get sunstroke," I said. "Here's your cap." And I pulled it out of my pocket and tossed it to him.

"Thanks," he said, as cool as you please. "And here's your horse-shoe. Fair exchange!"

I burst out laughing, and he looked disconcerted, as I hoped he would.

"I thought you'd be in Brooklyn by now," I said, "at 600 Abingdon Avenue, laying out Chapter One. What do you mean by following me this way? You nearly frightened me to death last night. I felt like one of Fenimore Cooper's heroines, shut up in the blockhouse while the redskins prowled about."

He flushed and looked very uncomfortable.

"I owe you an apology," he said. "I certainly never intended that you should see me. I bought a ticket for New York and checked my bag through. And then while I was waiting for the train it came over me that your brother was right, and that it was a darned risky thing for you to go jaunting about alone in Parnassus. I was afraid something might happen. I followed along the road behind you, keeping well out of sight."

"Where were you while I was at Pratt's?"

"Sitting not far down the road eating bread and cheese," he said. "Also I wrote a poem, a thing I very rarely do."

"Well, I hope your ears burned," I said, "for those Pratts have certainly raised you to the peerage."

He got more uncomfortable than ever.

"Well," he said, "I dare say it was all an error, but anyway I *did* follow you. When you turned off into that lane, I kept pretty close behind you. As it happens, I know this bit of country, and there are very often some hoboes hanging around the old quarry up that lane. They have a cave there where they go into winter quarters. I was afraid some of them might bother you. You could hardly have chosen a worse place to camp out. By the bones of George Eliot, Pratt ought to have warned you. I can't conceive why you didn't stop at his house overnight anyway."

"If you must know, I got weary of hearing them sing your praises."

I could see that he was beginning to get nettled.

"I regret having alarmed you," he said. "I see that Peg has dropped a shoe. If you'll let me fix it for you, after that I won't bother you."

We turned back again along the road, and I noticed the right side of his face for the first time. Under the ear was a large livid bruise.

"That hobo, or whoever he was," I said, "must have been a better fighter than Andrew. I see he landed on your cheek. Are you always fighting?"

His annoyance disappeared. Apparently the Professor enjoyed a fight almost as much as he did a good book.

"Please don't regard the last twenty-four hours as typical of me," he said with a chuckle. "I am so unused to being a squire of dames that perhaps I take the responsibilities too seriously."

"Did you sleep at all last night?" I asked. I think I began to realize for the first time that the gallant little creature had been out all night in a drizzling rain, simply to guard me from possible annoyance; and I had been unforgivably churlish about it.

"I found a very fine haystack in a field overlooking the quarry. I crawled into the middle of it. A haystack is sometimes more comfortable than a boarding-house."

"Well," I said penitently, "I can never forgive myself for the trouble I've caused you. It was awfully good of you to do what you did. Please put your cap on and don't catch cold."

We walked for several minutes in silence. I watched him out of the corner of my eye. I was afraid he might have caught his death of cold from being out all night in the wet, to say nothing of the scuffle he had had with the tramp; but he really looked as chipper as ever.

"How do you like the wild life of a bookseller?" he said. "You must read George Borrow. He would have enjoyed Parnassus."

"I was just thinking, when I met you, that I could write a book about my adventures."

"Good!" he said. "We might collaborate."

"There's another thing we might collaborate on," I said, "and that's breakfast. I'm sure you haven't had any."

"No," he said, "I don't think I have. I never lie when I know I shan't be believed."

"I haven't had any, either," I said. I thought that to tell an untruth would be the least thing I could do to reward the little man for his unselfishness.

"Well," he said, "I really thought that by this time—"

He broke off. "Was that Bock barking?" he asked sharply.

We had been walking slowly, and had not yet reached the spot where the lane branched from the main road. We were still about three quarters of a mile from the place where I had camped overnight. We both listened carefully, but I could hear nothing but the singing of the telephone wires along the road.

"No matter," he said. "I thought I heard a dog." But I noticed that he quickened his pace.

"I was saying," he continued, "that I had really thought to have lost Parnassus for good by this morning, but I'm tickled to death to have a chance to see her again. I hope she'll be as good a friend to you as she has been to me. I suppose you'll sell her when you return to the Sage?"

"I don't know I'm sure," I said. "I must confess I'm still a little at sea. My desire for an adventure seems to have let me in deeper than I expected. I begin to see that there's more in this bookselling game than I thought. Honestly, it's getting into my blood."

"Well, that's fine," he said heartily. "I couldn't have left Parnassus in better hands. You must let me know what you do with her, and then perhaps, when I've finished my book, I can buy her back."

We struck off into the lane. The ground was slippery under the trees and we went single file, Mifflin in front. I looked at my watch—it was nine o'clock, just an hour since I had left the van. As we neared the spot Mifflin kept looking ahead through the birch trees in a queer way.

"What's the matter?" I said. "We're almost there, aren't we?"

"We *are* there," he said. "Here's the place."

Parnassus was gone!

## Chapter Ten

We stood in complete dismay—I did, at any rate—for about as long as it takes to peel a potato. There could be no doubt in which direction the van had moved, for the track of the wheels was plain. It had gone farther up the lane toward the quarry. In the earth, which was still soggy, were a number of footprints.

"By the bones of Polycarp!" exclaimed the Professor, "those hoboes have stolen the van. I guess they think it'll make a fine Pullman sleeper for them. If I'd realized there was more than one of them I'd have hung around closer. They need a lesson."

Good Lord! I thought, here's Don Quixote about to wade into another fight.

"Hadn't we better go back and get Mr. Pratt?" I asked.

This was obviously the wrong thing to say. It put the fiery little man all the more on his mettle. His beard bristled. "Nothing of the sort!" he said. "Those fellows are cowards and vagabonds anyway. They can't be far off; you haven't been away more than an hour, have you? If they've done anything to Bock, by the bones of Chaucer, I'll harry them. I *thought* I heard him bark."

He hurried up the lane, and I followed in a panicky frame of mind. The track wound along a hillside, between a high bank and a forest of birch trees. I think the distance can't have been more than a quarter of a mile. Anyway, in a very few minutes the road made a sharp twist to the right and we found ourselves looking down into the quarry, over a sheer rocky drop of a hundred feet at least. Below, drawn over to one side of the wall of rock, stood Parnassus. Peg was between the shafts. Bock was nowhere to be seen. Sitting by the van were three disreputable looking men. The smoke of a cooking fire rose into the air; evidently they were making free with my little larder.

"Keep back," said the Professor softly. "Don't let them see us." He flattened himself in the grass and crawled to the edge of the cliff. I did the same, and we lay there, invisible from below, but quite able to see everything in the quarry. The three tramps were evidently enjoying an excellent breakfast.

"This place is a regular hang-out for these fellows," Mifflin whispered. "I've seen hoboes about here every year. They go into winter quarters about the end of October, usually. There's an old blasted-out section of this quarry that makes a sheltered dormitory for them, and as the place isn't worked any more they're not disturbed here so long as they don't make mischief in the neighbourhood. We'll give them...."

"Hands up!" said a rough voice behind us. I looked round. There was a fat, red-faced villainous-looking creature covering us with a shiny revolver. It was an awkward situation. Both the Professor and I were lying full length on the ground. We were quite helpless.

"Get up!" said the tramp in a husky, nasty voice. "I guess youse thought we wasn't covering our trail? Well, we'll have to tie you up, I reckon, while we get away with this Crystal Pallis of yourn."

I scrambled to my feet, but to my surprise the Professor continued to lie at full length.

"Get up, deacon!" said the tramp again. "Get up on them graceful limbs, *if* you please."

I guess he thought himself safe from attack by a woman. At any rate, he bent over as if to grab Mifflin by the neck. I saw my chance and jumped on him from behind. I am heavy, as I have said, and he sprawled on the ground. My doubts as to the pistol being loaded were promptly dissolved, for it went off like a cannon. Nobody was in front of it, however, and Mifflin was on his feet like a flash. He had the ruffian by the throat and kicked the weapon out of his hand. I ran to seize it.

"You son of Satan!" said the valiant Redbeard. "Thought you could bully us, did you? Miss McGill, you were as quick as Joan of Arc. Hand me the pistol, please."

I gave it to him, and he shoved it under the hobo's nose.

"Now," he said, "take off that rag around your neck."

The rag was an old red handkerchief, inconceivably soiled. The tramp removed it, grumbling and whining. Mifflin gave me the pistol to hold while he tied our prisoner's wrists together. In the meantime we heard a shout from the quarry. The three vagabonds were gazing up in great excitement.

"You tell those fashion plates down there," said Mifflin, as he knotted the tramp's hands together, "that if they make any fight I'll shoot them like crows." His voice was cold and savage and he seemed quite master of the situation, but I must confess I wondered how we could handle four of them.

The greasy ruffian shouted down to his pals in the quarry, but I did not hear what he said, as just then the Professor asked me to keep our captive covered while he got a stick. I stood with the pistol pointed at his head while Mifflin ran back into the birchwood to cut a cudgel.

The tramp's face became the colour of the under side of a fried egg as he looked into the muzzle of his own gun.

"Say, lady," he pleaded, "that gun goes off awful easy, point her somewhere else or you'll croak me by mistake."

I thought a good scare wouldn't do him any harm and kept the barrel steadily on him.

The rascals down below seemed debating what to do. I don't know whether they were armed or not; but probably they imagined that there were more than two of us. At all events, by the time Mifflin came back with a stout birch staff they were hustling out of the quarry on the lower side. The Professor swore, and looked as if he would gladly give chase, but he refrained.

"Here, you," he said in crisp tones to the tramp, "march on ahead of us, down to the quarry."

The fat ruffian shambled awkwardly down the trail. We had to make quite a detour to get into the quarry, and by the time we reached there the other three tramps had got clean away. I was not sorry, to tell the truth. I thought the Professor had had enough scrapping for one twenty-four hours.

Peg whinneyed loudly as she saw us coming, but Bock was not in sight.

"What have you done with the dog, you swine?" said Mifflin. "If you've hurt him I'll make you pay with your own hide."

Our prisoner was completely cowed. "No, boss, we ain't hurt the dog," he fawned. "We tied him up so he couldn't bark, that's all. He's in the 'bus." And sure enough, by this time we could hear smothered yelping and whining from Parnassus.

I hurried to open the door, and there was Bock, his jaws tied together with a rope-end. He bounded out and made super-canine efforts to express his joy at seeing the Professor again. He paid very little attention to me.

"Well," said Mifflin, after freeing the dog's muzzle, and with difficulty restraining him from burying his teeth in the tramp's shin, "what shall we do with this heroic specimen of manhood? Shall we cart him over to the jail in Port Vigor, or shall we let him go?"

The tramp burst into a whining appeal that was almost funny, it was so abject. The Professor cut it short.

"I ought to pack you into quod," he said. "Are you the Phoebus Apollo I scuffled with down the lane last night? Was it you skulking around this wagon then?"

"No, boss, that was Splitlip Sam, honest to Gawd it was. He come back, boss; said he'd been fightin' with a cat-o'-mountain! Say, boss, you sure hit him hard. One of his lamps is a pudding! Boss, I'll swear I ain't had nothin' to do with it."

"I don't like your society," said the Professor, "and I'm going to turn you loose. I'm going to count ten, and if you're not out of this quarry by then, I'll shoot. And if I see you again I'll skin you alive. Now get out!"

He cut the knotted handkerchief in two. The hobo needed no urging. He spun on his heel and fled like a rabbit. The Professor watched him go, and as the fat, ungainly figure burst through a hedge and disappeared he fired the revolver into the air to frighten him still more. Then he tossed the weapon into the pool near by.

"Well, Miss McGill," he said with a chuckle, "if you like to undertake breakfast, I'll fix up Peg." And he drew the horse-shoe from his pocket once more.

A brief inspection of Parnassus satisfied me that the thieves had not had time to do any real damage. They had got out most of the eatables and spread them on a flat rock in preparation for a feast; and they had tracked a good deal of mud into the van; but otherwise I could see nothing amiss. So while Mifflin busied himself with Peg's foot it was easy for me to get a meal under way. I found a gush of clean water trickling down the face of the rock. There were still some eggs and bread and cheese in the little cupboard, and an unopened tin of condensed milk. I gave Peg her nose bag of oats, and fed Bock, who was frisking about in high spirits. By that time the shoeing was done, and the Professor and I sat down to an improvised meal. I was beginning to feel as if this gipsy existence were the normal course of my life.

"Well, Professor," I said, as I handed him a cup of coffee and a plate of scrambled eggs and cheese, "for a man who slept in a wet haystack, you acquit yourself with excellent valour."

"Old Parnassus is quite a stormy petrel," he said. "I used to think the chief difficulty in writing a book would be to invent things to happen, but if I were to sit down and write the adventures I'd had with her it would be a regular Odyssey."

"How about Peg's foot?" I asked. "Can she travel on it?"

"It'll be all right if you go easy. I've scraped out the injured part and put the shoe back. I keep a little kit of tools under the van for emergencies of all sorts."

It was chilly, and we didn't dawdle over our meal. I only made a feint of eating, as I had had a little breakfast before, and also as the events of the last few hours had left me rather restless. I wanted to get Parnassus out on the highway again, to jog along in the sun and think things over. The quarry was a desolate, forbidding place anyway. But before we left we explored the cave where the tramps had been preparing to make themselves comfortable for the winter. It was not really a cave, but only a shaft into the granite cliff. A screen of evergreen boughs protected the opening against the weather, and inside were piles of sacking that had evidently been used as beds, and many old grocery boxes for tables and chairs. It amused me to notice a cracked fragment of mirror balanced on a corner of rock. Even these ragamuffins apparently were not totally unconscious of personal appearance. I seized the opportunity, while the Professor was giving Peg's foot a final look, to rearrange my hair, which was emphatically a sight. I hardly think Andrew would have recognized me that morning.

We led Peg up the steep incline, back into the lane where I had strayed, and at length we reached the main road again. Here I began to lay down the law to Redbeard.

"Now look here, Professor," I said, "I'm not going to have you tramp all the way back to Port Vigor. After the night you've had you need a rest. You just climb into that Parnassus and lie down for a good snooze. I'll drive you into Woodbridge and you can take your train there. Now you get right into that bunk. I'll sit out here and drive."

He demurred, but without much emphasis. I think the little fool was just about fagged out, and no wonder. I was a trifle groggy myself. In the end he was quite docile. He climbed into the van, took off his boots, and lay down under a blanket. Bock followed him, and I think they both fell asleep on the instant. I got on the front seat and took the reins. I didn't let Peg go more quickly than a walk as I wanted to spare her sore foot.

My, what a morning that was after the rain! The road ran pretty close to the shore, and every now and then I could catch a glimpse of the water. The air was keen—not just the ordinary, unnoticed air that we breathe in and out and don't think about, but a sharp and tingling essence, as strong in the nostrils as camphor or ammonia. The sun seemed focussed upon Parnassus, and we moved along the white road in a flush of golden light. The flat fronds of the cedars swayed gently in the salty air, and for the first time in ten years, I should think, I began amusing myself by selecting words to describe the goodness of the morning. I even imagined myself writing a description of it, as if I were Andrew or Thoreau. The crazy little Professor had inoculated me with his literary bug, I guess.

And then I did a dishonourable thing. Just by chance I put my hand into the little pocket beside the seat where Mifflin kept a few odds and ends. I meant to have another look at that card of his with the poem on it. And there I found a funny, battered little notebook, evidently forgotten. On the cover was written, in ink, "Thoughts on the Present Discontents." That title seemed vaguely familiar. I seemed to recall something of the kind from my school days—more than twenty years ago, goodness me! Of course if I had been honourable I wouldn't have looked into it. But in a kind of quibbling self-justification I recalled that

I had bought Parnassus and all it contained, "lock, stock, barrel and bung" as Andrew used to say. And so....

The notebook was full of little jottings, written in pencil in the Professor's small, precise hand. The words were rubbed and soiled, but plainly legible. I read this:

*I don't suppose Bock or Peg get lonely, but by the bones of Ben Gunn, I do. Seems silly when Herrick and Hans Andersen and Tennyson and Thoreau and a whole wagonload of other good fellows are riding at my back. I can hear them all talking as we trundle along. But books aren't a substantial world after all, and every now and then we get hungry for some closer, more human relationships. I've been totally alone now for eight years—except for Runt, and he might be dead and never say so. This wandering about is fine in its way, but it must come to an end some day. A man needs to put down a root somewhere to be really happy.*

*What absurd victims of contrary desires we are! If a man is settled in one place he yearns to wander; when he wanders he yearns to have a home. And yet how bestial is content—all the great things in life are done by discontented people.*

There are three ingredients in the good life: learning, earning, and yearning. A man should be learning as he goes; and he should be earning bread for himself and others; and he should be yearning, too: yearning to know the unknowable.

*What a fine old poem is "The Pulley" by George Herbert! Those Elizabethan fellows knew how to write! They were marred perhaps by their idea that poems must be "witty." (Remember how Bacon said that reading poets makes one witty? There he gave a clue to the literature of his time.) Their fantastic puns and conceits are rather out of our fashion nowadays. But Lord! the root of the matter was in them! How gallantly, how reverently, they tackle the problems of life!*

*When God at first made man (says George Herbert) He had a "glass of blessings standing by." So He pours on man all the blessings in His reservoir: strength, beauty, wisdom, honour, pleasure—and then He refrains from giving him the last of them, which is rest, i.e., contentment. God sees that if man is contented he will never win his way to Him. Let man be restless, so that*

> *"If goodness lead him not, yet weariness*
> *May toss him to My breast."*

*Some day I shall write a novel on that theme, and call it "The Pulley." In this tragic, restless world there must be some place where at last we can lay our heads and be at rest. Some people call it death. Some call it God.*

*My ideal of a man is not the Omar who wants to shatter into bits this sorry scheme of things, and then remould it nearer to the heart's desire. Old Omar was a coward, with his silk pajamas and his glass of wine. The real man is George Herbert's "seasoned timber"—the fellow who does handily and well whatever comes to him. Even if it's only shovelling coal into a furnace he can balance the shovel neatly, swing the coal square on the fire and not spill it on the floor. If it's only splitting kindling or running a trolley car he can make a good, artistic job of it. If it's only writing a book or peeling potatoes he can put into it the best he has. Even if he's only a bald-headed old fool over forty selling books on a country road, he can make an ideal of it. Good old Parnassus! It's a great game.... I think I'll have to give her up soon, though: I must get that book of mine written. But Parnassus has been a true glass of blessings to me.*

There was much more in the notebook; indeed it was half full of jotted paragraphs, memoranda, and scraps of writing—poems I believe some of them were—but I had seen enough. It seemed as if I had stumbled unawares on the pathetic, brave, and lonely heart of the little man. I'm a commonplace creature, I'm afraid, insensible to many of the deeper things in life, but every now and then, like all of us, I come face to face with something that thrills me. I saw how this little, red-bearded pedlar was like a cake of yeast in the big, heavy dough of humanity: how he travelled about trying to fulfil in his own way his ideals of beauty. I felt almost motherly toward him: I wanted to tell him that I understood him. And in a way I felt ashamed of having run away from my own homely tasks, my kitchen and my hen yard and dear old, hot-tempered, absent-minded Andrew. I fell into a sober mood. As soon as I was alone, I thought, I would sell Parnassus and hurry back to the farm. That was my job, that was my glass of blessings. What was I doing—a fat, middle-aged woman—trapesing along the roads with a cartload of books I didn't understand?

I slipped the little notebook back into its hiding-place. I would have died rather than let the Professor know I had seen it.

## Chapter Eleven

We were coming into Woodbridge; and I was just wondering whether to wake the Professor when the little window behind me slid back and he stuck his head out.

"Hello!" he said. "I think I must have been asleep!"

"Well, I should hope so," I said. "You needed it."

Indeed he looked much better, and I was relieved to see it. I had been really afraid he would be ill after sleeping out all night, but I guess he was tougher than I thought. He joined me on the seat, and we drove into the town. While he went to the station to ask about the trains I had a fine time selling books. I was away from the locality where I was known, and had no shyness in attempting to imitate Mifflin's methods. I even went him one better by going into a hardware store where I bought a large dinner bell. This I rang lustily until a crowd gathered, then I put up the flaps and displayed my books. As a matter of fact, I sold only one, but I enjoyed myself none the less.

By and by Mifflin reappeared. I think he had been to a barber: at any rate he looked very spry: he had bought a clean collar and a flowing tie of a bright electric blue which really suited him rather well.

"Well," he said, "the Sage is going to get back at me for that punch on the nose! I've been to the bank to cash your check. They telephoned over to Redfield, and apparently your brother has stopped payment on it. It's rather awkward: they seem to think I'm a crook."

I was furious. What right had Andrew to do that?

"The brute!" I said. "What on earth shall I do?"

"I suggest that you telephone to the Redfield Bank," he said, "and countermand your brother's instructions—that is, unless you think you've made a mistake? I don't want to take advantage of you."

"Nonsense!" I said. "I'm not going to let Andrew spoil my holiday. That's always his way: if he gets an idea into his head he's like a mule. I'll telephone to Redfield, and then we'll go to see the bank here."

We put Parnassus up at the hotel, and I went to the telephone. I was thoroughly angry at Andrew, and tried to get him on the wire first. But Sabine Farm didn't answer. Then I telephoned to the bank in Redfield, and got Mr. Shirley. He's the cashier, and I know him well. I guess he recognized my voice, for he made no objection when I told him what I wanted.

"Now you telephone to the bank in Woodbridge," I said, "and tell them to let Mr. Mifflin have the money. I'll go there with him to identify him. Will that be all right?"

"Perfectly," he said. The deceitful little snail! If I had only known what he was concocting!

Mifflin said there was a train at three o'clock which he could take. We stopped at a little lunch room for a bite to eat, then he went again to the bank, and I with him. We asked the cashier whether they had had a message from Redfield.

"Yes," he said. "We've just heard." And he looked at me rather queerly.

"Are you Miss McGill?" he said.

"I am," I said.

"Will you just step this way a moment?" he asked politely.

He led me into a little sitting-room and asked me to sit down. I supposed that he was going to get some paper for me to sign, so I waited quite patiently for several minutes. I had left the Professor at the cashier's window, where they would give him his money.

I waited some time, and finally I got tired of looking at the Life Insurance calendars. Then I happened to glance out of the window. Surely that was the Professor, just disappearing round the corner with another man?

I returned to the cashier's desk.

"What's the matter?" I said. "Your mahogany furniture is charming, but I'm tired of it. Do I have to sit here any longer? And where's Mr. Mifflin? Did he get his money?"

The cashier was a horrid little creature with side whiskers.

"I'm sorry you had to wait, Madam," he said. "The transaction is just concluded. We gave Mr. Mifflin what was due him. There is no need for you to stay longer."

I thought this was very extraordinary. Surely the Professor would not leave without saying good-bye? However, I noticed that the clock said three minutes to three, so I thought that perhaps he had had to run to catch his train. He was such a strange little man, anyway....

Well, I went back to the hotel, quite a little upset by this sudden parting. At least I was glad the little man had got his money all right. Probably he would write from Brooklyn, but of course I wouldn't get the letter till I returned to the farm as that was the only address he would have. Perhaps that wouldn't be so long after all: but I did not feel like going back now, when Andrew had been so horrid.

I drove Parnassus on the ferry, and we crossed the river. I felt lost and disagreeable. Even the fresh movement through the air gave me no pleasure. Bock whined dismally inside the van.

It didn't take me long to discover that Parnassing all alone had lost some of its charms. I missed the Professor: missed his abrupt, direct way of saying things, and his whimsical wit. And I was annoyed by his skipping off without a word of good-bye. It didn't seem natural. I partially appeased my irritation by stopping at a farmhouse on the other side of the river and selling a cook book. Then I started along the road for Bath—about five miles farther on. Peg's foot didn't seem to bother her so I thought it would be safe to travel that far before stopping for the night. Counting up the days (with some difficulty: it seemed as though I had been away from home a month), I remembered that this was Saturday night. I thought I would stay in Bath over Sunday and get a good rest. We jogged sedately along the road, and I got out a copy of *Vanity Fair*. I was so absorbed in Becky Sharp that I wouldn't even interrupt myself to sell books at the houses we passed. I think reading a good book makes one modest. When you see the marvellous insight into human nature which a truly great book shows, it is bound to make you feel small—like looking at the Dipper on a clear night, or seeing the winter sunrise when you go out to collect the morning eggs. And anything that makes you feel small is mighty good for you.

"What do you mean by a great book?" said the Professor—I mean,
I imagined him saying it. It seemed to me as if I could see him sitting
there, with his corncob pipe in his hand and that quizzical little face of
his looking sharply at me. Somehow, talking with the Professor had
made me think. He was as good as one of those Scranton
correspondence courses, I do believe, and no money to pay for postage.

Well, I said to the Professor—to myself I mean—let's see: what *is*
a good book? I don't mean books like Henry James's (he's Andrew's
great idol. It always seemed to me that he had a kind of rush of words
to the head and never stopped to sort them out properly). A good book
ought to have something simple about it. And, like Eve, it ought to
come from somewhere near the third rib: there ought to be a heart
beating in it. A story that's all forehead doesn't amount to much.
Anyway, it'll never get over at a Dorcas meeting. That was the trouble
with Henry James. Andrew talked so much about him that I took one of
his books to read aloud at our sewing circle over at Redfield. Well,
after one try we had to fall back on "Pollyanna."

I haven't been doing chores and running a farmhouse for fifteen
years without getting some ideas about life—and even about books. I
wouldn't set my lit'ry views up against yours, Professor (I was still
talking to Mifflin in my mind), no, nor even against Andrew's—but as
I say, I've got some ideas of my own. I've learned that honest work
counts in writing books just as much as it does in washing dishes. I
guess Andrew's books must be some good after all because he surely
does mull over them without end. I can forgive his being a shiftless
farmer so long as he really does his literary chores up to the hilt. A man
can be slack in everything else, if he does one thing as well as he
possibly can. And I guess it won't matter my being an ignoramus in
literature so long as I'm rated A-1 in the kitchen. That's what I used to
think as I polished and scoured and scrubbed and dusted and swept and
then set about getting dinner. If I ever sat down to read for ten minutes
the cat would get into the custard. No woman in the country sits down
for fifteen consecutive minutes between sunrise and sunset, anyway,
unless she has half a dozen servants. And nobody knows anything
about literature unless he spends most of his life sitting down. So there
you are.

The cultivation of philosophic reflection was a new experience for
me. Peg ambled along contentedly and the dog trailed under Parnassus
where I had tied him. I read *Vanity Fair* and thought about all sorts of
things. Once I got out to pick some scarlet maple leaves that attracted
me. The motors passing annoyed me with their dust and noise, but by
and by one of them stopped, looked at my outfit curiously, and then
asked to see some books. I put up the flaps for them and we pulled off
to one side of the road and had a good talk. They bought two or three
books, too.

By the time I neared Bath the hands of my watch pointed to supper. I was still a bit shy of Mifflin's scheme of stopping overnight at farmhouses, so I thought I'd go right into the town and look for a hotel. The next day was Sunday, so it seemed reasonable to give the horse a good rest and stay in Bath two nights. The Hominy House looked clean and old-fashioned, and the name amused me, so in I went. It was a kind of high-class boarding-house, with mostly old women around. It looked to me almost literary and Elbert Hubbardish compared to the Grand Central in Shelby. The folks there stared at me somewhat suspiciously and I half thought they were going to say they didn't take pedlars; but when I flashed a new five-dollar bill at the desk I got good service. A five-dollar bill is a patent of nobility in New England.

My! how I enjoyed that creamed chicken on toast, and buckwheat cakes with syrup! After you get used to cooking all your own grub, a meal off some one else's stove is the finest kind of treat. After supper I was all prepared to sit out on the porch with my sweater on and give a rocking chair a hot box, but then I remembered that it was up to me to carry on the traditions of Parnassus. I was there to spread the gospel of good books. I got to thinking how the Professor never shirked carrying on his campaign, and I determined that I would be worthy of the cause.

When I think back about the experience, it seems pretty crazy, but at the time I was filled with a kind of evangelistic zeal. I thought if I was going to try to sell books I might as well have some fun out of it. Most of the old ladies were squatting about in the parlour, knitting or reading or playing cards. In the smoking-room I could see two dried-up men. Mrs. Hominy, the manager of the place, was sitting at her desk behind a brass railing, going over accounts with a quill pen. I thought that the house probably hadn't had a shock since Walt Whitman wrote "Leaves of Grass." In a kind of do-or-die spirit I determined to give them a rouse.

In the dining-room I had noticed a huge dinner bell that stood behind the door. I stepped in there, and got it. Standing in the big hall I began ringing it as hard as I could shake my arm.

You might have thought it was a fire alarm. Mrs. Hominy dropped her pen in horror. The colonial dames in the parlour came to life and ran into the hall like cockroaches. In a minute I had gathered quite a respectable audience. It was up to me to do the spellbinding.

"Friends," I said (unconsciously imitating the Professor's tricks of the trade, I guess), "this bell which generally summons you to the groaning board now calls you to a literary repast. With the permission of the management, and with apologies for disturbing your tranquillity, I will deliver a few remarks on the value of good books. I see that several of you are fond of reading, so perhaps the topic will be congenial?"

They gazed at me about as warmly as a round of walnut sundaes.

"Ladies and Gentlemen," I continued, "of course you remember the story of Abe Lincoln when he said, 'if you call a leg a tail, how many tails has a dog?' 'Five,' you answer. Wrong; because, as Mr. Lincoln said, calling a leg a tail...."

I still think it was a good beginning. But that was as far as I got. Mrs. Hominy came out of her trance, hastened from the cage, and grabbed my arm. She was quite red with anger.

"Really!" she said. "Well, really!... I must ask you to continue this in some other place. We do not allow commercial travellers in this house."

And within fifteen minutes they had hitched up Peg and asked me to move on. Indeed I was so taken aback by my own zeal that I could hardly protest. In a kind of daze I found myself at the Moose Hotel, where they assured me that they catered to mercantile people. I went straight to my room and fell asleep as soon as I reached the straw mattress.

That was my first and only public speech.

### *Chapter Twelve*

The next day was Sunday, October sixth. I well remember the date.

I woke up as chipper as any Robert W. Chambers heroine. All my doubts and depressions of the evening before had fled, and I was single-heartedly delighted with the world and everything in it. The hotel was a poor place, but it would have taken more than that to mar my composure. I had a bitterly cold bath in a real country tin tub, and then eggs and pancakes for breakfast. At the table was a drummer who sold lightning rods, and several other travelling salesmen. I'm afraid my conversation was consciously modelled along the line of what the Professor would have said if he had been there, but at any rate I got along swimmingly. The travelling men, after a moment or two of embarrassed diffidence, treated me quite as one of themselves and asked me about my "line" with interest. I described what I was doing and they all said they envied me my freedom to come and go independently of trains. We talked cheerfully for a long time, and almost without intending to, I started preaching about books. In the end they insisted on my showing them Parnassus. We all went out to the stable, where the van was quartered, and they browsed over the shelves. Before I knew it I had sold five dollars' worth, although I had decided not to do any business at all on Sunday. But I couldn't refuse to sell them the stuff as they all seemed so keen on getting something really good to read. One man kept on talking about Harold Bell Wright, but I had to admit that I hadn't heard of him. Evidently the Professor hadn't stocked any of his works. I was tickled to see that after all little Redbeard didn't know *everything* about literature.

After that I debated whether to go to church or to write letters. Finally I decided in favour of the letters. First I tackled Andrew. I wrote:

The Moose Hotel, Bath,
Sunday morning.

DEAR ANDREW:

It seems absurd to think that it's only three days since I left Sabine Farm. Honestly, more has happened to me in these three days than in three years at home.

I'm sorry that you and Mr. Mifflin disagreed but I quite understood your feelings. But I'm very angry that you should have tried to stop that check I gave him. It was none of your business, Andrew. I telephoned Mr. Shirley and made him send word to the bank in Woodbridge to give Mifflin the money. Mr. Mifflin did not swindle me into buying Parnassus. I did it of my own free will. If you want to know the truth, it was your fault! I bought it because I was scared *you* would if I didn't. And I didn't want to be left all alone on the farm from now till Thanksgiving while you went off on another trip. So I decided to do the thing myself. I thought I'd see how you would like being left all alone to run the house. I thought it'd be pretty nice for me to get things off my mind a while and have an adventure of my own.

Now, Andrew, here are some directions for you:

1. Don't forget to feed the chickens twice a day, and collect *all* the eggs. There's a nest behind the wood pile, and some of the Wyandottes have been laying under the ice house.

2. Don't let Rosie touch grandmother's blue china, because she'll break it as sure as fate if she lays her big, thick Swedish fingers on it.

3. Don't forget your warmer underwear. The nights are getting chilly.

4. I forgot to put the cover on the sewing machine. Please do that for me or it'll get all dusty.

5. Don't let the cat run loose in the house at night: he always breaks something.

6. Send your socks and anything else that needs darning over to Mrs. McNally, she can do it for you.

7. Don't forget to feed the pigs.

8. Don't forget to mend the weathervane on the barn.

9. Don't forget to send that barrel of apples over to the cider mill or you won't have any cider to drink when Mr. Decameron comes up to see us later in the fall.

10. Just to make ten commandments, I'll add one more: You might 'phone to Mrs. Collins that the Dorcas will have to meet at some one else's house next week, because I don't know just when I'll get back. I

may be away a fortnight more. This is my first holiday in a long time and I'm going to chew it before I swallow it.

The Professor (Mr. Mifflin, I mean) has gone back to Brooklyn to work on his book. I'm sorry you and he had to mix it up on the high road like a couple of hooligans. He's a nice little man and you'd like him if you got to know him.

I'm spending Sunday in Bath: to-morrow I'm going on toward Hastings. I've sold five dollars' worth of books this morning even if it is Sunday.

Your affte sister<br>HELEN McGILL.

P.S. Don't forget to clean the separator after using it, or it'll get in a fearful state.

After writing to Andrew I thought I would send a message to the Professor. I had already written him a long letter in my mind, but somehow when I began putting it on paper a sort of awkwardness came over me. I didn't know just how to begin. I thought how much more fun it would be if he were there himself and I could listen to him talk. And then, while I was writing the first few sentences, some of the drummers came back into the room.

"Thought you'd like to see a Sunday paper," said one of them.

I picked up the newspaper with a word of thanks and ran an eye over the headlines. The ugly black letters stood up before me, and my heart gave a great contraction. I felt my fingertips turn cold.

DISASTROUS WRECK<br>ON THE SHORE LINE<br>EXPRESS RUNS INTO OPEN SWITCH<br>—<br><br>TEN LIVES LOST, AND<br>MORE THAN A SCORE INJURED<br>—<br><br>FAILURE OF BLOCK SIGNALS

The letters seemed to stand up before me as large as a Malted Milk signboard. With a shuddering apprehension I read the details. Apparently the express that left Providence at four o'clock on Saturday afternoon had crashed into an open siding near Willdon about six o'clock, and collided with a string of freight empties. The baggage car had been demolished and the smoker had turned over and gone down an embankment. There were ten men killed... my head swam. Was that the train the Professor had taken? Let me see. He left Woodbridge on a local train at three. He had said the day before that the express left Port

Vigor at five.... If he had changed to the express.....
In a kind of fascinated horror my eye caught the list of the dead. I
ran down the names. Thank God, no, Mifflin was not among them.
Then I saw the last entry:

UNIDENTIFIED MAN, MIDDLE-AGED.

What if that should be the Professor?
And I suddenly felt dizzy, and for the first time in my life I fainted.
Thank goodness, no one else was in the room. The drummers had
gone outside again, and no one heard me flop off the chair. I came to in
a moment, my heart whirling like a spinning top. At first I did not
realize what was wrong. Then my eye fell on the newspaper again.
Feverishly I re-read the account, and the names of the injured, too,
which I had missed before. Nowhere was there a name I knew. But the
tragic words "unidentified man" danced before my eyes. Oh! if it were
the Professor....
In a wave the truth burst upon me. I loved that little man: I loved
him, I loved him. He had brought something new into my life, and his
brave, quaint ways had warmed my fat old heart. For the first time, in
an intolerable gush of pain, I seemed to know that my life could never
again be endurable without him. And now—what was I to do?
How could I learn the truth? Certainly if he *had* been on the train,
and had escaped from the wreck unhurt, he would have sent a message
to Sabine Farm to let me know. At any rate, that was a possibility. I
rushed to the telephone to call up Andrew.
Oh! the agonizing slowness of telephone connections when urgent
hurry is needed! My voice shook as I said "Redfield 158 J" to the
operator. Throbbing with nervousness I waited to hear the familiar click
of the receiver at the other end. I could hear the Redfield switchboard
receive the call, and put in the plug to connect with our wire. In
imagination I could see the telephone against the wall in the old
hallway at Sabine Farm. I could see the soiled patch of plaster where
Andrew rests his elbow when he talks into the 'phone, and the place
where he jots numbers down in pencil and I rub them off with bread
crumbs. I could see Andrew coming out of the sitting-room to answer
the bell. And then the operator said carelessly, "Doesn't answer." My
forehead was wet as I came out of the booth.
I hope I may never have to re-live the horrors of the next hour. In
spite of my bluff and hearty ways, in times of trouble I am as reticent as
a clam. I was determined to hide my agony and anxiety from the well-
meaning people of the Moose Hotel. I hurried to the railway station to
send a telegram to the Professor's address in Brooklyn, but found the
place closed. A boy told me it would not be open until the afternoon.
From a drugstore I called "information" in Willdon, and finally got

connected with some undertaker to whom the Willdon operator referred me. A horrible, condoling voice (have you ever talked to an undertaker over the telephone?) answered me that no one by the name of Mifflin had been among the dead, but admitted that there was one body still unidentified. He used one ghastly word that made me shudder—*unrecognizable*. I rang off.

I knew then for the first time the horror of loneliness. I thought of the poor little man's notebook that I had seen. I thought of his fearless and lovable ways—of his pathetic little tweed cap, of the missing button of his jacket, of the bungling darns on his frayed sleeve. It seemed to me that heaven could mean nothing more than to roll creaking along country roads, in Parnassus, with the Professor beside me on the seat. What if I had known him only—how long was it? He had brought the splendour of an ideal into my humdrum life. And now—had I lost it forever? Andrew and the farm seemed faint and far away. I was a homely old woman, mortally lonely and helpless. In my perplexity I walked to the outskirts of the village and burst into tears.

Finally I got a grip on myself again. I am not ashamed to say that I now admitted frankly what I had been hiding from myself. I was in love—in love with a little, red-bearded bookseller who seemed to me more splendid than Sir Galahad. And I vowed that if he would have me, I would follow him to the other end of nowhere.

I walked back to the hotel. I thought I would make one more try to get Andrew on the telephone. My whole soul quivered when at last I heard the receiver click.

"Hello?" said Andrew's voice.

"Oh, Andrew," I said, "this is Helen."

"Where are you?" (His voice sounded cross.)

"Andrew, is there any—any message from Mr. Mifflin? That wreck yesterday—he might have been on that train—I've been so frightened; do you think he was—hurt?"

"Stuff and nonsense," said Andrew. "If you want to know about Mifflin, he's in jail in Port Vigor."

And then I think Andrew must have been surprised. I began to laugh and cry simultaneously, and in my agitation I set down the receiver.

### *Chapter Thirteen*

My first impulse was to hide myself in some obscure corner where I could vent my feelings without fear or favour. I composed my face as well as I could before leaving the 'phone booth; then I sidled across the lobby and slipped out of the side door. I found my way into the stable, where good old Peg was munching in her stall. The fine, homely smell of horseflesh and long-worn harness leather went right to my heart, and while Bock frisked at my knees I laid my head on Peg's neck and cried. I think that fat old mare understood me. She was as tubby and prosaic and middle-aged as I—but she loved the Professor.

Suddenly Andrew's words echoed again in my mind. I had barely heeded them before, in the great joy of my relief, but now their significance came to me. "In jail." The Professor in jail! That was the meaning of his strange disappearance at Woodbridge. That little brute of a man Shirley must have telephoned from Redfield, and when the Professor came to the Woodbridge bank to cash that check they had arrested him. That was why they had shoved me into that mahogany sitting-room. Andrew must be behind this. The besotted old fool! My face burned with anger and humiliation.

I never knew before what it means to be really infuriated. I could feel my brain tingle. The Professor in jail! The gallant, chivalrous little man, penned up with hoboes and sneak thieves suspected of being a crook... as if I couldn't take care of myself! What did they think he was, anyway? A kidnapper?

Instantly I decided I would hurry back to Port Vigor without delay. If Andrew had had the Professor locked up, it could only be on the charge of defrauding me. Certainly it couldn't be for giving him a bloody nose on the road from Shelby. And if I appeared to deny the charge, surely they would have to let Mr. Mifflin go.

I believe I must have been talking to myself in Peg's stall—at any rate, just at this moment the stableman appeared and looked very bewildered when he saw me, with flushed face and in obvious excitement, talking to the horse. I asked him when was the next train to Port Vigor.

"Well, ma'am," he said, "they say that all the local trains is held up till the wreck at Willdon's cleared away. This being Sunday, I don't think you'll get anything from here until to-morrow morning."

I reflected. It wasn't so awfully far back to Port Vigor. A flivver from the local garage could spin me back there in a couple of hours at the most. But somehow it seemed more fitting to go to the Professor's rescue in his own Parnassus, even if it would take longer to get there. To tell the truth, while I was angry and humiliated at the thought of his being put in jail by Andrew, I couldn't help, deep down within me, being rather thankful. Suppose he had been in the wreck? The Sage of Redfield had played the part of Providence after all. And if I set out right away with Parnassus, I could get to Port Vigor—well, by Monday morning anyway.

The good people of the Moose Hotel were genuinely surprised at the hurry with which I dispatched my lunch. But I gave them no explanations. Goodness knows, my head was full of other thoughts and the apple sauce might have been asbestos. You know, a woman only falls in love once in her life, and if it waits until she's darn near forty—

well, it *takes!* You see I hadn't even been vaccinated against it by girlish flirtations. I began to be a governess when I was just a kid, and a governess doesn't get many chances to be skittish. So now when it came, it hit me hard. That's when a woman finds herself—when she's in love. I don't care if she *is* old or fat or homely or prosy. She feels that little flutter under her ribs and she drops from the tree like a ripe plum. I didn't care if Roger Mifflin and I were as odd a couple as old Dr. Johnson and his wife, I only knew one thing: that when I saw that little red devil again I was going to be all his—if he'd have me. That's why the old Moose Hotel in Bath is always sacred to me. That's where I learned that life still held something fresh for me—something better than baking champlain biscuits for Andrew.

\* \* \* \* \* \* \* \* \*

That Sunday was one of those mellow, golden days that we New Englanders get in October. The year really begins in March, as every farmer knows, and by the end of September or the beginning of October the season has come to its perfect, ripened climax. There are a few days when the world seems to hang still in a dreaming, sweet hush, at the very fulness of the fruit before the decline sets in. I have no words (like Andrew) to describe it, but every autumn for years I have noticed it. I remember that sometimes at the farm I used to lean over the wood pile for a moment just before supper to watch those purple October sunsets. I would hear the sharp ting of Andrew's little typewriter bell as he was working in his study. And then I would try to swallow down within me the beauty and wistfulness of it all, and run back to mash the potatoes.

Peg drew Parnassus along the backward road with a merry little rumble. I think she knew we were going back to the Professor. Bock careered mightily along the wayside. And I had much time for thinking. On the whole, I was glad; for I had much to ponder. An adventure that had started as a mere lark or whim had now become for me the very gist of life itself. I was fanciful, I guess, and as romantic as a young hen, but by the bones of George Eliot, I'm sorry for the woman that never has a chance to be fanciful. Mifflin was in jail; aye, but he might have been dead and—*unrecognizable!* My heart refused to be altogether sad. I was on my way to deliver him from durance vile. There seemed a kinship between the season and myself, I mused, seeing the goldenrod turning bronze and droopy along the way. Here was I, in the full fruition of womanhood, on the verge of my decline into autumn, and lo! by the grace of God, I had found my man, my master. He had touched me with his own fire and courage. I didn't care what happened to Andrew, or to Sabine Farm, or to anything else in the world. Here were my hearth and my home—Parnassus, or wherever

Roger should pitch his tent. I dreamed of crossing the Brooklyn Bridge with him at dusk, watching the skyscrapers etched against a burning sky. I believed in calling things by their true names. Ink is ink, even if the bottle is marked "commercial fluid." I didn't try to blink the fact that I was in love. In fact, I gloried in it. As Parnassus rolled along the road, and the scarlet maple leaves eddied gently down in the blue October air, I made up a kind of chant which I called

*Hymn for a Middle-Aged Woman* (*Fat*)
*Who Has Fallen into Love*

*O God, I thank Thee who sent this great adventure my way! I am grateful to have come out of the barren land of spinsterhood, seeing the glory of a love greater than myself. I thank Thee for teaching me that mixing, and kneading, and baking are not all that life holds for me. Even if he doesn't love me, God, I shall always be his.*

I was crooning some such babble as this to myself when, near Woodbridge, I came upon a big, shiny motor car stranded by the roadside. Several people, evidently intelligent and well-to-do, sat under a tree while their chauffeur fussed with a tire. I was so absorbed in my own thoughts that I think I should have gone by without paying them much heed, but suddenly I remembered the Professor's creed—to preach the gospel of books in and out of season. Sunday or no Sunday, I thought I could best honour Mifflin by acting on his own principle. I pulled up by the side of the road.

I noticed the people turn to one another in a kind of surprise, and whisper something. There was an elderly man with a lean, hard-worked face; a stout woman, evidently his wife; and two young girls and a man in golfing clothes. Somehow the face of the older man seemed familiar. I wondered whether he were some literary friend of Andrew's whose photo I had seen.

Bock stood by the wheel with his long, curly tongue running in and out over his teeth. I hesitated a moment, thinking just how to phrase my attack, when the elderly gentleman called out:

"Where's the Professor?"

I was beginning to realize that Mifflin was indeed a public character.

"Heavens!" I said. "Do you know him, too?"

"Well, I should think so," he said. "Didn't he come to see me last spring about an appropriation for school libraries, and wouldn't leave till I'd promised to do what he wanted! He stayed the night with us and we talked literature till four o'clock in the morning. Where is he now? Have you taken over Parnassus?"

"Just at present," I said, "Mr. Mifflin is in the jail at Port Vigor."

The ladies gave little cries of astonishment, and the gentleman himself (I had sized him up as a school commissioner or something of that sort) seemed not less surprised.

"In jail!" he said. "What on earth for? Has he sandbagged somebody for reading Nick Carter and Bertha M. Clay? That's about the only crime he'd be likely to commit."

"He's supposed to have cozened me out of four hundred dollars," I said, "and my brother has had him locked up. But as a matter of fact he wouldn't swindle a hen out of a new-laid egg. I bought Parnassus of my own free will. I'm on my way to Port Vigor now to get him out. Then I'm going to ask him to marry me—if he will. It's not leap year, either."

He looked at me, his thin, lined face working with friendliness. He was a fine-looking man—short, gray hair brushed away from a broad, brown forehead. I noticed his rich, dark suit and the spotless collar. This was a man of breeding, evidently.

"Well, Madam," he said, "any friend of the Professor is a friend of ours." (His wife and the girls chimed in with assent.) "If you would like a lift in our car to speed you on your errand, I'm sure Bob here would be glad to drive Parnassus into Port Vigor. Our tire will soon be mended."

The young man assented heartily, but as I said before, I was bent on taking Parnassus back myself. I thought the sight of his own tabernacle would be the best balm for Mifflin's annoying experience. So I refused the offer, and explained the situation a little more fully.

"Well," he said, "then let me help in any way I can." He took a card from his pocket-book and scribbled something on it. "When you get to Port Vigor," he said, "show this at the jail and I don't think you'll have any trouble. I happen to know the people there."

So after a hand-shake all round I went on again, much cheered by this friendly little incident. It wasn't till I was some way along the road that I thought of looking at the card he had given me. Then I realized why the man's face had been familiar. The card read quite simply:

RALEIGH STONE STAFFORD

The Executive Mansion,
Darlington.

It was the Governor of the State!

## Chapter Fourteen

I couldn't help chuckling, as Parnassus came over the brow of the hill, and I saw the river in the distance once more. How different all this was from my girlhood visions of romance. That has been characteristic of my life all along—it has been full of homely, workaday happenings, and often rather comic in spite of my best resolves to be highbrow and serious. All the same I was something near to tears as I thought of the tragic wreck at Willdon and the grief-laden hearts that must be mourning. I wondered whether the Governor was now returning from Willdon after ordering an inquiry.

On his card he had written: "Please release R. Mifflin at once and show this lady all courtesies." So I didn't anticipate any particular trouble. This made me all the more anxious to push on, and after crossing the ferry we halted in Woodbridge only long enough for supper. I drove past the bank where I had waited in the anteroom, and would have been glad of a chance to horsewhip that sneaking little cashier. I wondered how they had transported the Professor to Port Vigor, and thought ironically that it was only that Saturday morning when he had suggested taking the hoboes to the same jail. Still I do not doubt that his philosophic spirit had made the best of it all.

Woodbridge was as dead as any country town is on Sunday night. At the little hotel where I had supper there was no topic of conversation except the wreck. But the proprietor, when I paid my bill, happened to notice Parnassus in the yard.

"That's the bus that pedlar sold you, ain't it?" he asked with a leer.

"Yes," I said, shortly.

"Goin' back to prosecute him, I guess?" he suggested. "Say, that feller's a devil, believe *me*. When the sheriff tried to put the cuffs on him he gave him a black eye and pretty near broke his jaw. Some scrapper fer a midget!"

My own brave little fighter, I thought, and flushed with pride.

The road back to Port Vigor seemed endless. I was a little nervous, remembering the tramps in Pratt's quarry, but with Bock sitting beside me on the seat I thought it craven to be alarmed. We rumbled gently through the darkness, between aisles of inky pines where the strip of starlight ran like a ribbon overhead, then on the rolling dunes that overlook the water. There was a moon, too, but I was mortally tired and lonely and longed only to see my little Redbeard. Peg was weary, too, and plodded slowly. It must have been midnight before we saw the red and green lights of the railway signals and I knew that Port Vigor was at hand.

I decided to camp where I was. I guided Peg into a field beside the road, hitched her to a fence, and took the dog into the van with me. I was too tired to undress. I fell into the bunk and drew the blankets over me. As I did so, something dropped down behind the bunk with a sharp rap. It was a forgotten corncob pipe of the Professor's, blackened and sooty. I put it under my pillow, and fell asleep.

Monday, October seventh. If this were a novel about some charming, slender, pansy-eyed girl, how differently I would have to describe the feelings with which I woke the next morning. But these being only a few pages from the life of a fat, New England housewife, I must be candid. I woke feeling dull and sour. The day was gray and cool: faint shreds of mist sifting up from the Sound and a desolate mewing of seagulls in the air. I was unhappy, upset, and—yes—shy. Passionately I yearned to run to the Professor, to gather him into my arms, to be alone with him in Parnassus, creaking up some sunny by-road. But his words came back to me: I was nothing to him. What if he didn't love me after all?

I walked across two fields, down to the beach where little waves were slapping against the shingle. I washed my face and hands in salt water. Then I went back to Parnassus and brewed some coffee with condensed milk. I gave Peg and Bock their breakfasts. Then I hitched Peg to the van again, and felt better. As I drove into the town I had to wait at the grade crossing while a wrecking train rumbled past, on its way back from Willdon. That meant that the line was clear again. I watched the grimy men on the cars, and shuddered to think what they had been doing.

The Vigor county jail lies about a mile out of the town, an ugly, gray stone barracks with a high, spiked wall about it. I was thankful that it was still fairly early in the morning, and I drove through the streets without seeing any one I knew. Finally I reached the gate in the prison wall. Here some kind of a keeper barred my way. "Can't get in, lady," he said. "Yesterday was visitors' day. No more visitors till next month."

"I *must* get in," I said. "You've got a man in there on a false charge."

"So they all say," he retorted, calmly, and spat halfway across the road. "You wouldn't believe any of our boarders had a right to be here if you could hear their friends talk."

I showed him Governor Stafford's card. He was rather impressed by this, and retired into a sentry-box in the wall—to telephone, I suppose.

Presently he came back.

"The sheriff says he'll see you, ma'am. But you'll have to leave this here dynamite caboose behind." He unlocked a little door in the immense iron gate, and turned me over to another man inside. "Take this here lady to the sheriff," he said.

Some of Vigor county's prisoners must have learned to be pretty good gardeners, for certainly the grounds were in good condition. The grass was green and trimly mowed; there were conventional beds of flowers in very ugly shapes; in the distance I saw a gang of men in striped overalls mending a roadway. The guide led me to an attractive cottage to one side of the main building. There were two children playing outside, and I remember thinking that within the walls of a jail was surely a queer place to bring up youngsters.

But I had other things to think about. I looked up at that grim, gray building. Behind one of those little barred windows was the Professor. I should have been angry at Andrew, but somehow it all seemed a kind of dream. Then I was taken into the hallway of the sheriff's cottage and in a minute I was talking to a big, bull-necked man with a political moustache.

"You have a prisoner here called Roger Mifflin?" I said.

"My dear Madam, I don't keep a list of all our inmates in my head. If you will come to the office we will look up the records."

I showed him the Governor's card. He took it and kept looking at it as though he expected to see the message written there change or fade away. We walked across a strip of lawn to the prison building. There, in a big bare office, he ran over a card index.

"Here we are," he said. "Roger Mifflin; age, 41; face, oval; complexion, florid; hair, red but not much of it; height, 64 inches; weight, stripped, 120; birthmark...."

"Never mind," I said. "That's the man. What's he here for?"

"He's held in default of bail, pending trial. The charge is attempt to defraud one Helen McGill, spinster, age..."

"Rubbish!" I said. "I'm Helen McGill, and the man made no attempt to defraud me."

"The charge was entered and warrant applied for by your brother, Andrew McGill, acting on your behalf."

"I never authorized Andrew to act on my behalf."

"Then do you withdraw the charge?"

"By all means," I said. "I've a great mind to enter a counter-charge against Andrew and have *him* arrested."

"This is all very irregular," said the sheriff, "but if the prisoner is known to the Governor, I suppose there is no alternative. I cannot annul the warrant without some recognizance. According to the laws of this State the next of kin must stand surety for the prisoner's good behaviour after release. There is no next of kin...."

"Surely there is!" I said. "I am the prisoner's next of kin."

"What do you mean?" he said. "In what relationship do you stand to this Roger Mifflin?"

"I intend to marry him just as soon as I can get him away from here."

He burst into a roar of laughter. "I guess there's no stopping you," he said. He pinned the Governor's card to a blue paper on the desk, and began filling in some blanks.

"Well, Miss McGill," he went on, "don't take away more than one of my prisoners or I'll lose my job. The turnkey will take you up to the cell. I'm exceedingly sorry: you can see that the mistake was none of our fault. Tell the Governor that, will you, when you see him?"

I followed the attendant up two flights of bare, stone stairs, and down a long, whitewashed corridor. It was a gruesome place; rows and rows of heavy doors with little, barred windows. I noticed that each door had a combination knob, like a safe. My knees felt awfully shaky.

But it wasn't really so heart-throbby as I had expected. The jailer stopped at the end of a long passageway. He spun the clicking dial, while I waited in a kind of horror. I think I expected to see the Professor with shaved head (they couldn't shave much off his head, poor lamb!) and striped canvas suit, and a ball and chain on his ankle.

The door swung open heavily. There was a narrow, clean little room with a low camp bed, and under the barred window a table strewn with sheets of paper. It was the Professor in his own clothes, writing busily, with his back toward me. Perhaps he thought it was only an attendant with food, or perhaps he didn't even hear the interruption. I could hear his pen running busily. I might have known you never would get any heroics out of that man! Trust him to make the best of it!

"Lemon sole and a glass of sherry, please, James," said the Professor over his shoulder, and the warder, who evidently had joked with him before, broke into a cackle of laughter.

"A lady to see yer Lordship," he said.

The Professor turned round. His face went quite white. For the first time in my experience of him he seemed to be at a loss for speech.

"Miss—Miss McGill," he stammered. "You *are* the good Samaritan. I'm doing the John Bunyan act, see? Writing in prison. I've really started my book at last. And I find the fellows here know nothing whatever about literature. There isn't even a library in the place."

For the life of me, I couldn't utter the tenderness in my heart with that gorilla of a jailer standing behind us.

Somehow we made our way downstairs, after the Professor had gathered together the sheets of his manuscript. It had already reached formidable proportions, as he had written fifty pages in the thirty-six hours he had been in prison. In the office we had to sign some papers. The sheriff was very apologetic to Mifflin, and offered to take him back to town in his car, but I explained that Parnassus was waiting at the gate. The Professor's eyes brightened when he heard that, but I had to hurry him away from an argument about putting good books in prisons. The sheriff walked with us to the gate and there shook hands again.

Peg whickered as we came up to her, and the Professor patted her soft nose. Bock tugged at his chain in a frenzy of joy. At last we were alone.

## Chapter Fifteen

I never knew just how it happened. Instead of driving back through Port Vigor, we turned into a side road leading up over the hill and across the heath where the air came fresh and sweet from the sea. The Professor sat very silent, looking about him. There was a grove of birches on the hill, and the sunlight played upon their satin boles.

"It feels good to be out again," he said calmly. "The Sage cannot be so keen a lover of open air as his books would indicate, or he wouldn't be so ready to clap a man into quod. Perhaps I owe him another punch on the nose for that."

"Oh, Roger," I said—and I'm afraid my voice was trembly—"I'm *sorry. I'm sorry.*"

Not very eloquent, was it? And then, somehow or other, his arm was around me.

"Helen," he said. "Will you marry me? I'm not rich, but I've saved up enough to live on. We'll always have Parnassus, and this winter we'll go and live in Brooklyn and write the book. And we'll travel around with Peg, and preach the love of books and the love of human beings. Helen—you're just what I need, God bless you. Will you come with me and make me the happiest bookseller in the world?"

Peg must have been astonished at the length of time she had for cropping the grass, undisturbed. I know that Roger and I sat careless of time. And when he told me that ever since our first afternoon together he had determined to have me, sooner or later, I was the proudest woman in New England. I told Roger about the ghastly wreck, and my agony of apprehension. I think it was the wreck that made us both feel inclined to forgive Andrew.

We had a light luncheon together there on the dunes above the Sound. By taking a short cut over the ridge we struck into the Shelby road without going down into Port Vigor again. Peg pulled us along toward Greenbriar, and we talked as we went.

Perhaps the best of it was that a cold drizzle of rain began to fall as we moved along the hill road. The Professor—as I still call him, by force of habit—curtained in the front of the van with a rubber sheet. Bock hopped up and curled himself against his master's leg. Roger got out his corncob pipe, and I sat close to him. In the gathering gloom we plodded along, as happy a trio—or quartet, if you include fat, cheery old Peg—as any on this planet. Summer was over, and we were no longer young, but there were great things before us. I listened to the drip of the rain, and the steady creak of Parnassus on her axles. I thought of my "anthology" of loaves of bread and vowed to bake a million more if Roger wanted me to. It was after supper time when we got to Greenbriar. Roger had suggested that we take a shorter road that would have brought us through to Redfield sooner, but I begged him to go by way of Shelby and Greenbriar, just as we had come before. I did not tell him why I wanted this. And when finally we came to a halt in front of Kirby's store at the crossroads it was raining heavily and we were ready for a rest.

"Well, sweetheart," said Roger, "shall we go and see what sort of rooms the hotel has?"

"I can think of something better than that," said I. "Let's go up to Mr. Kane and have him marry us. Then we can get back to Sabine Farm afterward, and give Andrew a surprise."

"By the bones of Hymen!" said Roger. "You're right!"

It must have been ten o'clock when we turned in at the red gate of Sabine Farm. The rain had stopped, but the wheels sloshed through mud and water at every turn. The light was burning in the sitting-room, and through the window I could see Andrew bent over his work table. We climbed out, stiff and sore from the long ride. I saw Roger's face set in a comical blend of sternness and humour.

"Well, here goes to surprise the Sage!" he whispered.

We picked our way between puddles and rapped on the door. Andrew appeared, carrying the lamp in one hand. When he saw us he grunted.

"Let me introduce my wife," said Roger.

"Well, I'll be damned," said Andrew.

But Andrew isn't quite so black as I've painted him. When he's once convinced of the error of his ways, he is almost pathetically eager to make up. I remember only one remark in the subsequent conversation, because I was so appalled by the state of everything at Sabine Farm that I immediately set about putting the house to rights. The two men, however, as soon as Parnassus was housed in the barn and the animals under cover, sat down by the stove to talk things over.

"I tell you what," said Andrew—"do whatever you like with your wife; she's too much for me. But I'd like to buy that Parnassus."

"Not on your life!" said the Professor.

### The Haunted Bookshop

## TO THE BOOKSELLERS

Be pleased to know, most worthy, that this little book is dedicated to you in affection and respect. The faults of the composition are plain to you all. I begin merely in the hope of saying something further of the adventures of ROGER MIFFLIN, whose exploits in "Parnassus on Wheels" some of you have been kind enough to applaud. But then came Miss Titania Chapman, and my young advertising man fell in love with her, and the two of them rather ran away with the tale.

I think I should explain that the passage in Chapter VIII, dealing with the delightful talent of Mr. Sidney Drew, was written before the lamented death of that charming artist. But as it was a sincere tribute, sincerely meant, I have seen no reason for removing it.

Chapters I, II, III, and VI appeared originally in *The Bookman*, and to the editor of that admirable magazine I owe thanks for his permission to reprint.

Now that Roger is to have ten Parnassuses on the road, I am emboldened to think that some of you may encounter them on their travels. And if you do, I hope you will find that these new errants of the Parnassus on Wheels Corporation are living up to the ancient and honourable traditions of our noble profession.

CHRISTOPHER MORLEY.

Philadelphia,
April 28, 1919.

### *Chapter I. The Haunted Bookshop*

If you are ever in Brooklyn, that borough of superb sunsets and magnificent vistas of husband-propelled baby-carriages, it is to be hoped you may chance upon a quiet by-street where there is a very remarkable bookshop.

This bookshop, which does business under the unusual name "Parnassus at Home," is housed in one of the comfortable old brown-stone dwellings which have been the joy of several generations of plumbers and cockroaches. The owner of the business has been at pains to remodel the house to make it a more suitable shrine for his trade, which deals entirely in second-hand volumes. There is no second-hand bookshop in the world more worthy of respect.

It was about six o'clock of a cold November evening, with gusts of rain splattering upon the pavement, when a young man proceeded uncertainly along Gissing Street, stopping now and then to look at shop

windows as though doubtful of his way. At the warm and shining face
of a French rotisserie he halted to compare the number enamelled on
the transom with a memorandum in his hand. Then he pushed on for a
few minutes, at last reaching the address he sought. Over the entrance
his eye was caught by the sign:

> PARNASSUS AT HOME
> R. AND H. MIFFLIN
> BOOKLOVERS WELCOME!
> THIS SHOP IS HAUNTED

He stumbled down the three steps that led into the dwelling of the
muses, lowered his overcoat collar, and looked about.

It was very different from such bookstores as he had been
accustomed to patronize. Two stories of the old house had been thrown
into one: the lower space was divided into little alcoves; above, a
gallery ran round the wall, which carried books to the ceiling. The air
was heavy with the delightful fragrance of mellowed paper and leather
surcharged with a strong bouquet of tobacco. In front of him he found a
large placard in a frame:

> THIS SHOP IS HAUNTED by the ghosts
> Of all great literature, in hosts;
>     We sell no fakes or trashes.
> Lovers of books are welcome here,
> No clerks will babble in your ear,
>     Please smoke—but don't drop ashes!
>
> ———
>
> Browse as long as you like.
> Prices of all books plainly marked.
> If you want to ask questions, you'll find the proprietor
>     where the tobacco smoke is thickest.
> We pay cash for books.
>     We have what you want, though you may not know
>     you want it.
>         Malnutrition of the reading faculty is a serious thing.
>     Let us prescribe for you.
>         By R. & H. MIFFLIN,
>
>                                           Proprs.

The shop had a warm and comfortable obscurity, a kind of drowsy
dusk, stabbed here and there by bright cones of yellow light from
green-shaded electrics. There was an all-pervasive drift of tobacco
smoke, which eddied and fumed under the glass lamp shades. Passing
down a narrow aisle between the alcoves the visitor noticed that some

of the compartments were wholly in darkness; in others where lamps were glowing he could see a table and chairs. In one corner, under a sign lettered ESSAYS, an elderly gentleman was reading, with a face of fanatical ecstasy illumined by the sharp glare of electricity; but there was no wreath of smoke about him so the newcomer concluded he was not the proprietor.

As the young man approached the back of the shop the general effect became more and more fantastic. On some skylight far overhead he could hear the rain drumming; but otherwise the place was completely silent, peopled only (so it seemed) by the gurgitating whorls of smoke and the bright profile of the essay reader. It seemed like a secret fane, some shrine of curious rites, and the young man's throat was tightened by a stricture which was half agitation and half tobacco. Towering above him into the gloom were shelves and shelves of books, darkling toward the roof. He saw a table with a cylinder of brown paper and twine, evidently where purchases might be wrapped; but there was no sign of an attendant.

"This place may indeed be haunted," he thought, "perhaps by the delighted soul of Sir Walter Raleigh, patron of the weed, but seemingly not by the proprietors."

His eyes, searching the blue and vaporous vistas of the shop, were caught by a circle of brightness that shone with a curious egg-like lustre. It was round and white, gleaming in the sheen of a hanging light, a bright island in a surf of tobacco smoke. He came more close, and found it was a bald head.

This head (he then saw) surmounted a small, sharp-eyed man who sat tilted back in a swivel chair, in a corner which seemed the nerve centre of the establishment. The large pigeon-holed desk in front of him was piled high with volumes of all sorts, with tins of tobacco and newspaper clippings and letters. An antiquated typewriter, looking something like a harpsichord, was half-buried in sheets of manuscript. The little bald-headed man was smoking a corn-cob pipe and reading a cook-book.

"I beg your pardon," said the caller, pleasantly; "is this the proprietor?"

Mr. Roger Mifflin, the proprietor of "Parnassus at Home," looked up, and the visitor saw that he had keen blue eyes, a short red beard, and a convincing air of competent originality.

"It is," said Mr. Mifflin. "Anything I can do for you?"

"My name is Aubrey Gilbert," said the young man. "I am representing the Grey-Matter Advertising Agency. I want to discuss with you the advisability of your letting us handle your advertising account, prepare snappy copy for you, and place it in large circulation mediums. Now the war's over, you ought to prepare some constructive campaign for bigger business."

The bookseller's face beamed. He put down his cook-book, blew an expanding gust of smoke, and looked up brightly.

"My dear chap," he said, "I don't do any advertising."

"Impossible!" cried the other, aghast as at some gratuitous indecency.

"Not in the sense you mean. Such advertising as benefits me most is done for me by the snappiest copywriters in the business."

"I suppose you refer to Whitewash and Gilt?" said Mr. Gilbert wistfully.

"Not at all. The people who are doing my advertising are Stevenson, Browning, Conrad and Company."

"Dear me," said the Grey-Matter solicitor. "I don't know that agency at all. Still, I doubt if their copy has more pep than ours."

"I don't think you get me. I mean that my advertising is done by the books I sell. If I sell a man a book by Stevenson or Conrad, a book that delights or terrifies him, that man and that book become my living advertisements."

"But that word-of-mouth advertising is exploded," said Gilbert. "You can't get Distribution that way. You've got to keep your trademark before the public."

"By the bones of Tauchnitz!" cried Mifflin. "Look here, you wouldn't go to a doctor, a medical specialist, and tell him he ought to advertise in papers and magazines? A doctor is advertised by the bodies he cures. My business is advertised by the minds I stimulate. And let me tell you that the book business is different from other trades. People don't know they want books. I can see just by looking at you that your mind is ill for lack of books but you are blissfully unaware of it! People don't go to a bookseller until some serious mental accident or disease makes them aware of their danger. Then they come here. For me to advertise would be about as useful as telling people who feel perfectly well that they ought to go to the doctor. Do you know why people are reading more books now than ever before? Because the terrific catastrophe of the war has made them realize that their minds are ill. The world was suffering from all sorts of mental fevers and aches and disorders, and never knew it. Now our mental pangs are only too manifest. We are all reading, hungrily, hastily, trying to find out—after the trouble is over—what was the matter with our minds."

The little bookseller was standing up now, and his visitor watched him with mingled amusement and alarm.

"You know," said Mifflin, "I am interested that you should have thought it worth while to come in here. It reinforces my conviction of the amazing future ahead of the book business. But I tell you that future lies not merely in systematizing it as a trade. It lies in dignifying it as a profession. It is small use to jeer at the public for craving shoddy books, quack books, untrue books. Physician, cure thyself! Let the bookseller learn to know and revere good books, he will teach the customer. The hunger for good books is more general and more insistent than you would dream. But it is still in a way subconscious. People need books, but they don't know they need them. Generally they are not aware that the books they need are in existence."

"Why wouldn't advertising be the way to let them know?" asked the young man, rather acutely.

"My dear chap, I understand the value of advertising. But in my own case it would be futile. I am not a dealer in merchandise but a specialist in adjusting the book to the human need. Between ourselves, there is no such thing, abstractly, as a 'good' book. A book is 'good' only when it meets some human hunger or refutes some human error. A book that is good for me would very likely be punk for you. My pleasure is to prescribe books for such patients as drop in here and are willing to tell me their symptoms. Some people have let their reading faculties decay so that all I can do is hold a *post mortem* on them. But most are still open to treatment. There is no one so grateful as the man to whom you have given just the book his soul needed and he never knew it. No advertisement on earth is as potent as a grateful customer.

"I will tell you another reason why I don't advertise," he continued. "In these days when everyone keeps his trademark before the public, as you call it, not to advertise is the most original and startling thing one can do to attract attention. It was the fact that I do *not* advertise that drew you here. And everyone who comes here thinks he has discovered the place himself. He goes and tells his friends about the book asylum run by a crank and a lunatic, and they come here in turn to see what it is like."

"I should like to come here again myself and browse about," said the advertising agent. "I should like to have you prescribe for me."

"The first thing needed is to acquire a sense of pity. The world has been printing books for 450 years, and yet gunpowder still has a wider circulation. Never mind! Printer's ink is the greater explosive: it will win. Yes, I have a few of the good books here. There are only about 30,000 really important books in the world. I suppose about 5,000 of them were written in the English language, and 5,000 more have been translated."

"You are open in the evenings?"

"Until ten o'clock. A great many of my best customers are those who are at work all day and can only visit bookshops at night. The real book-lovers, you know, are generally among the humbler classes. A man who is impassioned with books has little time or patience to grow rich by concocting schemes for cozening his fellows."

The little bookseller's bald pate shone in the light of the bulb hanging over the wrapping table. His eyes were bright and earnest, his short red beard bristled like wire. He wore a ragged brown Norfolk jacket from which two buttons were missing.

A bit of a fanatic himself, thought the customer, but a very entertaining one. "Well, sir," he said, "I am ever so grateful to you. I'll come again. Good-night." And he started down the aisle for the door.

As he neared the front of the shop, Mr. Mifflin switched on a cluster of lights that hung high up, and the young man found himself beside a large bulletin board covered with clippings, announcements, circulars, and little notices written on cards in a small neat script. The following caught his eye:

R

If your mind needs phosphorus, try "Trivia," by Logan Pearsall Smith.

If your mind needs a whiff of strong air, blue and cleansing, from hilltops and primrose valleys, try "The Story of My Heart," by Richard Jefferies.

If your mind needs a tonic of iron and wine, and a thorough rough-and-tumbling, try Samuel Butler's "Notebooks" or "The Man Who Was Thursday," by Chesterton.

If you need "all manner of Irish," and a relapse into irresponsible freakishness, try "The Demi-Gods," by James Stephens. It is a better book than one deserves or expects.

It's a good thing to turn your mind upside down now and then, like an hour-glass, to let the particles run the other way.

One who loves the English tongue can have a lot of fun with a Latin dictionary.

ROGER MIFFLIN.

Human beings pay very little attention to what is told them unless they know something about it already. The young man had heard of none of these books prescribed by the practitioner of bibliotherapy. He was about to open the door when Mifflin appeared at his side.

"Look here," he said, with a quaint touch of embarrassment. "I was very much interested by our talk. I'm all alone this evening—my wife is away on a holiday. Won't you stay and have supper with me? I was just looking up some new recipes when you came in."

The other was equally surprised and pleased by this unusual invitation.

"Why—that's very good of you," he said. "Are you sure I won't be intruding?"

"Not at all!" cried the bookseller. "I detest eating alone: I was hoping someone would drop in. I always try to have a guest for supper when my wife is away. I have to stay at home, you see, to keep an eye on the shop. We have no servant, and I do the cooking myself. It's great fun. Now you light your pipe and make yourself comfortable for a few minutes while I get things ready. Suppose you come back to my den."

On a table of books at the front of the shop Mifflin laid a large card lettered:

PROPRIETOR AT SUPPER
IF YOU WANT ANYTHING
RING THIS BELL

Beside the card he placed a large old-fashioned dinner bell, and then led the way to the rear of the shop.

Behind the little office in which this unusual merchant had been studying his cook-book a narrow stairway rose on each side, running up to the gallery. Behind these stairs a short flight of steps led to the domestic recesses. The visitor found himself ushered into a small room on the left, where a grate of coals glowed under a dingy mantelpiece of yellowish marble. On the mantel stood a row of blackened corn-cob pipes and a canister of tobacco. Above was a startling canvas in emphatic oils, representing a large blue wagon drawn by a stout white animal—evidently a horse. A background of lush scenery enhanced the forceful technique of the limner. The walls were stuffed with books. Two shabby, comfortable chairs were drawn up to the iron fender, and a mustard-coloured terrier was lying so close to the glow that a smell of singed hair was sensible.

"There," said the host; "this is my cabinet, my chapel of ease. Take off your coat and sit down."

"Really," began Gilbert, "I'm afraid this is——"

"Nonsense! Now you sit down and commend your soul to Providence and the kitchen stove. I'll bustle round and get supper." Gilbert pulled out his pipe, and with a sense of elation prepared to enjoy an unusual evening. He was a young man of agreeable parts, amiable and sensitive. He knew his disadvantages in literary conversation, for he had gone to an excellent college where glee clubs and theatricals had left him little time for reading. But still he was a lover of good books, though he knew them chiefly by hearsay. He was twenty-five years old, employed as a copywriter by the Grey-Matter Advertising Agency.

The little room in which he found himself was plainly the bookseller's sanctum, and contained his own private library. Gilbert browsed along the shelves curiously. The volumes were mostly shabby and bruised; they had evidently been picked up one by one in the humble mangers of the second-hand vendor. They all showed marks of use and meditation.

Mr. Gilbert had the earnest mania for self-improvement which has blighted the lives of so many young men—a passion which, however, is commendable in those who feel themselves handicapped by a college career and a jewelled fraternity emblem. It suddenly struck him that it would be valuable to make a list of some of the titles in Mifflin's collection, as a suggestion for his own reading. He took out a memorandum book and began jotting down the books that intrigued him:

> *The Works of Francis Thompson* (*3 vols.*)
> *Social History of Smoking: Apperson*
> *The Path to Rome: Hilaire Belloc*
> *The Book of Tea: Kakuzo*
> *Happy Thoughts: F. C. Burnand*
> *Dr. Johnson's Prayers and Meditations*
> *Margaret Ogilvy: J. M. Barrie*
> *Confessions of a Thug: Taylor*
> *General Catalogue of the Oxford University Press*
> *The Morning's War: C. E. Montague*
> *The Spirit of Man: edited by Robert Bridges*
> *The Romany Rye: Borrow*
> *Poems: Emily Dickinson*
> *Poems: George Herbert*
> *The House of Cobwebs: George Gissing*

So far had he got, and was beginning to say to himself that in the interests of Advertising (who is a jealous mistress) he had best call a halt, when his host entered the room, his small face eager, his eyes blue points of light.

"Come, Mr. Aubrey Gilbert!" he cried. "The meal is set. You want to wash your hands? Make haste then, this way: the eggs are hot and waiting."

The dining-room into which the guest was conducted betrayed a feminine touch not visible in the smoke-dimmed quarters of shop and cabinet. At the windows were curtains of laughing chintz and pots of pink geranium. The table, under a drop-light in a flame-coloured silk screen, was brightly set with silver and blue china. In a cut-glass decanter sparkled a ruddy brown wine. The edged tool of Advertising felt his spirits undergo an unmistakable upward pressure.

"Sit down, sir," said Mifflin, lifting the roof of a platter. "These are eggs Samuel Butler, an invention of my own, the apotheosis of hen fruit."

Gilbert greeted the invention with applause. An *Egg Samuel Butler*, for the notebook of housewives, may be summarized as a pyramid, based upon toast, whereof the chief masonries are a flake of bacon, an egg poached to firmness, a wreath of mushrooms, a cap-sheaf of red peppers; the whole dribbled with a warm pink sauce of which the inventor retains the secret. To this the bookseller *chef* added fried potatoes from another dish, and poured for his guest a glass of wine. "This is California catawba," said Mifflin, "in which the grape and the sunshine very pleasantly (and cheaply) fulfil their allotted destiny. I pledge you prosperity to the black art of Advertising!"

The psychology of the art and mystery of Advertising rests upon tact, an instinctive perception of the tone and accent which will be *en rapport* with the mood of the hearer. Mr. Gilbert was aware of this, and felt that quite possibly his host was prouder of his whimsical avocation as gourmet than of his sacred profession as a bookman.

"Is it possible, sir," he began, in lucid Johnsonian, "that you can concoct so delicious an entree in so few minutes? You are not hoaxing me? There is no secret passage between Gissing Street and the laboratories of the Ritz?"

"Ah, you should taste Mrs. Mifflin's cooking!" said the bookseller. "I am only an amateur, who dabbles in the craft during her absence. She is on a visit to her cousin in Boston. She becomes, quite justifiably, weary of the tobacco of this establishment, and once or twice a year it does her good to breathe the pure serene of Beacon Hill. During her absence it is my privilege to inquire into the ritual of housekeeping. I find it very sedative after the incessant excitement and speculation of the shop."

"I should have thought," said Gilbert, "that life in a bookshop would be delightfully tranquil."

"Far from it. Living in a bookshop is like living in a warehouse of explosives. Those shelves are ranked with the most furious combustibles in the world—the brains of men. I can spend a rainy afternoon reading, and my mind works itself up to such a passion and anxiety over mortal problems as almost unmans me. It is terribly nerve-racking. Surround a man with Carlyle, Emerson, Thoreau, Chesterton, Shaw, Nietzsche, and George Ade—would you wonder at his getting excited? What would happen to a cat if she had to live in a room tapestried with catnip? She would go crazy!"

"Truly, I had never thought of that phase of bookselling," said the young man. "How is it, though, that libraries are shrines of such austere calm? If books are as provocative as you suggest, one would expect every librarian to utter the shrill screams of a hierophant, to clash ecstatic castanets in his silent alcoves!"

"Ah, my boy, you forget the card index! Librarians invented that soothing device for the febrifuge of their souls, just as I fall back upon the rites of the kitchen. Librarians would all go mad, those capable of concentrated thought, if they did not have the cool and healing card index as medicament! Some more of the eggs?"

"Thank you," said Gilbert. "Who was the butler whose name was associated with the dish?"

"What?" cried Mifflin, in agitation, "you have not heard of Samuel

Butler, the author of *The Way of All Flesh?* My dear young man, whoever permits himself to die before he has read that book, and also *Erewhon*, has deliberately forfeited his chances of paradise. For paradise in the world to come is uncertain, but there is indeed a heaven on this earth, a heaven which we inhabit when we read a good book. Pour yourself another glass of wine, and permit me——"

(Here followed an enthusiastic development of the perverse philosophy of Samuel Butler, which, in deference to my readers, I omit. Mr. Gilbert took notes of the conversation in his pocketbook, and I am pleased to say that his heart was moved to a realization of his iniquity, for he was observed at the Public Library a few days later asking for a copy of *The Way of All Flesh*. After inquiring at four libraries, and finding all copies of the book in circulation, he was compelled to buy one. He never regretted doing so.)

"But I am forgetting my duties as host," said Mifflin. "Our dessert consists of apple sauce, gingerbread, and coffee." He rapidly cleared the empty dishes from the table and brought on the second course.

"I have been noticing the warning over the sideboard," said Gilbert. "I hope you will let me help you this evening?" He pointed to a card hanging near the kitchen door. It read:

> ALWAYS WASH DISHES
> IMMEDIATELY AFTER MEALS
> IT SAVES TROUBLE

"I'm afraid I don't always obey that precept," said the bookseller as he poured the coffee. "Mrs. Mifflin hangs it there whenever she goes away, to remind me. But, as our friend Samuel Butler says, he that is stupid in little will also be stupid in much. I have a different theory about dish-washing, and I please myself by indulging it.

"I used to regard dish-washing merely as an ignoble chore, a kind of hateful discipline which had to be undergone with knitted brow and brazen fortitude. When my wife went away the first time, I erected a reading stand and an electric light over the sink, and used to read while my hands went automatically through base gestures of purification. I made the great spirits of literature partners of my sorrow, and learned by heart a good deal of *Paradise Lost* and of Walt Mason, while I soused and wallowed among pots and pans. I used to comfort myself with two lines of Keats:

> 'The moving waters at their priest-like task
> Of pure ablution round earth's human shores——'

Then a new conception of the matter struck me. It is intolerable for a human being to go on doing any task as a penance, under duress. No matter what the work is, one must spiritualize it in some way, shatter the old idea of it into bits and rebuild it nearer to the heart's desire. How was I to do this with dish-washing? "I broke a good many plates while I was pondering over the matter. Then it occurred to me that here was just the relaxation I needed. I had been worrying over the mental strain of being surrounded all day long by vociferous books, crying out at me their conflicting views as to the glories and agonies of life. Why not make dish-washing my balm and poultice?

"When one views a stubborn fact from a new angle, it is amazing how all its contours and edges change shape! Immediately my dishpan began to glow with a kind of philosophic halo! The warm, soapy water became a sovereign medicine to retract hot blood from the head; the homely act of washing and drying cups and saucers became a symbol of the order and cleanliness that man imposes on the unruly world about him. I tore down my book rack and reading lamp from over the sink.

"Mr. Gilbert," he went on, "do not laugh at me when I tell you that I have evolved a whole kitchen philosophy of my own. I find the kitchen the shrine of our civilization, the focus of all that is comely in life. The ruddy shine of the stove is as beautiful as any sunset. A well-polished jug or spoon is as fair, as complete and beautiful, as any sonnet. The dish mop, properly rinsed and wrung and hung outside the back door to dry, is a whole sermon in itself. The stars never look so bright as they do from the kitchen door after the ice-box pan is emptied and the whole place is 'redd up,' as the Scotch say."

"A very delightful philosophy indeed," said Gilbert. "And now that we have finished our meal, I insist upon your letting me give you a hand with the washing up. I am eager to test this dish-pantheism of yours!"

"My dear fellow," said Mifflin, laying a restraining hand on his impetuous guest, "it is a poor philosophy that will not abide denial now and then. No, no—I did not ask you to spend the evening with me to wash dishes." And he led the way back to his sitting room.

"When I saw you come in," said Mifflin, "I was afraid you might be a newspaper man, looking for an interview. A young journalist came to see us once, with very unhappy results. He wheedled himself into Mrs. Mifflin's good graces, and ended by putting us both into a book, called *Parnassus on Wheels*, which has been rather a trial to me. In that book he attributes to me a number of shallow and sugary observations upon bookselling that have been an annoyance to the trade. I am happy to say, though, that his book had only a trifling sale."

"I have never heard of it," said Gilbert.

"If you are really interested in bookselling you should come here some evening to a meeting of the Corn Cob Club. Once a month a number of booksellers gather here and we discuss matters of bookish concern over corn-cobs and cider. We have all sorts and conditions of booksellers: one is a fanatic on the subject of libraries. He thinks that every public library should be dynamited. Another thinks that moving pictures will destroy the book trade. What rot! Surely everything that arouses people's minds, that makes them alert and questioning, increases their appetite for books."

"The life of a bookseller is very demoralizing to the intellect," he went on after a pause. "He is surrounded by innumerable books; he cannot possibly read them all; he dips into one and picks up a scrap from another. His mind gradually fills itself with miscellaneous flotsam, with superficial opinions, with a thousand half-knowledges. Almost unconsciously he begins to rate literature according to what people ask for. He begins to wonder whether Ralph Waldo Trine isn't really greater than Ralph Waldo Emerson, whether J. M. Chapple isn't as big a man as J. M. Barrie. That way lies intellectual suicide.

"One thing, however, you must grant the good bookseller. He is tolerant. He is patient of all ideas and theories. Surrounded, engulfed by the torrent of men's words, he is willing to listen to them all. Even to the publisher's salesman he turns an indulgent ear. He is willing to be humbugged for the weal of humanity. He hopes unceasingly for good books to be born.

"My business, you see, is different from most. I only deal in second-hand books; I only buy books that I consider have some honest reason for existence. In so far as human judgment can discern, I try to keep trash out of my shelves. A doctor doesn't traffic in quack remedies. I don't traffic in bogus books.

"A comical thing happened the other day. There is a certain wealthy man, a Mr. Chapman, who has long frequented this shop——"

"I wonder if that could be Mr. Chapman of the Chapman Daintybits Company?" said Gilbert, feeling his feet touch familiar soil.

"The same, I believe," said Mifflin. "Do you know him?"

"Ah," cried the young man with reverence. "There is a man who can tell you the virtues of advertising. If he is interested in books, it is advertising that made it possible. We handle all his copy—I've written a lot of it myself. We have made the Chapman prunes a staple of civilization and culture. I myself devised that slogan 'We preen ourselves on our prunes' which you see in every big magazine. Chapman prunes are known the world over. The Mikado eats them once a week. The Pope eats them. Why, we have just heard that thirteen cases of them are to be put on board the *George Washington* for the President's voyage to the peace Conference. The Czecho-Slovak armies were fed largely on prunes. It is our conviction in the office that our campaign for the Chapman prunes did much to win the war."

"I read in an ad the other day—perhaps you wrote that, too?" said the bookseller, "that the Elgin watch had won the war. However, Mr. Chapman has long been one of my best customers. He heard about the Corn Cob Club, and though of course he is not a bookseller he begged to come to our meetings. We were glad to have him do so, and he has entered into our discussions with great zeal. Often he has offered many a shrewd comment. He has grown so enthusiastic about the bookseller's way of life that the other day he wrote to me about his daughter (he is a widower). She has been attending a fashionable girls' school where, he says, they have filled her head with absurd, wasteful, snobbish notions. He says she has no more idea of the usefulness and beauty of life than a Pomeranian dog. Instead of sending her to college, he has asked me if Mrs. Mifflin and I will take her in here to learn to sell books. He wants her to think she is earning her keep, and is going to pay me privately for the privilege of having her live here. He thinks that being surrounded by books will put some sense in her head. I am rather nervous about the experiment, but it is a compliment to the shop, isn't it?"

"Ye gods," cried Gilbert, "what advertising copy that would make!"

At this point the bell in the shop rang, and Mifflin jumped up. "This part of the evening is often rather busy," he said. "I'm afraid I'll have to go down on the floor. Some of my habitués rather expect me to be on hand to gossip about books."

"I can't tell you how much I've enjoyed myself," said Gilbert. "I'm going to come again and study your shelves."

"Well, keep it dark about the young lady," said the bookseller. "I don't want all you young blades dropping in here to unsettle her mind. If she falls in love with anybody in this shop, it'll have to be Joseph Conrad or John Keats!"

As he passed out, Gilbert saw Roger Mifflin engaged in argument with a bearded man who looked like a college professor. "Carlyle's *Oliver Cromwell?*" he was saying. "Yes, indeed! Right over here! Hullo, that's odd! It *was* here."

## Chapter II. The Corn Cob Club[1]

The Haunted Bookshop was a delightful place, especially of an evening, when its drowsy alcoves were kindled with the brightness of lamps shining on the rows of volumes. Many a passer-by would stumble down the steps from the street in sheer curiosity; others, familiar visitors, dropped in with the same comfortable emotion that a man feels on entering his club. Roger's custom was to sit at his desk in

---

[1] The latter half of this chapter may be omitted by all readers who are not booksellers.

the rear, puffing his pipe and reading; though if any customer started a conversation, the little man was quick and eager to carry it on. The lion of talk lay only sleeping in him; it was not hard to goad it up.

It may be remarked that all bookshops that are open in the evening are busy in the after-supper hours. Is it that the true book-lovers are nocturnal gentry, only venturing forth when darkness and silence and the gleam of hooded lights irresistibly suggest reading? Certainly night-time has a mystic affinity for literature, and it is strange that the Esquimaux have created no great books. Surely, for most of us, an arctic night would be insupportable without O. Henry and Stevenson. Or, as Roger Mifflin remarked during a passing enthusiasm for Ambrose Bierce, the true *noctes ambrosianae* are the *noctes ambrose bierceianae.*

But Roger was prompt in closing Parnassus at ten o'clock. At that hour he and Bock (the mustard-coloured terrier, named for Boccaccio) would make the round of the shop, see that everything was shipshape, empty the ash trays provided for customers, lock the front door, and turn off the lights. Then they would retire to the den, where Mrs. Mifflin was generally knitting or reading. She would brew a pot of cocoa and they would read or talk for half an hour or so before bed. Sometimes Roger would take a stroll along Gissing Street before turning in. All day spent with books has a rather exhausting effect on the mind, and he used to enjoy the fresh air sweeping up the dark Brooklyn streets, meditating some thought that had sprung from his reading, while Bock sniffed and padded along in the manner of an elderly dog at night.

While Mrs. Mifflin was away, however, Roger's routine was somewhat different. After closing the shop he would return to his desk and with a furtive, shamefaced air take out from a bottom drawer an untidy folder of notes and manuscript. This was the skeleton in his closet, his secret sin. It was the scaffolding of his book, which he had been compiling for at least ten years, and to which he had tentatively assigned such different titles as "Notes on Literature," "The Muse on Crutches," "Books and I," and "What a Young Bookseller Ought to Know." It had begun long ago, in the days of his odyssey as a rural book huckster, under the title of "Literature Among the Farmers," but it had branched out until it began to appear that (in bulk at least) Ridpath would have to look to his linoleum laurels. The manuscript in its present state had neither beginning nor end, but it was growing strenuously in the middle, and hundreds of pages were covered with Roger's minute script. The chapter on "Ars Bibliopolae," or the art of bookselling, would be, he hoped, a classic among generations of book vendors still unborn. Seated at his disorderly desk, caressed by a counterpane of drifting tobacco haze, he would pore over the manuscript, crossing out, interpolating, re-arguing, and then referring to volumes on his shelves. Bock would snore under the chair, and soon Roger's brain would begin to waver. In the end he would fall asleep over his papers, wake with a cramp about two o'clock, and creak irritably to a lonely bed.

All this we mention only to explain how it was that Roger was dozing at his desk about midnight, the evening after the call paid by Aubrey Gilbert. He was awakened by a draught of chill air passing like a mountain brook over his bald pate. Stiffly he sat up and looked about. The shop was in darkness save for the bright electric over his head. Bock, of more regular habit than his master, had gone back to his couch in the kitchen, made of a packing case that had once coffined a set of the Encyclopædia Britannica.

"That's funny," said Roger to himself. "Surely I locked the door?" He walked to the front of the shop, switching on the cluster of lights that hung from the ceiling. The door was ajar, but everything else seemed as usual. Bock, hearing his footsteps, came trotting out from the kitchen, his claws rattling on the bare wooden floor. He looked up with the patient inquiry of a dog accustomed to the eccentricities of his patron.

"I guess I'm getting absent-minded," said Roger. "I must have left the door open." He closed and locked it. Then he noticed that the terrier was sniffing in the History alcove, which was at the front of the shop on the left-hand side.

"What is it, old man?" said Roger. "Want something to read in bed?" He turned on the light in that alcove. Everything appeared normal. Then he noticed a book that projected an inch or so beyond the even line of bindings. It was a fad of Roger's to keep all his books in a flat row on the shelves, and almost every evening at closing time he used to run his palm along the backs of the volumes to level any irregularities left by careless browsers. He put out a hand to push the book into place. Then he stopped.

"Queer again," he thought. "Carlyle's *Oliver Cromwell!* I looked for that book last night and couldn't find it. When that professor fellow was here. Maybe I'm tired and can't see straight. I'll go to bed."

The next day was a date of some moment. Not only was it Thanksgiving Day, with the November meeting of the Corn Cob Club scheduled for that evening, but Mrs. Mifflin had promised to get home from Boston in time to bake a chocolate cake for the booksellers. It was said that some of the members of the club were faithful in attendance more by reason of Mrs. Mifflin's chocolate cake, and the cask of cider that her brother Andrew McGill sent down from the Sabine Farm every autumn, than on account of the bookish conversation.

Roger spent the morning in doing a little housecleaning, in preparation for his wife's return. He was a trifle abashed to find how many mingled crumbs and tobacco cinders had accumulated on the dining-room rug. He cooked himself a modest lunch of lamb chops and baked potatoes, and was pleased by an epigram concerning food that came into his mind. "It's not the food you dream about that matters," he said to himself; "it's the vittles that walk right in and become a member of the family." He felt that this needed a little polishing and rephrasing, but that there was a germ of wit in it. He had a habit of encountering ideas at his solitary meals.

After this, he was busy at the sink scrubbing the dishes, when he was surprised by feeling two very competent arms surround him, and a pink gingham apron was thrown over his head. "Mifflin," said his wife, "how many times have I told you to put on an apron when you wash up!"

They greeted each other with the hearty, affectionate simplicity of those congenially wedded in middle age. Helen Mifflin was a buxom, healthy creature, rich in good sense and good humour, well nourished both in mind and body. She kissed Roger's bald head, tied the apron around his shrimpish person, and sat down on a kitchen chair to watch him finish wiping the china. Her cheeks were cool and ruddy from the keen air, her face lit with the tranquil satisfaction of those who have sojourned in the comfortable city of Boston.

"Well, my dear," said Roger, "this makes it a real Thanksgiving. You look as plump and full of matter as *The Home Book of Verse*."

"I've had a stunning time," she said, patting Bock who stood at her knee, imbibing the familiar and mysterious fragrance by which dogs identify their human friends. "I haven't even heard of a book for three weeks. I did stop in at the Old Angle Book Shop yesterday, just to say hullo to Joe Jillings. He says all booksellers are crazy, but that you are the craziest of the lot. He wants to know if you're bankrupt yet."

Roger's slate-blue eyes twinkled. He hung up a cup in the china closet and lit his pipe before replying.

"What did you say?"

"I said that our shop was haunted, and mustn't be supposed to come under the usual conditions of the trade."

"Bully for you! And what did Joe say to that?"

"'Haunted by the nuts!'"

"Well," said Roger, "when literature goes bankrupt I'm willing to go with it. Not till then. But by the way, we're going to be haunted by a beauteous damsel pretty soon. You remember my telling you that Mr. Chapman wants to send his daughter to work in the shop? Well, here's a letter I had from him this morning."

He rummaged in his pocket, and produced the following, which Mrs. Mifflin read:

DEAR MR. MIFFLIN,

I am so delighted that you and Mrs. Mifflin are willing to try the experiment of taking my daughter as an apprentice. Titania is really a very charming girl, and if only we can get some of the "finishing school" nonsense out of her head she will make a fine woman. She has had (it was my fault, not hers) the disadvantage of being brought up, or rather brought down, by having every possible want and whim gratified. Out of kindness for herself and her future husband, if she should have one, I want her to learn a little about earning a living. She is nearly nineteen, and I told her if she would try the bookshop job for a while I would take her to Europe for a year afterward.

As I explained to you, I want her to think she is really earning her way. Of course I don't want the routine to be too hard for her, but I do want her to get some idea of what it means to face life on one's own. If you will pay her ten dollars a week as a beginner, and deduct her board from that, I will pay you twenty dollars a week, privately, for your responsibility in caring for her and keeping your and Mrs. Mifflin's friendly eyes on her. I'm coming round to the Corn Cob meeting to-morrow night, and we can make the final arrangements.

Luckily, she is very fond of books, and I really think she is looking forward to the adventure with much anticipation. I overheard her saying to one of her friends yesterday that she was going to do some "literary work" this winter. That's the kind of nonsense I want her to outgrow. When I hear her say that she's got a job in a bookstore, I'll know she's cured.

Cordially yours,
GEORGE CHAPMAN.

"Well?" said Roger, as Mrs. Mifflin made no comment. "Don't you think it will be rather interesting to get a naive young girl's reactions toward the problems of our tranquil existence?"

"Roger, you blessed innocent!" cried his wife. "Life will no longer be tranquil with a girl of nineteen round the place. You may fool yourself, but you can't fool me. A girl of nineteen doesn't *react* toward things. She explodes. Things don't 'react' anywhere but in Boston and in chemical laboratories. I suppose you know you're taking a human bombshell into the arsenal?"

Roger looked dubious. "I remember something in *Weir of Hermiston* about a girl being 'an explosive engine,'" he said. "But I don't see that she can do any very great harm round here. We're both pretty well proof against shell shock. The worst that could happen would be if she got hold of my private copy of *Fireside Conversation in the Age of Queen Elizabeth*. Remind me to lock it up somewhere, will you?"

This secret masterpiece by Mark Twain was one of the bookseller's treasures. Not even Helen had ever been permitted to read it; and she had shrewdly judged that it was not in her line, for though she knew perfectly well where he kept it (together with his life insurance policy, some Liberty Bonds, an autograph letter from Charles Spencer Chaplin, and a snapshot of herself taken on their honeymoon) she had never made any attempt to examine it.

"Well," said Helen; "Titania or no Titania, if the Corn Cobs want their chocolate cake to-night, I must get busy. Take my suitcase upstairs like a good fellow."

A gathering of booksellers is a pleasant sanhedrim to attend. The members of this ancient craft bear mannerisms and earmarks just as definitely recognizable as those of the cloak and suit business or any other trade. They are likely to be a little—shall we say—worn at the bindings, as becomes men who have forsaken worldly profit to pursue a noble calling ill rewarded in cash. They are possibly a trifle embittered, which is an excellent demeanour for mankind in the face of inscrutable heaven. Long experience with publishers' salesmen makes them suspicious of books praised between the courses of a heavy meal. When a publisher's salesman takes you out to dinner, it is not surprising if the conversation turns toward literature about the time the last of the peas are being harried about the plate. But, as Jerry Gladfist says (he runs a shop up on Thirty-Eighth Street) the publishers' salesmen supply a long-felt want, for they do now and then buy one a dinner the like of which no bookseller would otherwise be likely to commit.

"Well, gentlemen," said Roger as his guests assembled in his little cabinet, "it's a cold evening. Pull up toward the fire. Make free with the cider. The cake's on the table. My wife came back from Boston specially to make it."

"Here's Mrs. Mifflin's health!" said Mr. Chapman, a quiet little man who had a habit of listening to what he heard. "I hope she doesn't mind keeping the shop while we celebrate?"

"Not a bit," said Roger. "She enjoys it."

"I see *Tarzan of the Apes* is running at the Gissing Street movie palace," said Gladfist. "Great stuff. Have you seen it?"

"Not while I can still read *The Jungle Book*," said Roger.

"You make me tired with that talk about literature," cried Jerry. "A book's a book, even if Harold Bell Wright wrote it."

"A book's a book if you enjoy reading it," amended Meredith, from a big Fifth Avenue bookstore. "Lots of people enjoy Harold Bell Wright just as lots of people enjoy tripe. Either of them would kill me. But let's be tolerant."

"Your argument is a whole succession of *non sequiturs*," said

Jerry, stimulated by the cider to unusual brilliance.

"That's a long putt," chuckled Benson, the dealer in rare books and first editions.

"What I mean is this," said Jerry. "We aren't literary critics. It's none of our business to say what's good and what isn't. Our job is simply to supply the public with the books it wants when it wants them. How it comes to want the books it does is no concern of ours."

"You're the guy that calls bookselling the worst business in the world," said Roger warmly, "and you're the kind of guy that makes it so. I suppose you would say that it is no concern of the bookseller to try to increase the public appetite for books?"

"Appetite is too strong a word," said Jerry. "As far as books are concerned the public is barely able to sit up and take a little liquid nourishment. Solid foods don't interest it. If you try to cram roast beef down the gullet of an invalid you'll kill him. Let the public alone, and thank God when it comes round to amputate any of its hard-earned cash."

"Well, take it on the lowest basis," said Roger. "I haven't any facts to go upon——"

"You never have," interjected Jerry.

"But I'd like to bet that the Trade has made more money out of Bryce's *American Commonwealth* than it ever did out of all Parson Wright's books put together."

"What of it? Why shouldn't they make both?"

This preliminary tilt was interrupted by the arrival of two more visitors, and Roger handed round mugs of cider, pointed to the cake and the basket of pretzels, and lit his corn-cob pipe. The new arrivals were Quincy and Fruehling; the former a clerk in the book department of a vast drygoods store, the latter the owner of a bookshop in the Hebrew quarter of Grand Street—one of the best-stocked shops in the city, though little known to uptown book-lovers.

"Well," said Fruehling, his bright dark eyes sparkling above richly tinted cheek-bones and bushy beard, "what's the argument?"

"The usual one," said Gladfist, grinning, "Mifflin confusing merchandise with metaphysics."

MIFFLIN—Not at all. I am simply saying that it is good business to sell only the best.

GLADFIST—Wrong again. You must select your stock according to your customers. Ask Quincy here. Would there be any sense in his loading up his shelves with Maeterlinck and Shaw when the department-store trade wants Eleanor Porter and the Tarzan stuff? Does a country grocer carry the same cigars that are listed on the wine card of a Fifth Avenue hotel? Of course not. He gets in the cigars that his trade enjoys and is accustomed to. Bookselling must obey the ordinary rules of commerce.

MIFFLIN—A fig for the ordinary rules of commerce! I came over here to Gissing Street to get away from them. My mind would blow out its fuses if I had to abide by the dirty little considerations of supply and demand. As far as I am concerned, supply *creates* demand.

GLADFIST—Still, old chap, you have to abide by the dirty little consideration of earning a living, unless someone has endowed you?

BENSON—Of course my line of business isn't strictly the same as you fellows'. But a thought that has often occurred to me in selling rare editions may interest you. The customer's willingness to part with his money is usually in inverse ratio to the permanent benefit he expects to derive from what he purchases.

MEREDITH—Sounds a bit like John Stuart Mill.

BENSON—Even so, it may be true. Folks will pay a darned sight more to be amused than they will to be exalted. Look at the way a man shells out five bones for a couple of theatre seats, or spends a couple of dollars a week on cigars without thinking of it. Yet two dollars or five dollars for a book costs him positive anguish. The mistake you fellows in the retail trade have made is in trying to persuade your customers that books are necessities. Tell them they're luxuries. That'll get them! People have to work so hard in this life they're shy of necessities. A man will go on wearing a suit until it's threadbare, much sooner than smoke a threadbare cigar.

GLADFIST—Not a bad thought. You know, Mifflin here calls me a material-minded cynic, but by thunder, I think I'm more idealistic than he is. I'm no propagandist incessantly trying to cajole poor innocent customers into buying the kind of book *I* think they ought to buy. When I see the helpless pathos of most of them, who drift into a bookstore without the slightest idea of what they want or what is worth reading, I would disdain to take advantage of their frailty. They are absolutely at the mercy of the salesman. They will buy whatever he tells them to. Now the honourable man, the high-minded man (by which I mean myself) is too proud to ram some shimmering stuff at them just because he thinks they ought to read it. Let the boobs blunder around and grab what they can. Let natural selection operate. I think it is fascinating to watch them, to see their helpless groping, and to study the weird ways in which they make their choice. Usually they will buy a book either because they think the jacket is attractive, or because it costs a dollar and a quarter instead of a dollar and a half, or because they say they saw a review of it. The "review" usually turns out to be an ad. I don't think one book-buyer in a thousand knows the difference.

MIFFLIN—Your doctrine is pitiless, base, and false! What would you think of a physician who saw men suffering from a curable disease and did nothing to alleviate their sufferings?

GLADFIST—Their sufferings (as you call them) are nothing to what mine would be if I stocked up with a lot of books that no one but highbrows would buy. What would you think of a base public that would go past my shop day after day and let the high-minded occupant die of starvation?

MIFFLIN—Your ailment, Jerry, is that you conceive yourself as merely a tradesman. What I'm telling you is that the bookseller is a public servant. He ought to be pensioned by the state. The honour of his profession should compel him to do all he can to spread the distribution of good stuff.

QUINCY—I think you forget how much we who deal chiefly in new books are at the mercy of the publishers. We have to stock the new stuff, a large proportion of which is always punk. Why it is punk, goodness knows, because most of the bum books don't sell.

MIFFLIN—Ah, that is a mystery indeed! But I can give you a fair reason. First, because there isn't enough good stuff to go round. Second, because of the ignorance of the publishers, many of whom honestly don't know a good book when they see it. It is a matter of sheer heedlessness in the selection of what they intend to publish. A big drug factory or a manufacturer of a well-known jam spends vast sums of money on chemically assaying and analyzing the ingredients that are to go into his medicines or in gathering and selecting the fruit that is to be stewed into jam. And yet they tell me that the most important department of a publishing business, which is the gathering and sampling of manuscripts, is the least considered and the least remunerated. I knew a reader for one publishing house: he was a babe recently out of college who didn't know a book from a frat pin. If a jam factory employs a trained chemist, why isn't it worth a publisher's while to employ an expert book analyzer? There are some of them. Look at the fellow who runs the *Pacific Monthly's* book business for example! He knows a thing or two.

CHAPMAN—I think perhaps you exaggerate the value of those trained experts. They are likely to be fourflushers. We had one once at our factory, and as far as I could make out he never thought we were doing good business except when we were losing money.

MIFFLIN—As far as I have been able to observe, making money is the easiest thing in the world. All you have to do is to turn out an honest product, something that the public needs. Then you have to let them know that you have it, and teach them that they need it. They will batter down your front door in their eagerness to get it. But if you begin to hand them gold bricks, if you begin to sell them books built like an apartment house, all marble front and all brick behind, you're cutting your own throat, or rather cutting your own pocket, which is the same thing.

MEREDITH—I think Mifflin's right. You know the kind of place our shop is: a regular Fifth Avenue store, all plate glass front and marble columns glowing in the indirect lighting like a birchwood at full moon. We sell hundreds of dollars' worth of bunkum every day because people ask for it; but I tell you we do it with reluctance. It's rather the custom in our shop to scoff at the book-buying public and call them boobs, but they really want good books—the poor souls don't know how to get them. Still, Jerry has a certain grain of truth to his credit. I get ten times more satisfaction in selling a copy of Newton's *The Amenities of Book-Collecting* than I do in selling a copy of—well, *Tarzan;* but it's poor business to impose your own private tastes on your customers. All you can do is to hint them along tactfully, when you get a chance, toward the stuff that counts.

QUINCY—You remind me of something that happened in our book department the other day. A flapper came in and said she had forgotten the name of the book she wanted, but it was something about a young man who had been brought up by the monks. I was stumped. I tried her with *The Cloister and the Hearth* and *Monastery Bells* and *Legends of the Monastic Orders* and so on, but her face was blank. Then one of the salesgirls overheard us talking, and she guessed it right off the bat. Of course it was *Tarzan.*

MIFFLIN—You poor simp, there was your chance to introduce her to Mowgli and the bandar-log.

QUINCY—True—I didn't think of it.

MIFFLIN—I'd like to get you fellows' ideas about advertising. There was a young chap in here the other day from an advertising agency, trying to get me to put some copy in the papers. Have you found that it pays?

FRUEHLING—It always pays—somebody. The only question is, does it pay the man who pays for the ad?

MEREDITH—What do you mean?

FRUEHLING—Did you ever consider the problem of what I call tangential advertising? By that I mean advertising that benefits your rival rather than yourself? Take an example. On Sixth Avenue there is a lovely delicatessen shop, but rather expensive. Every conceivable kind of sweetmeat and relish is displayed in the brightly lit window. When you look at that window it simply makes your mouth water. You decide to have something to eat. But do you get it there? Not much! You go a little farther down the street and get it at the Automat or the Crystal Lunch. The delicatessen fellow pays the overhead expense of that beautiful food exhibit, and the other man gets the benefit of it. It's the same way in my business. I'm in a factory district, where people can't afford to have any but the best books. (Meredith will bear me out in saying that only the wealthy can afford the poor ones.) They read the book ads in the papers and magazines, the ads of Meredith's shop and others, and then they come to me to buy them. I believe in advertising, but I believe in letting someone else pay for it.

MIFFLIN—I guess perhaps I can afford to go on riding on

Christopher Morley                                                    99

Meredith's ads. I hadn't thought of that. But I think I shall put a little notice in one of the papers some day, just a little card saying

PARNASSUS AT HOME
GOOD BOOKS BOUGHT
AND SOLD
THIS SHOP IS HAUNTED

It will be fun to see what come-back I get.

QUINCY—The book section of a department store doesn't get much chance to enjoy that tangential advertising, as Fruehling calls it. Why, when our interior decorating shark puts a few volumes of a pirated Kipling bound in crushed oilcloth or a copy of "Knock-kneed Stories," into the window to show off a Louis XVIII boudoir suite, display space is charged up against my department! Last summer he asked me for "something by that Ring fellow, I forget the name," to put a punchy finish on a layout of porch furniture. I thought perhaps he meant Wagner's Nibelungen operas, and began to dig them out. Then I found he meant Ring Lardner.

GLADFIST—There you are. I keep telling you bookselling is an impossible job for a man who loves literature. When did a bookseller ever make any real contribution to the world's happiness?

MIFFLIN—Dr. Johnson's father was a bookseller.

GLADFIST—Yes, and couldn't afford to pay for Sam's education.

FRUEHLING—There's another kind of tangential advertising that interests me. Take, for instance, a Coles Phillips painting for some brand of silk stockings. Of course the high lights of the picture are cunningly focussed on the stockings of the eminently beautiful lady; but there is always something else in the picture—an automobile or a country house or a Morris chair or a parasol—which makes it just as effective an ad for those goods as it is for the stockings. Every now and then Phillips sticks a book into his paintings, and I expect the Fifth Avenue book trade benefits by it. A book that fits the mind as well as a silk stocking does the ankle will be sure to sell.

MIFFLIN—You are all crass materialists. I tell you, books are the depositories of the human spirit, which is the only thing in this world that endures. What was it Shakespeare said—

Not marble nor the gilded monuments
Of princes shall outlive this powerful rhyme—

By the bones of the Hohenzollerns, he was right! And wait a minute! There's something in Carlyle's *Cromwell* that comes back to me.

He ran excitedly out of the room, and the members of the Corn Cob fraternity grinned at each other. Gladfist cleaned his pipe and poured out some more cider. "He's off on his hobby," he chuckled. "I love baiting him."

"Speaking of Carlyle's *Cromwell*," said Fruehling, "that's a book I don't often hear asked for. But a fellow came in the other day hunting for a copy, and to my chagrin I didn't have one. I rather pride myself on keeping that sort of thing in stock. So I called up Brentano's to see if I could pick one up, and they told me they had just sold the only copy they had. Somebody must have been boosting Thomas! Maybe he's quoted in *Tarzan*, or somebody has bought up the film rights."

Mifflin came in, looking rather annoyed.

"Here's an odd thing," he said. "I know damn well that copy of *Cromwell* was on the shelf because I saw it there last night. It's not there now."

"That's nothing," said Quincy. "You know how people come into a second-hand store, see a book they take a fancy to but don't feel like buying just then, and tuck it away out of sight or on some other shelf where they think no one else will spot it, but they'll be able to find it when they can afford it. Probably someone's done that with your *Cromwell*."

"Maybe, but I doubt it," said Mifflin. "Mrs. Mifflin says she didn't sell it this evening. I woke her up to ask her. She was dozing over her knitting at the desk. I guess she's tired after her trip."

"I'm sorry to miss the Carlyle quotation," said Benson. "What was the gist?"

"I think I've got it jotted down in a notebook," said Roger, hunting along a shelf. "Yes, here it is." He read aloud:

*"The works of a man, bury them under what guano-mountains and obscene owl-droppings you will, do not perish, cannot perish. What of Heroism, what of Eternal Light was in a Man and his Life, is with very great exactness added to the Eternities, remains forever a new divine portion of the Sum of Things.*

"Now, my friends, the bookseller is one of the keys in that universal adding machine, because he aids in the cross-fertilization of men and books. His delight in his calling doesn't need to be stimulated even by the bright shanks of a Coles Phillips picture.

"Roger, my boy," said Gladfist, "your innocent enthusiasm makes me think of Tom Daly's favourite story about the Irish priest who was rebuking his flock for their love of whisky. 'Whisky,' he said, 'is the bane of this congregation. Whisky, that steals away a man's brains. Whisky, that makes you shoot at landlords—and not hit them!' Even so, my dear Roger, your enthusiasm makes you shoot at truth and never come anywhere near it."

"Jerry," said Roger, "you are a upas tree. Your shadow is

poisonous!"

"Well, gentlemen," said Mr. Chapman, "I know Mrs. Mifflin wants to be relieved of her post. I vote we adjourn early. Your conversation is always delightful, though I am sometimes a bit uncertain as to the conclusions. My daughter is going to be a bookseller, and I shall look forward to hearing her views on the business."

As the guests made their way out through the shop, Mr. Chapman drew Roger aside. "It's perfectly all right about sending Titania?" he asked.

"Absolutely," said Roger. "When does she want to come?"

"Is to-morrow too soon?"

"The sooner the better. We've got a little spare room upstairs that she can have. I've got some ideas of my own about furnishing it for her. Send her round to-morrow afternoon."

### Chapter III. Titania Arrives

The first pipe after breakfast is a rite of some importance to seasoned smokers, and Roger applied the flame to the bowl as he stood at the bottom of the stairs. He blew a great gush of strong blue reek that eddied behind him as he ran up the flight, his mind eagerly meditating the congenial task of arranging the little spare room for the coming employee. Then, at the top of the steps, he found that his pipe had already gone out. "What with filling my pipe and emptying it, lighting it and relighting it," he thought, "I don't seem to get much time for the serious concerns of life. Come to think of it, smoking, soiling dishes and washing them, talking and listening to other people talk, take up most of life anyway."

This theory rather pleased him, so he ran downstairs again to tell it to Mrs. Mifflin.

"Go along and get that room fixed up," she said, "and don't try to palm off any bogus doctrines on me so early in the morning. Housewives have no time for philosophy after breakfast."

Roger thoroughly enjoyed himself in the task of preparing the guest-room for the new assistant. It was a small chamber at the back of the second storey, opening on to a narrow passage that connected through a door with the gallery of the bookshop. Two small windows commanded a view of the modest roofs of that quarter of Brooklyn, roofs that conceal so many brave hearts, so many baby carriages, so many cups of bad coffee, and so many cartons of the Chapman prunes.

"By the way," he called downstairs, "better have some of the prunes for supper to-night, just as a compliment to Miss Chapman."

Mrs. Mifflin preserved a humorous silence.

Over these noncommittal summits the bright eye of the bookseller, as he tacked up the freshly ironed muslin curtains Mrs. Mifflin had

allotted, could discern a glimpse of the bay and the leviathan ferries
that link Staten Island with civilization. "Just a touch of romance in the
outlook," he thought to himself. "It will suffice to keep a blasée young
girl aware of the excitements of existence."

The room, as might be expected in a house presided over by Helen
Mifflin, was in perfect order to receive any occupant, but Roger had
volunteered to psychologize it in such a fashion as (he thought) would
convey favourable influences to the misguided young spirit that was to
be its tenant. Incurable idealist, he had taken quite gravely his
responsibility as landlord and employer of Mr. Chapman's daughter.
No chambered nautilus was to have better opportunity to expand the
tender mansions of its soul.

Beside the bed was a bookshelf with a reading lamp. The problem
Roger was discussing was what books and pictures might be the best
preachers to this congregation of one. To Mrs. Mifflin's secret
amusement he had taken down the picture of Sir Galahad which he had
once hung there, because (as he had said) if Sir Galahad were living to-
day he would be a bookseller. "We don't want her feasting her
imagination on young Galahads," he had remarked at breakfast. "That
way lies premature matrimony. What I want to do is put up in her room
one or two good prints representing actual men who were so delightful
in their day that all the young men she is likely to see now will seem
tepid and prehensile. Thus she will become disgusted with the present
generation of youths and there will be some chance of her really putting
her mind on the book business."

Accordingly he had spent some time in going through a bin where
he kept photos and drawings of authors that the publishers' "publicity
men" were always showering upon him. After some thought he
discarded promising engravings of Harold Bell Wright and Stephen
Leacock, and chose pictures of Shelley, Anthony Trollope, Robert
Louis Stevenson, and Robert Burns. Then, after further meditation, he
decided that neither Shelley nor Burns would quite do for a young
girl's room, and set them aside in favour of a portrait of Samuel Butler.
To these he added a framed text that he was very fond of and had hung
over his own desk. He had once clipped it from a copy of *Life* and
found much pleasure in it. It runs thus:

## ON THE RETURN OF A BOOK
## LENT TO A FRIEND

I GIVE humble and hearty thanks for the safe return of this book
which having endured the perils of my friend's bookcase, and the
bookcases of my friend's friends, now returns to me in reasonably good
condition.

I GIVE humble and hearty thanks that my friend did not see fit to give this book to his infant as a plaything, nor use it as an ash-tray for his burning cigar, nor as a teething-ring for his mastiff.

WHEN I lent this book I deemed it as lost: I was resigned to the bitterness of the long parting: I never thought to look upon its pages again.

BUT NOW that my book is come back to me, I rejoice and am exceeding glad! Bring hither the fatted morocco and let us rebind the volume and set it on the shelf of honour: for this my book was lent, and is returned again.

PRESENTLY, therefore, I may return some of the books that I myself have borrowed.

"There!" he thought. "That will convey to her the first element of book morality."

These decorations having been displayed on the walls, he bethought himself of the books that should stand on the bedside shelf.

This is a question that admits of the utmost nicety of discussion. Some authorities hold that the proper books for a guest-room are of a soporific quality that will induce swift and painless repose. This school advises *The Wealth of Nations, Rome under the Caesars, The Statesman's Year Book*, certain novels of Henry James, and *The Letters of Queen Victoria* (in three volumes). It is plausibly contended that books of this kind cannot be read (late at night) for more than a few minutes at a time, and that they afford useful scraps of information.

Another branch of opinion recommends for bedtime reading short stories, volumes of pithy anecdote, swift and sparkling stuff that may keep one awake for a space, yet will advantage all the sweeter slumber in the end. Even ghost stories and harrowing matter are maintained seasonable by these pundits. This class of reading comprises O. Henry, Bret Harte, Leonard Merrick, Ambrose Bierce, W. W. Jacobs, Daudet, de Maupassant, and possibly even *On a Slow Train Through Arkansaw*, that grievous classic of the railway bookstalls whereof its author, Mr. Thomas W. Jackson, has said "It will sell forever, and a thousand years afterward." To this might be added another of Mr. Jackson's onslaughts on the human intelligence, *I'm From Texas, You Can't Steer Me*, whereof is said (by the author) "It is like a hard-boiled egg, you can't beat it." There are other of Mr. Jackson's books, whose titles escape memory, whereof he has said "They are a dynamite for sorrow." Nothing used to annoy Mifflin more than to have someone come in and ask for copies of these works. His brother-in-law, Andrew McGill, the writer, once gave him for Christmas (just to annoy him) a copy of *On a Slow Train Through Arkansaw* sumptuously bound and gilded in what is known to the trade as "dove-coloured ooze." Roger retorted by sending Andrew (for his next birthday) two volumes of *Brann the Iconoclast* bound in what Robert Cortes Holliday calls "embossed toadskin." But that is apart from the story.

To the consideration of what to put on Miss Titania's bookshelf Roger devoted the delighted hours of the morning. Several times Helen called him to come down and attend to the shop, but he was sitting on the floor, unaware of numbed shins, poring over the volumes he had carted upstairs for a final culling. "It will be a great privilege," he said to himself, "to have a young mind to experiment with. Now my wife, delightful creature though she is, was—well, distinctly mature when I had the good fortune to meet her; I have never been able properly to supervise her mental processes. But this Chapman girl will come to us wholly unlettered. Her father said she had been to a fashionable school: that surely is a guarantee that the delicate tendrils of her mind have never begun to sprout. I will test her (without her knowing it) by the books I put here for her. By noting which of them she responds to, I will know how to proceed. It might be worth while to shut up the shop one day a week in order to give her some brief talks on literature. Delightful! Let me see, a little series of talks on the development of the English novel, beginning with *Tom Jones*—hum, that would hardly do! Well, I have always longed to be a teacher, this looks like a chance to begin. We might invite some of the neighbours to send in their children once a week, and start a little school. *Causeries du lundi*, in fact! Who knows I may yet be the Sainte Beuve of Brooklyn."

Across his mind flashed a vision of newspaper clippings—"*This remarkable student of letters, who hides his brilliant parts under the unassuming existence of a second-hand bookseller, is now recognized as the——*"

"Roger!" called Mrs. Mifflin from downstairs: "Front! someone wants to know if you keep back numbers of *Foamy Stories*."

After he had thrown out the intruder, Roger returned to his meditation. "This selection," he mused, "is of course only tentative. It is to act as a preliminary test, to see what sort of thing interests her. First of all, her name naturally suggests Shakespeare and the Elizabethans. It's a remarkable name, Titania Chapman: there must be great virtue in prunes! Let's begin with a volume of Christopher Marlowe. Then Keats, I guess: every young person ought to shiver over St. Agnes' Eve on a bright cold winter evening. *Over Bemerton's*, certainly, because it's a bookshop story. Eugene Field's *Tribune Primer* to try out her sense of humour. And Archy, by all means, for the same reason. I'll go down and get the Archy scrapbook."

It should be explained that Roger was a keen admirer of Don Marquis, the humourist of the New York *Evening Sun*. Mr. Marquis once lived in Brooklyn, and the bookseller was never tired of saying that he was the most eminent author who had graced the borough since the days of Walt Whitman. Archy, the imaginary cockroach whom Mr. Marquis uses as a vehicle for so much excellent fun, was a constant delight to Roger, and he had kept a scrapbook of all Archy's clippings. This bulky tome he now brought out from the grotto by his desk where his particular treasures were kept. He ran his eye over it, and Mrs. Mifflin heard him utter shrill screams of laughter.

"What on earth is it?" she asked.

"Only Archy," he said, and began to read aloud—

down in a wine vault underneath the city
   two old men were sitting they were drinking booze
torn were their garments hair and beards were gritty
   one had an overcoat but hardly any shoes

overhead the street cars through the streets were running
   filled with happy people going home to christmas
in the adirondacks the hunters all were gunning
   big ships were sailing down by the isthmus

in came a little tot for to kiss her granny
   such a little totty she could scarcely tottle
saying kiss me grandpa kiss your little nanny
   but the old man beaned her with a whisky bottle.

outside the snowflakes began for to flutter
   far at sea the ships were sailing with the seamen
not another word did angel nanny utter
   her grandsire chuckled and pledged the whisky demon

up spake the second man he was worn and weary
   tears washed his face which otherwise was pasty
she loved her parents who commuted on the erie
   brother im afraid you struck a trifle hasty

she came to see you all her pretty duds on
   bringing christmas posies from her mothers garden
riding in the tunnel underneath the hudson
   brother was it rum caused your heart to harden——

"What on earth is there funny in that?" said Mrs. Mifflin. "Poor little lamb, I think it was terrible."

"There's more of it," cried Roger, and opened his mouth to continue.

"No more, thank you," said Helen. "There ought to be a fine for using the meter of *Love in the Valley* that way. I'm going out to market so if the bell rings you'll have to answer it."

Roger added the Archy scrapbook to Miss Titania's shelf, and went on browsing over the volumes he had collected.

"*The Nigger of the Narcissus*," he said to himself, "for even if she doesn't read the story perhaps she'll read the preface, which not marble nor the monuments of princes will outlive. Dickens' *Christmas Stories* to introduce her to Mrs. Lirriper, the queen of landladies. Publishers tell me that Norfolk Street, Strand, is best known for the famous literary agent that has his office there, but I wonder how many of them know that that was where Mrs. Lirriper had her immortal lodgings? *The Notebooks of Samuel Butler*, just to give her a little intellectual jazz. *The Wrong Box*, because it's the best farce in the language. *Travels with a Donkey*, to show her what good writing is like. *The Four Horsemen of the Apocalypse* to give her a sense of pity for human woes—wait a minute, though: that's a pretty broad book for young ladies. I guess we'll put it aside and see what else there is. Some of Mr. Mosher's catalogues: fine! they'll show her the true spirit of what one book-lover calls biblio-bliss. *Walking-Stick Papers*—yes, there are still good essayists running around. A bound file of The Publishers' Weekly to give her a smack of trade matters. *Jo's Boys* in case she needs a little relaxation. *The Lays of Ancient Rome* and Austin Dobson to show her some good poetry. I wonder if they give them *The Lays* to read in school nowadays? I have a horrible fear they are brought up on the battle of Salamis and the brutal redcoats of '76. And now we'll be exceptionally subtle: we'll stick in a Robert Chambers to see if she falls for it."

He viewed the shelf with pride. "Not bad," he said to himself. "I'll just add this Leonard Merrick, *Whispers about Women*, to amuse her. I bet that title will start her guessing. Helen will say I ought to have included the Bible, but I'll omit it on purpose, just to see whether the girl misses it."

With typical male curiosity he pulled out the bureau drawers to see what disposition his wife had made of them, and was pleased to find a little muslin bag of lavender dispersing a quiet fragrance in each. "Very nice," he remarked. "Very nice indeed! About the only thing missing is an ashtray. If Miss Titania is as modern as some of them, that'll be the first thing she'll call for. And maybe a copy of Ezra Pound's poems. I do hope she's not what Helen calls a bolshevixen."

There was nothing bolshevik about a glittering limousine that drew up at the corner of Gissing and Swinburne streets early that afternoon. A chauffeur in green livery opened the door, lifted out a suitcase of beautiful brown leather, and gave a respectful hand to the vision that emerged from depths of lilac-coloured upholstery.

"Where do you want me to carry the bag, miss?"

"This is the bitter parting," replied Miss Titania. "I don't want you to know my address, Edwards. Some of my mad friends might worm it out of you, and I don't want them coming down and bothering me. I am going to be very busy with literature. I'll walk the rest of the way."

Edwards saluted with a grin—he worshipped the original young heiress—and returned to his wheel.

"There's one thing I want you to do for me," said Titania. "Call up my father and tell him I'm on the job."

"Yes, miss," said Edwards, who would have run the limousine into a government motor truck if she had ordered it.

Miss Chapman's small gloved hand descended into an interesting purse that was cuffed to her wrist with a bright little chain. She drew out a nickel—it was characteristic of her that it was a very bright and engaging looking nickel—and handed it gravely to her charioteer. Equally gravely he saluted, and the car, after moving through certain dignified arcs, swam swiftly away down Thackeray Boulevard.

Titania, after making sure that Edwards was out of sight, turned up Gissing Street with a fluent pace and an observant eye. A small boy cried, "Carry your bag, lady?" and she was about to agree, but then remembered that she was now engaged at ten dollars a week and waved him away. Our readers would feel a justifiable grudge if we did not attempt a description of the young lady, and we will employ the few blocks of her course along Gissing Street for this purpose.

Walking behind her, the observer, by the time she had reached Clemens Place, would have seen that she was faultlessly tailored in genial tweeds; that her small brown boots were sheltered by spats of that pale tan complexion exhibited by Pullman porters on the Pennsylvania Railroad; that her person was both slender and vigorous; that her shoulders were carrying a sumptuous fur of the colour described by the trade as nutria, or possibly opal smoke. The word chinchilla would have occurred irresistibly to this observer from behind; he might also, if he were the father of a family, have had a fleeting vision of many autographed stubs in a check book. The general impression that he would have retained, had he turned aside at Clemens Place, would be "expensive, but worth the expense."

It is more likely, however, that the student of phenomena would have continued along Gissing Street to the next corner, being that of Hazlitt Street. Taking advantage of opportunity, he would overtake the lady on the pavement, with a secret, sidelong glance. If he were wise, he would pass her on the right side where her tilted bonnet permitted a wider angle of vision. He would catch a glimpse of cheek and chin belonging to the category known (and rightly) as adorable; hair that held sunlight through the dullest day; even a small platinum wrist watch that might pardonably be excused, in its exhilarating career, for beating a trifle fast. Among the greyish furs he would note a bunch of such violets as never bloom in the crude springtime, but reserve themselves for November and the plate glass windows of Fifth Avenue.

It is probable that whatever the errand of this spectator he would have continued along Gissing Street a few paces farther. Then, with calculated innocence, he would have halted halfway up the block that leads to the Wordsworth Avenue "L," and looked backward with carefully simulated irresolution, as though considering some forgotten matter. With apparently unseeing eyes he would have scanned the bright pedestrian, and caught the full impact of her rich blue gaze. He would have seen a small resolute face rather vivacious in effect, yet with a quaint pathos of youth and eagerness. He would have noted the cheeks lit with excitement and rapid movement in the bracing air. He would certainly have noted the delicate contrast of the fur of the wild nutria with the soft V of her bare throat. Then, to his surprise, he would have seen this attractive person stop, examine her surroundings, and run down some steps into a rather dingy-looking second-hand bookshop. He would have gone about his affairs with a new and surprised conviction that the Almighty had the borough of Brooklyn under His especial care.

Roger, who had conceived a notion of some rather peevish foundling of the Ritz-Carlton lobbies and Central Park riding academies, was agreeably amazed by the sweet simplicity of the young lady.

"Is this Mr. Mifflin?" she said, as he advanced all agog from his smoky corner.

"Miss Chapman?" he replied, taking her bag. "Helen!" he called. "Miss Titania is here."

She looked about the sombre alcoves of the shop. "I do think it's adorable of you to take me in," she said. "Dad has told me so much about you. He says I'm impossible. I suppose this is the literature he talks about. I want to know all about it."

"And here's Bock!" she cried. "Dad says he's the greatest dog in the world, named after Botticelli or somebody. I've brought him a present. It's in my bag. Nice old Bocky!"

Bock, who was unaccustomed to spats, was examining them after his own fashion.

"Well, my dear," said Mrs. Mifflin. "We are delighted to see you. I hope you'll be happy with us, but I rather doubt it. Mr. Mifflin is a hard man to get along with."

"Oh, I'm sure of it!" cried Titania. "I mean, I'm sure I shall be happy! You mustn't believe a word of what Dad says about me. I'm crazy about books. I don't see how you can bear to sell them. I brought these violets for you, Mrs. Mifflin."

"How perfectly sweet of you," said Helen, captivated already. "Come along, we'll put them right in water. I'll show you your room."

Roger heard them moving about overhead. It suddenly occurred to him that the shop was rather a dingy place for a young girl. "I wish I had thought to get in a cash register," he mused. "She'll think I'm terribly unbusiness-like."

"Now," said Mrs. Mifflin, as she and Titania came downstairs again, "I'm making some pastry, so I'm going to turn you over to your employer. He can show you round the shop and tell you where all the books are."

"Before we begin," said Titania, "just let me give Bock his present." She showed a large package of tissue paper and, unwinding innumerable layers, finally disclosed a stalwart bone. "I was lunching at Sherry's, and I made the head waiter give me this. He was awfully amused."

"Come along into the kitchen and give it to him," said Helen. "He'll be your friend for life."

"What an adorable kennel!" cried Titania, when she saw the remodelled packing-case that served Bock as a retreat. The bookseller's ingenious carpentry had built it into the similitude of a Carnegie library, with the sign READING-ROOM over the door; and he had painted imitation book-shelves along the interior.

"You'll get used to Mr. Mifflin after a while," said Helen amusedly. "He spent all one winter getting that kennel fixed to his liking. You might have thought he was going to live in it instead of Bock. All the titles that he painted in there are books that have dogs in them, and a lot of them he made up."

Titania insisted on getting down to peer inside. Bock was much flattered at this attention from the new planet that had swum into his kennel.

"Gracious!" she said, "here's 'The Rubaiyat of Omar Canine.' I do think that's clever!"

"Oh, there are a lot more," said Helen. "The works of Bonar Law, and Bohn's 'Classics,' and 'Catechisms on Dogma' and goodness knows what. If Roger paid half as much attention to business as he does to jokes of that sort, we'd be rich. Now, you run along and have a look at the shop."

Titania found the bookseller at his desk. "Here I am, Mr. Mifflin," she said. "See, I brought a nice sharp pencil along with me to make out sales slips. I've been practicing sticking it in my hair. I can do it quite nicely now. I hope you have some of those big red books with all the carbon paper in them and everything. I've been watching the girls up at Lord and Taylor's make them out, and I think they're fascinating. And you must teach me to run the elevator. I'm awfully keen about elevators."

"Bless me," said Roger, "You'll find this very different from Lord and Taylor's! We haven't any elevators, or any sales slips, or even a cash register. We don't wait on customers unless they ask us to. They come in and browse round, and if they find anything they want they

come back here to my desk and ask about it. The price is marked in
every book in red pencil. The cash-box is here on this shelf. This is the
key hanging on this little hook. I enter each sale in this ledger. When
you sell a book you must write it down here, and the price paid for it."

"But suppose it's charged?" said Titania.

"No charge accounts. Everything is cash. If someone comes in to
sell books, you must refer him to me. You mustn't be surprised to see
people drop in here and spend several hours reading. Lots of them look
on this as a kind of club. I hope you don't mind the smell of tobacco,
for almost all the men that come here smoke in the shop. You see, I put
ash trays around for them."

"I love tobacco smell," said Titania. "Daddy's library at home
smells something like this, but not quite so strong. And I want to see
the worms, bookworms you know. Daddy said you had lots of them."

"You'll see them, all right," said Roger, chuckling. "They come in
and out. To-morrow I'll show you how my stock is arranged. It'll take
you quite a while to get familiar with it. Until then I just want you to
poke around and see what there is, until you know the shelves so well
you could put your hand on any given book in the dark. That's a game
my wife and I used to play. We would turn off all the lights at night,
and I would call out the title of a book and see how near she could
come to finding it. Then I would take a turn. When we came more than
six inches away from it we would have to pay a forfeit. It's great fun."

"What larks we'll have," cried Titania. "I do think this is a cunning
place!"

"This is the bulletin board, where I put up notices about books that
interest me. Here's a card I've just been writing."

Roger drew from his pocket a square of cardboard and affixed it to
the board with a thumbtack. Titania read:

THE BOOK THAT SHOULD HAVE PREVENTED THE WAR

Now that the fighting is over is a good time to read Thomas
Hardy's *The Dynasts*. I don't want to sell it, because it is one of the
greatest treasures I own. But if any one will guarantee to read all three
volumes, and let them sink into his mind, I'm willing to lend them.

If enough thoughtful Germans had read *The Dynasts* before July,
1914, there would have been no war.

If every delegate to the Peace Conference could be made to read it
before the sessions begin, there will be no more wars.

R. MIFFLIN.

"Dear me," said Titania, "Is it so good as all that? Perhaps I'd
better read it."

"It is so good that if I knew any way of doing so I'd insist on Mr.

Wilson reading it on his voyage to France. I wish I could get it onto his ship. My, what a book! It makes one positively ill with pity and terror. Sometimes I wake up at night and look out of the window and imagine I hear Hardy laughing. I get him a little mixed up with the Deity, I fear. But he's a bit too hard for you to tackle."

Titania was puzzled, and said nothing. But her busy mind made a note of its own: *Hardy, hard to read, makes one ill, try it.*

"What did you think of the books I put in your room?" said Roger. He had vowed to wait until she made some comment unsolicited, but he could not restrain himself.

"In my room?" she said. "Why, I'm sorry, I never noticed them!"

### Chapter IV. The Disappearing Volume

"Well, my dear," said Roger after supper that evening, "I think perhaps we had better introduce Miss Titania to our custom of reading aloud."

"Perhaps it would bore her?" said Helen. "You know it isn't everybody that likes being read to."

"Oh, I should love it!" exclaimed Titania. "I don't think anybody ever read to me, that is not since I was a child."

"Suppose we leave you to look after the shop," said Helen to Roger, in a teasing mood, "and I'll take Titania out to the movies. I think *Tarzan* is still running."

Whatever private impulses Miss Chapman may have felt, she saw by the bookseller's downcast face that a visit to *Tarzan* would break his heart, and she was prompt to disclaim any taste for the screen classic.

"Dear me," she said; "*Tarzan*—that's all that nature stuff by John Burroughs; isn't it? Oh, Mrs. Mifflin, I think it would be very tedious. Let's have Mr. Mifflin read to us. I'll get down my knitting bag."

"You mustn't mind being interrupted," said Helen. "When anybody rings the bell Roger has to run out and tend the shop."

"You must let me do it," said Titania. "I want to earn my wages, you know."

"All right," said Mrs. Mifflin; "Roger, you settle Miss Chapman in the den and give her something to look at while we do the dishes."

But Roger was all on fire to begin the reading. "Why don't we postpone the dishes," he said, "just to celebrate?"

"Let me help," insisted Titania. "I should think washing up would be great fun."

"No, no, not on your first evening," said Helen. "Mr. Mifflin and I will finish them in a jiffy."

So Roger poked up the coal fire in the den, disposed the chairs, and gave Titania a copy of *Sartor Resartus* to look at. He then vanished into the kitchen with his wife, whence Titania heard the cheerful clank of crockery in a dishpan and the splashing of hot water. "The best thing about washing up," she heard Roger say, "is that it makes one's hands so clean, a novel sensation for a second-hand bookseller."

She gave *Sartor Resartus* what is graphically described as a "once over," and then seeing the morning *Times* lying on the table, picked it up, as she had not read it. Her eye fell upon the column headed

LOST AND FOUND
Fifty cents an agate line

and as she had recently lost a little pearl brooch, she ran hastily through it. She chuckled a little over

Lost—Hotel Imperial lavatory, set of teeth. Call or communicate Steel, 134 East 43 St. Reward, no questions asked.

Then she saw this:

Lost—Copy of Thomas Carlyle's "Oliver Cromwell," between Gissing Street, Brooklyn, and the Octagon Hotel. If found before midnight, Tuesday, Dec. 3, return to assistant chef, Octagon Hotel.

"Why" she exclaimed, "Gissing Street—that's here! And what a funny kind of book for an assistant chef to read. No wonder their lunches have been so bad lately!"

When Roger and Helen rejoined her in the den a few minutes later she showed the bookseller the advertisement. He was very much excited.

"That's a funny thing," he said. "There's something queer about that book. Did I tell you about it? Last Tuesday—I know it was then because it was the evening young Gilbert was here—a man with a beard came in asking for it, and it wasn't on the shelf. Then the next night, Wednesday, I was up very late writing, and fell asleep at my desk. I must have left the front door ajar, because I was waked up by the draught, and when I went to close the door I saw the book sticking out a little beyond the others, in its usual place. And last night, when the Corn Cobs were here, I went out to look up a quotation in it, and it was gone again."

"Perhaps the assistant chef stole it?" said Titania.

"But if so, why the deuce would he advertise having done so?" asked Roger.

"Well, if he did steal it," said Helen, "I wish him joy of it. I tried to read it once, you talked so much about it, and I found it dreadfully dull."

"If he did steal it," cried the bookseller, "I'm perfectly delighted. It shows that my contention is right: people *do* really care for good books.

If an assistant chef is so fond of good books that he has to steal them, the world is safe for democracy. Usually the only books any one wants to steal are sheer piffle, like *Making Life Worth While* by Douglas Fairbanks or Mother Shipton's *Book of Oracles*. I don't mind a man stealing books if he steals good ones!"

"You see the remarkable principles that govern this business," said Helen to Titania. They sat down by the fire and took up their knitting while the bookseller ran out to see if the volume had by any chance returned to his shelves.

"Is it there?" said Helen, when he came back.

"No," said Roger, and picked up the advertisement again. "I wonder why he wants it returned before midnight on Tuesday?"

"So he can read it in bed, I guess," said Helen. "Perhaps he suffers from insomnia."

"It's a darn shame he lost it before he had a chance to read it. I'd like to have known what he thought of it. I've got a great mind to go up and call on him."

"Charge it off to profit and loss and forget about it," said Helen. "How about that reading aloud?"

Roger ran his eye along his private shelves, and pulled down a well-worn volume.

"Now that Thanksgiving is past," he said, "my mind always turns to Christmas, and Christmas means Charles Dickens. My dear, would it bore you if we had a go at the old *Christmas Stories?*"

Mrs. Mifflin held up her hands in mock dismay. "He reads them to me every year at this time," she said to Titania. "Still, they're worth it. I know good old Mrs. Lirriper better than I do most of my friends."

"What is it, the Christmas Carol?" said Titania. "We had to read that in school."

"No," said Roger; "the other stories, infinitely better. Everybody gets the Carol dinned into them until they're weary of it, but no one nowadays seems to read the others. I tell you, Christmas wouldn't be Christmas to me if I didn't read these tales over again every year. How homesick they make one for the good old days of real inns and real beefsteak and real ale drawn in pewter. My dears, sometimes when I am reading Dickens I get a vision of rare sirloin with floury boiled potatoes and plenty of horse-radish, set on a shining cloth not far from a blaze of English coal——"

"He's an incorrigible visionary," said Mrs. Mifflin. "To hear him talk you might think no one had had a square meal since Dickens died. You might think that all landladies died with Mrs. Lirriper."

"Very ungrateful of him," said Titania. "I'm sure I couldn't ask for better potatoes, or a nicer hostess, than I've found in Brooklyn."

"Well, well," said Roger. "You are right, of course. And yet something went out of the world when Victorian England vanished, something that will never come again. Take the stagecoach drivers, for instance. What a racy, human type they were! And what have we now to compare with them? Subway guards? Taxicab drivers? I have hung around many an all-night lunchroom to hear the chauffeurs talk. But they are too much on the move, you can't get the picture of them the way Dickens could of his types. You can't catch that sort of thing in a snapshot, you know: you have to have a time exposure. I'll grant you, though, that lunchroom food is mighty good. The best place to eat is always a counter where the chauffeurs congregate. They get awfully hungry, you see, driving round in the cold, and when they want food they want it hot and tasty. There's a little hash-alley called Frank's, up on Broadway near 77th, where I guess the ham and eggs and French fried is as good as any Mr. Pickwick ever ate."

"I must get Edwards to take me there," said Titania. "Edwards is our chauffeur. I've been to the Ansonia for tea, that's near there."

"Better keep away," said Helen. "When Roger comes home from those places he smells so strong of onions it brings tears to my eyes."

"We've just been talking about an assistant chef," said Roger; "that suggests that I read you *Somebody's Luggage*, which is all about a head waiter. I have often wished I could get a job as a waiter or a bus boy, just to learn if there really are any such head waiters nowadays. You know there are all sorts of jobs I'd like to have, just to fructify my knowledge of human nature and find out whether life is really as good as literature. I'd love to be a waiter, a barber, a floorwalker——"

"Roger, my dear," said Helen, "why don't you get on with the reading?"

Roger knocked out his pipe, turned Bock out of his chair, and sat down with infinite relish to read the memorable character sketch of Christopher, the head waiter, which is dear to every lover of taverns. "The writer of these humble lines being a Waiter," he began. The knitting needles flashed with diligence, and the dog by the fender stretched himself out in the luxuriant vacancy of mind only known to dogs surrounded by a happy group of their friends. And Roger, enjoying himself enormously, and particularly pleased by the chuckles of his audience, was approaching the ever-delightful items of the coffee-room bill which is to be found about ten pages on in the first chapter—how sad it is that hotel bills are not so rendered in these times—when the bell in the shop clanged. Picking up his pipe and matchbox, and grumbling "It's always the way," he hurried out of the room.

He was agreeably surprised to find that his caller was the young advertising man, Aubrey Gilbert.

"Hullo!" he said. "I've been saving something for you. It's a quotation from Joseph Conrad about advertising."

"Good enough," said Aubrey. "And I've got something for you.

You were so nice to me the other evening I took the liberty of bringing you round some tobacco. Here's a tin of Blue-Eyed Mixture, it's my favourite. I hope you'll like it."

"Bully for you. Perhaps I ought to let you off the Conrad quotation since you're so kind."

"Not a bit. I suppose it's a knock. Shoot!"

The bookseller led the way back to his desk, where he rummaged among the litter and finally found a scrap of paper on which he had written:

Being myself animated by feelings of affection toward my fellowmen, I am saddened by the modern system of advertising. Whatever evidence it offers of enterprise, ingenuity, impudence, and resource in certain individuals, it proves to my mind the wide prevalence of that form of mental degradation which is called gullibility.

JOSEPH CONRAD.

"What do you think of that?" said Roger. "You'll find that in the story called *The Anarchist*."

"I think less than nothing of it," said Aubrey. "As your friend Don Marquis observed the other evening, an idea isn't always to be blamed for the people who believe in it. Mr. Conrad has been reading some quack ads, that's all. Because there are fake ads, that doesn't condemn the principle of Publicity. But look here, what I really came round to see you for is to show you this. It was in the *Times* this morning."

He pulled out of his pocket a clipping of the LOST insertion to which Roger's attention had already been drawn.

"Yes, I've just seen it," said Roger. "I missed the book from my shelves, and I believe someone must have stolen it."

"Well, now, I want to tell you something," said Aubrey. "To-night I had dinner at the Octagon with Mr. Chapman." "Is that so?" said Roger. "You know his daughter's here now."

"So he told me. It's rather interesting how it all works out. You see, after you told me the other day that Miss Chapman was coming to work for you, that gave me an idea. I knew her father would be specially interested in Brooklyn, on that account, and it suggested to me an idea for a window-display campaign here in Brooklyn for the Daintybits Products. You know we handle all his sales promotion campaigns. Of course I didn't let on that I knew about his daughter coming over here, but he told me about it himself in the course of our talk. Well, here's what I'm getting at. We had dinner in the Czecho-Slovak Grill, up on the fourteenth floor, and going up in the elevator I saw a man in a chef's uniform carrying a book. I looked over his shoulder to see what it was. I thought of course it would be a cook-book. It was a copy of *Oliver Cromwell*."

"So he found it again, eh? I must go and have a talk with that chap. If he's a Carlyle fan I'd like to know him."

"Wait a minute. I had seen the LOST ad in the paper this morning, because I always look over that column. Often it gives me ideas for advertising stunts. If you keep an eye on the things people are anxious to get back, you know what they really prize, and if you know what they prize you can get a line on what goods ought to be advertised more extensively. This was the first time I had ever noticed a LOST ad for a book, so I thought to myself "the book business is coming up." Well, when I saw the chef with the book in his hand, I said to him jokingly, "I see you found it again." He was a foreign-looking fellow, with a big beard, which is unusual for a chef, because I suppose it's likely to get in the soup. He looked at me as though I'd run a carving knife into him, almost scared me the way he looked. "Yes, yes," he said, and shoved the book out of sight under his arm. He seemed half angry and half frightened, so I thought maybe he had no right to be riding in the passenger elevator and was scared someone would report him to the manager. Just as we were getting to the fourteenth floor I said to him in a whisper, "It's all right, old chap, I'm not going to report you." I give you my word he looked more scared than before. He went quite white. I got off at the fourteenth, and he followed me out. I thought he was going to speak to me, but Mr. Chapman was there in the lobby, and he didn't have a chance. But I noticed that he watched me into the grill room as though I was his last chance of salvation."

"I guess the poor devil was scared you'd report him to the police for stealing the book," said Roger. "Never mind, let him have it."

"Did he steal it?"

"I haven't a notion. But somebody did, because it disappeared from here."

"Well, now, wait a minute. Here's the queer part of it. I didn't think anything more about it, except that it was a funny coincidence my seeing him after having noticed that ad in the paper. I had a long talk with Mr. Chapman, and we discussed some plans for a prune and Saratoga chip campaign, and I showed him some suggested copy I had prepared. Then he told me about his daughter, and I let on that I knew you. I left the Octagon about eight o'clock, and I thought I'd run over here on the subway just to show you the LOST notice and give you this tobacco. And when I got off the subway at Atlantic Avenue, who should I see but friend chef again. He got off the same train I did. He had on civilian clothes then, of course, and when he was out of his white uniform and pancake hat I recognized him right off. Who do you suppose it was?"

"Can't imagine," said Roger, highly interested by this time.

"Why, the professor-looking guy who came in to ask for the book the first night I was here."

"Humph! Well, he must be keen about Carlyle, because he was horribly disappointed that evening when he asked for the book and I couldn't find it. I remember how he insisted that I *must* have it, and I hunted all through the History shelves to make sure it hadn't got misplaced. He said that some friend of his had seen it here, and he had come right round to buy it. I told him he could certainly get a copy at the Public Library, and he said that wouldn't do at all."

"Well, I think he's nuts," said Aubrey, "because I'm damn sure he followed me down the street after I left the subway. I stopped in at the drug store on the corner to get some matches, and when I came out, there he was underneath the lamp-post."

"If it was a modern author, instead of Carlyle," said Roger, "I'd say it was some publicity stunt pulled off by the publishers. You know they go to all manner of queer dodges to get an author's name in print. But Carlyle's copyrights expired long ago, so I don't see the game."

"I guess he's picketing your place to try and steal the formula for eggs Samuel Butler," said Aubrey, and they both laughed.

"You'd better come in and meet my wife and Miss Chapman," said Roger. The young man made some feeble demur, but it was obvious to the bookseller that he was vastly elated at the idea of making Miss Chapman's acquaintance.

"Here's a friend of mine," said Roger, ushering Aubrey into the little room where Helen and Titania were still sitting by the fire. "Mrs. Mifflin, Mr. Aubrey Gilbert, Miss Chapman, Mr. Gilbert."

Aubrey was vaguely aware of the rows of books, of the shining coals, of the buxom hostess and the friendly terrier; but with the intense focus of an intelligent young male mind these were all merely appurtenances to the congenial spectacle of the employee. How quickly a young man's senses assemble and assimilate the data that are really relevant! Without seeming even to look in that direction he had performed the most amazing feat of lightning calculation known to the human faculties. He had added up all the young ladies of his acquaintance, and found the sum total less than the girl before him. He had subtracted the new phenomenon from the universe as he knew it, including the solar system and the advertising business, and found the remainder a minus quantity. He had multiplied the contents of his intellect by a factor he had no reason to assume "constant," and was startled at what teachers call (I believe) the "product." And he had divided what was in the left-hand armchair into his own career, and found no room for a quotient. All of which transpired in the length of time necessary for Roger to push forward another chair.

With the politeness desirable in a well-bred youth, Aubrey's first instinct was to make himself square with the hostess. Resolutely he occluded blue eyes, silk shirtwaist, and admirable chin from his mental vision.

"It's awfully good of you to let me come in," he said to Mrs. Mifflin. "I was here the other evening and Mr. Mifflin insisted on my staying to supper with him."

"I'm very glad to see you," said Helen. "Roger told me about you. I hope he didn't poison you with any of his outlandish dishes. Wait till he tries you with brandied peaches a la Harold Bell Wright."

Aubrey uttered some genial reassurance, still making the supreme sacrifice of keeping his eyes away from where (he felt) they belonged.

"Mr. Gilbert has just had a queer experience," said Roger. "Tell them about it."

In the most reckless way, Aubrey permitted himself to be impaled upon a direct and interested flash of blue lightning. "I was having dinner with your father at the Octagon."

The high tension voltage of that bright blue current felt like ohm sweet ohm, but Aubrey dared not risk too much of it at once. Fearing to blow out a fuse, he turned in panic to Mrs. Mifflin. "You see," he explained, "I write a good deal of Mr. Chapman's advertising for him. We had an appointment to discuss some business matters. We're planning a big barrage on prunes."

"Dad works much too hard, don't you think?" said Titania.

Aubrey welcomed this as a pleasant avenue of discussion leading into the parkland of Miss Chapman's family affairs; but Roger insisted on his telling the story of the chef and the copy of *Cromwell*.

"And he followed you here?" exclaimed Titania. "What fun! I had no idea the book business was so exciting."

"Better lock the door to-night, Roger," said Mrs. Mifflin, "or he may walk off with a set of the Encyclopædia Britannica."

"Why, my dear," said Roger, "I think this is grand news. Here's a man, in a humble walk of life, so keen about good books that he even pickets a bookstore on the chance of swiping some. It's the most encouraging thing I've ever heard of. I must write to the Publishers' Weekly about it."

"Well," said Aubrey, "you mustn't let me interrupt your little party."

"You're not interrupting," said Roger. "We were only reading aloud. Do you know Dickens' *Christmas Stories?*"

"I'm afraid I don't."

"Suppose we go on reading, shall we?"

"Please do."

"Yes, do go on," said Titania. "Mr. Mifflin was just reading about a most adorable head waiter in a London chop house."

Aubrey begged permission to light his pipe, and Roger picked up the book. "But before we read the items of the coffee-room bill," he said, "I think it only right that we should have a little refreshment. This passage should never be read without something to accompany it. My dear, what do you say to a glass of sherry all round?"

"It is sad to have to confess it," said Mrs. Mifflin to Titania, "Mr. Mifflin can never read Dickens without having something to drink. I think the sale of Dickens will fall off terribly when prohibition comes in."

"I once took the trouble to compile a list of the amount of liquor drunk in Dickens' works," said Roger, "and I assure you the total was astounding: 7,000 hogsheads, I believe it was. Calculations of that sort are great fun. I have always intended to write a little essay on the rainstorms in the stories of Robert Louis Stevenson. You see R. L. S. was a Scot, and well acquainted with wet weather. Excuse me a moment, I'll just run down cellar and get up a bottle."

Roger left the room, and they heard his steps passing down into the cellar. Bock, after the manner of dogs, followed him. The smells of cellars are a rare treat to dogs, especially ancient Brooklyn cellars which have a cachet all their own. The cellar of the Haunted Bookshop was, to Bock, a fascinating place, illuminated by a warm glow from the furnace, and piled high with split packing-cases which Roger used as kindling. From below came the rasp of a shovel among coal, and the clear, musical slither as the lumps were thrown from the iron scoop onto the fire. Just then the bell rang in the shop.

"Let me go," said Titania, jumping up.

"Can't I?" said Aubrey.

"Nonsense!" said Mrs. Mifflin, laying down her knitting. "Neither of you knows anything about the stock. Sit down and be comfortable. I'll be right back."

Aubrey and Titania looked at each other with a touch of embarrassment.

"Your father sent you his—his kind regards," said Aubrey. That was not what he had intended to say, but somehow he could not utter the word. "He said not to read all the books at once."

Titania laughed. "How funny that you should run into him just when you were coming here. He's a duck, isn't he?"

"Well, you see I only know him in a business way, but he certainly is a corker. He believes in advertising, too."

"Are you crazy about books?"

"Why, I never really had very much to do with them. I'm afraid you'll think I'm terribly ignorant——"

"Not at all. I'm awfully glad to meet someone who doesn't think it's a crime not to have read all the books there are."

"This is a queer kind of place, isn't it?"

"Yes, it's a funny idea to call it the Haunted Bookshop. I wonder what it means."

"Mr. Mifflin told me it meant haunted by the ghosts of great literature. I hope they won't annoy you. The ghost of Thomas Carlyle seems to be pretty active."

"I'm not afraid of ghosts," said Titania.

Aubrey gazed at the fire. He wanted to say that he intended from now on to do a little haunting on his own account but he did not know just how to break it gently. And then Roger returned from the cellar with the bottle of sherry. As he was uncorking it, they heard the shop door close, and Mrs. Mifflin came in.

"Well, Roger," she said; "if you think so much of your old *Cromwell*, you'd better keep it in here. Here it is." She laid the book on the table.

"For the love of Mike!" exclaimed Roger. "Who brought it back?"

"I guess it was your friend the assistant chef," said Mrs. Mifflin. "Anyway, he had a beard like a Christmas tree. He was mighty polite. He said he was terribly absent minded, and that the other day he was in here looking at some books and just walked off with it without knowing what he was doing. He offered to pay for the trouble he had caused, but of course I wouldn't let him. I asked if he wanted to see you, but he said he was in a hurry."

"I'm almost disappointed," said Roger. "I thought that I had turned up a real booklover. Here we are, all hands drink the health of Mr. Thomas Carlyle."

The toast was drunk, and they settled themselves in their chairs.

"And here's to the new employee," said Helen.

This also was dispatched, Aubrey draining his glass with a zeal which did not escape Miss Chapman's discerning eye. Roger then put out his hand for the Dickens. But first he picked up his beloved *Cromwell*. He looked at it carefully, and then held the volume close to the light.

"The mystery's not over yet," he said. "It's been rebound. This isn't the original binding."

"Are you sure?" said Helen in surprise. "It looks the same."

"The binding has been cleverly imitated, but it can't fool me. In the first place, there was a rubbed corner at the top; and there was an ink stain on one of the end papers."

"There's still a stain there," said Aubrey, looking over his shoulder.

"Yes, but not the same stain. I've had that book long enough to know it by heart. Now what the deuce would that lunatic want to have it rebound for?"

"Goodness gracious," said Helen, "put it away and forget about it. We'll all be dreaming about Carlyle if you're not careful."

### Chapter V. *Aubrey Walks Part Way Home—and*
### *Rides the Rest of the Way*

It was a cold, clear night as Mr. Aubrey Gilbert left the Haunted Bookshop that evening, and set out to walk homeward. Without making a very conscious choice, he felt instinctively that it would be agreeable to walk back to Manhattan rather than permit the roaring disillusion of the subway to break in upon his meditations.

It is to be feared that Aubrey would have badly flunked any quizzing on the chapters of *Somebody's Luggage* which the bookseller had read aloud. His mind was swimming rapidly in the agreeable, unfettered fashion of a stream rippling downhill. As O. Henry puts it in one of his most delightful stories: "He was outwardly decent and managed to preserve his aquarium, but inside he was impromptu and full of unexpectedness." To say that he was thinking of Miss Chapman would imply too much power of ratiocination and abstract scrutiny on his part. He was not thinking: he was being thought. Down the accustomed channels of his intellect he felt his mind ebbing with the irresistible movement of tides drawn by the blandishing moon. And across these shimmering estuaries of impulse his will, a lost and naked athlete, was painfully attempting to swim, but making much leeway and already almost resigned to being carried out to sea.

He stopped a moment at Weintraub's drug store, on the corner of Gissing Street and Wordsworth Avenue, to buy some cigarettes, unfailing solace of an agitated bosom.

It was the usual old-fashioned pharmacy of those parts of Brooklyn: tall red, green, and blue vases of liquid in the windows threw blotches of coloured light onto the pavement; on the panes was affixed white china lettering: H. WE TRAUB, DEUT CHE APOTHEKER. Inside, the customary shelves of labelled jars, glass cases holding cigars, nostrums and toilet knick-knacks, and in one corner an ancient revolving bookcase deposited long ago by the Tabard Inn Library. The shop was empty, but as he opened the door a bell buzzed sharply. In a back chamber he could hear voices. As he waited idly for the druggist to appear, Aubrey cast a tolerant eye over the dusty volumes in the twirling case. There were the usual copies of Harold MacGrath's *The Man on the Box*, *A Girl of the Limberlost*, and *The Houseboat on the Styx*. *The Divine Fire*, much grimed, leaned against Joe Chapple's *Heart Throbs*. Those familiar with the Tabard Inn bookcases still to be found in outlying drug-shops know that the stock has not been "turned" for many a year. Aubrey was the more surprised, on spinning the the case round, to find wedged in between two other volumes the empty cover of a book that had been torn loose from the pages to which it belonged. He glanced at the lettering on the back. It ran thus:

CARLYLE

---

OLIVER CROMWELL'S
LETTERS
AND
SPEECHES

Obeying a sudden impulse, he slipped the book cover in his overcoat pocket.

Mr. Weintraub entered the shop, a solid Teutonic person with discoloured pouches under his eyes and a face that was a potent argument for prohibition. His manner, however, was that of one anxious to please. Aubrey indicated the brand of cigarettes he wanted. Having himself coined the advertising catchword for them—*They're mild—but they satisfy*—he felt a certain loyal compulsion always to smoke this kind. The druggist held out the packet, and Aubrey noticed that his fingers were stained a deep saffron colour.

"I see you're a cigarette smoker, too," said Aubrey pleasantly, as he opened the packet and lit one of the paper tubes at a little alcohol flame burning in a globe of blue glass on the counter.

"Me? I never smoke," said Mr. Weintraub, with a smile which somehow did not seem to fit his surly face. "I must have steady nerves in my profession. Apothecaries who smoke make up bad prescriptions."

"Well, how do you get your hands stained that way?"

Mr. Weintraub removed his hands from the counter.

"Chemicals," he grunted. "Prescriptions—all that sort of thing."

"Well," said Aubrey, "smoking's a bad habit. I guess I do too much of it." He could not resist the impression that someone was listening to their talk. The doorway at the back of the shop was veiled by a portiere of beads and thin bamboo sections threaded on strings. He heard them clicking as though they had been momentarily pulled aside. Turning, just as he opened the door to leave, he noticed the bamboo curtain swaying.

"Well, good-night," he said, and stepped out onto the street.

As he walked down Wordsworth Avenue, under the thunder of the L, past lighted lunchrooms, oyster saloons, and pawnshops, Miss Chapman resumed her sway. With the delightful velocity of thought his mind whirled in a narrowing spiral round the experience of the evening. The small book-crammed sitting room of the Mifflins, the sparkling fire, the lively chirrup of the bookseller reading aloud—and there, in the old easy chair whose horsehair stuffing was bulging out, that blue-eyed vision of careless girlhood! Happily he had been so seated that he could study her without seeming to do so. The line of her ankle where the firelight danced upon it put Coles Phillips to shame, he averred.

Extraordinary, how these creatures are made to torment us with their intolerable comeliness! Against the background of dusky bindings her head shone with a soft haze of gold. Her face, that had an air of naive and provoking independence, made him angry with its unnecessary surplus of enchantment. An unaccountable gust of rage drove him rapidly along the frozen street. "Damn it," he cried, "what right has any girl to be as pretty as that? Why—why, I'd like to beat her!" he muttered, amazed at himself. "What the devil right has a girl got to look so innocently adorable?"

It would be unseemly to follow poor Aubrey in his vacillations of rage and worship as he thrashed along Wordsworth Avenue, hearing and seeing no more than was necessary for the preservation of his life at street crossings. Half-smoked cigarette stubs glowed in his wake;[2] his burly bosom echoed with incoherent oratory. In the darker stretches of Fulton Street that lead up to the Brooklyn Bridge he fiercely exclaimed: "By God, it's not such a bad world." As he ascended the slope of that vast airy span, a black midget against a froth of stars, he was gravely planning such vehemence of exploit in the advertising profession as would make it seem less absurd to approach the President of the Daintybits Corporation with a question for which no progenitor of loveliness is ever quite prepared.

In the exact centre of the bridge something diluted his mood; he halted, leaning against the railing, to consider the splendour of the scene. The hour was late—moving on toward midnight—but in the tall black precipices of Manhattan scattered lights gleamed, in an odd, irregular pattern like the sparse punctures on the raffle-board—"take a chance on a Milk-Fed Turkey"—the East Indian elevator-boy presents to apartment-house tenants about Hallowe'en. A fume of golden light eddied over uptown merriment: he could see the ruby beacon on the Metropolitan Tower signal three quarters. Underneath the airy decking of the bridge a tug went puffing by, her port and starboard lamps trailing red and green threads over the tideway. Some great argosy of the Staten Island fleet swept serenely down to St. George, past Liberty in her soft robe of light, carrying theatred commuters, dazed with weariness and blinking at the raw fury of the electric bulbs. Overhead the night was a superb arch of clear frost, sifted with stars. Blue sparks crackled stickily along the trolley wires as the cars groaned over the bridge.

Aubrey surveyed all this splendid scene without exact observation. He was of a philosophic turn, and was attempting to console his discomfiture in the overwhelming lustre of Miss Titania by the thought

---

[2] NOTE WHILE PROOFREADING: Surely this phrase was unconsciously lifted from R. L. S. But where does the original occur? C. D. M.

that she was, after all, the creature and offspring of the science he worshipped—that of Advertising. Was not the fragrance of her presence, the soft compulsion of her gaze, even the delirious frill of muslin at her wrist, to be set down to the credit of his chosen art? Had he not, pondering obscurely upon "attention-compelling" copy and lay-out and type-face, in a corner of the Grey-Matter office, contributed to the triumphant prosperity and grace of this unconscious beneficiary? Indeed she seemed to him, fiercely tormenting himself with her loveliness, a symbol of the mysterious and subtle power of publicity. It was Advertising that had done this—that had enabled Mr. Chapman, a shy and droll little person, to surround this girl with all the fructifying glories of civilization—to foster and cherish her until she shone upon the earth like a morning star! Advertising had clothed her, Advertising had fed her, schooled, roofed, and sheltered her. In a sense she was the crowning advertisement of her father's career, and her innocent perfection taunted him just as much as the bright sky-sign he knew was flashing the words CHAPMAN PRUNES above the teeming pavements of Times Square. He groaned to think that he himself, by his conscientious labours, had helped to put this girl in such a position that he could hardly dare approach her.

He would never have approached her again, on any pretext, if the intensity of his thoughts had not caused him, unconsciously, to grip the railing of the bridge with strong and angry hands. For at that moment a sack was thrown over his head from behind and he was violently seized by the legs, with the obvious intent of hoisting him over the parapet. His unexpected grip on the railing delayed this attempt just long enough to save him. Swept off his feet by the fury of the assault, he fell sideways against the barrier and had the good fortune to seize his enemy by the leg. Muffled in the sacking, it was vain to cry out; but he held furiously to the limb he had grasped and he and his attacker rolled together on the footway. Aubrey was a powerful man, and even despite the surprise could probably have got the better of the situation; but as he wrestled desperately and tried to rid himself of his hood, a crashing blow fell upon his head, half stunning him. He lay sprawled out, momentarily incapable of struggle, yet conscious enough to expect, rather curiously, the dizzying sensation of a drop through insupportable air into the icy water of the East River. Hands seized him—and then, passively, he heard a shout, the sound of footsteps running on the planks, and other footsteps hurrying away at top speed. In a moment the sacking was torn from his head and a friendly pedestrian was kneeling beside him.

"Say, are you all right?" said the latter anxiously. "Gee, those guys nearly got you."

Aubrey was too faint and dizzy to speak for a moment. His head was numb and he felt certain that several inches of it had been caved in.

Putting up his hand, feebly, he was surprised to find the contours of his skull much the same as usual. The stranger propped him against his knee and wiped away a trickle of blood with his handkerchief. "Say, old man, I thought you was a goner," he said sympathetically. "I seen those fellows jump you. Too bad they got away. Dirty work, I'll say so."

Aubrey gulped the night air, and sat up. The bridge rocked under him; against the star-speckled sky he could see the Woolworth Building bending and jazzing like a poplar tree in a gale. He felt very sick. "Ever so much obliged to you," he stammered. "I'll be all right in a minute."

"D'you want me to go and ring up a nambulance?" said his assistant.

"No, no," said Aubrey; "I'll be all right." He staggered to his feet and clung to the rail of the bridge, trying to collect his wits. One phrase ran over and over in his mind with damnable iteration—"*Mild, but they satisfy!*"

"Where were you going?" said the other, supporting him.

"Madison Avenue and Thirty-Second——"

"Maybe I can flag a jitney for you. Here," he cried, as another citizen approached afoot, "Give this fellow a hand. Someone beat him over the bean with a club. I'm going to get him a lift."

The newcomer readily undertook the friendly task, and tied Aubrey's handkerchief round his head, which was bleeding freely. After a few moments the first Samaritan succeeded in stopping a touring car which was speeding over from Brooklyn. The driver willingly agreed to take Aubrey home, and the other two helped him in. Barring a nasty gash on his scalp he was none the worse.

"A fellow needs a tin hat if he's going to wander round Long Island at night," said the motorist genially. "Two fellows tried to hold me up coming in from Rockville Centre the other evening. Maybe they were the same two that picked on you. Did you get a look at them?"

"No," said Aubrey. "That piece of sacking might have helped me trace them, but I forgot it."

"Want to run back for it?"

"Never mind," said Aubrey. "I've got a hunch about this."

"Think you know who it is? Maybe you're in politics, hey?"

The car ran swiftly up the dark channel of the Bowery, into Fourth Avenue, and turned off at Thirty-Second Street to deposit Aubrey in front of his boarding house. He thanked his convoy heartily, and refused further assistance. After several false shots he got his latch key in the lock, climbed four creaking flights, and stumbled into his room. Groping his way to the wash-basin, he bathed his throbbing head, tied a towel round it, and fell into bed.

*Chapter VI. Titania Learns the Business*

Although he kept late hours, Roger Mifflin was a prompt riser. It is only the very young who find satisfaction in lying abed in the morning. Those who approach the term of the fifth decade are sensitively aware of the fluency of life, and have no taste to squander it among the blankets.

The bookseller's morning routine was brisk and habitual. He was generally awakened about half-past seven by the jangling bell that balanced on a coiled spring at the foot of the stairs. This ringing announced the arrival of Becky, the old scrubwoman who came each morning to sweep out the shop and clean the floors for the day's traffic. Roger, in his old dressing gown of vermilion flannel, would scuffle down to let her in, picking up the milk bottles and the paper bag of baker's rolls at the same time. As Becky propped the front door wide, opened window transoms, and set about buffeting dust and tobacco smoke, Roger would take the milk and rolls back to the kitchen and give Bock a morning greeting. Bock would emerge from his literary kennel, and thrust out his forelegs in a genial obeisance. This was partly politeness, and partly to straighten out his spine after its all-night curvature. Then Roger would let him out into the back yard for a run, himself standing on the kitchen steps to inhale the bright freshness of the morning air.

This Saturday morning was clear and crisp. The plain backs of the homes along Whittier Street, irregular in profile as the margins of a free verse poem, offered Roger an agreeable human panorama. Thin strands of smoke were rising from chimneys; a belated baker's wagon was joggling down the alley; in bedroom bay-windows sheets and pillows were already set to sun and air. Brooklyn, admirable borough of homes and hearty breakfasts, attacks the morning hours in cheery, smiling spirit. Bock sniffed and rooted about the small back yard as though the earth (every cubic inch of which he already knew by rote) held some new entrancing flavour. Roger watched him with the amused and tender condescension one always feels toward a happy dog—perhaps the same mood of tolerant paternalism that Gott is said to have felt in watching his boisterous Hohenzollerns.

The nipping air began to infiltrate his dressing gown, and Roger returned to the kitchen, his small, lively face alight with zest. He opened the draughts in the range, set a kettle on to boil, and went down to resuscitate the furnace. As he came upstairs for his bath, Mrs. Mifflin was descending, fresh and hearty in a starchy morning apron. Roger hummed a tune as he picked up the hairpins on the bedroom floor, and wondered to himself why women are always supposed to be more tidy than men.

Titania was awake early. She smiled at the enigmatic portrait of Samuel Butler, glanced at the row of books over her bed, and dressed rapidly. She ran downstairs, eager to begin her experience as a bookseller. The first impression the Haunted Bookshop had made on her was one of superfluous dinginess, and as Mrs. Mifflin refused to let her help get breakfast—except set out the salt cellars—she ran down Gissing Street to a little florist's shop she had noticed the previous afternoon. Here she spent at least a week's salary in buying chrysanthemums and a large pot of white heather. She was distributing these about the shop when Roger found her.

"Bless my soul!" he said. "How are you going to live on your wages if you do that sort of thing? Pay-day doesn't come until next Friday!"

"Just one blow-out," she said cheerfully. "I thought it would be fun to brighten the place up a bit. Think how pleased your floorwalker will be when he comes in!"

"Dear me," said Roger. "I hope you don't really think we have floorwalkers in the second-hand book business."

After breakfast he set about initiating his new employee into the routine of the shop. As he moved about, explaining the arrangement of his shelves, he kept up a running commentary.

"Of course all the miscellaneous information that a bookseller has to have will only come to you gradually," he said. "Such tags of bookshop lore as the difference between Philo Gubb and Philip Gibbs, Mrs. Wilson Woodrow and Mrs. Woodrow Wilson, and all that sort of thing. Don't be frightened by all the ads you see for a book called "Bell and Wing," because no one was ever heard to ask for a copy. That's one of the reasons why I tell Mr. Gilbert I don't believe in advertising. Someone may ask you who wrote *The Winning of the Best*, and you'll have to know it wasn't Colonel Roosevelt but Mr. Ralph Waldo Trine. The beauty of being a bookseller is that you don't have to be a literary critic: all you have to do to books is enjoy them. A literary critic is the kind of fellow who will tell you that Wordsworth's *Happy Warrior* is a poem of 85 lines composed entirely of two sentences, one of 26 lines and one of 59. What does it matter if Wordsworth wrote sentences almost as long as those of Walt Whitman or Mr. Will H. Hays, if only he wrote a great poem? Literary critics are queer birds. There's Professor Phelps of Yale, for instance. He publishes a book in 1918 and calls it *The Advance of English Poetry in the Twentieth Century*. To my way of thinking a book of that title oughtn't to be published until 2018. Then somebody will come along and ask you for a book of poems about a typewriter, and by and by you'll learn that what they want is Stevenson's *Underwoods*. Yes, it's a complicated life. Never argue with customers. Just give them the book they ought to have even if they don't know they want it."

They went outside the front door, and Roger lit his pipe. In the little area in front of the shop windows stood large empty boxes supported on trestles. "The first thing I always do——," he said.

"The first thing you'll both do is catch your death of cold," said Helen over his shoulder. "Titania, you run and get your fur. Roger, go and find your cap. With your bald head, you ought to know better!"

When they returned to the front door, Titania's blue eyes were sparkling above her soft tippet.

"I applaud your taste in furs," said Roger. "That is just the colour of tobacco smoke." He blew a whiff against it to prove the likeness. He felt very talkative, as most older men do when a young girl looks as delightfully listenable as Titania.

"What an adorable little place," said Titania, looking round at the bookshop's space of private pavement, which was sunk below the street level. "You could put tables out here and serve tea in summer time."

"The first thing every morning," continued Roger, "I set out the ten-cent stuff in these boxes. I take it in at night and stow it in these bins. When it rains, I shove out an awning, which is mighty good business. Someone is sure to take shelter, and spend the time in looking over the books. A really heavy shower is often worth fifty or sixty cents. Once a week I change my pavement stock. This week I've got mostly fiction out here. That's the sort of thing that comes in in unlimited numbers. A good deal of it's tripe, but it serves its purpose."

"Aren't they rather dirty?" said Titania doubtfully, looking at some little blue Rollo books, on which the siftings of generations had accumulated. "Would you mind if I dusted them off a bit?"

"It's almost unheard of in the second-hand trade," said Roger; "but it might make them look better."

Titania ran inside, borrowed a duster from Helen, and began housecleaning the grimy boxes, while Roger chatted away in high spirits. Bock already noticing the new order of things, squatted on the doorstep with an air of being a party to the conversation. Morning pedestrians on Gissing Street passed by, wondering who the bookseller's engaging assistant might be. "I wish *I* could find a maid like that," thought a prosperous Brooklyn housewife on her way to market. "I must ring her up some day and find out how much she gets."

Roger brought out armfuls of books while Titania dusted.

"One of the reasons I'm awfully glad you've come here to help me," he said, "is that I'll be able to get out more. I've been so tied down by the shop, I haven't had a chance to scout round, buy up libraries, make bids on collections that are being sold, and all that sort of thing. My stock is running a bit low. If you just wait for what comes in, you don't get much of the really good stuff."

Titania was polishing a copy of *The Late Mrs. Null*. "It must be wonderful to have read so many books," she said. "I'm afraid I'm not a very deep reader, but at any rate Dad has taught me a respect for good books. He gets so mad because when my friends come to the house, and he asks them what they've been reading, the only thing they seem to know about is *Dere Mable*."

Roger chuckled. "I hope you don't think I'm a mere highbrow," he said. "As a customer said to me once, without meaning to be funny, 'I like both the *Iliad* and the *Argosy*.' The only thing I can't stand is literature that is unfairly and intentionally flavoured with vanilla. Confectionery soon disgusts the palate, whether you find it in Marcus Aurelius or Doctor Crane. There's an odd aspect of the matter that sometimes strikes me: Doc Crane's remarks are just as true as Lord Bacon's, so how is it that the Doctor puts me to sleep in a paragraph, while my Lord's essays keep me awake all night?"

Titania, being unacquainted with these philosophers, pursued the characteristic feminine course of clinging to the subject on which she was informed. The undiscerning have called this habit of mind irrelevant, but wrongly. The feminine intellect leaps like a grasshopper; the masculine plods as the ant.

"I see there's a new Mable book coming," she said. "It's called *That's Me All Over Mable*, and the newsstand clerk at the Octagon says he expects to sell a thousand copies."

"Well, there's a meaning in that," said Roger. "People have a craving to be amused, and I'm sure I don't blame 'em. I'm afraid I haven't read *Dere Mable*. If it's really amusing, I'm glad they read it. I suspect it isn't a very great book, because a Philadelphia schoolgirl has written a reply to it called *Dere Bill*, which is said to be as good as the original. Now you can hardly imagine a Philadelphia flapper writing an effective companion to Bacon's Essays. But never mind, if the stuff's amusing, it has its place. The human yearning for innocent pastime is a pathetic thing, come to think about it. It shows what a desperately grim thing life has become. One of the most significant things I know is that breathless, expectant, adoring hush that falls over a theatre at a Saturday matinee, when the house goes dark and the footlights set the bottom of the curtain in a glow, and the latecomers tank over your feet climbing into their seats——"

"Isn't it an adorable moment!" cried Titania.

"Yes, it is," said Roger; "but it makes me sad to see what tosh is handed out to that eager, expectant audience, most of the time. There they all are, ready to be thrilled, eager to be worked upon, deliberately putting themselves into that glorious, rare, receptive mood when they are clay in the artist's hand—and Lord! what miserable substitutes for joy and sorrow are put over on them! Day after day I see people streaming into theatres and movies, and I know that more than half the time they are on a blind quest, thinking they are satisfied when in truth they are fed on paltry husks. And the sad part about it is that if you let yourself think you are satisfied with husks, you'll have no appetite left for the real grain."

Titania wondered, a little panic-stricken, whether she had been permitting herself to be satisfied with husks. She remembered how greatly she had enjoyed a Dorothy Gish film a few evenings before. "But," she ventured, "you said people want to be amused. And if they laugh and look happy, surely they're amused?"

"They only think they are!" cried Mifflin. "They think they're amused because they don't know what real amusement is! Laughter and prayer are the two noblest habits of man; they mark us off from the brutes. To laugh at cheap jests is as base as to pray to cheap gods. To laugh at Fatty Arbuckle is to degrade the human spirit."

Titania thought she was getting in rather deep, but she had the tenacious logic of every healthy girl. She said:

"But a joke that seems cheap to you doesn't seem cheap to the person who laughs at it, or he wouldn't laugh."

Her face brightened as a fresh idea flooded her mind:

"The wooden image a savage prays to may seem cheap to you, but it's the best god he knows, and it's all right for him to pray to it."

"Bully for you," said Roger. "Perfectly true. But I've got away from the point I had in mind. Humanity is yearning now as it never did before for truth, for beauty, for the things that comfort and console and make life seem worth while. I feel this all round me, every day. We've been through a frightful ordeal, and every decent spirit is asking itself what we can do to pick up the fragments and remould the world nearer to our heart's desire. Look here, here's something I found the other day in John Masefield's preface to one of his plays: "*The truth and rapture of man are holy things, not lightly to be scorned. A carelessness of life and beauty marks the glutton, the idler, and the fool in their deadly path across history.*" I tell you, I've done some pretty sober thinking as I've sat here in my bookshop during the past horrible years. Walt Whitman wrote a little poem during the Civil War—*Year that trembled and reeled beneath me*, said Walt, *Must I learn to chant the cold dirges of the baffled, and sullen hymns of defeat?*—I've sat here in my shop at night, and looked round at my shelves, looked at all the brave books that house the hopes and gentlenesses and dreams of men and women, and wondered if they were all wrong, discredited, defeated. Wondered if the world were still merely a jungle of fury. I think I'd have gone balmy if it weren't for Walt Whitman. Talk about Mr. Britling—Walt was the man who 'saw it through.'

"The glutton, the idler, and the fool in their deadly path across history.... Aye, a deadly path indeed. The German military men weren't idlers, but they were gluttons and fools to the nth power. Look at their deadly path! And look at other deadly paths, too. Look at our slums, jails, insane asylums...."

"I used to wonder what I could do to justify my comfortable existence here during such a time of horror. What right had I to shirk in a quiet bookshop when so many men were suffering and dying through no fault of their own? I tried to get into an ambulance unit, but I've had no medical training and they said they didn't want men of my age unless they were experienced doctors."

"I know how you felt," said Titania, with a surprising look of comprehension. "Don't you suppose that a great many girls, who couldn't do anything real to help, got tired of wearing neat little uniforms with Sam Browne belts?"

"Well," said Roger, "it was a bad time. The war contradicted and denied everything I had ever lived for. Oh, I can't tell you how I felt about it. I can't even express it to myself. Sometimes I used to feel as I think that truly noble simpleton Henry Ford may have felt when he organized his peace voyage—that I would do anything, however stupid, to stop it all. In a world where everyone was so wise and cynical and cruel, it was admirable to find a man so utterly simple and hopeful as Henry. A boob, they called him. Well, I say bravo for boobs! I daresay most of the apostles were boobs—or maybe they called them bolsheviks."

Titania had only the vaguest notion about bolsheviks, but she had seen a good many newspaper cartoons.

"I guess Judas was a bolshevik," she said innocently.

"Yes, and probably George the Third called Ben Franklin a bolshevik," retorted Roger. "The trouble is, truth and falsehood don't come laid out in black and white—Truth and Huntruth, as the wartime joke had it. Sometimes I thought Truth had vanished from the earth," he cried bitterly. "Like everything else, it was rationed by the governments. I taught myself to disbelieve half of what I read in the papers. I saw the world clawing itself to shreds in blind rage. I saw hardly any one brave enough to face the brutalizing absurdity as it really was, and describe it. I saw the glutton, the idler, and the fool applauding, while brave and simple men walked in the horrors of hell. The stay-at-home poets turned it to pretty lyrics of glory and sacrifice. Perhaps half a dozen of them have told the truth. Have you read Sassoon? Or Latzko's *Men in War*, which was so damned true that the government suppressed it? Humph! Putting Truth on rations!"

He knocked out his pipe against his heel, and his blue eyes shone with a kind of desperate earnestness.

"But I tell you, the world is going to have the truth about War. We're going to put an end to this madness. It's not going to be easy. Just now, in the intoxication of the German collapse, we're all rejoicing in our new happiness. I tell you, the real Peace will be a long time coming. When you tear up all the fibres of civilization it's a slow job to knit things together again. You see those children going down the street

to school? Peace lies in their hands. When they are taught in school that
war is the most loathsome scourge humanity is subject to, that it
smirches and fouls every lovely occupation of the mortal spirit, then
there may be some hope for the future. But I'd like to bet they are
having it drilled into them that war is a glorious and noble sacrifice.

"The people who write poems about the divine frenzy of going
over the top are usually those who dipped their pens a long, long way
from the slimy duckboards of the trenches. It's funny how we hate to
face realities. I knew a commuter once who rode in town every day on
the 8.13. But he used to call it the 7.73. He said it made him feel more
virtuous."

There was a pause, while Roger watched some belated urchins
hurrying toward school.

"I think any man would be a traitor to humanity who didn't pledge
every effort of his waking life to an attempt to make war impossible in
future."

"Surely no one would deny that," said Titania. "But I do think the
war was very glorious as well as very terrible. I've known lots of men
who went over, knowing well what they were to face, and yet went
gladly and humbly in the thought they were going for a true cause."

"A cause which is so true shouldn't need the sacrifice of millions
of fine lives," said Roger gravely. "Don't imagine I don't see the
dreadful nobility of it. But poor humanity shouldn't be asked to be
noble at such a cost. That's the most pitiful tragedy of it all. Don't you
suppose the Germans thought they too were marching off for a noble
cause when they began it and forced this misery on the world? They
had been educated to believe so, for a generation. That's the terrible
hypnotism of war, the brute mass-impulse, the pride and national spirit,
the instinctive simplicity of men that makes them worship what is their
own above everything else. I've thrilled and shouted with patriotic
pride, like everyone. Music and flags and men marching in step have
bewitched me, as they do all of us. And then I've gone home and sworn
to root this evil instinct out of my soul. God help us—let's love the
world, love humanity—not just our own country! That's why I'm so
keen about the part we're going to play at the Peace Conference. Our
motto over there will be America Last! Hurrah for us, I say, for we
shall be the only nation over there with absolutely no axe to grind.
Nothing but a pax to grind!"

It argued well for Titania's breadth of mind that she was not
dismayed nor alarmed at the poor bookseller's anguished harangue. She
surmised sagely that he was cleansing his bosom of much perilous
stuff. In some mysterious way she had learned the greatest and rarest of
the spirit's gifts—toleration.

"You can't help loving your country," she said.

"Let's go indoors," he answered. "You'll catch cold out here. I want to show you my alcove of books on the war."

"Of course one can't help loving one's country," he added. "I love mine so much that I want to see her take the lead in making a new era possible. She has sacrificed least for war, she should be ready to sacrifice most for peace. As for me," he said, smiling, "I'd be willing to sacrifice the whole Republican party!"

"I don't see why you call the war an absurdity," said Titania. "We *had* to beat Germany, or where would civilization have been?"

"We had to beat Germany, yes, but the absurdity lies in the fact that we had to beat ourselves in doing it. The first thing you'll find, when the Peace Conference gets to work, will be that we shall have to help Germany onto her feet again so that she can be punished in an orderly way. We shall have to feed her and admit her to commerce so that she can pay her indemnities—we shall have to police her cities to prevent revolution from burning her up—and the upshot of it all will be that men will have fought the most terrible war in history, and endured nameless horrors, for the privilege of nursing their enemy back to health. If that isn't an absurdity, what is? That's what happens when a great nation like Germany goes insane.

"Well, we're up against some terribly complicated problems. My only consolation is that I think the bookseller can play as useful a part as any man in rebuilding the world's sanity. When I was fretting over what I could do to help things along, I came across two lines in my favourite poet that encouraged me. Good old George Herbert says:

"A grain of glory mixed with humblenesse
 Cures both a fever and lethargicknesse.

"Certainly running a second-hand bookstore is a pretty humble calling, but I've mixed a grain of glory with it, in my own imagination at any rate. You see, books contain the thoughts and dreams of men, their hopes and strivings and all their immortal parts. It's in books that most of us learn how splendidly worth-while life is. I never realized the greatness of the human spirit, the indomitable grandeur of man's mind, until I read Milton's *Areopagitica*. To read that great outburst of splendid anger ennobles the meanest of us simply because we belong to the same species of animal as Milton. Books are the immortality of the race, the father and mother of most that is worth while cherishing in our hearts. To spread good books about, to sow them on fertile minds, to propagate understanding and a carefulness of life and beauty, isn't that high enough mission for a man? The bookseller is the real Mr. Valiant-For-Truth.

"Here's my War-alcove," he went on. "I've stacked up here most of the really good books the War has brought out. If humanity has sense enough to take these books to heart, it will never get itself into this mess again. Printer's ink has been running a race against gunpowder these many, many years. Ink is handicapped, in a way, because you can blow up a man with gunpowder in half a second, while it may take twenty years to blow him up with a book. But the gunpowder destroys itself along with its victim, while a book can keep on exploding for centuries. There's Hardy's *Dynasts* for example. When you read that book you can feel it blowing up your mind. It leaves you gasping, ill, nauseated—oh, it's not pleasant to feel some really pure intellect filtered into one's brain! It hurts! There's enough T. N. T. in that book to blast war from the face of the globe. But there's a slow fuse attached to it. It hasn't really exploded yet. Maybe it won't for another fifty years.

"In regard to the War, think what books have accomplished. What was the first thing all the governments started to do—publish books! Blue Books, Yellow Books, White Books, Red Books—everything but Black Books, which would have been appropriate in Berlin. They knew that guns and troops were helpless unless they could get the books on their side, too. Books did as much as anything else to bring America into the war. Some German books helped to wipe the Kaiser off his throne—*I Accuse*, and Dr. Muehlon's magnificent outburst *The Vandal of Europe*, and Lichnowsky's private memorandum, that shook Germany to her foundations, simply because he told the truth. Here's that book *Men in War*, written I believe by a Hungarian officer, with its noble dedication "To Friend and Foe." Here are some of the French books—books in which the clear, passionate intellect of that race, with its savage irony, burns like a flame. Romain Rolland's *Au-Dessus de la Melee*, written in exile in Switzerland; Barbusse's terrible *Le Feu*; Duhamel's bitter *Civilization*; Bourget's strangely fascinating novel *The Meaning of Death*. And the noble books that have come out of England: *A Student in Arms*; *The Tree of Heaven*; *Why Men Fight*, by Bertrand Russell—I'm hoping he'll write one on *Why Men Are Imprisoned*: you know he was locked up for his sentiments! And here's one of the most moving of all—*The Letters of Arthur Heath*, a gentle, sensitive young Oxford tutor who was killed on the Western front. You ought to read that book. It shows the entire lack of hatred on the part of the English. Heath and his friends, the night before they enlisted, sat up singing the German music they had loved, as a kind of farewell to the old, friendly joyous life. Yes, that's the kind of thing War does—wipes out spirits like Arthur Heath. Please read it. Then you'll have to read Philip Gibbs, and Lowes Dickinson and all the young poets. Of course you've read Wells already. Everybody has."

"How about the Americans?" said Titania. "Haven't they written anything about the war that's worth while?"

"Here's one that I found a lot of meat in, streaked with philosophical gristle," said Roger, relighting his pipe. He pulled out a copy of *Professor Latimer's Progress.* "There was one passage that I remember marking—let's see now, what was it?—Yes, here!

"It is true that, if you made a poll of newspaper editors, you might find a great many who think that war is evil. But if you were to take a census among pastors of fashionable metropolitan churches—"

"That's a bullseye hit! The church has done for itself with most thinking men.... There's another good passage in Professor Latimer, where he points out the philosophical value of dishwashing. Some of Latimer's talk is so much in common with my ideas that I've been rather hoping he'd drop in here some day. I'd like to meet him. As for American poets, get wise to Edwin Robinson——"

There is no knowing how long the bookseller's monologue might have continued, but at this moment Helen appeared from the kitchen.

"Good gracious, Roger!" she exclaimed, "I've heard your voice piping away for I don't know how long. What are you doing, giving the poor child a Chautauqua lecture? You must want to frighten her out of the book business."

Roger looked a little sheepish. "My dear," he said, "I was only laying down a few of the principles underlying the art of bookselling——"

"It was very interesting, honestly it was," said Titania brightly. Mrs. Mifflin, in a blue check apron and with plump arms floury to the elbow, gave her a wink—or as near a wink as a woman ever achieves (ask the man who owns one).

"Whenever Mr. Mifflin feels very low in his mind about the business," she said, "he falls back on those highly idealized sentiments. He knows that next to being a parson, he's got into the worst line there is, and he tries bravely to conceal it from himself."

"I think it's too bad to give me away before Miss Titania," said Roger, smiling, so Titania saw this was merely a family joke.

"Really truly," she protested, "I'm having a lovely time. I've been learning all about Professor Latimer who wrote *The Handle of Europe,* and all sorts of things. I've been afraid every minute that some customer would come in and interrupt us."

"No fear of that," said Helen. "They're scarce in the early morning." She went back to her kitchen.

"Well, Miss Titania," resumed Roger. "You see what I'm driving at. I want to give people an entirely new idea about bookshops. The grain of glory that I hope will cure both my fever and my lethargicness is my conception of the bookstore as a power-house, a radiating place for truth and beauty. I insist books are not absolutely dead things: they are as lively as those fabulous dragons' teeth, and being sown up and down, may chance to spring up armed men. How about Bernhardi?

Some of my Corn Cob friends tell me books are just merchandise. Pshaw!"

"I haven't read much of Bernard Shaw" said Titania.

"Did you ever notice how books track you down and hunt you out? They follow you like the hound in Francis Thompson's poem. They know their quarry! Look at that book *The Education of Henry Adams!* Just watch the way it's hounding out thinking people this winter. And *The Four Horsemen*—you can see it racing in the veins of the reading people. It's one of the uncanniest things I know to watch a real book on its career—it follows you and follows you and drives you into a corner and *makes* you read it. There's a queer old book that's been chasing me for years: *The Life and Opinions of John Buncle, Esq.*, it's called. I've tried to escape it, but every now and then it sticks up its head somewhere. It'll get me some day, and I'll be compelled to read it. *Ten Thousand a Year* trailed me the same way until I surrendered. Words can't describe the cunning of some books. You'll think you've shaken them off your trail, and then one day some innocent-looking customer will pop in and begin to talk, and you'll know he's an unconscious agent of book-destiny. There's an old sea-captain who drops in here now and then. He's simply the novels of Captain Marryat put into flesh. He has me under a kind of spell; I know I shall have to read *Peter Simple* before I die, just because the old fellow loves it so. That's why I call this place the Haunted Bookshop. Haunted by the ghosts of the books I haven't read. Poor uneasy spirits, they walk and walk around me. There's only one way to lay the ghost of a book, and that is to read it."

"I know what you mean," said Titania. "I haven't read much Bernard Shaw, but I feel I shall have to. He meets me at every turn, bullying me. And I know lots of people who are simply terrorized by H. G. Wells. Every time one of his books comes out, and that's pretty often, they're in a perfect panic until they've read it."

Roger chuckled. "Some have even been stampeded into subscribing to the *New Republic* for that very purpose."

"But speaking of the Haunted Bookshop, what's your special interest in that Oliver Cromwell book?"

"Oh, I'm glad you mentioned it," said Roger. "I must put it back in its place on the shelf." He ran back to the den to get it, and just then the bell clanged at the door. A customer came in, and the one-sided gossip was over for the time being.

## Chapter VII. Aubrey Takes Lodgings

I am sensible that Mr. Aubrey Gilbert is by no means ideal as the leading juvenile of our piece. The time still demands some explanation why the leading juvenile wears no gold chevrons on his left sleeve. As a matter of fact, our young servant of the Grey-Matter Agency had been declined by a recruiting station and a draft board on account of flat feet; although I must protest that their flatness detracts not at all from his outward bearing nor from his physical capacity in the ordinary concerns of amiable youth. When the army "turned him down flat," as he put it, he had entered the service of the Committee on Public Information, and had carried on mysterious activities in their behalf for over a year, up to the time when the armistice was signed by the United Press. Owing to a small error of judgment on his part, now completely forgotten, but due to the regrettable delay of the German envoys to synchronize with over-exuberant press correspondents, the last three days of the war had been carried on without his active assistance. After the natural recuperation necessary on the 12th of November, he had been re-absorbed by the Grey-Matter Advertising Agency, with whom he had been connected for several years, and where his sound and vivacious qualities were highly esteemed. It was in the course of drumming up post-war business that he had swung so far out of his ordinary orbit as to call on Roger Mifflin. Perhaps these explanations should have been made earlier.

At any rate, Aubrey woke that Saturday morning, about the time Titania began to dust the pavement-boxes, in no very world-conquering humour. As it was a half-holiday, he felt no compunction in staying away from the office. The landlady, a motherly soul, sent him up some coffee and scrambled eggs, and insisted on having a doctor in to look at his damage. Several stitches were taken, after which he had a nap. He woke up at noon, feeling better, though his head still ached abominably. Putting on a dressing gown, he sat down in his modest chamber, which was furnished chiefly with a pipe-rack, ash trays, and a set of O. Henry, and picked up one of his favourite volumes for a bit of solace. We have hinted that Mr. Gilbert was not what is called "literary." His reading was mostly of the newsstand sort, and Printer's Ink, that naive journal of the publicity professions. His favourite diversion was luncheon at the Advertising Club where he would pore, fascinated, over displays of advertising booklets, posters, and pamphlets with such titles as *Tell Your Story in Bold-Face*. He was accustomed to remark that "the fellow who writes the Packard ads has Ralph Waldo Emerson skinned three ways from the Jack." Yet much must be forgiven this young man for his love of O. Henry. He knew, what many other happy souls have found, that O. Henry is one of those

rare and gifted tellers of tales who can be read at all times. No matter
how weary, how depressed, how shaken in morale, one can always find
enjoyment in that master romancer of the Cabarabian Nights. "Don't
talk to me of Dickens' *Christmas Stories*," Aubrey said to himself,
recalling his adventure in Brooklyn. "I'll bet O. Henry's *Gift of the
Magi* beats anything Dick ever laid pen to. What a shame he died
without finishing that Christmas story in *Rolling Stones!* I wish some
boss writer like Irvin Cobb or Edna Ferber would take a hand at
finishing it. If I were an editor I'd hire someone to wind up that yarn.
It's a crime to have a good story like that lying around half written."

He was sitting in a soft wreath of cigarette smoke when his
landlady came in with the morning paper.

"Thought you might like to see the Times, Mr. Gilbert," she said.
"I knew you'd been too sick to go out and buy one. I see the President's
going to sail on Wednesday."

Aubrey threaded his way through the news with the practiced eye
of one who knows what interests him. Then, by force of habit, he
carefully scanned the advertising pages. A notice in the HELP WANTED
columns leaped out at him.

WANTED—For temporary employment at Hotel Octagon, 3
chefs, 5 experienced cooks, 20 waiters. Apply chef's office, 11 P.M.
Tuesday.

"Hum," he thought. "I suppose, to take the place of those fellows
who are going to sail on the *George Washington* to cook for Mr.
Wilson. That's a grand ad for the Octagon, having their kitchen staff
chosen for the President's trip. Gee, I wonder why they don't play that
up in some real space? Maybe I can place some copy for them along
that line."

An idea suddenly occurred to him, and he went over to the chair
where he had thrown his overcoat the night before. From the pocket he
took out the cover of Carlyle's *Cromwell*, and looked at it carefully.

"I wonder what the jinx is on this book?" he thought. "It's a queer
thing the way that fellow trailed me last night—then my finding this in
the drug store, and getting that crack on the bean. I wonder if that
neighbourhood is a safe place for a girl to work in?"

He paced up and down the room, forgetting the pain in his head.

"Maybe I ought to tip the police off about this business," he
thought. "It looks wrong to me. But I have a hankering to work the
thing out on my own. I'd have a wonderful stand-in with old man
Chapman if I saved that girl from anything.... I've heard of gangs of
kidnappers.... No, I don't like the looks of things a little bit. I think that
bookseller is half cracked, anyway. He doesn't believe in advertising!
The idea of Chapman trusting his daughter in a place like that——"

The thought of playing knight errant to something more personal and romantic than an advertising account was irresistible. "I'll slip over to Brooklyn as soon as it gets dark this evening," he said to himself. "I ought to be able to get a room somewhere along that street, where I can watch that bookshop without being seen, and find out what's haunting it. I've got that old .22 popgun of mine that I used to use up at camp. I'll take it along. I'd like to know more about Weintraub's drug store, too. I didn't fancy the map of Herr Weintraub, not at all. To tell the truth, I had no idea old man Carlyle would get mixed up in anything as interesting as this."

He found a romantic exhilaration in packing a handbag. Pyjamas, hairbrushes, toothbrush, toothpaste—("What an ad it would be for the Chinese Paste people," he thought, "if they knew I was taking a tube of their stuff on this adventure!")—his .22 revolver, a small green box of cartridges of the size commonly used for squirrel-shooting, a volume of O. Henry, a safety razor and adjuncts, a pad of writing paper.… At least six nationally advertised articles, he said to himself, enumerating his kit. He locked his bag, dressed, and went downstairs for lunch. After lunch he lay down for a rest, as his head was still very painful. But he was not able to sleep. The thought of Titania Chapman's blue eyes and gallant little figure came between him and slumber. He could not shake off the conviction that some peril was hanging over her. Again and again he looked at his watch, rebuking the lagging dusk. At half-past four he set off for the subway. Half-way down Thirty-third Street a thought struck him. He returned to his room, got out a pair of opera glasses from his trunk, and put them in his bag.

It was blue twilight when he reached Gissing Street. The block between Wordsworth Avenue and Hazlitt Street is peculiar in that on one side—the side where the Haunted Bookshop stands—the old brownstone dwellings have mostly been replaced by small shops of a bright, lively character. At the Wordsworth Avenue corner, where the L swings round in a lofty roaring curve, stands Weintraub's drug store; below it, on the western side, a succession of shining windows beacon through the evening. Delicatessen shops with their appetizing medley of cooked and pickled meats, dried fruits, cheeses, and bright coloured jars of preserves; small modistes with generously contoured wax busts of coiffured ladies; lunch rooms with the day's menu typed and pasted on the outer pane; a French rotisserie where chickens turn hissing on the spits before a tall oven of rosy coals; florists, tobacconists, fruit-dealers, and a Greek candy-shop with a long soda fountain shining with onyx marble and coloured glass lamps and nickel tanks of hot chocolate; a stationery shop, now stuffed for the holiday trade with Christmas cards, toys, calendars, and those queer little suede-bound volumes of Kipling, Service, Oscar Wilde, and Omar Khayyam that appear every year toward Christmas time—such modest and cheerful merchandising makes the western pavement of Gissing Street a jolly place when the lights are lit. All the shops were decorated for the Christmas trade; the Christmas issues of the magazines were just out and brightened the newsstands with their glowing covers. This section of Brooklyn has a tone and atmosphere peculiarly French in some parts: one can quite imagine oneself in some smaller Parisian boulevard frequented by the *petit bourgeois*. Midway in this engaging and animated block stands the Haunted Bookshop. Aubrey could see its windows lit, and the shelved masses of books within. He felt a severe temptation to enter, but a certain bashfulness added itself to his desire to act in secret. There was a privy exhilaration in his plan of putting the bookshop under an unsuspected surveillance, and he had the emotion of one walking on the frontiers of adventure.

So he kept on the opposite side of the street, which still maintains an unbroken row of quiet brown fronts, save for the movie theatre at the upper corner, opposite Weintraub's. Some of the basements on this side are occupied now by small tailors, laundries, and lace-curtain cleaners (lace curtains are still a fetish in Brooklyn), but most of the houses are still merely dwellings. Carrying his bag, Aubrey passed the bright halo of the movie theatre. Posters announcing THE RETURN OF TARZAN showed a kind of third chapter of Genesis scene with an Eve in a sports suit. ADDED ATTRACTION, MR. AND MRS. SIDNEY DREW, he read.

A little way down the block he saw a sign VACANCIES in a parlour window. The house was nearly opposite the bookshop, and he at once mounted the tall steps to the front door and rang.

A fawn-tinted coloured girl, of the kind generally called "Addie," arrived presently. "Can I get a room here?" he asked. "I don't know, you'd better see Miz' Schiller," she said, without rancor. Adopting the customary compromise of untrained domestics, she did not invite him inside, but departed, leaving the door open to show that there was no ill will.

Aubrey stepped into the hall and closed the door behind him. In an immense mirror the pale cheese-coloured flutter of a gas jet was remotely reflected. He noticed the Landseer engraving hung against wallpaper designed in facsimile of large rectangles of gray stone, and the usual telephone memorandum for the usual Mrs. J. F. Smith (who abides in all lodging houses) tucked into the frame of the mirror. *Will Mrs. Smith please call Stockton 6771*, it said. A carpeted stair with a fine old mahogany balustrade rose into the dimness. Aubrey, who was thoroughly familiar with lodgings, knew instinctively that the fourth, ninth, tenth, and fourteenth steps would be creakers. A soft musk sweetened the warm, torpid air: he divined that someone was toasting marshmallows over a gas jet. He knew perfectly well that somewhere in the house would be a placard over a bathtub with the legend: *Please leave this tub as you would wish to find it*. Roger Mifflin would have said, after studying the hall, that someone in the house was sure to be reading the poems of Rabbi Tagore; but Aubrey was not so caustic. Mrs. Schiller came up the basement stairs, followed by a small pug dog. She was warm and stout, with a tendency to burst just under the armpits. She was friendly. The pug made merry over Aubrey's ankles. "Stop it, Treasure!" said Mrs. Schiller.

"Can I get a room here?" asked Aubrey, with great politeness.

"Third floor front's the only thing I've got," she said. "You don't smoke in bed, do you? The last young man I had burned holes in three of my sheets——"

Aubrey reassured her.

"I don't give meals."

"That's all right," said Aubrey. "Suits me."

"Five dollars a week," she said.

"May I see it?"

Mrs. Schiller brightened the gas and led the way upstairs. Treasure skipped up the treads beside her. The sight of the six feet ascending together amused Aubrey. The fourth, ninth, tenth, and fourteenth steps creaked, as he had guessed they would. On the landing of the second storey a transom gushed orange light. Mrs. Schiller was secretly pleased at not having to augment the gas on that landing. Under the transom and behind a door Aubrey could hear someone having a bath, with a great sloshing of water. He wondered irreverently whether it was Mrs. J. F. Smith. At any rate (he felt sure), it was some experienced habitué of lodgings, who knew that about five-thirty in the afternoon is the best time for a bath—before cooking supper and the homecoming ablutions of other tenants have exhausted the hot water boiler.

They climbed one more flight. The room was small, occupying half the third-floor frontage. A large window opened onto the street, giving a plain view of the bookshop and the other houses across the way. A wash-stand stood modestly inside a large cupboard. Over the mantel was the familiar picture—usually, however, reserved for the fourth floor back—of a young lady having her shoes shined by a ribald small boy.

Aubrey was delighted. "This is fine," he said. "Here's a week in advance."

Mrs. Schiller was almost disconcerted by the rapidity of the transaction. She preferred to solemnize the reception of a new lodger by a little more talk—remarks about the weather, the difficulty of getting "help," the young women guests who empty tea-leaves down wash-basin pipes, and so on. All this sort of gossip, apparently aimless, has a very real purpose: it enables the defenceless landlady to size up the stranger who comes to prey upon her. She had hardly had a good look at this gentleman, nor even knew his name, and here he had paid a week's rent and was already installed.

Aubrey divined the cause of her hesitation, and gave her his business card.

"All right, Mr. Gilbert," she said. "I'll send up the girl with some clean towels and a latchkey."

Aubrey sat down in a rocking chair by the window, tucked the muslin curtain to one side, and looked out upon the bright channel of Gissing Street. He was full of the exhilaration that springs from any change of abode, but his romantic satisfaction in being so close to the adorable Titania was somewhat marred by a sense of absurdity, which is feared by young men more than wounds and death. He could see the lighted windows of the Haunted Bookshop quite plainly, but he could not think of any adequate excuse for going over there. And already he realized that to be near Miss Chapman was not at all the consolation he had expected it would be. He had a powerful desire to see her. He turned off the gas, lit his pipe, opened the window, and focussed the opera glasses on the door of the bookshop. It brought the place tantalizingly near. He could see the table at the front of the shop, Roger's bulletin board under the electric light, and one or two nondescript customers gleaning along the shelves. Then something bounded violently under the third button of his shirt. There she was! In the bright, prismatic little circle of the lenses he could see Titania. Heavenly creature, in her white V-necked blouse and brown skirt, there she was looking at a book. He saw her put out one arm and caught the twinkle of her wrist-watch. In the startling familiarity of the magnifying glass he could see her bright, unconscious face, the merry profile of her cheek and chin.... "The idea of that girl working in a second-hand bookstore!" he exclaimed. "It's positive sacrilege! Old man Chapman must be crazy."

He took out his pyjamas and threw them on the bed; put his toothbrush and razor on the wash-basin, laid hairbrushes and O. Henry on the bureau. Feeling rather serio-comic he loaded his small revolver and hipped it. It was six o'clock, and he wound his watch. He was a little uncertain what to do: whether to keep a vigil at the window with the opera glasses, or go down in the street where he could watch the bookshop more nearly. In the excitement of the adventure he had forgotten all about the cut on his scalp, and felt quite chipper. In leaving Madison Avenue he had attempted to excuse the preposterousness of his excursion by thinking that a quiet week-end in Brooklyn would give him an opportunity to jot down some tentative ideas for Daintybits advertising copy which he planned to submit to his chief on Monday. But now that he was here he felt the impossibility of attacking any such humdrum task. How could he sit down in cold blood to devise any "attention-compelling" lay-outs for Daintybits Tapioca and Chapman's Cherished Saratoga Chips, when the daintiest bit of all was only a few yards away? For the first time was made plain to him the amazing power of young women to interfere with the legitimate commerce of the world. He did get so far as to take out his pad of writing paper and jot down

### CHAPMAN'S CHERISHED CHIPS

These delicate wafers, crisped by a secret process, cherish in their unique tang and flavour all the life-giving nutriment that has made the potato the King of Vegetables——

But the face of Miss Titania kept coming between his hand and brain. Of what avail to flood the world with Chapman Chips if the girl herself should come to any harm? "Was this the face that launched a thousand chips?" he murmured, and for an instant wished he had brought The *Oxford Book of English Verse* instead of O. Henry.

A tap sounded at his door, and Mrs. Schiller appeared. "Telephone for you, Mr. Gilbert," she said.

"For *me?*" said Aubrey in amazement. How could it be for him, he thought, for no one knew he was there.

"The party on the wire asked to speak to the gentleman who arrived about half an hour ago, and I guess you must be the one he means."

"Did he say who he is?" asked Aubrey.

"No, sir."

For a moment Aubrey thought of refusing to answer the call. Then it occurred to him that this would arouse Mrs. Schiller's suspicions. He ran down to the telephone, which stood under the stairs in the front hall.

"Hello," he said.

"Is this the new guest?" said a voice—a deep, gargling kind of voice.

"Yes," said Aubrey.

"Is this the gentleman that arrived half an hour ago with a handbag?"

"Yes; who are you?"

"I'm a friend," said the voice; "I wish you well."

"How do you do, friend and well-wisher," said Aubrey genially.

"I schust want to warn you that Gissing Street is not healthy for you," said the voice.

"Is that so?" said Aubrey sharply. "Who are you?"

"I am a friend," buzzed the receiver. There was a harsh, bass note in the voice that made the diaphragm at Aubrey's ear vibrate tinnily. Aubrey grew angry.

"Well, Herr Freund," he said, "if you're the well-wisher I met on the Bridge last night, watch your step. I've got your number."

There was a pause. Then the other repeated, ponderously, "I am a friend. Gissing Street is not healthy for you." There was a click, and he had rung off.

Aubrey was a good deal perplexed. He returned to his room, and sat in the dark by the window, smoking a pipe and thinking, with his eyes on the bookshop.

There was no longer any doubt in his mind that something sinister was afoot. He reviewed in memory the events of the past few days.

It was on Monday that a bookloving friend had first told him of the existence of the shop on Gissing Street. On Tuesday evening he had gone round to visit the place, and had stayed to supper with Mr. Mifflin. On Wednesday and Thursday he had been busy at the office, and the idea of an intensive Daintybit campaign in Brooklyn had occurred to him. On Friday he had dined with Mr. Chapman, and had run into a curious string of coincidences. He tabulated them:—

(1) The Lost ad in the *Times* on Friday morning.
(2) The chef in the elevator carrying the book that was supposed to be lost—he being the same man Aubrey had seen in the bookshop on Tuesday evening.
(3) Seeing the chef again on Gissing Street.
(4) The return of the book to the bookshop.
(5) Mifflin had said that the book had been stolen from him. Then why should it be either advertised or returned?
(6) The rebinding of the book.
(7) Finding the original cover of the book in Weintraub's drug store.
(8) The affair on the Bridge.
(9) The telephone message from "a friend"—a friend with an obviously Teutonic voice.

He remembered the face of anger and fear displayed by the Octagon chef when he had spoken to him in the elevator. Until this oddly menacing telephone message, he could have explained the attack on the Bridge as merely a haphazard foot-pad enterprise; but now he was forced to conclude that it was in some way connected with his visits to the bookshop. He felt, too, that in some unknown way Weintraub's drug store had something to do with it. Would he have been attacked if he had not taken the book cover from the drug store? He got the cover out of his bag and looked at it again. It was of plain blue cloth, with the title stamped in gold on the back, and at the bottom the lettering *London: Chapman and Hall*. From the width of the backstrap it was evident that the book had been a fat one. Inside the front cover the figure 60 was written in red pencil—this he took to be Roger Mifflin's price mark. Inside the back cover he found the following notations—

vol. 3—166, 174, 210, 329, 349
329 ff. cf. W. W.

These references were written in black ink, in a small, neat hand. Below them, in quite a different script and in pale violet ink, was written

153 (3) 1, 2

"I suppose these are page numbers," Aubrey thought. "I think I'd better have a look at that book."

He put the cover in his pocket and went out for a bite of supper. "It's a puzzle with three sides to it," he thought, as he descended the crepitant stairs, "The Bookshop, the Octagon, and Weintraub's; but that book seems to be the clue to the whole business."

*Chapter VIII. Aubrey Goes to the Movies, and*
*Wishes He Knew More German*

A few doors from the bookshop was a small lunchroom named after the great city of Milwaukee, one of those pleasant refectories where the diner buys his food at the counter and eats it sitting in a flat-armed chair. Aubrey got a bowl of soup, a cup of coffee, beef stew, and bran muffins, and took them to an empty seat by the window. He ate with one eye on the street. From his place in the corner he could command the strip of pavement in front of Mifflin's shop. Halfway through the stew he saw Roger come out onto the pavement and begin to remove the books from the boxes.

After finishing his supper he lit one of his "mild but they satisfy" cigarettes and sat in the comfortable warmth of a near-by radiator. A large black cat lay sprawled on the next chair. Up at the service counter there was a pleasant clank of stout crockery as occasional customers came in and ordered their victuals. Aubrey began to feel a relaxation swim through his veins. Gissing Street was very bright and orderly in its Saturday evening bustle. Certainly it was grotesque to imagine melodrama hanging about a second-hand bookshop in Brooklyn. The revolver felt absurdly lumpy and uncomfortable in his hip pocket. What a different aspect a little hot supper gives to affairs! The most resolute idealist or assassin had better write his poems or plan his atrocities before the evening meal. After the narcosis of that repast the spirit falls into a softer mood, eager only to be amused. Even Milton would hardly have had the inhuman fortitude to sit down to the manuscript of *Paradise Lost* right after supper. Aubrey began to wonder if his unpleasant suspicions had not been overdrawn. He thought how delightful it would be to stop in at the bookshop and ask Titania to go to the movies with him.

Curious magic of thought! The idea was still sparkling in his mind when he saw Titania and Mrs. Mifflin emerge from the bookshop and pass briskly in front of the lunchroom. They were talking and laughing merrily. Titania's face, shining with young vitality, seemed to him more "attention-compelling" than any ten-point Caslon type-arrangement he had ever seen. He admired the layout of her face from the standpoint of his cherished technique. "Just enough 'white space,'" he thought, "to set off her eyes as the 'centre of interest.' Her features aren't this modern bold-face stuff, set solid," he said to himself, thinking typographically. "They're rather French old-style italic, slightly leaded. Set on 22-point body, I guess. Old man Chapman's a pretty good typefounder, you have to hand it to him."

He smiled at this conceit, seized hat and coat, and dashed out of the lunchroom.

Mrs. Mifflin and Titania had halted a few yards up the street, and were looking at some pert little bonnets in a window. Aubrey hurried across the street, ran up to the next corner, recrossed, and walked down the eastern pavement. In this way he would meet them as though he were coming from the subway. He felt rather more excited than King Albert re-entering Brussels. He saw them coming, chattering together in the delightful fashion of women out on a spree. Helen seemed much younger in the company of her companion. "A lining of pussy-willow taffeta and an embroidered slip-on," she was saying.

Aubrey steered onto them with an admirable gesture of surprise.

"Well, I never!" said Mrs. Mifflin. "Here's Mr. Gilbert. Were you coming to see Roger?" she added, rather enjoying the young man's predicament.

Titania shook hands cordially. Aubrey, searching the old-style italics with the desperate intensity of a proof-reader, saw no evidence of chagrin at seeing him again so soon.

"Why," he said rather lamely, "I was coming to see you all. I—I wondered how you were getting along."

Mrs. Mifflin had pity on him. "We've left Mr. Mifflin to look after the shop," she said. "He's busy with some of his old crony customers. Why don't you come with us to the movies?"

"Yes, do," said Titania. "It's Mr. and Mrs. Sidney Drew, you know how adorable they are!"

No one needs to be told how quickly Aubrey assented. Pleasure coincided with duty in that the outer wing of the party placed him next to Titania.

"Well, how do you like bookselling?" he asked.

"Oh, it's the greatest fun!" she cried. "But it'll take me ever and ever so long to learn about all the books. People ask such questions! A woman came in this afternoon looking for a copy of *Blasé Tales*. How

was I to know she wanted *The Blazed Trail?*"
"You'll get used to that," said Mrs. Mifflin. "Just a minute, people, I want to stop in at the drug store."
They went into Weintraub's pharmacy. Entranced as he was by the proximity of Miss Chapman, Aubrey noticed that the druggist eyed him rather queerly. And being of a noticing habit, he also observed that when Weintraub had occasion to write out a label for a box of powdered alum Mrs. Mifflin was buying, he did so with a pale violet ink.
At the glass sentry-box in front of the theatre Aubrey insisted on buying the tickets.
"We came out right after supper," said Titania as they entered, "so as to get in before the crowd."
It is not so easy, however, to get ahead of Brooklyn movie fans. They had to stand for several minutes in a packed lobby while a stern young man held the waiting crowd in check with a velvet rope. Aubrey sustained delightful spasms of the protective instinct in trying to shelter Titania from buffets and pushings. Unknown to her, his arm extended behind her like an iron rod to absorb the onward impulses of the eager throng. A rustling groan ran through these enthusiasts as they saw the preliminary footage of the great *Tarzan* flash onto the screen, and realized they were missing something. At last, however, the trio got through the barrier and found three seats well in front, at one side. From this angle the flying pictures were strangely distorted, but Aubrey did not mind.
"Isn't it lucky I got here when I did," whispered Titania. "Mr. Mifflin has just had a telephone call from Philadelphia asking him to go over on Monday to make an estimate on a library that's going to be sold so I'll be able to look after the shop for him while he's gone."
"Is that so?" said Aubrey. "Well, now, I've got to be in Brooklyn on Monday, on business. Maybe Mrs. Mifflin would let me come in and buy some books from you."
"Customers always welcome," said Mrs. Mifflin.
"I've taken a fancy to that Cromwell book," said Aubrey. "What do you suppose Mr. Mifflin would sell it for?"
"I think that book must be valuable," said Titania. "Somebody came in this afternoon and wanted to buy it, but Mr. Mifflin wouldn't part with it. He says it's one of his favourites. Gracious, what a weird film this is!"
The fantastic absurdities of Tarzan proceeded on the screen, tearing celluloid passions to tatters, but Aubrey found the strong man of the jungle coming almost too close to his own imperious instincts. Was not he, too—he thought naively—a poor Tarzan of the advertising jungle, lost among the elephants and alligators of commerce, and sighing for this dainty and unattainable vision of girlhood that had burst

upon his burning gaze! He stole a perilous side-glance at her profile, and saw the racing flicker of the screen reflected in tiny spangles of light that danced in her eyes. He was even so unknowing as to imagine that she was not aware of his contemplation. And then the lights went up.

"What nonsense, wasn't it?" said Titania. "I'm so glad it's over! I was quite afraid one of those elephants would walk off the screen and tread on us."

"I never can understand," said Helen, "why they don't film some of the really good books—think of Frank Stockton's stuff, how delightful that would be. Can't you imagine Mr. and Mrs. Drew playing in *Rudder Grange!*"

"Thank goodness!" said Titania. "Since I entered the book business, that's the first time anybody's mentioned a book that I've read. Yes—do you remember when Pomona and Jonas visit an insane asylum on their honeymoon? Do you know, you and Mr. Mifflin remind me a little of Mr. and Mrs. Drew."

Helen and Aubrey chuckled at this innocent correlation of ideas. Then the organ began to play "O How I Hate To Get Up in the Morning" and the ever-delightful Mr. and Mrs. Drew appeared on the screen in one of their domestic comedies. Lovers of the movies may well date a new screen era from the day those whimsical pantomimers set their wholesome and humane talent at the service of the arc light and the lens. Aubrey felt a serene and intimate pleasure in watching them from a seat beside Titania. He knew that the breakfast table scene shadowed before them was only a makeshift section of lath propped up in some barnlike motion picture studio; yet his rocketing fancy imagined it as some arcadian suburb where he and Titania, by a jugglery of benign fate, were bungalowed together. Young men have a pioneering imagination: it is doubtful whether any young Orlando ever found himself side by side with Rosalind without dreaming himself wedded to her. If men die a thousand deaths before this mortal coil is shuffled, even so surely do youths contract a thousand marriages before they go to the City Hall for a license.

Aubrey remembered the opera glasses, which were still in his pocket, and brought them out. The trio amused themselves by watching Sidney Drew's face through the magnifying lenses. They were disappointed in the result, however, as the pictures, when so enlarged, revealed all the cobweb of fine cracks on the film. Mr. Drew's nose, the most amusing feature known to the movies, lost its quaintness when so augmented.

"Why," cried Titania, "it makes his lovely nose look like the map of Florida."

"How on earth did you happen to have these in your pocket?" asked Mrs. Mifflin, returning the glasses.

Aubrey was hard pressed for a prompt and reasonable fib, but advertising men are resourceful.

"Oh," he said, "I sometimes carry them with me at night to study the advertising sky-signs. I'm a little short sighted. You see, it's part of my business to study the technique of the electric signs."

After some current event pictures the programme prepared to repeat itself, and they went out. "Will you come in and have some cocoa with us?" said Helen as they reached the door of the bookshop. Aubrey was eager enough to accept, but feared to overplay his hand. "I'm sorry," he said, "but I think I'd better not. I've got some work to do to-night. Perhaps I can drop in on Monday when Mr. Mifflin's away, and put coal on the furnace for you, or something of that sort?"

Mrs. Mifflin laughed. "Surely!" she said. "You're welcome any time." The door closed behind them, and Aubrey fell into a profound melancholy. Deprived of the heavenly rhetoric of her eye, Gissing Street seemed flat and dull.

It was still early—not quite ten o'clock—and it occurred to Aubrey that if he was going to patrol the neighbourhood he had better fix its details in his head. Hazlitt, the next street below the bookshop, proved to be a quiet little byway, cheerfully lit with modest dwellings. A few paces down Hazlitt Street a narrow cobbled alley ran through to Wordsworth Avenue, passing between the back yards of Gissing Street and Whittier Street. The alley was totally dark, but by counting off the correct number of houses Aubrey identified the rear entrance of the bookshop. He tried the yard gate cautiously, and found it unlocked. Glancing in he could see a light in the kitchen window and assumed that the cocoa was being brewed. Then a window glowed upstairs, and he was thrilled to see Titania shining in the lamplight. She moved to the window and pulled down the blind. For a moment he saw her head and shoulders silhouetted against the curtain; then the light went out.

Aubrey stood briefly in sentimental thought. If he only had a couple of blankets, he mused, he could camp out here in Roger's back yard all night. Surely no harm could come to the girl while he kept watch beneath her casement! The idea was just fantastic enough to appeal to him. Then, as he stood in the open gateway, he heard distant footfalls coming down the alley, and a grumble of voices. Perhaps two policemen on their rounds, he thought: it would be awkward to be surprised skulking about back doors at this time of night. He slipped inside the gate and closed it gently behind him, taking the precaution to slip the bolt.

The footsteps came nearer, stumbling down the uneven cobbles in the darkness. He stood still against the back fence. To his amazement the men halted outside Mifflin's gate, and he heard the latch quietly lifted.

"It's no use," said a voice—"the gate is locked. We must find some other way, my friend."

Aubrey tingled to hear the rolling, throaty "r" in the last word. There was no mistaking—this was the voice of his "friend and well-wisher" over the telephone.

The other said something in German in a hoarse whisper. Having studied that language in college, Aubrey caught only two words—*Thür* and *Schlüssel*, which he knew meant *door* and *key*.

"Very well," said the first voice. "That will be all right, but we must act to-night. The damned thing must be finished to-morrow. Your idiotic stupidity—"

Again followed some gargling in German, in a rapid undertone too fluent for Aubrey's grasp. The latch of the alley gate clicked once more, and his hand was on his revolver; but in a moment the two had passed on down the alley.

The young advertising agent stood against the fence in silent horror, his heart bumping heavily. His hands were clammy, his feet seemed to have grown larger and taken root. What damnable complot was this? A sultry wave of anger passed over him. This bland, slick, talkative bookseller, was he arranging some blackmailing scheme to kidnap the girl and wring blood-money out of her father? And in league with Germans, too, the scoundrel! What an asinine thing for old Chapman to send an unprotected girl over here into the wilds of Brooklyn ... and in the meantime, what was he to do? Patrol the back yard all night? No, the friend and well-wisher had said "We must find some other way." Besides, Aubrey remembered something having been said about the old terrier sleeping in the kitchen. He felt sure Bock would not let any German in at night without raising the roof. Probably the best way would be to watch the front of the shop. In miserable perplexity he waited several minutes until the two Germans would be well out of earshot. Then he unbolted the gate and stole up the alley on tiptoe, in the opposite direction. It led into Wordsworth Avenue just behind Weintraub's drug store, over the rear of which hung the great girders and trestles of the "L" station, a kind of Swiss chalet straddling the street on stilts. He thought it prudent to make a detour, so he turned east on Wordsworth Avenue until he reached Whittier Street, then sauntered easily down Whittier for a block, spying sharply for evidences of pursuit. Brooklyn was putting out its lights for the night, and all was quiet. He turned into Hazlitt Street and so back onto Gissing, noticing now that the Haunted Bookshop lights were off. It was nearly eleven o'clock: the last audience was filing out of the movie theatre, where two workmen were already perched on ladders taking down the Tarzan electric light sign, to substitute the illuminated lettering for the next feature.

After some debate he decided that the best thing to do was to return to his room at Mrs. Schiller's, from which he could keep a sharp watch on the front door of the bookshop. By good fortune there was a lamp post almost directly in front of Mifflin's house, which cast plenty of light on the little sunken area before the door. With his opera glasses he could see from his bedroom whatever went on. As he crossed the street he cast his eyes upward at the facade of Mrs. Schiller's house. Two windows in the fourth storey were lit, and the gas burned minutely in the downstairs hall, elsewhere all was dark. And then, as he glanced at the window of his own chamber, where the curtain was still tucked back behind the pane, he noticed a curious thing. A small point of rosy light glowed, faded, and glowed again by the window. Someone was smoking a cigar in his room.

Aubrey continued walking in even stride, as though he had seen nothing. Returning down the street, on the opposite side, he verified his first glance. The light was still there, and he judged himself not far out in assuming the smoker to be the friend and well-wisher or one of his gang. He had suspected the other man in the alley of being Weintraub, but he could not be sure. A cautious glance through the window of the drug store revealed Weintraub at his prescription counter. Aubrey determined to get even with the guttural gentleman who was waiting for him, certainly with no affectionate intent. He thanked the good fortune that had led him to stick the book cover in his overcoat pocket when leaving Mrs. Schiller's. Evidently, for reasons unknown, someone was very anxious to get hold of it.

An idea occurred to him as he passed the little florist's shop, which was just closing. He entered and bought a dozen white carnations, and then, as if by an afterthought, asked "Have you any wire?"

The florist produced a spool of the slender, tough wire that is sometimes used to nip the buds of expensive roses, to prevent them from blossoming too quickly.

"Let me have about eight feet," said Aubrey. "I need some to-night and I guess the hardware stores are all closed."

With this he returned to Mrs. Schiller's, picking his way carefully and close to the houses so as to be out of sight from the upstairs windows. He climbed the steps and unlatched the door with bated breath. It was half-past eleven, and he wondered how long he would have to wait for the well-wisher to descend.

He could not help chuckling as he made his preparations, remembering an occasion at college somewhat similar in setting though far less serious in purpose. First he took off his shoes, laying them carefully to one side where he could find them again in a hurry. Then, choosing a banister about six feet from the bottom of the stairs he attached one end of the wire tightly to its base and spread the slack in a large loop over two of the stair treads. The remaining end of the wire he passed out through the banisters, twisting it into a small loop so that he could pull it easily. Then he turned out the hall gas and sat down in the dark to wait events.

He sat for a long time, in some nervousness lest the pug dog might come prowling and find him. He was startled by a lady in a dressing gown—perhaps Mrs. J. F. Smith—who emerged from a ground-floor room passed very close to him in the dark, and muttered upstairs. He twitched his noose out of the way just in time. Presently, however, his patience was rewarded. He heard a door squeak above, and then the groaning of the staircase as someone descended slowly. He relaid his trap and waited, smiling to himself. A clock somewhere in the house was chiming twelve as the man came groping down the last flight, feeling his way in the dark. Aubrey heard him swearing under his breath.

At the precise moment, when both his victim's feet were within the loop, Aubrey gave the wire a gigantic tug. The man fell like a safe, crashing against the banisters and landing in a sprawl on the floor. It was a terrific fall, and shook the house. He lay there groaning and cursing.

Barely retaining his laughter, Aubrey struck a match and held it over the sprawling figure. The man lay with his face twisted against one out-spread arm, but the beard was unmistakable. It was the assistant chef again, and he seemed partly unconscious. "Burnt hair is a grand restorative," said Aubrey to himself, and applied the match to the bush of beard. He singed off a couple of inches of it with intense delight, and laid his carnations on the head of the stricken one. Then, hearing stirrings in the basement, he gathered up his wire and shoes and fled upstairs. He gained his room roaring with inward mirth, but entered cautiously, fearing some trap. Save for a strong tincture of cigar smoke, everything seemed correct. Listening at his door he heard Mrs. Schiller exclaiming shrilly in the hall, assisted by yappings from the pug. Doors upstairs were opened, and questions were called out. He heard guttural groans from the bearded one, mingled with oaths and some angry remark about having fallen downstairs. The pug, frenzied with excitement, yelled insanely. A female voice—possibly Mrs. J. F. Smith—cried out "What's that smell of burning?" Someone else said, "They're burning feathers under his nose to bring him to."

"Yes, Hun's feathers," chuckled Aubrey to himself. He locked his door, and sat down by the window with his opera glasses.

### Chapter IX. Again the Narrative is Retarded

Roger had spent a quiet evening in the bookshop. Sitting at his desk under a fog of tobacco, he had honestly intended to do some writing on the twelfth chapter of his great work on bookselling. This chapter was to be an (alas, entirely conjectural) "Address Delivered by a Bookseller on Being Conferred the Honorary Degree of Doctor of

Letters by a Leading University," and it presented so many alluring possibilities that Roger's mind always wandered from the paper into entranced visions of his imagined scene. He loved to build up in fancy the flattering details of that fine ceremony when bookselling would at last be properly recognized as one of the learned professions. He could see the great auditorium, filled with cultivated people: men with Emersonian profiles, ladies whispering behind their fluttering programmes. He could see the academic beadle, proctor, dean (or whatever he is, Roger was a little doubtful) pronouncing the august words of presentation—

A man who, in season and out of season, forgetting private gain for public weal, has laboured with Promethean and sacrificial ardour to instil the love of reasonable letters into countless thousands; to whom, and to whose colleagues, amid the perishable caducity of human affairs, is largely due the pullulation of literary taste; in honouring whom we seek to honour the noble and self-effacing profession of which he is so representative a member——

Then he could see the modest bookseller, somewhat clammy in his extremities and lost within his academic robe and hood, nervously fidgeting his mortar-board, haled forward by ushers, and tottering rubescent before the chancellor, provost, president (or whoever it might be) who hands out the diploma. Then (in Roger's vision) he could see the garlanded bibliopole turning to the expectant audience, giving his trailing gown a deft rearward kick as the ladies do on the stage, and uttering, without hesitation or embarrassment, with due interpolation of graceful pleasantry, that learned and unlaboured discourse on the delights of bookishness that he had often dreamed of. Then he could see the ensuing reception: the distinguished savants crowding round; the plates of macaroons, the cups of untasted tea; the ladies twittering, "Now there's something I want to ask you—why are there so many statues to generals, admirals, parsons, doctors, statesmen, scientists, artists, and authors, but no statues to booksellers?"

Contemplation of this glittering scene always lured Roger into fantastic dreams. Ever since he had travelled country roads, some years before, selling books from a van drawn by a fat white horse, he had nourished a secret hope of some day founding a Parnassus on Wheels Corporation which would own a fleet of these vans and send them out into the rural byways where bookstores are unknown. He loved to imagine a great map of New York State, with the daily location of each travelling Parnassus marked by a coloured pin. He dreamed of himself, sitting in some vast central warehouse of second-hand books, poring over his map like a military chief of staff and forwarding cases of literary ammunition to various bases where his vans would re-stock.

His idea was that his travelling salesmen could be recruited largely from college professors, parsons, and newspaper men, who were weary of their thankless tasks, and would welcome an opportunity to get out on the road. One of his hopes was that he might interest Mr. Chapman in this superb scheme, and he had a vision of the day when the shares of the Parnassus on Wheels Corporation would pay a handsome dividend and be much sought after by serious investors.

These thoughts turned his mind toward his brother-in-law Andrew McGill, the author of several engaging books on the joys of country living, who dwells at the Sabine Farm in the green elbow of a Connecticut valley. The original Parnassus, a quaint old blue wagon in which Roger had lived and journeyed and sold books over several thousand miles of country roads in the days before his marriage, was now housed in Andrew's barn. Peg, his fat white horse, had lodging there also. It occurred to Roger that he owed Andrew a letter, and putting aside his notes for the bookseller's collegiate oration, he began to write:

THE HAUNTED BOOKSHOP
163 Gissing Street, Brooklyn,
November 30, 1918.

MY DEAR ANDREW:

It is scandalous not to have thanked you sooner for the annual cask of cider, which has given us even more than the customary pleasure. This has been an autumn when I have been hard put to it to keep up with my own thoughts, and I've written no letters at all. Like everyone else I am thinking constantly of this new peace that has marvellously come upon us. I trust we may have statesmen who will be able to turn it to the benefit of humanity. I wish there could be an international peace conference of booksellers, for (you will smile at this) my own conviction is that the future happiness of the world depends in no small measure on them and on the librarians. I wonder what a German bookseller is like?

I've been reading *The Education of Henry Adams* and wish he might have lived long enough to give us his thoughts on the War. I fear it would have bowled him over. He thought that this is not a world "that sensitive and timid natures can regard without a shudder." What would he have said of the four-year shambles we have watched with sickened hearts?

You remember my favourite poem—old George Herbert's *Church Porch*—where he says—

By all means use sometimes to be alone;
Salute thyself; see what thy soul doth wear;
Dare to look in thy chest, for 'tis thine own,
And tumble up and down what thou find'st there—

Well, I've been tumbling my thoughts up and down a good deal. Melancholy, I suppose, is the curse of the thinking classes; but I confess my soul wears a great uneasiness these days! The sudden and amazing turnover in human affairs, dramatic beyond anything in history, already seems to be taken as a matter of course. My great fear is that humanity will forget the atrocious sufferings of the war, which have never been told. I am hoping and praying that men like Philip Gibbs may tell us what they really saw.

You will not agree with me on what I am about to say, for I know you as a stubborn Republican; but I thank fortune that Wilson is going to the Peace Conference. I've been mulling over one of my favourite books—it lies beside me as I write—*Cromwell's Letters and Speeches*, edited by Carlyle, with what Carlyle amusingly calls "Elucidations." (Carlyle is not very good at "elucidating" anything!) I have heard somewhere or other that this is one of Wilson's favourite books, and indeed, there is much of the Cromwell in him. With what a grim, covenanting zeal he took up the sword when at last it was forced into his hand! And I have been thinking that what he will say to the Peace Conference will smack strongly of what old Oliver used to say to Parliament in 1657 and 1658—"If we will have Peace without a worm in it, lay we foundations of Justice and Righteousness." What makes Wilson so irritating to the unthoughtful is that he operates exclusively upon reason, not upon passion. He contradicts Kipling's famous lines, which apply to most men—

Very rarely will he squarely push the logic of a fact
To its ultimate conclusion in unmitigated act.

In this instance, I think, Reason is going to win. I feel the whole current of the world setting in that direction.

It's quaint to think of old Woodrow, a kind of Cromwell-Wordsworth, going over to do his bit among the diplomatic shell-craters. What I'm waiting for is the day when he'll get back into private life and write a book about it. There's a job, if you like, for a man who might reasonably be supposed to be pretty tired in body and soul! When that book comes out I'll spend the rest of my life in selling it. I ask nothing better! Speaking of Wordsworth, I've often wondered whether Woodrow hasn't got some poems concealed somewhere among his papers! I've always imagined that he may have written

poems on the sly. And by the way, you needn't make fun of me for
being so devoted to George Herbert. Do you realize that two of the
most familiar quotations in our language come from his pen, viz.:

>  Wouldst thou both eat thy cake, and have it?

and

>  Dare to be true: nothing can need a ly;
>  A fault, which needs it most, grows two thereby.

Forgive this tedious sermon! My mind has been so tumbled up and
down this autumn that I am in a queer state of mingled melancholy and
exaltation. You know how much I live in and for books. Well, I have a
curious feeling, a kind of premonition that there are great books coming
out of this welter of human hopes and anguishes, perhaps A book in
which the tempest-shaken soul of the race will speak out as it never has
before. The Bible, you know, is rather a disappointment: it has never
done for humanity what it should have done. I wonder why? Walt
Whitman is going to do a great deal, but he is not quite what I mean.
There is something coming—I don't know just what! I thank God I am
a bookseller, trafficking in the dreams and beauties and curiosities of
humanity rather than some mere huckster of merchandise. But how
helpless we all are when we try to tell what goes on within us! I found
this in one of Lafcadio Hearn's letters the other day—I marked the
passage for you

Baudelaire has a touching poem about an albatross, which you
would like—describing the poet's soul superb in its own free azure—
but helpless, insulted, ugly, clumsy when striving to walk on common
earth—or rather, on a deck, where sailors torment it with tobacco pipes,
etc.

You can imagine what evenings I have here among my shelves,
now the long dark nights are come! Of course until ten o'clock, when I
shut up shop, I am constantly interrupted—as I have been during this
letter, once to sell a copy of *Helen's Babies* and once to sell *The Ballad
of Reading Gaol*, so you can see how varied are my clients' tastes! But
later on, after we have had our evening cocoa and Helen has gone to
bed, I prowl about the place, dipping into this and that, fuddling myself
with speculation. How clear and bright the stream of the mind flows in
those late hours, after all the sediment and floating trash of the day has
drained off! Sometimes I seem to coast the very shore of Beauty or
Truth, and hear the surf breaking on those shining sands. Then some
offshore wind of weariness or prejudice bears me away again. Have

you ever come across Andreyev's *Confessions of a Little Man During Great Days?* One of the honest books of the War. The Little Man ends his confession thus—

My anger has left me, my sadness returned, and once more the tears flow. Whom can I curse, whom can I judge, when we are all alike unfortunate? Suffering is universal; hands are outstretched to each other, and when they touch ... the great solution will come. My heart is aglow, and I stretch out my hand and cry, "Come, let us join hands! I love you, I love you!"

And of course, as soon as one puts one's self in that frame of mind someone comes along and picks your pocket.... I suppose we must teach ourselves to be too proud to mind having our pockets picked!

Did it ever occur to you that the world is really governed by *books?* The course of this country in the War, for instance, has been largely determined by the books Wilson has read since he first began to think! If we could have a list of the principal books he has read since the War began, how interesting it would be.

Here's something I'm just copying out to put up on my bulletin board for my customers to ponder. It was written by Charles Sorley, a young Englishman who was killed in France in 1915. He was only twenty years old—

TO GERMANY

You are blind like us. Your hurt no man designed,
And no man claimed the conquest of your land.
But gropers both through fields of thought confined
We stumble and we do not understand.
You only saw your future bigly planned,
And we, the tapering paths of our own mind,
And in each other's dearest ways we stand,
And hiss and hate. And the blind fight the blind.

When it is peace, then we may view again
With new-won eyes each other's truer form
And wonder. Grown more loving-kind and warm
We'll grasp firm hands and laugh at the old pain,
When it is peace. But until peace, the storm
The darkness and the thunder and the rain.

Isn't that noble? You see what I am dumbly groping for—some way of thinking about the War that will make it seem (to future ages) a purification for humanity rather than a mere blackness of stinking cinders and tortured flesh and men shot to ribbons in marshes of blood and sewage. Out of such unspeakable desolation men *must* rise to some new conception of national neighbourhood. I hear so much apprehension that Germany won't be punished sufficiently for her crime. But how can any punishment be devised or imposed for such a huge panorama of sorrow? I think she has already punished herself horribly, and will continue to do so. My prayer is that what we have gone through will startle the world into some new realization of the sanctity of life—all life, animal as well as human. Don't you find that a visit to a zoo can humble and astound you with all that amazing and grotesque variety of living energy?

What is it that we find in every form of life? Desire of some sort— some unexplained motive power that impels even the smallest insect on its queer travels. You must have watched some infinitesimal red spider on a fence rail, bustling along—why and whither? Who knows? And when you come to man, what a chaos of hungers and impulses keep thrusting him through his cycle of quaint tasks! And in every human heart you find some sorrow, some frustration, some lurking pang. I often think of Lafcadio Hearn's story of his Japanese cook. Hearn was talking of the Japanese habit of not showing their emotions on their faces. His cook was a smiling, healthy, agreeable-looking young fellow whose face was always cheerful. Then one day, by chance, Hearn happened to look through a hole in the wall and saw his cook alone. His face was not the same face. It was thin and drawn and showed strange lines worn by old hardships or sufferings. Hearn thought to himself, "He will look just like that when he is dead." He went into the kitchen to see him, and instantly the cook was all changed, young and happy again. Never again did Hearn see that face of trouble; but he knew the man wore it when he was alone.

Don't you think there is a kind of parable there for the race as a whole? Have you ever met a man without wondering what shining sorrows he hides from the world, what contrast between vision and accomplishment torments him? Behind every smiling mask is there not some cryptic grimace of pain? Henry Adams puts it tersely. He says the human mind appears suddenly and inexplicably out of some unknown and unimaginable void. It passes half its known life in the mental chaos of sleep. Even when awake it is a victim of its own ill-adjustment, of disease, of age, of external suggestion, of nature's compulsions; it doubts its own sensations and trusts only in instruments and averages. After sixty years or so of growing astonishment the mind wakes to find itself looking blankly into the void of death. And, as Adams says, that it should profess itself pleased by this performance is all that the highest rules of good breeding can ask. That the mind should actually be satisfied would prove that it exists only as idiocy!

I hope that you will write to tell me along what curves your mind is moving. For my own part I feel that we are on the verge of amazing things. Long ago I fell back on books as the only permanent consolers. They are the one stainless and unimpeachable achievement of the human race. It saddens me to think that I shall have to die with thousands of books unread that would have given me noble and unblemished happiness. I will tell you a secret. I have never read *King Lear*, and have purposely refrained from doing so. If I were ever very ill I would only need to say to myself "You can't die yet, you haven't read *Lear*." That would bring me round, I know it would.

You see, books are the answer to all our perplexities! Henry Adams grinds his teeth at his inability to understand the universe. The best he can do is to suggest a "law of acceleration," which seems to mean that Nature is hustling man along at an ever-increasing rate so that he will either solve all her problems or else die of fever in the effort. But Adams' candid portrait of a mind grappling helplessly with its riddles is so triumphantly delightful that one forgets the futility of the struggle in the accuracy of the picture. Man is unconquerable because he can make even his helplessness so entertaining. His motto seems to be "Even though He slay me, yet will I make fun of Him!"

Yes, books are man's supreme triumph, for they gather up and transmit all other triumphs. As Walter de la Mare writes, "How uncomprehendingly must an angel from heaven smile on a poor human sitting engrossed in a romance: angled upon his hams, motionless in his chair, spectacles on nose, his two feet as close together as the flukes of a merman's tail, only his strange eyes stirring in his time-worn face."

Well, I've been scribbling away all this time and haven't given you any news whatever. Helen came back the other day from a visit to Boston where she enjoyed herself greatly. To-night she has gone out to the movies with a young protégée of ours, Miss Titania Chapman, an engaging damsel whom we have taken in as an apprentice bookseller. It's a quaint idea, done at the request of her father, Mr. Chapman, the proprietor of Chapman's Daintybits which you see advertised everywhere. He is a great booklover, and is very eager to have the zeal transmitted to his daughter. So you can imagine my glee to have a neophyte of my own to preach books at! Also it will enable me to get away from the shop a little more. I had a telephone call from Philadelphia this afternoon asking me to go over there on Monday evening to make an estimate of the value of a private collection that is to be sold. I was rather flattered because I can't imagine how they got hold of my name.

Forgive this long, incoherent scrawl. How did you like *Erewhon?* It's pretty near closing time and I must say grace over the day's accounts.

Yours ever,<br>ROGER MIFFLIN.

## *Chapter X. Roger Raids the Ice-Box*

Roger had just put Carlyle's *Cromwell* back in its proper place in the History alcove when Helen and Titania returned from the movies. Bock, who had been dozing under his master's chair, rose politely and wagged a deferential tail.

"I do think Bock has the darlingest manners," said Titania.

"Yes," said Helen, "it's really a marvel that his wagging muscles aren't all worn out, he has abused them so."

"Well," said Roger, "did you have a good time?"

"An adorable time!" cried Titania, with a face and voice so sparkling that two musty habitués of the shop popped their heads out of the alcoves marked ESSAYS and THEOLOGY and peered in amazement. One of these even went so far as to purchase the copy of Leigh Hunt's *Wishing Cap Papers* he had been munching through, in order to have an excuse to approach the group and satisfy his bewildered eyes. When Miss Chapman took the book and wrapped it up for him, his astonishment was made complete.

Unconscious that she was actually creating business, Titania resumed.

"We met your friend Mr. Gilbert on the street," she said, "and he went to the movies with us. He says he's coming in on Monday to fix the furnace while you're away."

"Well," said Roger, "these advertising agencies are certainly enterprising, aren't they? Think of sending a man over to attend to my furnace, just on the slim chance of getting my advertising account."

"Did you have a quiet evening?" said Helen.

"I spent most of the time writing to Andrew," said Roger. "One amusing thing happened, though. I actually sold that copy of *Philip Dru*."

"No!" cried Helen.

"A fact," said Roger. "A man was looking at it, and I told him it was supposed to be written by Colonel House. He insisted on buying it. But what a sell when he tries to read it!"

"Did Colonel House really write it?" asked Titania.

"I don't know," said Roger. "I hope not, because I find in myself a secret tendency to believe that Mr. House is an able man. If he did write it, I devoutly hope none of the foreign statesmen in Paris will learn of that fact."

While Helen and Titania took off their wraps, Roger was busy closing up the shop. He went down to the corner with Bock to mail his letter, and when he returned to the den Helen had prepared a large jug of cocoa. They sat down by the fire to enjoy it.

"Chesterton has written a very savage poem against cocoa," said

Roger, "which you will find in *The Flying Inn*; but for my part I find it
the ideal evening drink. It lets the mind down gently, and paves the way
for slumber. I have often noticed that the most terrific philosophical
agonies can be allayed by three cups of Mrs. Mifflin's cocoa. A man
can safely read Schopenhauer all evening if he has a tablespoonful of
cocoa and a tin of condensed milk available. Of course it should be
made with condensed milk, which is the only way."

"I had no idea anything could be so good," said Titania. "Of
course, Daddy makes condensed milk in one of his factories, but I
never dreamed of trying it. I thought it was only used by explorers,
people at the North Pole, you know."

"How stupid of me!" exclaimed Roger. "I quite forgot to tell you!
Your father called up just after you had gone out this evening, and
wanted to know how you were getting on."

"Oh, dear," said Titania. "He must have been delighted to hear I
was at the movies, on the second day of my first job! He probably said
it was just like me."

"I explained that I had insisted on your going with Mrs. Mifflin,
because I felt she needed the change."

"I do hope," said Titania, "you won't let Daddy poison your mind
about me. He thinks I'm dreadfully frivolous, just because I *look*
frivolous. But I'm so keen to make good in this job. I've been
practicing doing up parcels all afternoon, so as to learn how to tie the
string nicely and not cut it until after the knot's tied. I found that when
you cut it beforehand either you get it too short and it won't go round,
or else too long and you waste some. Also I've learned how to make
wrapping paper cuffs to keep my sleeves clean."

"Well, I haven't finished yet," continued Roger. "Your father
wants us all to spend to-morrow out at your home. He wants to show us
some books he has just bought, and besides he thinks maybe you're
feeling homesick."

"What, with all these lovely books to read? Nonsense! I don't want
to go home for six months!"

"He wouldn't take No for an answer. He's going to send Edwards
round with the car the first thing to-morrow morning."

"What fun!" said Helen. "It'll be delightful."

"Goodness," said Titania. "Imagine leaving this adorable bookshop
to spend Sunday in Larchmont. Well, I'll be able to get that georgette
blouse I forgot."

"What time will the car be here?" asked Helen.

"Mr. Chapman said about nine o'clock. He begs us to get out there
as early as possible, as he wants to spend the day showing us his
books."

As they sat round the fading bed of coals, Roger began hunting
along his private shelves. "Have you ever read any Gissing?" he said.

Titania made a pathetic gesture to Mrs. Mifflin. "It's awfully embarrassing to be asked these things! No, I never heard of him."

"Well, as the street we live on is named after him, I think you ought to," he said. He pulled down his copy of *The House of Cobwebs*. "I'm going to read you one of the most delightful short stories I know. It's called 'A Charming Family.'"

"No, Roger," said Mrs. Mifflin firmly. "Not to-night. It's eleven o'clock, and I can see Titania's tired. Even Bock has left us and gone in to his kennel. He's got more sense than you have."

"All right," said the bookseller amiably. "Miss Chapman, you take the book up with you and read it in bed if you want to. Are you a librocubicularist?"

Titania looked a little scandalized.

"It's all right, my dear," said Helen. "He only means are you fond of reading in bed. I've been waiting to hear him work that word into the conversation. He made it up, and he's immensely proud of it."

"Reading in bed?" said Titania. "What a quaint idea! Does any one do it? It never occurred to me. I'm sure when I go to bed I'm far too sleepy to think of such a thing."

"Run along then, both of you," said Roger. "Get your beauty sleep. I shan't be very late."

He meant it when he said it, but returning to his desk at the back of the shop his eye fell upon his private shelf of books which he kept there "to rectify perturbations" as Burton puts it. On this shelf there stood *Pilgrim's Progress*, *Shakespeare*, *The Anatomy of Melancholy*, *The Home Book of Verse*, *George Herbert's Poems*, *The Notebooks of Samuel Butler*, and *Leaves of Grass*. He took down *The Anatomy of Melancholy*, that most delightful of all books for midnight browsing. Turning to one of his favourite passages—"A Consolatory Digression, Containing the Remedies of All Manner of Discontents"—he was happily lost to all ticking of the clock, retaining only such bodily consciousness as was needful to dump, fill, and relight his pipe from time to time. Solitude is a dear jewel for men whose days are spent in the tedious this-and-that of trade. Roger was a glutton for his midnight musings. To such tried companions as Robert Burton and George Herbert he was wont to exonerate his spirit. It used to amuse him to think of Burton, the lonely Oxford scholar, writing that vast book to "rectify" his own melancholy.

By and by, turning over the musty old pages, he came to the following, on Sleep—

*The fittest time is two or three hours after supper, whenas the meat is now settled at the bottom of the stomach, and 'tis good to lie on the right side first, because at that site the liver doth rest under the stomach, not molesting any way, but heating him as a fire doth a kettle, that is put to it. After the first sleep 'tis not amiss to lie on the left side, that the meat may the better descend, and sometimes again on the belly, but never on the back. Seven or eight hours is a competent time for a melancholy man to rest——*

In that case, thought Roger, it's time for me to be turning in. He looked at his watch, and found it was half-past twelve. He switched off his light and went back to the kitchen quarters to tend the furnace.

I hesitate to touch upon a topic of domestic bitterness, but candor compels me to say that Roger's evening vigils invariably ended at the ice-box. There are two theories as to this subject of ice-box plundering, one of the husband and the other of the wife. Husbands are prone to think (in their simplicity) that if they take a little of everything palatable they find in the refrigerator, but thus distributing their forage over the viands the general effect of the depradation will be almost unnoticeable. Whereas wives say (and Mrs. Mifflin had often explained to Roger) that it is far better to take all of any one dish than a little of each; for the latter course is likely to diminish each item below the bulk at which it is still useful as a left-over. Roger, however, had the obstinate viciousness of all good husbands, and he knew the delights of cold provender by heart. Many a stewed prune, many a mess of string beans or naked cold boiled potato, many a chicken leg, half apple pie, or sector of rice pudding, had perished in these midnight festivals. He made it a point of honour never to eat quite all of the dish in question, but would pass with unabated zest from one to another. This habit he had sternly repressed during the War, but Mrs. Mifflin had noticed that since the armistice he had resumed it with hearty violence. This is a custom which causes the housewife to be confronted the next morning with a tragical vista of pathetic scraps. Two slices of beet in a little earthenware cup, a sliver of apple pie one inch wide, three prunes lowly nestling in a mere trickle of their own syrup, and a tablespoonful of stewed rhubarb where had been one of those yellow basins nearly full—what can the most resourceful kitcheneer do with these oddments? This atrocious practice cannot be too bitterly condemned.

But we are what we are, and Roger was even more so. *The Anatomy of Melancholy* always made him hungry, and he dipped discreetly into various vessels of refreshment, sharing a few scraps with Bock whose pleading brown eye at these secret suppers always showed a comical realization of their shameful and furtive nature. Bock knew very well that Roger had no business at the ice-box, for the larger outlines of social law upon which every home depends are clearly understood by dogs. But Bock's face always showed his tremulous eagerness to participate in the sin, and rather than have him stand by as a silent and damning critic, Roger used to give him most of the cold potato. The censure of a dog is something no man can stand. But I rove, as Burton would say.

After the ice-box, the cellar. Like all true householders, Roger was fond of his cellar. It was something mouldy of smell, but it harboured a well-stocked little bin of liquors, and the florid glow of the furnace mouth upon the concrete floor was a great pleasure to the bookseller. He loved to peer in at the dancing flicker of small blue flames that played above the ruddy mound of coals in the firebox—tenuous, airy little flames that were as blue as violets and hovered up and down in the ascending gases. Before blackening the fire with a stoking of coal he pulled up a wooden Bushmills box, turned off the electric bulb overhead, and sat there for a final pipe, watching the rosy shine of the grate. The tobacco smoke, drawn inward by the hot inhaling fire, seemed dry and gray in the golden brightness. Bock, who had pattered down the steps after him, nosed and snooped about the cellar. Roger was thinking of Burton's words on the immortal weed—

Tobacco, divine, rare, superexcellent tobacco, which goes far beyond all the panaceas, potable gold, and philosopher's stones, a sovereign remedy to all diseases.... a virtuous herb, if it be well qualified, opportunely taken, and medicinally used; but as it is commonly abused by most men, which take it as tinkers do ale, 'tis a plague, a mischief, a violent purger of goods, lands, health, hellish, devilish, and damned tobacco, the ruin and overthrow of body and soul——

Bock was standing on his hind legs, looking up at the front wall of the cellar, in which two small iron-grated windows opened onto the sunken area by the front door of the shop. He gave a low growl, and seemed uneasy.

"What is it, Bock?" said Roger placidly, finishing his pipe.

Bock gave a short, sharp bark, with a curious note of protest in it. But Roger's mind was still with Burton.

"Rats?" he said. "Aye, very likely! This is Ratisbon, old man, but don't bark about it. *Incident of the French Camp:* 'Smiling, the rat fell dead.'"

Bock paid no heed to this persiflage, but prowled the front end of the cellar, looking upward in curious agitation. He growled again, softly.

"Shhh," said Roger gently. "Never mind the rats, Bock. Come on, we'll stoke up the fire and go to bed. Lord, it's one o'clock."

*Chapter XI. Titania Tries Reading in Bed*

Aubrey, sitting at his window with the opera glasses, soon realized that he was blind weary. Even the exalted heroics of romance are not proof against fatigue, most potent enemy of all who do and dream. He had had a long day, coming after the skull-smiting of the night before; it was only the frosty air at the lifted sash that kept him at all awake. He had fallen into a half drowse when he heard footsteps coming down the opposite side of the street.

He had forced himself awake several times before, to watch the passage of some harmless strollers through the innocent blackness of the Brooklyn night, but this time it was what he sought. The man stepped stealthily, with a certain blend of wariness and assurance. He halted under the lamp by the bookshop door, and the glasses gave him enlarged to Aubrey's eye. It was Weintraub, the druggist.

The front of the bookshop was now entirely dark save for a curious little glimmer down below the pavement level. This puzzled Aubrey, but he focussed his glasses on the door of the shop. He saw Weintraub pull a key out of his pocket, insert it very carefully in the lock, and open the door stealthily. Leaving the door ajar behind him, the druggist slipped into the shop.

"What devil's business is this?" thought Aubrey angrily. "The swine has even got a key of his own. There's no doubt about it. He and Mifflin are working together on this job."

For a moment he was uncertain what to do. Should he run downstairs and across the street? Then, as he hesitated, he saw a pale beam of light over in the front left-hand corner of the shop. Through the glasses he could see the yellow circle of a flashlight splotched upon dim shelves of books. He saw Weintraub pull a volume out of the case, and the light vanished. Another instant and the man reappeared in the doorway, closed the door behind him with a gesture of careful silence, and was off up the street quietly and swiftly. It was all over in a minute. Two yellow oblongs shone for a minute or two down in the area underneath the door. Through the glasses he now made out these patches as the cellar windows. Then they disappeared also, and all was placid gloom. In the quivering light of the street lamps he could see the bookseller's sign gleaming whitely, with its lettering THIS SHOP IS HAUNTED.

Aubrey sat back in his chair. "Well," he said to himself, "that guy certainly gave his shop the right name. This is by me. I do believe it's only some book-stealing game after all. I wonder if he and Weintraub go in for some first-edition faking, or some such stunt as that? I'd give a lot to know what it's all about."

He stayed by the window on the qui vive, but no sound broke the stillness of Gissing Street. In the distance he could hear the occasional rumble of the Elevated trains rasping round the curve on Wordsworth Avenue. He wondered whether he ought to go over and break into the shop to see if all was well. But, like every healthy young man, he had a horror of appearing absurd. Little by little weariness numbed his apprehensions. Two o'clock clanged and echoed from distant steeples. He threw off his clothes and crawled into bed.

It was ten o'clock on Sunday morning when he awoke. A broad swath of sunlight cut the room in half: the white muslin curtain at the window rippled outward like a flag. Aubrey exclaimed when he saw his watch. He had a sudden feeling of having been false to his trust. What had been happening across the way?

He gazed out at the bookshop. Gissing Street was bright and demure in the crisp quietness of the forenoon. Mifflin's house showed no sign of life. It was as he had last seen it, save that broad green shades had been drawn down inside the big front windows, making it impossible to look through into the book-filled alcoves.

Aubrey put on his overcoat in lieu of a dressing gown, and went in search of a bathtub. He found the bathroom on his floor locked, with sounds of leisurely splashing within. "Damn Mrs. J. F. Smith," he said. He was about to descend to the storey below, bashfully conscious of bare feet and pyjamaed shins, but looking over the banisters he saw Mrs. Schiller and the treasure-dog engaged in some household manoeuvres. The pug caught sight of his pyjama legs and began to yap. Aubrey retreated in the irritation of a man baulked of a cold tub. He shaved and dressed rapidly.

On his way downstairs he met Mrs. Schiller. He thought that her gaze was disapproving.

"A gentleman called to see you last night, sir," she said. "He said he was very sorry to miss you."

"I was rather late in getting in," said Aubrey. "Did he leave his name?"

"No, he said he'd see you some other time. He woke the whole house up by falling downstairs," she added sourly.

He left the lodging house swiftly, fearing to be seen from the bookshop. He was very eager to learn if everything was all right, but he did not want the Mifflins to know he was lodging just opposite. Hastening diagonally across the street, he found that the Milwaukee Lunch, where he had eaten the night before, was open. He went in and had breakfast, rejoicing in grapefruit, ham and eggs, coffee, and doughnuts. He lit a pipe and sat by the window wondering what to do next. "It's damned perplexing," he said to himself. "I stand to lose either way. If I don't do anything, something may happen to the girl; if I butt in too soon I'll get in dutch with her. I wish I knew what

Weintraub and that chef are up to."

The lunchroom was practically empty, and in two chairs near him the proprietor and his assistant were sitting talking. Aubrey was suddenly struck by what they said.

"Say, this here, now, bookseller guy must have struck it rich."

"Who, Mifflin?"

"Yeh; did ya see that car in front of his place this morning?"

"No."

"Believe me, some boat."

"Musta hired it, hey? Where'd he go at?"

"I didn't see. I just saw the bus standing front the door."

"Say, did you see that swell dame he's got clerking for him?"

"I sure did. What's he doing, taking her joy-riding?"

"Shouldn't wonder. I wouldn't blame him——"

Aubrey gave no sign of having heard, but got up and left the lunchroom. Had the girl been kidnapped while he overslept? He burned with shame to think what a pitiful failure his knight-errantry had been. His first idea was to beard Weintraub and compel him to explain his connection with the bookshop. His next thought was to call up Mr. Chapman and warn him of what had been going on. Then he decided it would be futile to do either of these before he really knew what had happened. He determined to get into the bookshop itself, and burst open its sinister secret.

He walked hurriedly round to the rear alley, and surveyed the domestic apartments of the shop. Two windows in the second storey stood slightly open, but he could discern no signs of life. The back gate was still unlocked, and he walked boldly into the yard.

The little enclosure was serene in the pale winter sunlight. Along one fence ran a line of bushes and perennials, their roots wrapped in straw. The grass plot was lumpy, the sod withered to a tawny yellow and granulated with a sprinkle of frost. Below the kitchen door—which stood at the head of a flight of steps—was a little grape arbour with a rustic bench where Roger used to smoke his pipe on summer evenings. At the back of this arbour was the cellar door. Aubrey tried it, and found it locked.

He was in no mood to stick at trifles. He was determined to unriddle the mystery of the bookshop. At the right of the door was a low window, level with the brick pavement. Through the dusty pane he could see it was fastened only by a hook on the inside. He thrust his heel through the pane. As the glass tinkled onto the cellar floor he heard a low growl. He unhooked the catch, lifted the frame of the broken window, and looked in. There was Bock, with head quizzically tilted, uttering a rumbling guttural vibration that seemed to proceed automatically from his interior.

Aubrey was a little dashed, but he said cheerily "Hullo, Bock!

Good old man! Well, well, nice old fellow!" To his surprise, Bock recognized him as a friend and wagged his tail slightly, but still continued to growl.

"I wish dogs weren't such sticklers for form," thought Aubrey. "Now if I went in by the front door, Bock wouldn't say anything. It's just because he sees me coming in this way that he's annoyed. Well, I'll have to take a chance."

He thrust his legs in through the window, carefully holding up the sash with its jagged triangles of glass. It will never be known how severely Bock was tempted by the extremities thus exposed to him, but he was an old dog and his martial instincts had been undermined by years of kindness. Moreover, he remembered Aubrey perfectly well, and the smell of his trousers did not seem at all hostile. So he contented himself with a small grumbling of protest. He was an Irish terrier, but there was nothing Sinn Fein about him.

Aubrey dropped to the floor, and patted the dog, thanking his good fortune. He glanced about the cellar as though expecting to find some lurking horror. Nothing more appalling than several cases of beer bottles met his eyes. He started quietly to go up the cellar stairs, and Bock, evidently consumed with legitimate curiosity, kept at his heels.

"Look here," thought Aubrey. "I don't want the dog following me all through the house. If I touch anything he'll probably take a hunk out of my shin."

He unlocked the door into the yard, and Bock obeying the Irish terrier's natural impulse to get into the open air, ran outside. Aubrey quickly closed the door again. Bock's face appeared at the broken window, looking in with so quaint an expression of indignant surprise that Aubrey almost laughed. "There, old man," he said, "it's all right. I'm just going to look around a bit."

He ascended the stairs on tiptoe and found himself in the kitchen. All was quiet. An alarm clock ticked with a stumbling, headlong hurry. Pots of geraniums stood on the window sill. The range, with its lids off and the fire carefully nourished, radiated a mild warmth. Through a dark little pantry he entered the dining room. Still no sign of anything amiss. A pot of white heather stood on the table, and a corncob pipe lay on the sideboard. "This is the most innocent-looking kidnapper's den I ever heard of," he thought. "Any moving-picture director would be ashamed not to provide a better stage-set."

At that instant he heard footsteps overhead. Curiously soft, muffled footsteps. Instantly he was on the alert. Now he would know the worst.

A window upstairs was thrown open. "Bock, what are you doing in the yard?" floated a voice—a very clear, imperious voice that somehow made him think of the thin ringing of a fine glass tumbler. It was Titania.

He stood aghast. Then he heard a door open, and steps on the stair.

Merciful heaven, the girl must not find him here. What *would* she think? He skipped back into the pantry, and shrank into a corner. He heard the footfalls reach the bottom of the stairs. There was a door into the kitchen from the central hall: it was not necessary for her to pass through the pantry, he thought. He heard her enter the kitchen.

In his anxiety he crouched down beneath the sink, and his foot, bent beneath him, touched a large tin tray leaning against the wall. It fell over with a terrible clang.

"Bock!" said Titania sharply, "what are you doing?"

Aubrey was wondering miserably whether he ought to counterfeit a bark, but it was too late to do anything. The pantry door opened, and Titania looked in.

They gazed at each other for several seconds in mutual horror. Even in his abasement, crouching under a shelf in the corner, Aubrey's stricken senses told him that he had never seen so fair a spectacle. Titania wore a blue kimono and a curious fragile lacy bonnet which he did not understand. Her dark, gold-spangled hair came down in two thick braids across her shoulders. Her blue eyes were very much alive with amazement and alarm which rapidly changed into anger.

"Mr. Gilbert!" she cried. For an instant he thought she was going to laugh. Then a new expression came into her face. Without another word she turned and fled. He heard her run upstairs. A door banged, and was locked. A window was hastily closed. Again all was silent.

Stupefied with chagrin, he rose from his cramped position. What on earth was he to do? How could he explain? He stood by the pantry sink in painful indecision. Should he slink out of the house? No, he couldn't do that without attempting to explain. And he was still convinced that some strange peril hung about this place. He must put Titania on her guard, no matter how embarrassing it proved. If only she hadn't been wearing a kimono—how much easier it would have been.

He stepped out into the hall, and stood at the bottom of the stairs in the throes of doubt. After waiting some time in silence he cleared the huskiness from his throat and called out:

"Miss Chapman!"

There was no answer, but he heard light, rapid movements above.

"Miss Chapman!" he called again.

He heard the door opened, and clear words edged with frost came downward. This time he thought of a thin tumbler with ice in it.

"Mr. Gilbert!"

"Yes?" he said miserably.

"Will you please call me a taxi?"

Something in the calm, mandatory tone nettled him. After all, he had acted in pure good faith.

"With pleasure," he said, "but not until I have told you something. It's very important. I beg your pardon most awfully for frightening you, but it's really very urgent."

There was a brief silence. Then she said:

"Brooklyn's a queer place. Wait a few minutes, please."

Aubrey stood absently fingering the pattern on the wallpaper. He suddenly experienced a great craving for a pipe, but felt that the etiquette of the situation hardly permitted him to smoke.

In a few moments Titania appeared at the head of the stairs in her customary garb. She sat down on the landing. Aubrey felt that everything was as bad as it could possibly be. If he could have seen her face his embarrassment would at least have had some compensation. But the light from a stair window shone behind her, and her features were in shadow. She sat clasping her hands round her knees. The light fell crosswise down the stairway, and he could see only a gleam of brightness upon her ankle. His mind unconsciously followed its beaten paths. "What a corking pose for a silk stocking ad!" he thought. "Wouldn't it make a stunning full-page layout. I must suggest it to the Ankleshimmer people."

"Well?" she said. Then she could not refrain from laughter, he looked so hapless. She burst into an engaging trill. "Why don't you light your pipe?" she said. "You look as doleful as the Kaiser."

"Miss Chapman," he said, "I'm afraid you think—I don't know what you must think. But I broke in here this morning because I—well, I don't think this is a safe place for you to be."

"So it seems. That's why I asked you to get me a taxi."

"There's something queer going on round this shop. It's not right for you to be here alone this way. I was afraid something had happened to you. Of course, I didn't know you were—were——"

Faint almond blossoms grew in her cheeks. "I was reading," she said. "Mr. Mifflin talks so much about reading in bed, I thought I'd try it. They wanted me to go with them to-day but I wouldn't. You see, if I'm going to be a bookseller I've got to catch up with some of this literature that's been accumulating. After they left I—I—well, I wanted to see if this reading in bed is what it's cracked up to be."

"Where has Mifflin gone?" asked Aubrey. "What business has he got to leave you here all alone?"

"I had Bock," said Titania. "Gracious, Brooklyn on Sunday morning doesn't seem very perilous to me. If you must know, he and Mrs. Mifflin have gone over to spend the day with father. I was to have gone, too, but I wouldn't. What business is it of yours? You're as bad as Morris Finsbury in *The Wrong Box*. That's what I was reading when I heard the dog barking."

Aubrey began to grow nettled. "You seem to think this was a mere impertinence on my part," he said. "Let me tell you a thing or two." And he briefly described to her the course of his experiences since leaving the shop on Friday evening, but omitting the fact that he was lodging just across the street.

"There's something mighty unpalatable going on," he said. "At first I thought Mifflin was the goat. I thought it might be some frame-up for swiping valuable books from his shop. But when I saw Weintraub come in here with his own latch-key, I got wise. He and Mifflin are in cahoots, that's what. I don't know what they're pulling off, but I don't like the looks of it. You say Mifflin has gone out to see your father? I bet that's just camouflage, to stall you. I've got a great mind to ring Mr. Chapman up and tell him he ought to get you out of here."

"I won't hear a word said against Mr. Mifflin," said Titania angrily. "He's one of my father's oldest friends. What would Mr. Mifflin say if he knew you had been breaking into his house and frightening me half to death? I'm sorry you got that knock on the head, because it seems that's your weak spot. I'm quite able to take care of myself, thank you. This isn't a movie."

"Well, how do you explain the actions of this man Weintraub?" said Aubrey. "Do you like to have a man popping in and out of the shop at all hours of the night, stealing books?"

"I don't have to explain it at all," said Titania. "I think it's up to you to do the explaining. Weintraub is a harmless old thing and he keeps delicious chocolates that cost only half as much as what you get on Fifth Avenue. Mr. Mifflin told me that he's a very good customer. Perhaps his business won't let him read in the daytime, and he comes in here late at night to borrow books. He probably reads in bed."

"I don't think anybody who talks German round back alleys at night is a harmless old thing," said Aubrey. "I tell you, your Haunted Bookshop is haunted by something worse than the ghost of Thomas Carlyle. Let me show you something." He pulled the book cover out of his pocket, and pointed to the annotations in it.

"That's Mifflin's handwriting," said Titania, pointing to the upper row of figures. "He puts notes like that in all his favourite books. They refer to pages where he has found interesting things."

"Yes, and that's Weintraub's," said Aubrey, indicating the numbers in violet ink. "If that isn't a proof of their complicity, I'd like to know what is. If that Cromwell book is here, I'd like to have a look at it."

They went into the shop. Titania preceded him down the musty aisle, and it made Aubrey angry to see the obstinate assurance of her small shoulders. He was horribly tempted to seize her and shake her. It annoyed him to see her bright, unconscious girlhood in that dingy vault of books. "She's as out of place here as—as a Packard ad in the *Liberator*" he said to himself.

They stood in the History alcove. "Here it is," she said. "No, it isn't—that's the *History of Frederick the Great.*"

There was a two-inch gap in the shelf. *Cromwell* was gone.

"Probably Mr. Mifflin has it somewhere around," said Titania. "It was there last night."

"Probably nothing," said Aubrey. "I tell you, Weintraub came in and took it. I saw him. Look here, if you really want to know what I think, I'll tell you. The War's not over by a long sight. Weintraub's a German. Carlyle was pro-German—I remember that much from college. I believe your friend Mifflin is pro-German, too. I've heard some of his talk!"

Titania faced him with cheeks aflame.

"That'll do for you!" she cried. "Next thing I suppose you'll say Daddy's pro-German, and me, too! I'd like to see you say that to Mr. Mifflin himself."

"I will, don't worry," said Aubrey grimly. He knew now that he had put himself hopelessly in the wrong in Titania's mind, but he refused to abate his own convictions. With sinking heart he saw her face relieved against the shelves of faded bindings. Her eyes shone with a deep and sultry blue, her chin quivered with anger.

"Look here," she said furiously. "Either you or I must leave this place. If you intend to stay, please call me a taxi."

Aubrey was as angry as she was.

"I'm going," he said. "But you've got to play fair with me. I tell you on my oath, these two men, Mifflin and Weintraub, are framing something up. I'm going to get the goods on them and show you. But you mustn't put them wise that I'm on their track. If you do, of course, they'll call it off. I don't care what you think of me. You've got to promise me that."

"I won't promise you *anything*," she said, "except never to speak to you again. I never saw a man like you before—and I've seen a good many."

"I won't leave here until you promise me not to warn them," he retorted. "What I told you, I said in confidence. They've already found out where I'm lodging. Do you think this is a joke? They've tried to put me out of the way twice. If you breathe a word of this to Mifflin he'll warn the other two."

"You're afraid to have Mr. Mifflin know you broke into his shop," she taunted.

"You can think what you like."

"I won't promise you anything!" she burst out. Then her face altered. The defiant little line of her mouth bent and her strength seemed to run out at each end of that pathetic curve. "Yes, I will," she said. "I suppose that's fair. I couldn't tell Mr. Mifflin, anyway. I'd be ashamed to tell him how you frightened me. I think you're hateful. I came over here thinking I was going to have such a good time, and you've spoilt it all!"

For one terrible moment he thought she was going to cry. But he remembered having seen heroines cry in the movies, and knew it was only done when there was a table and chair handy.

"Miss Chapman," he said, "I'm as sorry as a man can be. But I swear I did what I did in all honesty. If I'm wrong in this, you need never speak to me again. If I'm wrong, you—you can tell your father to take his advertising away from the Grey-Matter Company. I can't say more than that."

And, to do him justice, he couldn't. It was the supreme sacrifice. She let him out of the front door without another word.

*Chapter XII. Aubrey Determines to give Service that's Different*

Seldom has a young man spent a more desolate afternoon than Aubrey on that Sunday. His only consolation was that twenty minutes after he had left the bookshop he saw a taxi drive up (he was then sitting gloomily at his bedroom window) and Titania enter it and drive away. He supposed that she had gone to join the party in Larchmont, and was glad to know that she was out of what he now called the war zone. For the first time on record, O. Henry failed to solace him. His pipe tasted bitter and brackish. He was eager to know what Weintraub was doing, but did not dare make any investigations in broad daylight. His idea was to wait until dark. Observing the Sabbath calm of the streets, and the pageant of baby carriages wheeling toward Thackeray Boulevard, he wondered again whether he had thrown away this girl's friendship for a merely imaginary suspicion.

At last he could endure his cramped bedroom no longer. Downstairs someone was dolefully playing a flute, most horrible of all tortures to tightened nerves. While her lodgers were at church the tireless Mrs. Schiller was doing a little housecleaning: he could hear the monotonous rasp of a carpet-sweeper passing back and forth in an adjoining room. He creaked irritably downstairs, and heard the usual splashing behind the bathroom door. In the frame of the hall mirror he saw a pencilled note: *Will Mrs. Smith please call Tarkington 1565*, it said. Unreasonably annoyed, he tore a piece of paper out of his notebook and wrote on it *Will Mrs. Smith please call Bath 4200.* Mounting to the second floor he tapped on the bathroom door. "Don't come in!" cried an agitated female voice. He thrust the memorandum under the door, and left the house.

Walking the windy paths of Prospect Park he condemned himself to relentless self-scrutiny. "I've damned myself forever with her," he groaned, "unless I can prove something." The vision of Titania's face silhouetted against the shelves of books came maddeningly to his mind. "I was going to have such a good time, and you've spoilt it all!" With what angry conviction she had said: "I never saw a man like you before—and I've seen a good many!"

Even in his disturbance of soul the familiar jargon of his profession came naturally to utterance. "At least she admits I'm *different*," he said dolefully. He remembered the first item in the Grey-Matter Code, a neat little booklet issued by his employers for the information of their representatives:

Business is built upon *Confidence*. Before you can sell Grey-Matter Service to a Client, you must sell *Yourself.*

"How am I going to sell myself to her?" he wondered. "I've simply got to deliver, that's all. I've got to give her service that's *different*. If I fall down on this, she'll never speak to me again. Not only that, the firm will lose the old man's account. It's simply unthinkable."

Nevertheless, he thought about it a good deal, stimulated from time to time as in the course of his walk (which led him out toward the faubourgs of Flatbush) he passed long vistas of signboards, which he imagined placarded with vivid lithographs in behalf of the Chapman prunes. "Adam and Eve Ate Prunes on Their Honeymoon" was a slogan that flashed into his head, and he imagined a magnificent painting illustrating this text. Thus, in hours of stress, do all men turn for comfort to their chosen art. The poet, battered by fate, heals himself in the niceties of rhyme. The prohibitionist can weather the blackest melancholia by meditating the contortions of other people's abstinence. The most embittered citizen of Detroit will never perish by his own hand while he has an automobile to tinker.

Aubrey walked many miles, gradually throwing his despair to the winds. The bright spirits of Orison Swett Marden and Ralph Waldo Trine, Dioscuri of Good Cheer, seemed to be with him reminding him that nothing is impossible. In a small restaurant he found sausages, griddle cakes and syrup. When he got back to Gissing Street it was dark, and he girded his soul for further endeavour.

About nine o'clock he walked up the alley. He had left his overcoat in his room at Mrs. Schiller's and also the *Cromwell* bookcover—having taken the precaution, however, to copy the inscriptions into his pocket memorandum-book. He noticed lights in the rear of the bookshop, and concluded that the Mifflins and their employee had got home safely. Arrived at the back of Weintraub's pharmacy, he studied the contours of the building carefully.

The drug store lay, as we have explained before, at the corner of Gissing Street and Wordsworth Avenue, just where the Elevated railway swings in a long curve. The course of this curve brought the scaffolding of the viaduct out over the back roof of the building, and this fact had impressed itself on Aubrey's observant eye the day before. The front of the drug store stood three storeys, but in the rear it dropped to two, with a flat roof over the hinder portion. Two windows looked out upon this roof. Weintraub's back yard opened onto the alley, but the gate, he found, was locked. The fence would not be hard to scale, but he hesitated to make so direct an approach.

He ascended the stairs of the "L" station, on the near side, and paying a nickel passed through a turnstile onto the platform. Waiting until just after a train had left, and the long, windy sweep of planking was solitary, he dropped onto the narrow footway that runs beside the track. This required watchful walking, for the charged third rail was very near, but hugging the outer side of the path he proceeded without trouble. Every fifteen feet or so a girder ran sideways from the track, resting upon an upright from the street below. The fourth of these overhung the back corner of Weintraub's house, and he crawled cautiously along it. People were passing on the pavement underneath, and he greatly feared being discovered. But he reached the end of the beam without mishap. From here a drop of about twelve feet would bring him onto Weintraub's back roof. For a moment he reflected that, once down there, it would be impossible to return the same way. However, he decided to risk it. Where he was, with his legs swinging astride the girder, he was in serious danger of attracting attention.

He would have given a great deal, just then, to have his overcoat with him, for by lowering it first he could have jumped onto it and muffled the noise of his fall. He took off his coat and carefully dropped it on the corner of the roof. Then cannily waiting until a train passed overhead, drowning all other sounds with its roar, he lowered himself as far as he could hang by his hands, and let go.

For some minutes he lay prone on the tin roof, and during that time a number of distressing ideas occurred to him. If he really expected to get into Weintraub's house, why had he not laid his plans more carefully? Why (for instance) had he not made some attempt to find out how many there were in the household? Why had he not arranged with one of his friends to call Weintraub to the telephone at a given moment, so that he could be more sure of making an entry unnoticed? And what did he expect to see or do if he got inside the house? He found no answer to any of these questions.

It was unpleasantly cold, and he was glad to slip his coat on again. The small revolver was still in his hip pocket. Another thought occurred to him—that he should have provided himself with tennis shoes. However, it was some comfort to know that rubber heels of a nationally advertised brand were under him. He crawled quietly up to the sill of one of the windows. It was closed, and the room inside was dark. A blind was pulled most of the way down, leaving a gap of about four inches. Peeping cautiously over the sill, he could see farther inside the house a brightly lit door and a passageway.

"One thing I've got to look out for," he thought, "is children. There are bound to be some—who ever heard of a German without offspring? If I wake them, they'll bawl. This room is very likely a nursery, as it's on the southeastern side. Also, the window is shut tight, which is probably the German idea of bedroom ventilation."

His guess may not have been a bad one, for after his eyes became accustomed to the dimness of the room he thought he could perceive two cot beds. He then crawled over to the other window. Here the blind was pulled down flush with the bottom of the sash. Trying the window very cautiously, he found it locked. Not knowing just what to do, he returned to the first window, and lay there peering in. The sill was just high enough above the roof level to make it necessary to raise himself a little on his hands to see inside, and the position was very trying. Moreover, the tin roof had a tendency to crumple noisily when he moved. He lay for some time, shivering in the chill, and wondering whether it would be safe to light a pipe.

"There's another thing I'd better look out for," he thought, "and that's a dog. Who ever heard of a German without a dachshund?"

He had watched the lighted doorway for a long while without seeing anything, and was beginning to think he was losing time to no profit when a stout and not ill-natured looking woman appeared in the hallway. She came into the room he was studying, and closed the door. She switched on the light, and to his horror began to disrobe. This was not what he had counted on at all, and he retreated rapidly. It was plain that nothing was to be gained where he was. He sat timidly at one edge of the roof and wondered what to do next.

As he sat there, the back door opened almost directly below him, and he heard the clang of a garbage can set out by the stoop. The door stood open for perhaps half a minute, and he heard a male voice—Weintraub's, he thought—speaking in German. For the first time in his life he yearned for the society of his German instructor at college, and also wondered—in the rapid irrelevance of thought—what that worthy man was now doing to earn a living. In a rather long and poorly lubricated sentence, heavily verbed at the end, he distinguished one phrase that seemed important. "*Nach Philadelphia gehen*"—"Go to Philadelphia."

Did that refer to Mifflin? he wondered.

The door closed again. Leaning over the rain-gutter, he saw the light go out in the kitchen. He tried to look through the upper portion of the window just below him, but leaning out too far, the tin spout gave beneath his hands. Without knowing just how he did it, he slithered down the side of the wall, and found his feet on a window-sill. His hands still clung to the tin gutter above. He made haste to climb down from his position, and found himself outside the back door. He had managed the descent rather more quietly than if it had been carefully planned. But he was badly startled, and retreated to the bottom of the yard to see if he had aroused notice.

A wait of several minutes brought no alarm, and he plucked up courage. On the inner side of the house—away from Wordsworth Avenue—a narrow paved passage led to an outside cellar-way with old-fashioned slanting doors. He reconnoitred this warily. A bright light was shining from a window in this alley. He crept below it on hands and knees fearing to look in until he had investigated a little. He found that one flap of the cellar door was open, and poked his nose into the aperture. All was dark below, but a strong, damp stench of paints and chemicals arose. He sniffed gingerly. "I suppose he stores drugs down there," he thought.

Very carefully he crawled back, on hands and knees, toward the lighted window. Lifting his head a few inches at a time, finally he got his eyes above the level of the sill. To his disappointment he found the lower half of the window frosted. As he knelt there, a pipe set in the wall suddenly vomited liquid which gushed out upon his knees. He sniffed it, and again smelled a strong aroma of acids. With great care, leaning against the brick wall of the house, he rose to his feet and peeped through the upper half of the pane.

It seemed to be the room where prescriptions were compounded. As it was empty, he allowed himself a hasty survey. All manner of bottles were ranged along the walls; there was a high counter with scales, a desk, and a sink. At the back he could see the bamboo curtain which he remembered having noticed from the shop. The whole place was in the utmost disorder: mortars, glass beakers, a typewriter, cabinets of labels, dusty piles of old prescriptions strung on filing hooks, papers of pills and capsules, all strewn in an indescribable litter. Some infusion was heating in a glass bowl propped on a tripod over a blue gas flame. Aubrey noticed particularly a heap of old books several feet high piled carelessly at one end of the counter.

Looking more carefully, he saw that what he had taken for a mirror over the prescription counter was an aperture looking into the shop. Through this he could see Weintraub, behind the cigar case, waiting upon some belated customer with his shop-worn air of affability. The visitor departed, and Weintraub locked the door after him and pulled down the blinds. Then he returned toward the prescription room, and Aubrey ducked out of view.

Presently he risked looking again, and was just in time to see a curious sight. The druggist was bending over the counter, pouring some liquid into a glass vessel. His face was directly under a hanging bulb, and Aubrey was amazed at the transformation. The apparently genial apothecary of cigar stand and soda fountain was gone. He saw instead a heavy, cruel, jowlish face, with eyelids hooded down over the eyes, and a square thrusting chin buttressed on a mass of jaw and suetty cheek that glistened with an oily shimmer. The jaw quivered a little as though

with some intense suppressed emotion. The man was completely
absorbed in his task. The thick lower lip lapped upward over the mouth.
On the cheekbone was a deep red scar. Aubrey felt a pang of fascinated
amazement at the gross energy and power of that abominable relentless
mask.

"So this is the harmless old thing!" he thought.

Just then the bamboo curtain parted, and the woman whom he had
seen upstairs appeared. Forgetting his own situation, Aubrey still
stared. She wore a faded dressing gown and her hair was braided as
though for the night. She looked frightened, and must have spoken, for
Aubrey saw her lips move. The man remained bent over his counter
until the last drops of liquid had run out. His jaw tightened, he
straightened suddenly and took one step toward her, with outstretched
hand imperiously pointed. Aubrey could see his face plainly: it had a
savagery more than bestial. The woman's face, which had borne a
timid, pleading expression, appealed in vain against that fierce gesture.
She turned and vanished. Aubrey saw the druggist's pointing finger
tremble. Again he ducked out of sight. "That man's face would be
lonely in a crowd," he said to himself. "And I used to think the movies
exaggerated things. Say, he ought to play opposite Theda Bara."

He lay at full length in the paved alley and thought that a little
acquaintance with Weintraub would go a long way. Then the light in
the window above him went out, and he gathered himself together for
quick motion if necessary. Perhaps the man would come out to close
the cellar door——

The thought was in his mind when a light flashed on farther down
the passage, between him and the kitchen. It came from a small barred
window on the ground level. Evidently the druggist had gone down into
the cellar. Aubrey crawled silently along toward the yard. Reaching the
lit pane he lay against the wall and looked in.

The window was too grimed for him to see clearly, but what he
could make out had the appearance of a chemical laboratory and
machine shop combined. A long work bench was lit by several
electrics. On it he saw glass vials of odd shapes, and a medley of tools.
Sheets of tin, lengths of lead pipe, gas burners, a vise, boilers and
cylinders, tall jars of coloured fluids. He could hear a dull humming
sound, which he surmised came from some sort of revolving tool which
he could see was run by a belt from a motor. On trying to spy more
clearly he found that what he had taken for dirt was a coat of
whitewash which had been applied to the window on the inside, but the
coating had worn away in one spot which gave him a loophole. What
surprised him most was to spy the covers of a number of books strewn
about the work table. One, he was ready to swear, was the *Cromwell*.
He knew that bright blue cloth by this time.

For the second time that evening Aubrey wished for the presence of one of his former instructors. "I wish I had my old chemistry professor here," he thought. "I'd like to know what this bird is up to. I'd hate to swallow one of his prescriptions."

His teeth were chattering after the long exposure and he was wet through from lying in the little gutter that apparently drained off from the sink in Weintraub's prescription laboratory. He could not see what the druggist was doing in the cellar, for the man's broad back was turned toward him. He felt as though he had had quite enough thrills for one evening. Creeping along he found his way back to the yard, and stepped cautiously among the empty boxes with which it was strewn. An elevated train rumbled overhead, and he watched the brightly lighted cars swing by. While the train roared above him, he scrambled up the fence and dropped down into the alley.

"Well," he thought, "I'd give full-page space, preferred position, in the magazine Ben Franklin founded to the guy that'd tell me what's going on at this grand bolshevik headquarters. It looks to me as though they're getting ready to blow the Octagon Hotel off the map."

He found a little confectionery shop on Wordsworth Avenue that was still open, and went in for a cup of hot chocolate to warm himself. "The expense account on this business is going to be rather heavy," he said to himself. "I think I'll have to charge it up to the Daintybits account. Say, old Grey Matter gives service that's *different*, don't she! We not only keep Chapman's goods in the public eye, but we face all the horrors of Brooklyn to preserve his family from unlawful occasions. No, I don't like the company that bookseller runs with. If 'nach *Philadelphia*' is the word, I think I'll tag along. I guess it's off for Philadelphia in the morning!"

*Chapter XIII. The Battle of Ludlow Street*

Rarely was a more genuine tribute paid to entrancing girlhood than when Aubrey compelled himself, by sheer force of will and the ticking of his subconscious time-sense, to wake at six o'clock the next morning. For this young man took sleep seriously and with a primitive zest. It was to him almost a religious function. As a minor poet has said, he "made sleep a career."

But he did not know what train Roger might be taking, and he was determined not to miss him. By a quarter after six he was seated in the Milwaukee Lunch (which is never closed—*Open from Now Till the Judgment Day. Tables for Ladies*, as its sign says) with a cup of coffee and corned beef hash. In the mood of tender melancholy common to unaccustomed early rising he dwelt fondly on the thought of Titania, so near and yet so far away. He had leisure to give free rein to these musings, for it was ten past seven before Roger appeared, hurrying toward the subway. Aubrey followed at a discreet distance, taking care not to be observed.

The bookseller and his pursuer both boarded the eight o'clock train at the Pennsylvania Station, but in very different moods. To Roger, this expedition was a frolic, pure and simple. He had been tied down to the bookshop so long that a day's excursion seemed too good to be true. He bought two cigars—an unusual luxury—and let the morning paper lie unheeded in his lap as the train drummed over the Hackensack marshes. He felt a good deal of pride in having been summoned to appraise the Oldham library. Mr. Oldham was a very distinguished collector, a wealthy Philadelphia merchant whose choice Johnson, Lamb, Keats, and Blake items were the envy of connoisseurs all over the world. Roger knew very well that there were many better-known dealers who would have jumped at the chance to examine the collection and pocket the appraiser's fee. The word that Roger had had by long distance telephone was that Mr. Oldham had decided to sell his collection, and before putting it to auction desired the advices of an expert as to the prices his items should command in the present state of the market. And as Roger was not particularly conversant with current events in the world of rare books and manuscripts, he spent most of the trip in turning over some annotated catalogues of recent sales which Mr. Chapman had lent him. "This invitation," he said to himself, "confirms what I have always said, that the artist, in any line of work, will eventually be recognized above the mere tradesman. Somehow or other Mr. Oldham has heard that I am not only a seller of old books but a lover of them. He prefers to have me go over his treasures with him, rather than one of those who peddle these things like so much tallow."

Aubrey's humour was far removed from that of the happy bookseller. In the first place, Roger was sitting in the smoker, and as Aubrey feared to enter the same car for fear of being observed, he had to do without his pipe. He took the foremost seat in the second coach, and peering occasionally through the glass doors he could see the bald poll of his quarry wreathed with exhalements of cheap havana. Secondly, he had hoped to see Weintraub on the same train, but though he had tarried at the train-gate until the last moment, the German had not appeared. He had concluded from Weintraub's words the night before that druggist and bookseller were bound on a joint errand. Apparently he was mistaken. He bit his nails, glowered at the flying landscape, and revolved many grievous fancies in his prickling bosom. Among other discontents was the knowledge that he did not have enough money with him to pay his fare back to New York, and he would either have to borrow from someone in Philadelphia or wire to his office for funds. He had not anticipated, when setting out upon this series of adventures, that it would prove so costly.

The train drew into Broad Street station at ten o'clock, and Aubrey followed the bookseller through the bustling terminus and round the

City Hall plaza. Mifflin seemed to know his way, but Philadelphia was comparatively strange to the Grey-Matter solicitor. He was quite surprised at the impressive vista of South Broad Street, and chagrined to find people jostling him on the crowded pavement as though they did not know he had just come from New York.

Roger turned in at a huge office building on Broad Street and took an express elevator. Aubrey did not dare follow him into the car, so he waited in the lobby. He learned from the starter that there was a second tier of elevators on the other side of the building, so he tipped a boy a quarter to watch them for him, describing Mifflin so accurately that he could not be missed. By this time Aubrey was in a thoroughly ill temper, and enjoyed quarrelling with the starter on the subject of indicators for showing the position of the elevators. Observing that in this building the indicators were glass tubes in which the movement of the car was traced by a rising or falling column of coloured fluid, Aubrey remarked testily that that old-fashioned stunt had long been abandoned in New York. The starter retorted that New York was only two hours away if he liked it better. This argument helped to fleet the time rapidly.

Meanwhile Roger, with the pleasurable sensation of one who expects to be received as a distinguished visitor from out of town, had entered the luxurious suite of Mr. Oldham. A young lady, rather too transparently shirtwaisted but fair to look upon, asked what she could do for him.

"I want to see Mr. Oldham."

"What name shall I say?"

"Mr. Mifflin—Mr. Mifflin of Brooklyn."

"Have you an appointment?"

"Yes."

Roger sat down with agreeable anticipation. He noticed the shining mahogany of the office furniture, the sparkling green jar of drinking water, the hushed and efficient activity of the young ladies. "Philadelphia girls are amazingly comely," he said to himself, "but none of these can hold a candle to Miss Titania."

The young lady returned from the private office looking a little perplexed.

"Did you have an appointment with Mr. Oldham?" she said. "He doesn't seem to recall it."

"Why, certainly," said Roger. "It was arranged by telephone on Saturday afternoon. Mr. Oldham's secretary called me up."

"Have I got your name right?" she asked, showing a slip on which she had written *Mr. Miflin.*

"Two f's," said Roger. "Mr. Roger Mifflin, the bookseller."

The girl retired, and came back a moment later.

"Mr. Oldham's very busy," she said, "but he can see you for a moment."

Roger was ushered into the private office, a large, airy room lined with bookshelves. Mr. Oldham, a tall, thin man with short gray hair and lively black eyes, rose courteously from his desk.

"How do you do, sir," he said. "I'm sorry, I had forgotten our appointment."

"He must be very absent minded," thought Roger. "Arranges to sell a collection worth half a million, and forgets all about it."

"I came over in response to your message," he said. "About selling your collection."

Mr. Oldham looked at him, rather intently, Roger thought.

"Do you want to buy it?" he said.

"To buy it?" said Roger, a little peevishly. "Why, no. I came over to appraise it for you. Your secretary telephoned me on Saturday."

"My dear sir," replied the other, "there must be some mistake. I have no intention of selling my collection. I never sent you a message."

Roger was aghast.

"Why," he exclaimed, "your secretary called me up on Saturday and said you particularly wanted me to come over this morning, to examine your books with you. I've made the trip from Brooklyn for that purpose."

Mr. Oldham touched a buzzer, and a middle-aged woman came into the office. "Miss Patterson," he said, "did you telephone to Mr. Mifflin of Brooklyn on Saturday, asking him——"

"It was a man that telephoned," said Roger.

"I'm exceedingly sorry, Mr. Mifflin," said Mr. Oldham. "More sorry than I can tell you—I'm afraid someone has played a trick on you. As I told you, and Miss Patterson will bear me out, I have no idea of selling my books, and have never authorized any one even to suggest such a thing."

Roger was filled with confusion and anger. A hoax on the part of some of the Corn Cob Club, he thought to himself. He flushed painfully to recall the simplicity of his glee.

"Please don't be embarrassed," said Mr. Oldham, seeing the little man's vexation. "Don't let's consider the trip wasted. Won't you come out and dine with me in the country this evening, and see my things?"

But Roger was too proud to accept this balm, courteous as it was.

"I'm sorry," he said, "but I'm afraid I can't do it. I'm rather busy at home, and only came over because I believed this to be urgent."

"Some other time, perhaps," said Mr. Oldham. "Look here, you're a bookseller? I don't believe I know your shop. Give me your card. The next time I'm in New York I'd like to stop in."

Roger got away as quickly as the other's politeness would let him. He chafed savagely at the awkwardness of his position. Not until he reached the street again did he breathe freely.

"Some of Jerry Gladfist's tomfoolery, I'll bet a hat," he muttered. "By the bones of Fanny Kelly, I'll make him smart for it."

Even Aubrey, picking up the trail again, could see that Roger was angry.

"Something's got his goat," he reflected. "I wonder what he's peeved about?"

They crossed Broad Street and Roger started off down Chestnut. Aubrey saw the bookseller halt in a doorway to light his pipe, and stopped some yards behind him to look up at the statue of William Penn on the City Hall. It was a blustery day, and at that moment a gust of wind whipped off his hat and sent it spinning down Broad Street. He ran half a block before he recaptured it. When he got back to Chestnut, Roger had disappeared. He hurried down Chestnut Street, bumping pedestrians in his eagerness, but at Thirteenth he halted in dismay. Nowhere could he see a sign of the little bookseller. He appealed to the policeman at that corner, but learned nothing. Vainly he scoured the block and up and down Juniper Street. It was eleven o'clock, and the streets were thronged.

He cursed the book business in both hemispheres, cursed himself, and cursed Philadelphia. Then he went into a tobacconist's and bought a packet of cigarettes.

For an hour he patrolled up and down Chestnut Street, on both sides of the way, thinking he might possibly encounter Roger. At the end of this time he found himself in front of a newspaper office, and remembered that an old friend of his was an editorial writer on the staff. He entered, and went up in the elevator.

He found his friend in a small grimy den, surrounded by a sea of papers, smoking a pipe with his feet on the table. They greeted each other joyfully.

"Well, look who's here!" cried the facetious journalist. "Tamburlaine the Great, and none other! What brings you to this distant outpost?"

Aubrey grinned at the use of his old college nickname.

"I've come to lunch with you, and borrow enough money to get home with."

"On Monday?" cried the other. "Tuesday being the day of stipend in these quarters? Nay, say not so!"

They lunched together at a quiet Italian restaurant, and Aubrey narrated tersely the adventures of the past few days. The newspaper man smoked pensively when the story was concluded.

"I'd like to see the girl," he said. "Tambo, your tale hath the ring of sincerity. It is full of sound and fury, but it signifieth something. You say your man is a second-hand bookseller?"

"Yes."

"Then I know where you'll find him."

"Nonsense!"

"It's worth trying. Go up to Leary's, 9 South Ninth. It's right on this street. I'll show you."

"Let's go," said Aubrey promptly.

"Not only that," said the other, "but I'll lend you my last V. Not for your sake, but on behalf of the girl. Just mention my name to her, will you?

"Right up the block," he pointed as they reached Chestnut Street. "No, I won't come with you, Wilson's speaking to Congress to-day, and there's big stuff coming over the wire. So long, old man. Invite me to the wedding!"

Aubrey had no idea what Leary's was, and rather expected it to be a tavern of some sort. When he reached the place, however, he saw why his friend had suggested it as a likely lurking ground for Roger. It would be as impossible for any bibliophile to pass this famous second-hand bookstore as for a woman to go by a wedding party without trying to see the bride. Although it was a bleak day, and a snell wind blew down the street, the pavement counters were lined with people turning over disordered piles of volumes. Within, he could see a vista of white shelves, and the many-coloured tapestry of bindings stretching far away to the rear of the building.

He entered eagerly, and looked about. The shop was comfortably busy, with a number of people browsing. They seemed normal enough from behind, but in their eyes he detected the wild, peering glitter of the bibliomaniac. Here and there stood members of the staff. Upon their features Aubrey discerned the placid and philosophic tranquillity which he associated with second-hand booksellers—all save Mifflin.

He paced through the narrow aisles, scanning the blissful throng of seekers. He went down to the educational department in the basement, up to the medical books in the gallery, even back to the sections of Drama and Pennsylvania History in the raised quarterdeck at the rear. There was no trace of Roger.

At a desk under the stairway he saw a lean, studious, and kindly-looking bibliosoph, who was poring over an immense catalogue. An idea struck him.

"Have you a copy of Carlyle's *Letters and Speeches of Oliver Cromwell?*" he asked.

The other looked up.

"I'm afraid we haven't," he said. "Another gentleman was in here asking for it just a few minutes ago."

"Good God!" cried Aubrey. "Did he get it?"

This emphasis brought no surprise to the bookseller, who was accustomed to the oddities of edition hunters.

"No," he said. "We didn't have a copy. We haven't seen one for a long time."

"Was he a little bald man with a red beard and bright blue eyes?" asked Aubrey hoarsely.

"Yes—Mr. Mifflin of Brooklyn. Do you know him?"

"I should say I do!" cried Aubrey. "Where has he gone? I've been hunting him all over town, the scoundrel!"

The bookseller, douce man, had seen too many eccentric customers to be shocked by the vehemence of his questioner.

"He was here a moment ago," he said gently, and gazed with a mild interest upon the excited young advertising man. "I daresay you'll find him just outside, in Ludlow Street."

"Where's that?"

The tall man—and I don't see why I should scruple to name him, for it was Philip Warner—explained that Ludlow Street was the narrow alley that runs along one side of Leary's and elbows at right angles behind the shop. Down the flank of the store, along this narrow little street, run shelves of books under a penthouse. It is here that Leary's displays its stock of ragamuffin ten-centers—queer dingy volumes that call to the hearts of gentle questers. Along these historic shelves many troubled spirits have come as near happiness as they are like to get... for after all, happiness (as the mathematicians might say) lies on a curve, and we approach it only by asymptote.... The frequenters of this alley call themselves whimsically The Ludlow Street Business Men's Association, and Charles Lamb or Eugene Field would have been proud to preside at their annual dinners, at which the members recount their happiest book-finds of the year.

Aubrey rushed out of the shop and looked down the alley. Half a dozen Ludlow Street Business Men were groping among the shelves. Then, down at the far end, his small face poked into an open volume, he saw Roger. He approached with a rapid stride.

"Well," he said angrily, "here you are!"

Roger looked up from his book good-humouredly. Apparently, in the zeal of his favourite pastime, he had forgotten where he was.

"Hullo!" he said. "What are you doing in Brooklyn? Look here, here's a copy of Tooke's *Pantheon*——"

"What's the idea?" cried Aubrey harshly. "Are you trying to kid me? What are you and Weintraub framing up here in Philadelphia?"

Roger's mind came back to Ludlow Street. He looked with some surprise at the flushed face of the young man, and put the book back in its place on the shelf, making a mental note of its location. His disappointment of the morning came back to him with some irritation.

"What are you talking about?" he said. "What the deuce business is it of yours?"

"I'll make it my business," said Aubrey, and shook his fist in the bookseller's face. "I've been trailing you, you scoundrel, and I want to know what kind of a game you're playing."

A spot of red spread on Roger's cheekbones. In spite of his apparent demureness he had a pugnacious spirit and a quick fist.

"By the bones of Charles Lamb!" he said. "Young man, your manners need mending. If you're looking for display advertising, I'll give you one on each eye."

Aubrey had expected to find a cringing culprit, and this back talk infuriated him beyond control.

"You damned little bolshevik," he said, "if you were my size I'd give you a hiding. You tell me what you and your pro-German pals are up to or I'll put the police on you!"

Roger stiffened. His beard bristled, and his blue eyes glittered.

"You impudent dog," he said quietly, "you come round the corner where these people can't see us and I'll give you some private tutoring."

He led the way round the corner of the alley. In this narrow channel, between blank walls, they confronted each other.

"In the name of Gutenberg," said Roger, calling upon his patron saint, "explain yourself or I'll hit you."

"Who's he?" sneered Aubrey. "Another one of your Huns?"

That instant he received a smart blow on the chin, which would have been much harder but that Roger misgauged his footing on the uneven cobbles, and hardly reached the face of his opponent, who topped him by many inches.

Aubrey forgot his resolution not to hit a smaller man, and also calling upon his patron saints—the Associated Advertising Clubs of the World—he delivered a smashing slog which hit the bookseller in the chest and jolted him half across the alley.

Both men were furiously angry—Aubrey with the accumulated bitterness of several days' anxiety and suspicion, and Roger with the quick-flaming indignation of a hot-tempered man unwarrantably outraged. Aubrey had the better of the encounter in height, weight, and more than twenty years juniority, but fortune played for the bookseller. Aubrey's terrific punch sent the latter staggering across the alley onto the opposite curb. Aubrey followed him up with a rush, intending to crush the other with one fearful smite. But Roger, keeping cool, now had the advantage of position. Standing on the curb, he had a little the better in height. As Aubrey leaped at him, his face grim with hatred, Roger met him with a savage buffet on the jaw. Aubrey's foot struck against the curb, and he fell backward onto the stones. His head crashed violently on the cobbles, and the old cut on his scalp broke out afresh. Dazed and shaken, there was, for the moment, no more fight in him.

"You insolent pup," panted Roger, "do you want any more?" Then he saw that Aubrey was really hurt. With horror he observed a trickle of blood run down the side of the young man's face.

"Good Lord," he said. "Maybe I've killed him!"

In a panic he ran round the corner to get Leary's outside man, who stands in a little sentry box at the front angle of the store and sells the outdoor books.

"Quick," he said. "There's a fellow back here badly hurt."

They ran back around the corner, and found Aubrey walking rather shakily toward them. Immense relief swam through Roger's brain.

"Look here," he said, "I'm awfully sorry—are you hurt?"

Aubrey glared whitely at him, but was too stunned to speak. He grunted, and the others took him one on each side and supported him. Leary's man ran inside the store and opened the little door of the freight elevator at the back of the shop. In this way, avoiding notice save by a few book-prowlers, Aubrey was carted into the shop as though he had been a parcel of second-hand books.

Mr. Warner greeted them at the back of the shop, a little surprised, but gentle as ever.

"What's wrong?" he said.

"Oh, we've been fighting over a copy of Tooke's *Pantheon*," said Roger.

They led Aubrey into the little private office at the rear. Here they made him sit down in a chair and bathed his bleeding head with cold water. Philip Warner, always resourceful, produced some surgical plaster. Roger wanted to telephone for a doctor.

"Not on your life," said Aubrey, pulling himself together. "See here, Mr. Mifflin, don't flatter yourself you gave me this cut on the skull. I got that the other evening on Brooklyn Bridge, going home from your damned bookshop. Now if you and I can be alone for a few minutes, we've got to have a talk."

*Chapter XIV. The "Cromwell" Makes its Last Appearance*

"You utter idiot," said Roger, half an hour later. "Why didn't you tell me all this sooner? Good Lord, man, there's some devil's work going on!"

"How the deuce was I to know you knew nothing about it?" said Aubrey impatiently. "You'll grant everything pointed against you? When I saw that guy go into the shop with his own key, what could I think but that you were in league with him? Gracious, man, are you so befuddled in your old books that you don't see what's going on round you?"

"What time did you say that was?" said Roger shortly.

"One o'clock Sunday morning."

Roger thought a minute. "Yes, I was in the cellar with Bock," he said. "Bock barked, and I thought it was rats. That fellow must have taken an impression of the lock and made himself a key. He's been in the shop hundreds of times, and could easily do it. That explains the disappearing *Cromwell*. But *why?* What's the idea?"

"For the love of heaven," said Aubrey. "Let's get back to Brooklyn as soon as we can. God only knows what may have happened. Fool that I was, to go away and leave those women all alone. Triple-distilled lunacy!"

"My dear fellow," said Roger, "I was the fool to be lured off by a fake telephone call. Judging by what you say, Weintraub must have worked that also."

Aubrey looked at his watch. "Just after three," he said.

"We can't get a train till four," said Roger. "That means we can't get back to Gissing Street until nearly seven."

"Call them up," said Aubrey.

They were still in the private office at the rear of Leary's. Roger was well-known in the shop, and had no hesitation in using the telephone. He lifted the receiver.

"Long Distance, please," he said. "Hullo? I want to get Brooklyn, Wordsworth 1617-W."

They spent a sour twenty-five minutes waiting for the connection. Roger went out to talk with Warner, while Aubrey fumed in the back office. He could not sit still, and paced the little room in a fidget of impatience, tearing his watch out of his pocket every few minutes. He felt dull and sick with vague fear. To his mind recurred the spiteful buzz of that voice over the wire—"*Gissing Street is not healthy for you.*" He remembered the scuffle on the Bridge, the whispering in the alley, and the sinister face of the druggist at his prescription counter. The whole series of events seemed a grossly fantastic nightmare, yet it frightened him. "If only I were in Brooklyn," he groaned, "it wouldn't be so bad. But to be over here, a hundred miles away, in another cursed bookshop, while that girl may be in trouble—Gosh!" he muttered. "If I get through this business all right I'll lay off bookshops for the rest of my life!"

The telephone rang, and Aubrey frantically beckoned to Roger, who was outside, talking.

"Answer it, you chump!" said Roger. "We'll lose the connection!"

"Nix," said Aubrey. "If Titania hears my voice she'll ring off. She's sore at me."

Roger ran to the instrument. "Hullo, hullo?" he said, irritably. "Hullo, is that Wordsworth——? Yes, I'm calling Brooklyn—Hullo!"

Aubrey, leaning over Roger's shoulder, could hear a clucking in the receiver, and then, incredibly clear, a thin, silver, distant voice. How well he knew it! It seemed to vibrate in the air all about him. He could hear every syllable distinctly. A hot perspiration burst out on his forehead and in the palms of his hands.

"Hullo," said Roger. "Is that Mifflin's Bookshop?"

"Yes," said Titania. "Is that you, Mr. Mifflin? Where are you?"

"In Philadelphia," said Roger. "Tell me, is everything all right?"

"Everything's dandy," said Titania. "I'm selling loads of books. Mrs. Mifflin's gone out to do some shopping."

Aubrey shook to hear the tiny, airy voice, like a trill of birdsong, like a tinkling from some distant star. He could imagine her standing at the phone in the back of the shadowy bookshop, and seemed to see her as though through an inverted telescope, very minute and very perfect. How brave and exquisite she was!

"When are you coming home?" she was saying.

"About seven o'clock," said Roger. "Listen, is everything absolutely O. K.?"

"Why, yes," said Titania. "I've been having lots of fun. I went down just now and put some coal on the furnace. Oh, yes. Mr. Weintraub came in a little while ago and left a suitcase of books. He said you wouldn't mind. A friend of his is going to call for them this afternoon."

"Hold the wire a moment," said Roger, and clapped his hand over the mouthpiece. "She says Weintraub left a suitcase of books there to be called for. What do you make of that?"

"For the love of God, tell her not to touch those books."

"Hullo?" said Roger. Aubrey, leaning over him, noticed that the little bookseller's naked pate was ringed with crystal beads.

"Hullo?" replied Titania's elfin voice promptly.

"Did you open the suitcase?"

"No. It's locked. Mr. Weintraub said there were a lot of old books in it for a friend of his. It's very heavy."

"Look here," said Roger, and his voice rang sharply. "This is important. I don't want you to touch that suitcase. Leave it wherever it is, and *don't touch it*. Promise me."

"Yes, Mr. Mifflin. Had I better put it in a safe place?"

"*Don't touch it!*"

"Bock's sniffing at it now."

"Don't touch it, and don't let Bock touch it. It—it's got valuable papers in it."

"I'll be careful of it," said Titania.

"Promise me not to touch it. And another thing—if any one calls for it, don't let them take it until I get home."

Aubrey held out his watch in front of Roger. The latter nodded.

"Do you understand?" he said. "Do you hear me all right?"

"Yes, splendidly. I think it's wonderful! You know I never talked on long distance before——"

"Don't touch the bag," repeated Roger doggedly, "and don't let any one take it until we—until I get back."

"I promise," said Titania blithely.

"Good-bye," said Roger, and set down the receiver. His face

looked curiously pinched, and there was perspiration in the hollows under his eyes. Aubrey held out his watch impatiently.

"We've just time to make it," cried Roger, and they rushed from the shop.

It was not a sprightly journey. The train made its accustomed detour through West Philadelphia and North Philadelphia before getting down to business, and the two voyagers felt a personal hatred of the brakemen who permitted passengers from these suburbs to straggle leisurely aboard instead of flogging them in with knotted whips. When the express stopped at Trenton, Aubrey could easily have turned a howitzer upon that innocent city and blasted it into rubble. An unexpected stop at Princeton Junction was the last straw. Aubrey addressed the conductor in terms that were highly treasonable, considering that this official was a government servant.

The winter twilight drew in, gray and dreary, with a threat of snow. For some time they sat in silence, Roger buried in a Philadelphia afternoon paper containing the text of the President's speech announcing his trip to Europe, and Aubrey gloomily recapitulating the schedule of his past week. His head throbbed, his hands were wet with nervousness so that crumbs of tobacco adhered to them annoyingly.

"It's a funny thing," he said at last. "You know I never heard of your shop until a week ago to-day, and now it seems like the most important place on earth. It was only last Tuesday that we had supper together, and since then I've had my scalp laid open twice, had a desperado lie in wait for me in my own bedroom, spent two night vigils on Gissing Street, and endangered the biggest advertising account our agency handles. I don't wonder you call the place haunted!"

"I suppose it would all make good advertising copy?" said Roger peevishly.

"Well, I don't know" said Aubrey. "It's a bit too rough, I'm afraid. How do you dope it out?"

"I don't know what to think. Weintraub has run that drug store for twenty years or more. Years ago, before I ever got into the book business, I used to know his shop. He was always rather interested in books, especially scientific books, and we got quite friendly when I opened up on Gissing Street. I never fell for his face very hard, but he always seemed quiet and well-disposed. It sounds to me like some kind of trade in illicit drugs, or German incendiary bombs. You know what a lot of fires there were during the war—those big grain elevators in Brooklyn, and so on."

"I thought at first it was a kidnapping stunt," said Aubrey. "I thought you had got Miss Chapman planted in your shop so that these other guys could smuggle her away."

"You seem to have done me the honour of thinking me a very

complete rascal," said Roger.

Aubrey's lips trembled with irritable retort, but he checked himself heroically.

"What was your particular interest in the Cromwell book?" he asked after a pause.

"Oh, I read somewhere—two or three years ago—that it was one of Woodrow Wilson's favourite books. That interested me, and I looked it up."

"By the way," cried Aubrey excitedly, "I forgot to show you those numbers that were written in the cover." He pulled out his memorandum book, and showed the transcript he had made.

"Well, one of these is perfectly understandable," said Roger. "Here, where it says 329 *ff. cf. W. W.* That simply means 'pages 329 and following, compare Woodrow Wilson.' I remember jotting that down not long ago, because that passage in the book reminded me of some of Wilson's ideas. I generally note down in the back of a book the numbers of any pages that interest me specially. These other page numbers convey nothing unless I had the book before me."

"The first bunch of numbers was in your handwriting, then; but underneath were these others, in Weintraub's—or at any rate in his ink. When I saw that he was jotting down what I took to be code stuff in the backs of your books I naturally assumed you and he were working together——"

"And you found the cover in his drug store?"

"Yes."

Roger scowled. "I don't make it out," he said. "Well, there's nothing we can do till we get there. Do you want to look at the paper? There's the text of Wilson's speech to Congress this morning."

Aubrey shook his head dismally, and leaned his hot forehead against the pane. Neither of them spoke again until they reached Manhattan Transfer, where they changed for the Hudson Terminal.

It was seven o'clock when they hurried out of the subway terminus at Atlantic Avenue. It was a raw, damp evening, but the streets had already begun to bustle with their nightly exuberance of light and colour. The yellow glitter of a pawnshop window reminded Aubrey of the small revolver in his pocket. As they passed a dark alley, he stepped aside to load the weapon.

"Have you anything of this sort with you?" he said, showing it to Roger.

"Good Lord, no," said the bookseller. "What do you think I am, a moving-picture hero?"

Down Gissing Street the younger man set so rapid a pace that his companion had to trot to keep abreast. The placid vista of the little street was reassuring. Under the glowing effusion of the shop windows the pavement was a path of checkered brightness. In Weintraub's pharmacy they could see the pasty-faced assistant in his stained white coat serving a beaker of hot chocolate. In the stationer's shop people were looking over trays of Christmas cards. In the Milwaukee Lunch Aubrey saw (and envied) a sturdy citizen peacefully dipping a doughnut into a cup of coffee.

"This all seems very unreal," said Roger.

As they neared the bookshop, Aubrey's heart gave a jerk of apprehension. The blinds in the front windows had been drawn down. A dull shining came through them, showing that the lights were turned on inside. But why should the shades be lowered with closing time three hours away?

They reached the front door, and Aubrey was about to seize the handle when Roger halted him.

"Wait a moment," he said. "Let's go in quietly. There may be something queer going on."

Aubrey turned the knob gently. The door was locked.

Roger pulled out his latchkey and cautiously released the bolt. Then he opened the door slightly—about an inch.

"You're taller than I am," he whispered. "Reach up and muffle the bell above the door while I open it."

Aubrey thrust three fingers through the aperture and blocked the trigger of the gong. Then Roger pushed the door wide, and they tiptoed in.

The shop was empty, and apparently normal. They stood for an instant with pounding pulses.

From the back of the house came a clear voice, a little tremulous:

"You can do what you like, I shan't tell you where it is. Mr. Mifflin said——"

There followed the bang of a falling chair, and a sound of rapid movement.

Aubrey was down the aisle in a flash, followed by Roger, who had delayed just long enough to close the door. He tiptoed up the steps at the back of the shop and looked into the dining room. At the instant his eyes took in the scene it seemed as though the whole room was in motion.

The cloth was spread for supper and shone white under the drop lamp. In the far corner of the room Titania was struggling in the grasp of a bearded man whom Aubrey instantly recognized as the chef. On the near side of the table, holding a revolver levelled at the girl, stood Weintraub. His back was toward the door. Aubrey could see the druggist's sullen jaw crease and shake with anger.

Two strides took him into the room. He jammed the muzzle of his pistol against the oily cheek. "Drop it!" he said hoarsely. "You Hun!" With his left hand he seized the man's shirt collar and drew it tight against the throat. In his tremor of rage and excitement his arms felt curiously weak, and his first thought was how impossible it would be to strangle that swinish neck.

For an instant there was a breathless tableau. The bearded man still had his hands on Titania's shoulders. She, very pale but with brilliant eyes, gazed at Aubrey in unbelieving amazement. Weintraub stood quite motionless with both hands on the dining table, as though thinking. He felt the cold bruise of metal against the hollow of his cheek. Slowly he opened his right hand and his revolver fell on the linen cloth. Then Roger burst into the room.

Titania wrenched herself away from the chef.

"I wouldn't give them the suitcase!" she cried.

Aubrey kept his pistol pinned against Weintraub's face. With his left hand he picked up the druggist's revolver. Roger was about to seize the chef, who was standing uncertainly on the other side of the table.

"Here," said Aubrey, "take this gun. Cover this fellow and leave that one to me. I've got a score to settle with him."

The chef made a movement as though to jump through the window behind him, but Aubrey flung himself upon him. He hit the man square on the nose and felt a delicious throb of satisfaction as the rubbery flesh flattened beneath his knuckles. He seized the man's hairy throat and sank his fingers into it. The other tried to snatch the bread knife on the table, but was too late. He fell to the floor, and Aubrey throttled him savagely.

"You blasted Hun," he grunted. "Go wrestling with girls, will you?"

Titania ran from the room, through the pantry.

Roger was holding Weintraub's revolver in front of the German's face.

"Look here," he said, "what does this mean?"

"It's all a mistake," said the druggist suavely, though his eyes slid uneasily to and fro. "I just came in to get some books I left here earlier in the afternoon."

"With a revolver, eh?" said Roger. "Speak up, Hindenburg, what's the big idea?"

"It's not my revolver," said Weintraub. "It's Metzger's."

"Where's this suitcase of yours?" said Roger. "We're going to have a look at it."

"It's all a stupid mistake," said Weintraub. "I left a suitcase of old books here for Metzger, because I expected to go out of town this afternoon. He called for it, and your young woman wouldn't give it to him. He came to me, and I came down here to tell her it was all right."

"Is that Metzger?" said Roger, pointing to the bearded man who was trying to break Aubrey's grip. "Gilbert, don't choke that man, we want him to do some explaining."

Aubrey got up, picked his revolver from the floor where he had dropped it, and prodded the chef to his feet.

"Well, you swine," he said, "how did you enjoy falling downstairs the other evening? As for you, Herr Weintraub, I'd like to know what kind of prescriptions you make up in that cellar of yours."

Weintraub's face shone damply in the lamplight. Perspiration was thick on his forehead.

"My dear Mifflin," he said, "this is awfully stupid. In my eagerness, I'm afraid——"

Titania ran back into the room, followed by Helen, whose face was crimson.

"Thank God you're back, Roger," she said. "These brutes tied me up in the kitchen and gagged me with a roller-towel. They threatened to shoot Titania if she wouldn't give them the suitcase."

Weintraub began to say something, but Roger thrust the revolver between his eyes.

"Hold your tongue!" he said. "We're going to have a look at those books of yours."

"I'll get the suitcase," said Titania. "I hid it. When Mr. Weintraub came in and asked for it, at first I was going to give it to him, but he looked so queer I thought something must be wrong."

"Don't you get it," said Aubrey, and their eyes met for the first time. "Show me where it is, and we'll let friend Hun bring it."

Titania flushed a little. "It's in my bedroom cupboard," she said.

She led the way upstairs, Metzger following, and Aubrey behind Metzger with his pistol ready. Outside the bedroom door Aubrey halted. "Show him the suitcase and let him pick it up," he said. "If he makes a wrong movement, call me, and I'll shoot him."

Titania pointed out the suitcase, which she had stowed at the back of her cupboard behind some clothes. The chef showed no insubordination, and the three returned downstairs.

"Very well," said Roger. "We'll go down in the shop where we can see better. Perhaps he's got a first folio Shakespeare in here. Helen, you go to the phone and ring up the McFee Street police station. Ask them to send a couple of men round here at once."

"My dear Mifflin," said Weintraub, "this is very absurd. Only a few old books that I had collected from time to time."

"I don't call it absurd when a man comes into my house and ties my wife up with clothesline and threatens to shoot a young girl," said Roger. "We'll see what the police have to say about this, Weintraub. Don't make any mistake: if you try to bolt I'll blow your brains out."

Aubrey led the way down into the shop while Metzger carried the suitcase. Roger and Weintraub followed, and Titania brought up the rear. Under a bright light in the Essay alcove Aubrey made the chef lay the bag on the table.

"Open her up," he said curtly.

"It's nothing but some old books," said Metzger.

"If they're old enough they may be valuable," said Roger. "I'm interested in old books. Look sharp!"

Metzger drew a key from his pocket and unlocked the bag. Aubrey held the pistol at his head as he threw back the lid. The suitcase was full of second-hand books closely packed together. Roger, with great presence of mind, was keeping his eyes on Weintraub.

"Tell me what's in it," he said.

"Why, it's only a lot of books, after all," cried Titania.

"You see," said Weintraub surlily, "there's no mystery about it. I'm sorry I was so——"

"Oh, look!" said Titania; "There's the *Cromwell* book!"

For an instant Roger forgot himself. He looked instinctively at the suitcase, and in that moment the druggist broke away, ran down the aisle, and flew out of the door. Roger dashed after him, but was too late. Aubrey was holding Metzger by the collar with the pistol at his head.

"Good God," he said, "why didn't you shoot?"

"I don't know" said Roger in confusion. "I was afraid of hitting him. Never mind, we can fix him later."

"The police will be here in a minute," said Helen, calling from the telephone. "I'm going to let Bock in. He's in the back yard."

"I think they're both crazy," said Titania. "Let's put the *Cromwell* back on the shelf and let this creature go." She put out her hand for the book.

"Stop!" cried Aubrey, and seized her arm. "Don't touch that book!"

Titania shrank back, frightened by his voice. Had everyone gone insane?

"Here, Mr. Metzger," said Aubrey, "you put that book back on the shelf where it belongs. Don't try to get away. I've got this revolver pointed at you."

He and Roger were both startled by the chef's face. Above the unkempt beard his eyes shone with a half-crazed lustre, and his hands shook.

"Very well," he said. "Show me where it goes."

"I'll show you," said Titania.

Aubrey put out his arm in front of the girl. "Stay where you are," he said angrily.

"Down in the History alcove," said Roger. "The front alcove on the other side of the shop. We've both got you covered."

Instead of taking the volume from the suitcase, Metzger picked up the whole bag, holding it flat. He carried it to the alcove they indicated. He placed the case carefully on the floor, and picked the *Cromwell* volume out of it.

"Where would you want it to go?" he said in an odd voice. "This is a valuable book."

"On the fifth shelf," said Roger. "Over there——"

"For God's sake stand back," said Aubrey. "Don't go near him. There's something damnable about this."

"You poor fools!" cried Metzger harshly. "To hell with you and your old books." He drew his hand back as though to throw the volume at them.

There was a quick patter of feet, and Bock, growling, ran down the aisle. In the same instant, Aubrey, obeying some unexplained impulse, gave Roger a violent push back into the Fiction alcove, seized Titania roughly in his arms, and ran with her toward the back of the shop.

Metzger's arm was raised, about to throw the book, when Bock darted at him and buried his teeth in the man's leg. The *Cromwell* fell from his hand.

There was a shattering explosion, a dull roar, and for an instant Aubrey thought the whole bookshop had turned into a vast spinning top. The floor rocked and sagged, shelves of books were hurled in every direction. Carrying Titania, he had just reached the steps leading to the domestic quarters when they were flung sideways into the corner behind Roger's desk. The air was full of flying books. A row of encyclopedias crashed down upon his shoulders, narrowly missing Titania's head. The front windows were shivered into flying streamers of broken glass. The table near the door was hurled into the opposite gallery. With a splintering crash the corner of the gallery above the History alcove collapsed, and hundreds of volumes cascaded heavily on to the floor. The lights went out, and for an instant all was silence.

"Are you all right?" said Aubrey hastily. He and Titania had fallen sprawling against the bookseller's desk.

"I think so," she said faintly. "Where's Mr. Mifflin?"

Aubrey put out his hand to help her, and touched something wet on the floor. "Good heavens," he thought. "She's dying!" He struggled to his feet in the darkness. "Hullo, Mr. Mifflin," he called, "where are you?"

There was no answer.

A beam of light gushed out from the passageway behind the shop, and picking his way over fallen litter he found Mrs. Mifflin standing dazed by the dining-room door. In the back of the house the lights were still burning.

"For heaven's sake, have you a candle?" he said.

"Where's Roger?" she cried piteously, and stumbled into the kitchen.

With a candle Aubrey found Titania sitting on the floor, very faint, but unhurt. What he had thought was blood proved to be a pool of ink from a quart bottle that had stood over Roger's desk. He picked her up like a child and carried her into the kitchen. "Stay here and don't stir," he said.

By this time a crowd was already gathering on the pavement. Someone came in with a lantern. Three policemen appeared at the door.

"For God's sake," cried Aubrey, "get a light in here so we can see what's happened. Mifflin's buried in this mess somewhere. Someone ring for an ambulance."

The whole front of the Haunted Bookshop was a wreck. In the pale glimmer of the lantern it was a disastrous sight. Helen groped her way down the shattered aisle.

"Where was he?" she cried wildly.

"Thanks to that set of Trollope," said a voice in the remains of the Fiction alcove, "I think I'm all right. Books make good shock-absorbers. Is any one hurt?"

It was Roger, half stunned, but undamaged. He crawled out from under a case of shelves that had crumpled down upon him.

"Bring that lantern over here," said Aubrey, pointing to a dark heap lying on the floor under the broken fragments of Roger's bulletin board.

It was the chef. He was dead. And clinging to his leg was all that was left of Bock.

*Chapter XV. Mr. Chapman Waves His Wand*

Gissing Street will not soon forget the explosion at the Haunted Bookshop. When it was learned that the cellar of Weintraub's pharmacy contained just the information for which the Department of Justice had been looking for four years, and that the inoffensive German-American druggist had been the artisan of hundreds of incendiary bombs that had been placed on American and Allied shipping and in ammunition plants—and that this same Weintraub had committed suicide when arrested on Bromfield Street in Boston the next day—Gissing Street hummed with excitement. The Milwaukee Lunch did a roaring business among the sensation seekers who came to view the ruins of the bookshop. When it became known that fragments of a cabin plan of the *George Washington* had been found in Metzger's pocket, and the confession of an accomplice on the kitchen staff of the Octagon Hotel showed that the bomb, disguised as a copy of one of Woodrow Wilson's favourite books, was to have been placed in the Presidential suite of the steamship, indignation knew no bounds. Mrs. J. F. Smith left Mrs. Schiller's lodgings, declaring that she would stay no longer in a pro-German colony; and Aubrey was able at last to get a much-needed bath.

For the next three days he was too busy with agents of the

Department of Justice to be able to carry on an investigation of his own
that greatly occupied his mind. But late on Friday afternoon he called at
the bookshop to talk things over.

The debris had all been neatly cleared away, and the shattered front
of the building boarded up. Inside, Aubrey found Roger seated on the
floor, looking over piles of volumes that were heaped pell-mell around
him. Through Mr. Chapman's influence with a well-known firm of
builders, the bookseller had been able to get men to work at once in
making repairs, but even so it would be at least ten days, he said, before
he could reopen for business. "I hate to lose the value of all this
advertising," he lamented. "It isn't often that a second-hand bookstore
gets onto the front pages of the newspapers."

"I thought you didn't believe in advertising," said Aubrey.

"The kind of advertising I believe in," said Roger, "is the kind that
doesn't cost you anything."

Aubrey smiled as he looked round at the dismantled shop. "It
seems to me that this'll cost you a tidy bit when the bill comes in."

"My dear fellow," said Roger, "This is just what I needed. I was
getting into a rut. The explosion has blown out a whole lot of books I
had forgotten about and didn't even know I had. Look, here's an old
copy of *How to Be Happy Though Married*, which I see the publisher
lists as 'Fiction.' Here's *Urn Burial*, and *The Love Affairs of a
Bibliomaniac*, and Mistletoe's *Book of Deplorable Facts*. I'm going to
have a thorough house-cleaning. I'm thinking seriously of putting in a
vacuum cleaner and a cash register. Titania was quite right, the place
was too dirty. That girl has given me a lot of ideas."

Aubrey wanted to ask where she was, but didn't like to say so
point-blank.

"There's no question about it," said Roger, "an explosion now and
then does one good. Since the reporters got here and dragged the whole
yarn out of us, I've had half a dozen offers from publishers for my
book, a lyceum bureau wants me to lecture on Bookselling as a Form of
Public Service, I've had five hundred letters from people asking when
the shop will reopen for business, and the American Booksellers'
Association has invited me to give an address at its convention next
spring. It's the first recognition I've ever had. If it weren't for poor dear
old Bock—— Come, we've buried him in the back yard. I want to
show you his grave."

Over a pathetically small mound near the fence a bunch of big
yellow chrysanthemums were standing in a vase.

"Titania put those there," said Roger. "She says she's going to
plant a dogwood tree there in the spring. We intend to put up a little
stone for him, and I'm trying to think of an inscription, I thought of *De
Mortuis Nil Nisi Bonum*, but that's a bit too flippant."

The living quarters of the house had not been damaged by the explosion, and Roger took Aubrey back to the den. "You've come just at the right time," he said. "Mr. Chapman's coming to dinner this evening, and we'll all have a good talk. There's a lot about this business I don't understand yet."

Aubrey was still keeping his eye open for a sign of Titania's presence, and Roger noticed his wandering gaze.

"This is Miss Chapman's afternoon off," he said. "She got her first salary to-day, and was so much exhilarated that she went to New York to blow it in. She's out with her father. Excuse me, please, I'm going to help Helen get dinner ready."

Aubrey sat down by the fire, and lit his pipe. The burden of his meditation was that it was just a week since he had first met Titania, and in all that week there had been no waking moment when he had not thought of her. He was wondering how long it might take for a girl to fall in love? A man—he knew now—could fall in love in five minutes, but how did it work with girls? He was also thinking what unique Daintybits advertising copy he could build (like all ad men he always spoke of *building* an ad, never of writing one) out of this affair if he could only use the inside stuff.

He heard a rustle behind him, and there she was. She had on a gray fur coat and a lively little hat. Her cheeks were delicately tinted by the winter air. Aubrey rose.

"Why, Mr. Gilbert!" she said. "Where have you been keeping yourself when I wanted to see you so badly? I haven't seen you, not to talk to, since last Sunday."

He found it impossible to say anything intelligible. She threw off her coat, and went on, with a wistful gravity that became her even more than smiles:

"Mr. Mifflin has told me some more about what you did last week—I mean, how you took a room across the street and spied upon that hateful man and saw through the whole thing when we were too blind to know what was going on. And I want to apologize for the silly things I said that Sunday morning. Will you forgive me?"

Aubrey had never felt his self-salesmanship ability at such a low ebb. To his unspeakable horror, he felt his eyes betray him. They grew moist.

"Please don't talk like that," he said. "I had no right to do what I did, anyway. And I was wrong in what I said about Mr. Mifflin. I don't wonder you were angry."

"Now surely you're not going to deprive me of the pleasure of thanking you," she said. "You know as well as I do that you saved my life—all our lives, that night. I guess you'd have saved poor Bock's, too, if you could." Her eyes filled with tears.

"If anybody deserves credit, it's you," he said. "Why, if it hadn't been for you they'd have been away with that suitcase and probably

Metzger would have got his bomb on board the ship and blown up the President——"

"I'm not arguing with you," she said. "I'm just thanking you."

It was a happy little party that sat down in Roger's dining room that evening. Helen had prepared Eggs Samuel Butler in Aubrey's honour, and Mr. Chapman had brought two bottles of champagne to pledge the future success of the bookshop. Aubrey was called upon to announce the result of his conferences with the secret service men who had been looking up Weintraub's record.

"It all seems so simple now," he said, "that I wonder we didn't see through it at once. You see, we all made the mistake of assuming that German plotting would stop automatically when the armistice was signed. It seems that this man Weintraub was one of the most dangerous spies Germany had in this country. Thirty or forty fires and explosions on our ships at sea are said to have been due to his work. As he had lived here so long and taken out citizen's papers, no one suspected him. But after his death, his wife, whom he had treated very brutally, gave way and told a great deal about his activities. According to her, as soon as it was announced that the President would go to the Peace Conference, Weintraub made up his mind to get a bomb into the President's cabin on board the *George Washington*. Mrs. Weintraub tried to dissuade him from it, as she was in secret opposed to these murderous plots of his, but he threatened to kill her if she thwarted him. She lived in terror of her life. I can believe it, for I remember her face when her husband looked at her.

"Of course to make the bomb was simple enough for Weintraub. He had an infernally complete laboratory in the cellar of his house, where he had made hundreds. The problem was, how to make a bomb that would not look suspicious, and how to get it into the President's private cabin. He hit on the idea of binding it into the cover of a book. How he came to choose that particular volume, I don't know."

"I think probably I gave him the idea quite innocently," said Roger. "He used to come in here a good deal and one day he asked me whether Mr. Wilson was a great reader. I said that I believed he was, and then mentioned the *Cromwell*, which I had heard was one of Wilson's favourite books. Weintraub was much interested and said he must read the book some day. I remember now that he stood in that alcove for some time, looking over it."

"Well," said Aubrey, "it must have seemed to him that luck was playing into his hands. This man Metzger, who had been an assistant chef at the Octagon for years, was slated to go on board the *George Washington* with the party of cooks from that hotel who were to prepare the President's meals. Weintraub was informed of all this from someone higher up in the German spy organization. Metzger, who was known as Messier at the hotel, was a very clever chef, and had fake passports as a Swiss citizen. He was another tool of the organization. By the original scheme there would have been no direct communication between Weintraub and Metzger, but the go-between was spotted by the Department of Justice on another count, and is now behind bars at Atlanta.

"It seems that Weintraub had conceived the idea that the least suspicious way of passing his messages to Metzger would be to slip them into a copy of some book—a book little likely to be purchased— in a second-hand bookshop. Metzger had been informed what the book was, but—perhaps owing to the unexpected removal of the go- between—did not know in which shop he was to find it. That explains why so many booksellers had inquiries from him recently for a copy of the *Cromwell* volume.

"Weintraub, of course, was not at all anxious to have any direct dealings with Metzger, as the druggist had a high regard for his own skin. When the chef was finally informed where the bookshop was in which he was to see the book, he hurried over here. Weintraub had picked out this shop not only because it was as unlikely as any place on earth to be suspected as a channel of spy codes, but also because he had your confidence and could drop in frequently without arousing surprise. The first time Metzger came here happened to be the night I dined with you, as you remember."

Roger nodded. "He asked for the book, and to my surprise, it wasn't there."

"No: for the excellent reason that Weintraub had taken it some days before, to measure it so he could build his infernal machine to fit, and also to have it rebound. He needed the original binding as a case for his bomb. The following night, as you told me, it came back. He brought it himself, having provided himself with a key to your front door."

"It was gone again on Thursday night, when the Corn Cob Club met here," said Mr. Chapman.

"Yes, that time Metzger had taken it," said Aubrey. "He misunderstood his instructions, and thought he was to steal the book. You see, owing to the absence of their third man, they were working at cross purposes. Metzger, I think, was only intended to get his information out of the book, and leave it where it was. At any rate, he was puzzled, and inserted that ad in the *Times* the next morning—that LOST ad, you remember. By that, I imagine, he intended to convey the idea that he had located the bookshop, but didn't know what to do next. And the date he mentioned in the ad, midnight on Tuesday, December third, was to inform Weintraub (of whose identity he was still ignorant) when Metzger was to go on board the ship. Weintraub had been instructed by their spy organization to watch the LOST and FOUND ads."

"Think of it!" cried Titania.

"Well," continued Aubrey, "all this may not be 100 per cent. accurate, but after putting things together this is how it dopes out. Weintraub, who was as canny as they make them, saw he'd have to get into direct touch with Metzger. He sent him word, on the Friday, to come over to see him and bring the book. Metzger, meanwhile, had had a bad fright when I spoke to him in the hotel elevator. He returned the book to the shop that night, as Mrs. Mifflin remembers. Then, when I stopped in at the drug store on my way home, he must have been with Weintraub. I found the *Cromwell* cover in the drug-store bookcase— why Weintraub was careless enough to leave it there I can't guess—and they spotted me right away as having some kind of hunch. So they followed me over the Bridge and tried to get rid of me. It was because I got that cover on Friday night that Weintraub broke into the shop again early Sunday morning. He had to have the cover of the book to bind his bomb in."

Aubrey was agreeably conscious of the close attention of his audience. He caught Titania's gaze, and flushed a little.

"That's pretty nearly all there is to it," he said. "I knew that if those guys were so keen to put me out of the way there must be something rather rotten on foot. I came over to Brooklyn the next afternoon, Saturday, and took a room across the street."

"And we went to the movies," chirped Titania.

"The rest of it I think you all know—except Metzger's visit to my lodgings that night." He described the incident. "You see they were trailing me pretty close. If I hadn't happened to notice the cigar at my window I guess he'd have had me on toast. Of course you know how wrongly I doped it out. I thought Mr. Mifflin was running with them, and I owe him my apology for that. He's laid me out once on that score, over in Philadelphia."

Humourously, Aubrey narrated how he had sleuthed the bookseller to Ludlow Street, and had been worsted in battle.

"I think they counted on disposing of me sooner or later," said Aubrey. "They framed up that telephone call to get Mr. Mifflin out of town. The point in having Metzger come to the bookshop to get the suitcase was to clear Weintraub's skirts if possible. Apparently it was just a bag of old books. The bombed book, I guess, was perfectly harmless until any one tried to open it."

"You both got back just in the nick of time," said Titania admiringly. "You see I was all alone most of the afternoon. Weintraub left the suitcase about two o'clock. Metzger came for it about six. I refused to let him have it. He was very persistent, and I had to threaten to set Bock at him. It was all I could do to hold the dear old dog in, he was so keen to go for Metzger. The chef went away, and I suppose he went up to see Weintraub about it. I hid the suitcase in my room. Mr. Mifflin had forbidden me to touch it, but I thought that the safest thing to do. Then Mrs. Mifflin came in. We let Bock into the yard for a run, and were getting supper. I heard the bell ring, and went into the shop. There were the two Germans, pulling down the shades. I asked what they meant by it, and they grabbed me and told me to shut up. Then Metzger pointed a pistol at me while the other one tied up Mrs. Mifflin."

"The damned scoundrels!" cried Aubrey. "They got what was coming to them."

"Well, my friends," said Mr. Chapman, "Let's thank heaven that it ended no worse. Mr. Gilbert, I haven't told you yet how I feel about the whole affair. That'll come later. I'd like to propose the health of Mr. Aubrey Gilbert, who is certainly the hero of this film!"

They drank the toast with cheers, and Aubrey blushed becomingly.

"Oh, I forgot something!" cried Titania. "When I went shopping this afternoon I stopped in at Brentano's, and was lucky enough to find just what I wanted. It's for Mr. Gilbert, as a souvenir of the Haunted Bookshop."

She ran to the sideboard and brought back a parcel.

Aubrey opened it with delighted agitation. It was a copy of Carlyle's *Cromwell*. He tried to stammer his thanks, but what he saw— or thought he saw—in Titania's sparkling face—unmanned him.

"The same edition!" said Roger. "Now let's see what those mystic page numbers are! Gilbert, have you got your memorandum?"

Aubrey took out his notebook. "Here we are," he said. "This is what Weintraub wrote in the back of the cover."

153 (3) 1, 2.

Roger glanced at the notation.

"That ought to be easy," he said. "You see in this edition three volumes are bound in one. Let's look at page 153 in the third volume, the first and second lines."

Aubrey turned to the place. He read, and smiled.

"Right you are," he said.

"Read it!" they all cried.

"*To seduce the Protector's guard, to blow up the Protector in his bedroom, and do other little fiddling things.*"

"I shouldn't wonder if that's where he got his idea," said Roger. "What have I been saying right along—that books aren't merely dead things!"

"Good gracious," said Titania. "You told me that books are explosives. You were right, weren't you! But it's lucky Mr. Gilbert didn't hear you say it or he'd certainly have suspected you!"

"The joke is on me," said Roger.

"Well, *I've* got a toast to propose," said Titania. "Here's to the memory of Bock, the dearest, bravest dog I ever met!"

They drank it with due gravity.

"Well, good people," said Mr. Chapman, "there's nothing we can do for Bock now. But we can do something for the rest of us. I've been talking with Titania, Mr. Mifflin. I'm bound to say that after this disaster my first thought was to get her out of the book business as fast as I could. I thought it was a little too exciting for her. You know I sent her over here to have a quiet time and calm down a bit. But she wouldn't hear of leaving. And if I'm going to have a family interest in the book business I want to do something to justify it. I know your idea about travelling book-wagons, and taking literature into the countryside. Now if you and Mrs. Mifflin can find the proper people to run them, I'll finance a fleet of ten of those Parnassuses you're always talking about, and have them built in time to go on the road next spring. How about it?"

Roger and Helen looked at each other, and at Mr. Chapman. In a flash Roger saw one of his dearest dreams coming true. Titania, to whom this was a surprise, leaped from her chair and ran to kiss her father, crying, "Oh, Daddy, you *are* a darling!"

Roger rose solemnly and gave Mr. Chapman his hand.

"My dear sir," he said, "Miss Titania has found the right word. You are an honour to human nature, sir, and I hope you'll never live to regret it. This is the happiest moment of my life."

"Then that's settled," said Mr. Chapman. "We'll go over the details later. Now there's another thing on my mind. Perhaps I shouldn't bring up business matters here, but this is a kind of family party—Mr. Gilbert, it's my duty to inform you that I intend to take my advertising out of the hands of the Grey-Matter Agency."

Aubrey's heart sank. He had feared a catastrophe of this kind from the first. Naturally a hard-headed business man would not care to entrust such vast interests to a firm whose young men went careering about like secret service agents, hunting for spies, eavesdropping in alleys, and accusing people of pro-germanism. Business, Aubrey said to himself, is built upon Confidence, and what confidence could Mr. Chapman have in such vagabond and romantic doings? Still, he felt that he had done nothing to be ashamed of.

"I'm sorry, sir," he said. "We have tried to give you service. I assure you that I've spent by far the larger part of my time at the office in working up plans for your campaigns."

He could not bear to look at Titania, ashamed that she should be the witness of his humiliation.

"That's exactly it," said Mr. Chapman. "I don't want just the larger part of your time. I want all of it. I want you to accept the position of assistant advertising manager of the Daintybits Corporation."

They all cheered, and for the third time that evening Aubrey felt more overwhelmed than any good advertising man is accustomed to feel. He tried to express his delight, and then added:

"I think it's my turn to propose a toast. I give you the health of Mr. and Mrs. Mifflin, and their Haunted Bookshop, the place where I first—I first——"

His courage failed him, and he concluded, "First learned the meaning of literature."

"Suppose we adjourn to the den," said Helen. "We have so many delightful things to talk over, and I know Roger wants to tell you all about the improvements he is planning for the shop."

Aubrey lingered to be the last, and it is to be conjectured that Titania did not drop her handkerchief merely by accident. The others had already crossed the hall into the sitting room.

Their eyes met, and Aubrey could feel himself drowned in her steady, honest gaze. He was tortured by the bliss of being so near her, and alone. The rest of the world seemed to shred away and leave them standing in that little island of light where the tablecloth gleamed under the lamp.

In his hand he clutched the precious book. Out of all the thousand things he thought, there was only one he dared to say.

"Will you write my name in it?"

"I'd love to," she said, a little shakily, for she, too, was strangely alarmed at certain throbbings.

He gave her his pen, and she sat down at the table. She wrote quickly

*For Aubrey Gilbert*
*From Titania Chapman*
*With much gr*

She paused.

"Oh," she said quickly. "Do I have to finish it now?"

She looked up at him, with the lamplight shining on her vivid face. Aubrey felt oddly stupefied, and was thinking only of the little golden sparkle of her eyelashes. This time her eyes were the first to turn away.

"You see," she said with a funny little quaver, "I might want to change the wording." And she ran from the room.

As she entered the den, her father was speaking. "You know," he said, "I'm rather glad she wants to stay in the book business." Roger looked up at her.

"Well," he said, "I believe it agrees with her! You know, the beauty of living in a place like this is that you get so absorbed in the books you don't have any temptation to worry about anything else. The people in books become more real to you than any one in actual life."

Titania, sitting on the arm of Mrs. Mifflin's chair, took Helen's hand, unobserved by the others. They smiled at each other slyly.

## THE END

CPSIA information can be obtained
at www.ICGtesting.com
Printed in the USA
LVHW100706170422
716393LV00024B/121

9 781420 978933